BARNUM!

IN SECRET SERVICE TO THE USA

WRITERS

HOWARD CHAYKIN
& DAVID TISCHMAN

ARTIST

NIKO HENRICHON

LETTERER

JOHN COSTANZA

COLORIST

LEE LOUGHRIDGE

VERTIGO DC COMICS

Karen Berger VP-Executive Editor
Shelly Bond Senior Editor
Mariah Huehner Assistant Editor
Amie Brockway-Metcalf Art Director
Paul Levitz President & Publisher
Georg Brewer VP-Design & Retail Product Development
Richard Bruning VP-Creative Director
Patrick Caldon Senior VP-Finance & Operations
Chris Caramalis VP-Finance
Terri Cunningham VP-Managing Editor
Dan DiDio VP-Editorial
Joel Ehrlich Senior VP-Advertising & Promotions
Alison Gill VP-Manufacturing
Lillian Laserson Senior VP & General Counsel
David McKillips VP-Advertising
John Nee VP-Business Development
Cheryl Rubin VP-Licensing & Merchandising
Bob Wayne VP-Sales & Marketing

Barnum! Published by DC Comics,
1700 Broadway, New York, NY 10019.
Copyright © 2003 Howard Chaykin, Inc.
TM Howard Chaykin, Inc and DC Comics.
All Rights Reserved.
VERTIGO is a trademark of DC Comics.
The stories and incidents mentioned
in this magazine are entirely fictional.

Printed in Canada.
Hardcover ISBN: 1-4012-0072-9
Softcover ISBN: 1-4012-0073-7
DC Comics. A division of Warner Bros.
— An AOL Time Warner Company

Cover Artist: Niko Henrichon
Logo Design: John Roshell

CHAPTER 1

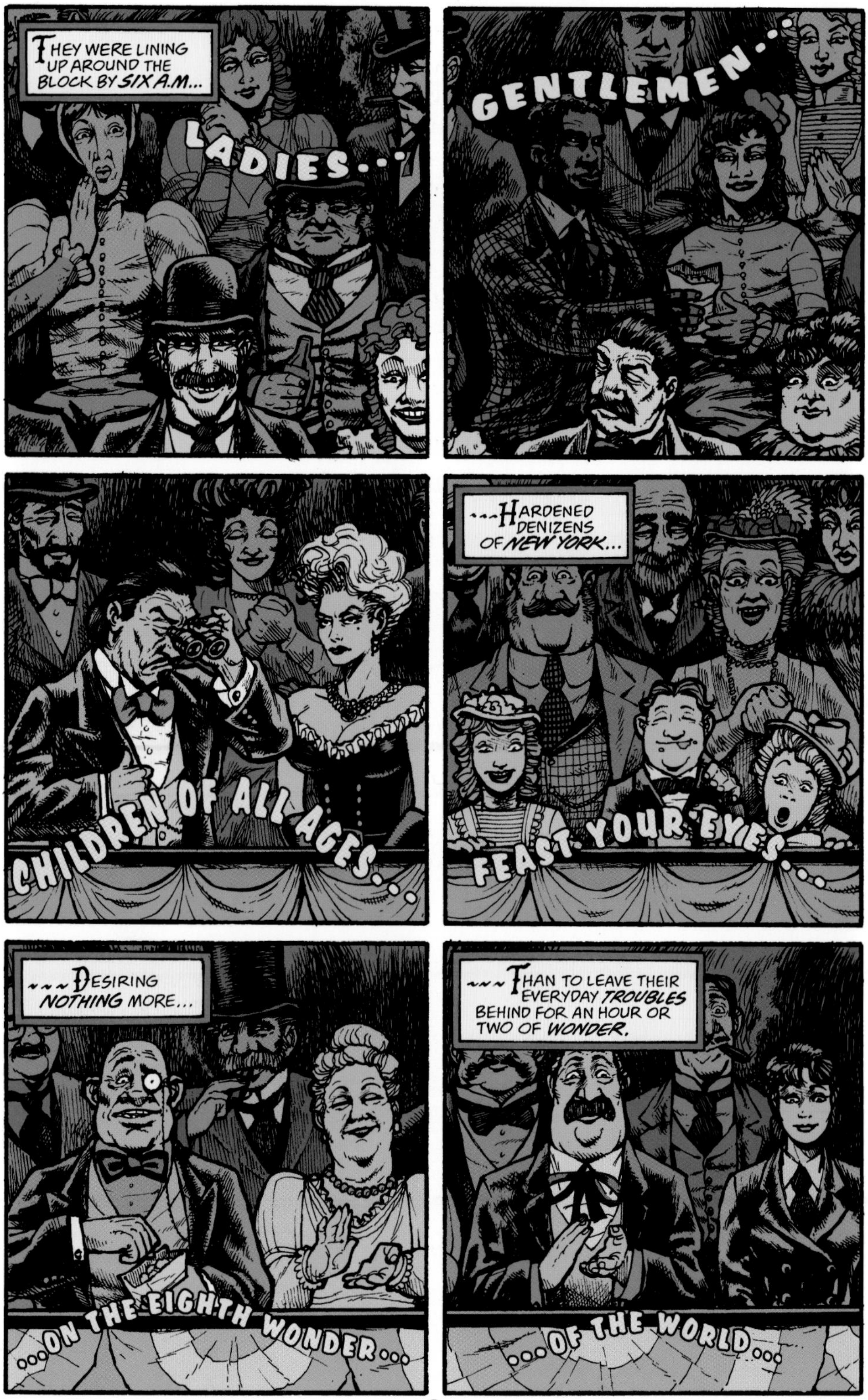
THEY WERE LINING UP AROUND THE BLOCK BY SIX A.M...
LADIES...
GENTLEMEN...
CHILDREN OF ALL AGES...
...HARDENED DENIZENS OF NEW YORK...
FEAST YOUR EYES...
...DESIRING NOTHING MORE...
...ON THE EIGHTH WONDER...
...THAN TO LEAVE THEIR EVERYDAY TROUBLES BEHIND FOR AN HOUR OR TWO OF WONDER.
...OF THE WORLD...

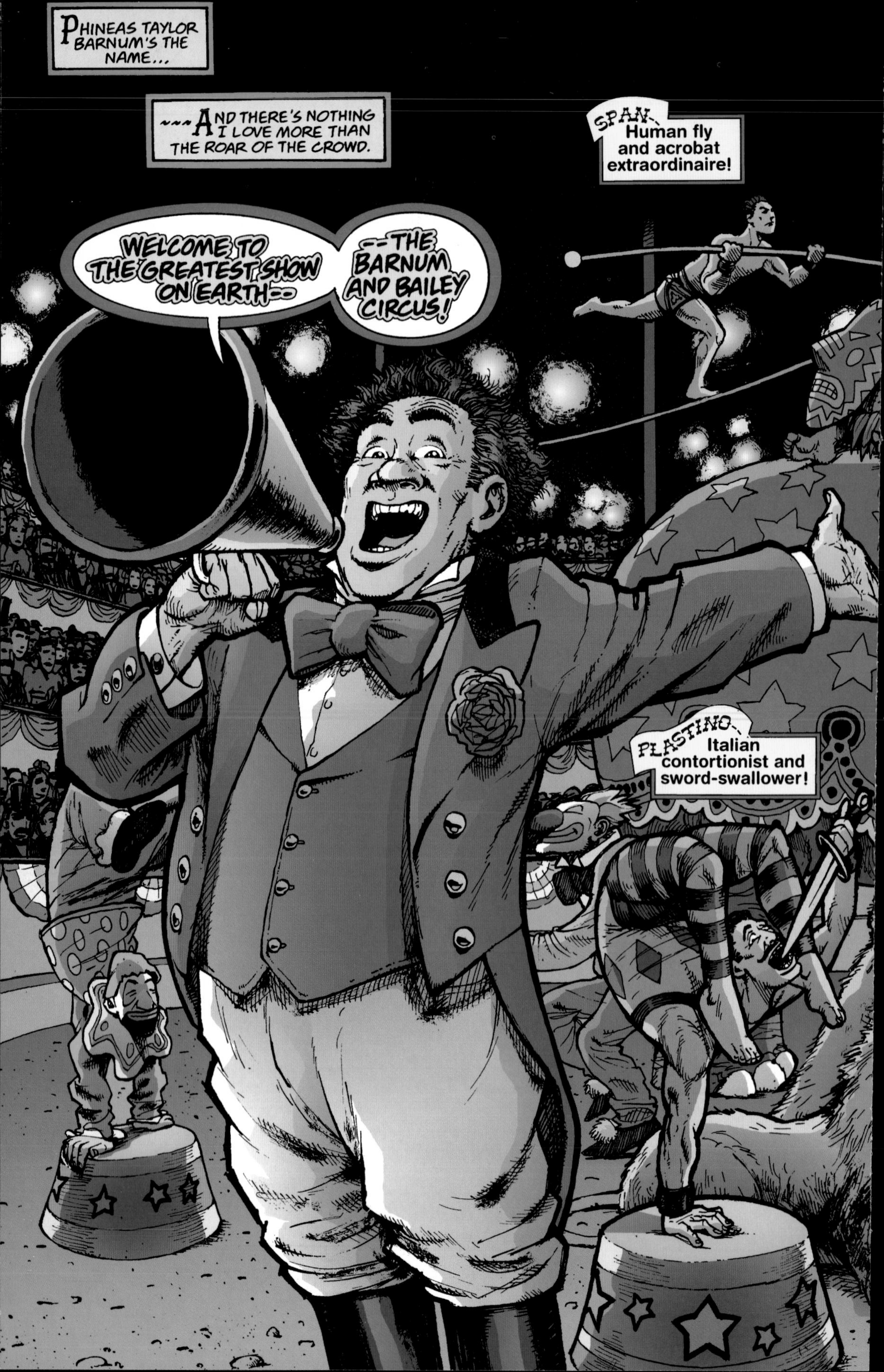
PHINEAS TAYLOR BARNUM'S THE NAME...
...AND THERE'S NOTHING I LOVE MORE THAN THE ROAR OF THE CROWD.
SPAN-- Human fly and acrobat extraordinaire!
WELCOME TO THE GREATEST SHOW ON EARTH--
--THE BARNUM AND BAILEY CIRCUS!
PLASTINO-- Italian contortionist and sword-swallower!

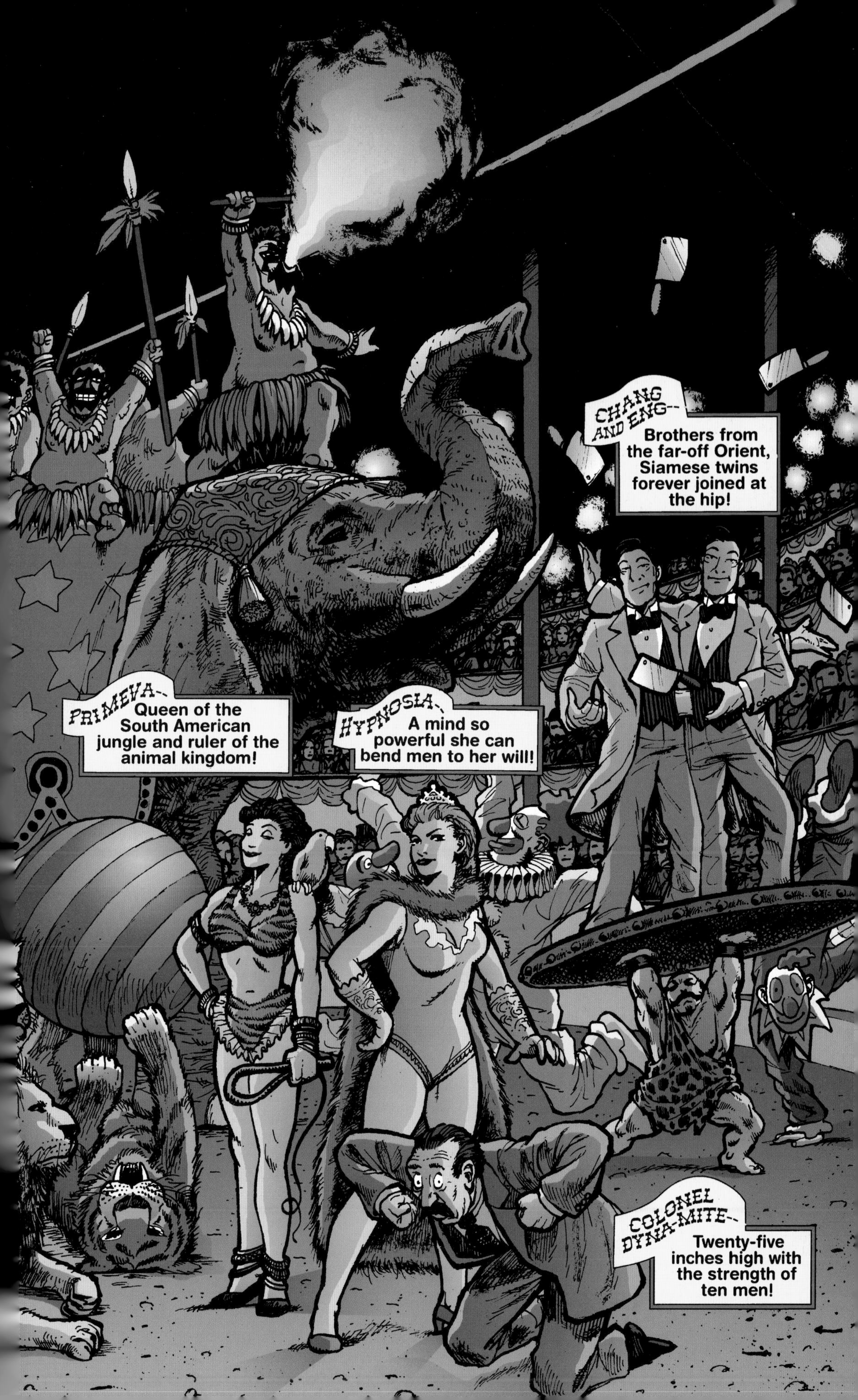
CHANG AND ENG--
Brothers from the far-off Orient, Siamese twins forever joined at the hip!
PRIMEVA--
Queen of the South American jungle and ruler of the animal kingdom!
HYPNOSIA--
A mind so powerful she can bend men to her will!
COLONEL DYNA-MITE--
Twenty-five inches high with the strength of ten men!

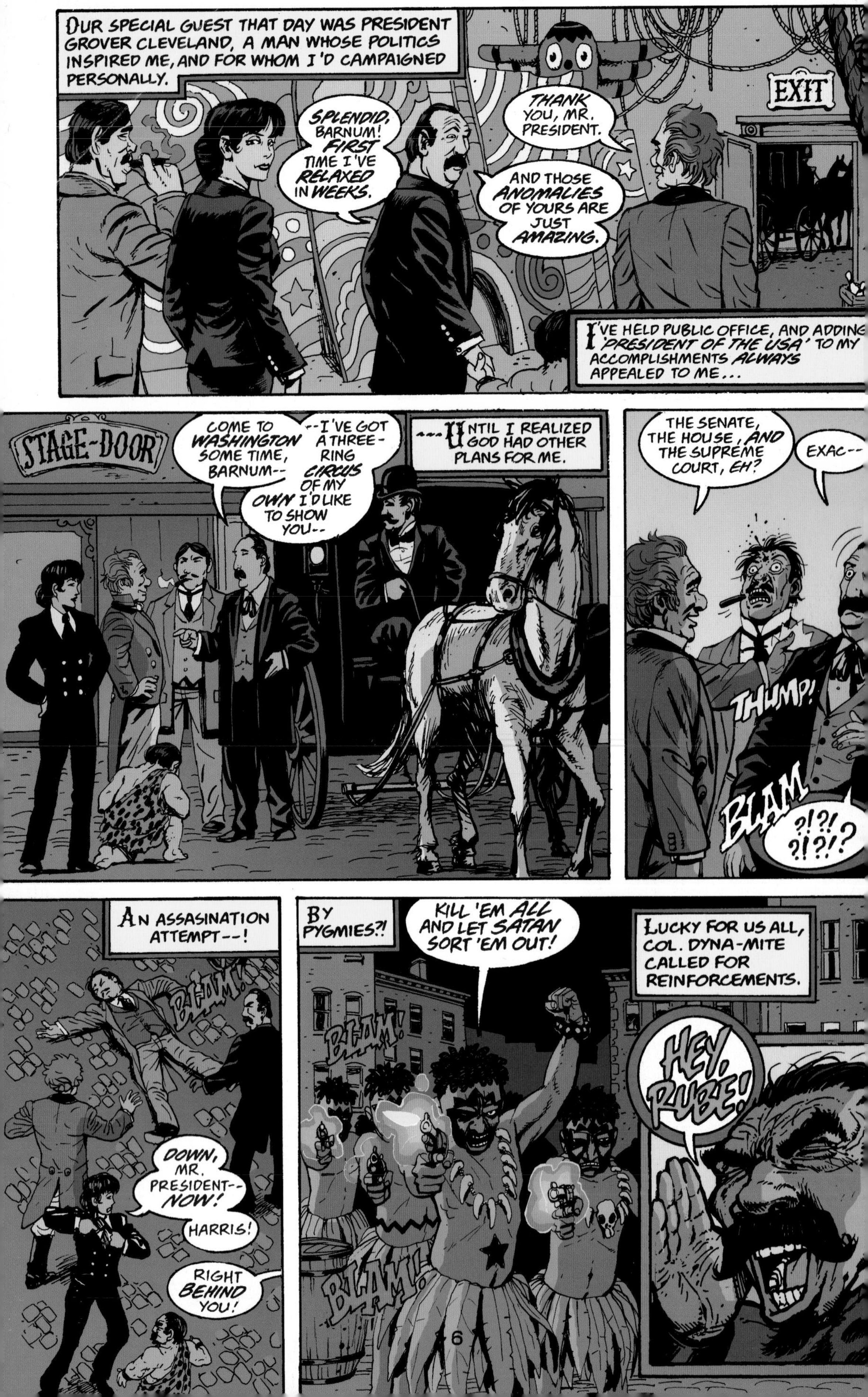

OUR SPECIAL GUEST THAT DAY WAS PRESIDENT GROVER CLEVELAND, A MAN WHOSE POLITICS INSPIRED ME, AND FOR WHOM I'D CAMPAIGNED PERSONALLY.
EXIT
SPLENDID, BARNUM! FIRST TIME I'VE RELAXED IN WEEKS.
THANK YOU, MR. PRESIDENT.
AND THOSE ANOMALIES OF YOURS ARE JUST AMAZING.
I'VE HELD PUBLIC OFFICE, AND ADDING 'PRESIDENT OF THE USA' TO MY ACCOMPLISHMENTS ALWAYS APPEALED TO ME...
STAGE-DOOR
COME TO WASHINGTON SOME TIME, BARNUM--
--I'VE GOT A THREE-RING CIRCUS OF MY OWN I'D LIKE TO SHOW YOU--
---UNTIL I REALIZED GOD HAD OTHER PLANS FOR ME.
THE SENATE, THE HOUSE, AND THE SUPREME COURT, EH?
EXAC--
THUMP!
BLAM
?!?!?!?!?
AN ASSASINATION ATTEMPT--!
BLAM!
DOWN, MR. PRESIDENT--NOW!
HARRIS!
RIGHT BEHIND YOU!
BY PYGMIES?!
KILL 'EM ALL AND LET SATAN SORT 'EM OUT!
BLAM!
BLAM!
LUCKY FOR US ALL, COL. DYNA-MITE CALLED FOR REINFORCEMENTS.
HEY, RUBE!

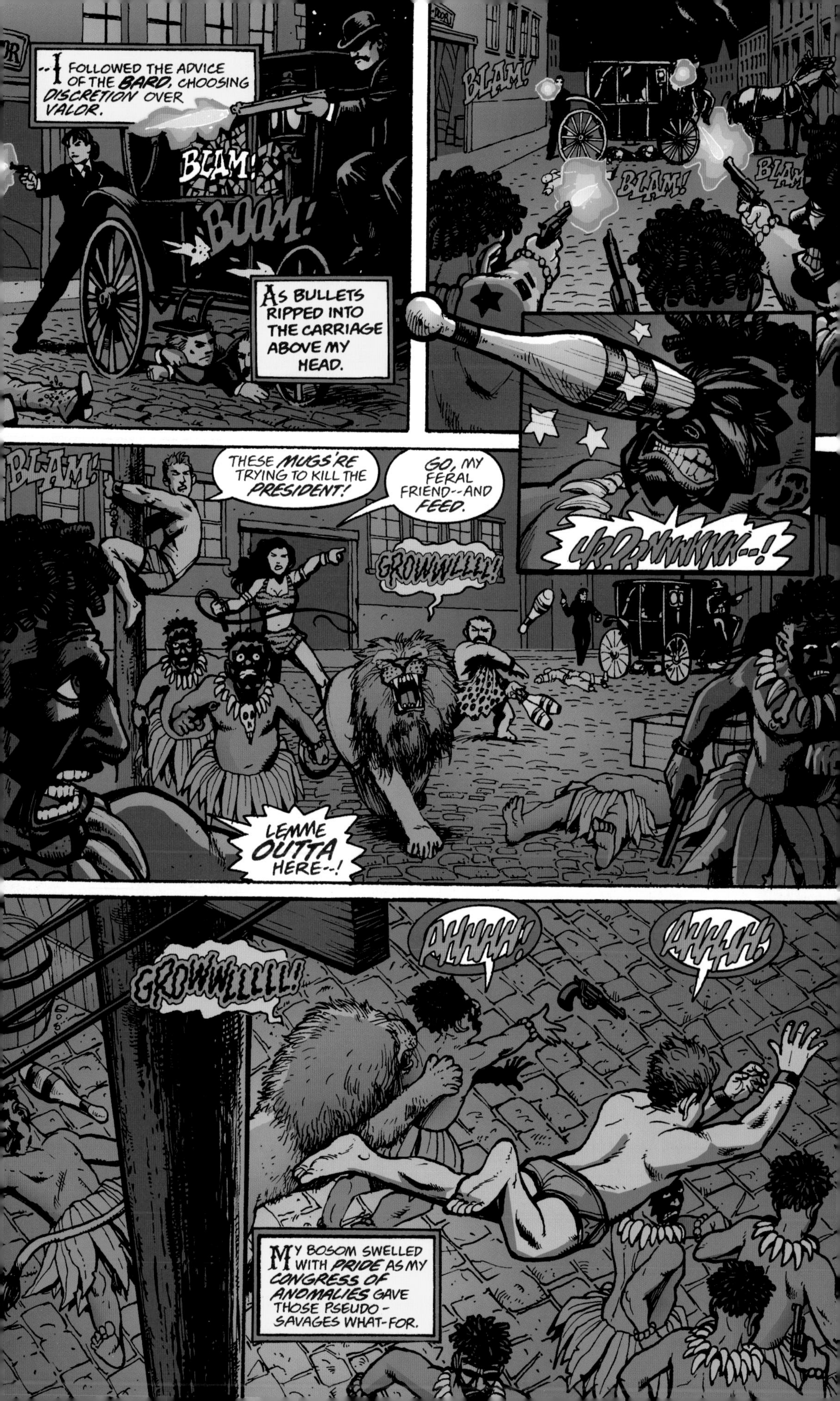
--I FOLLOWED THE ADVICE OF THE BARD, CHOOSING DISCRETION OVER VALOR.
BLAM!
BOOM!
AS BULLETS RIPPED INTO THE CARRIAGE ABOVE MY HEAD.
BLAM!
BLAM!
BLAM
URRRNNNKKK--!
BLAM!
THESE MUGS'RE TRYING TO KILL THE PRESIDENT!
GO, MY FERAL FRIEND--AND FEED.
GROWWLLLL!
LEMME OUTTA HERE--!
AHHHH!
AHHHH!
GROWWLLLLL!
MY BOSOM SWELLED WITH PRIDE AS MY CONGRESS OF ANOMALIES GAVE THOSE PSEUDO-SAVAGES WHAT-FOR.

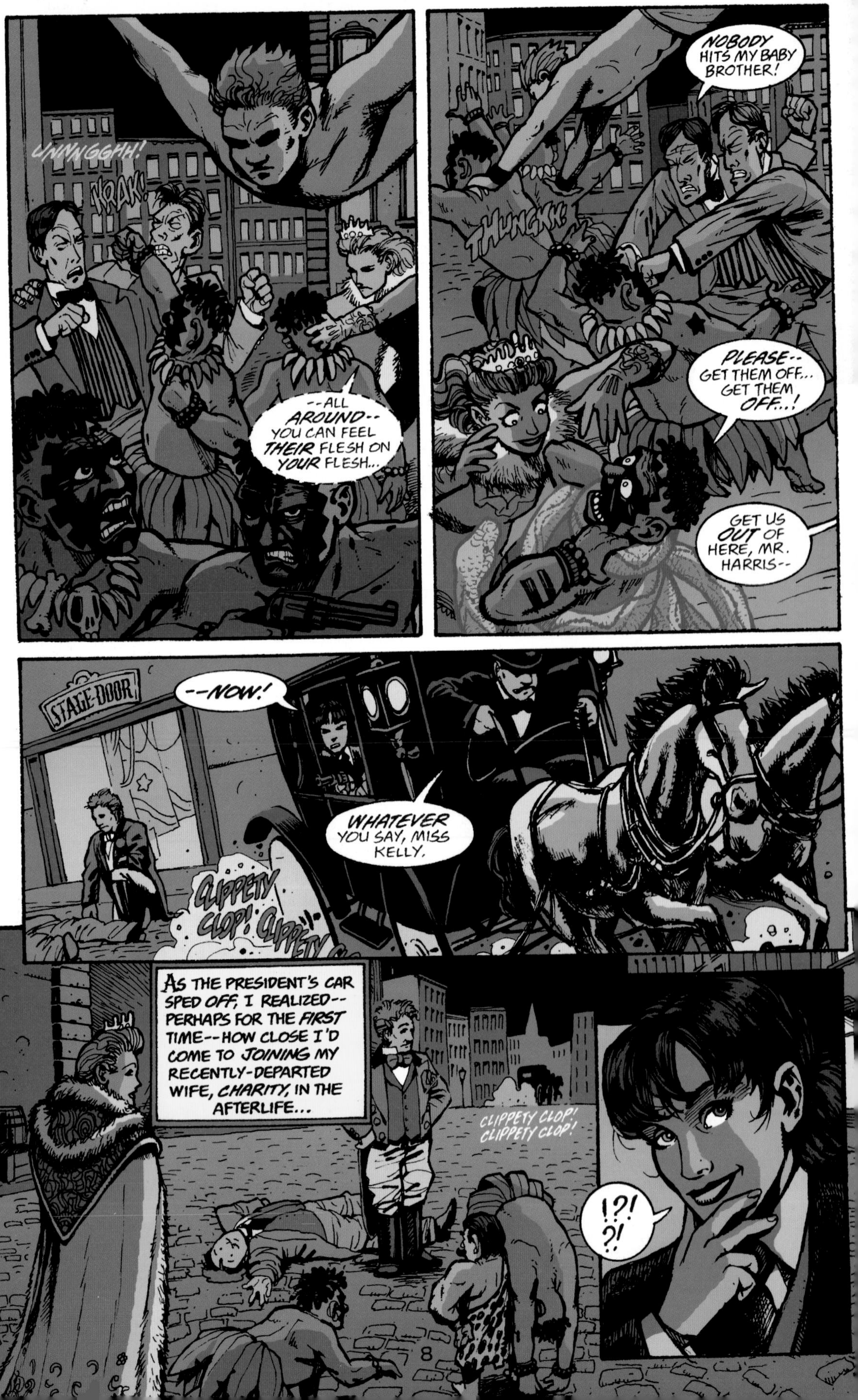

UNNNGGHH!
KRAK!
--ALL AROUND-- YOU CAN FEEL THEIR FLESH ON YOUR FLESH...
NOBODY HITS MY BABY BROTHER!
THUNCKK!
PLEASE-- GET THEM OFF... GET THEM OFF...!
GET US OUT OF HERE, MR. HARRIS--
STAGE DOOR
--NOW!
WHATEVER YOU SAY, MISS KELLY.
CLIPPETY CLOP! CLIPPETY
AS THE PRESIDENT'S CAR SPED OFF, I REALIZED-- PERHAPS FOR THE FIRST TIME--HOW CLOSE I'D COME TO JOINING MY RECENTLY-DEPARTED WIFE, CHARITY, IN THE AFTERLIFE...
CLIPPETY CLOP! CLIPPETY CLOP!
!?! ?!

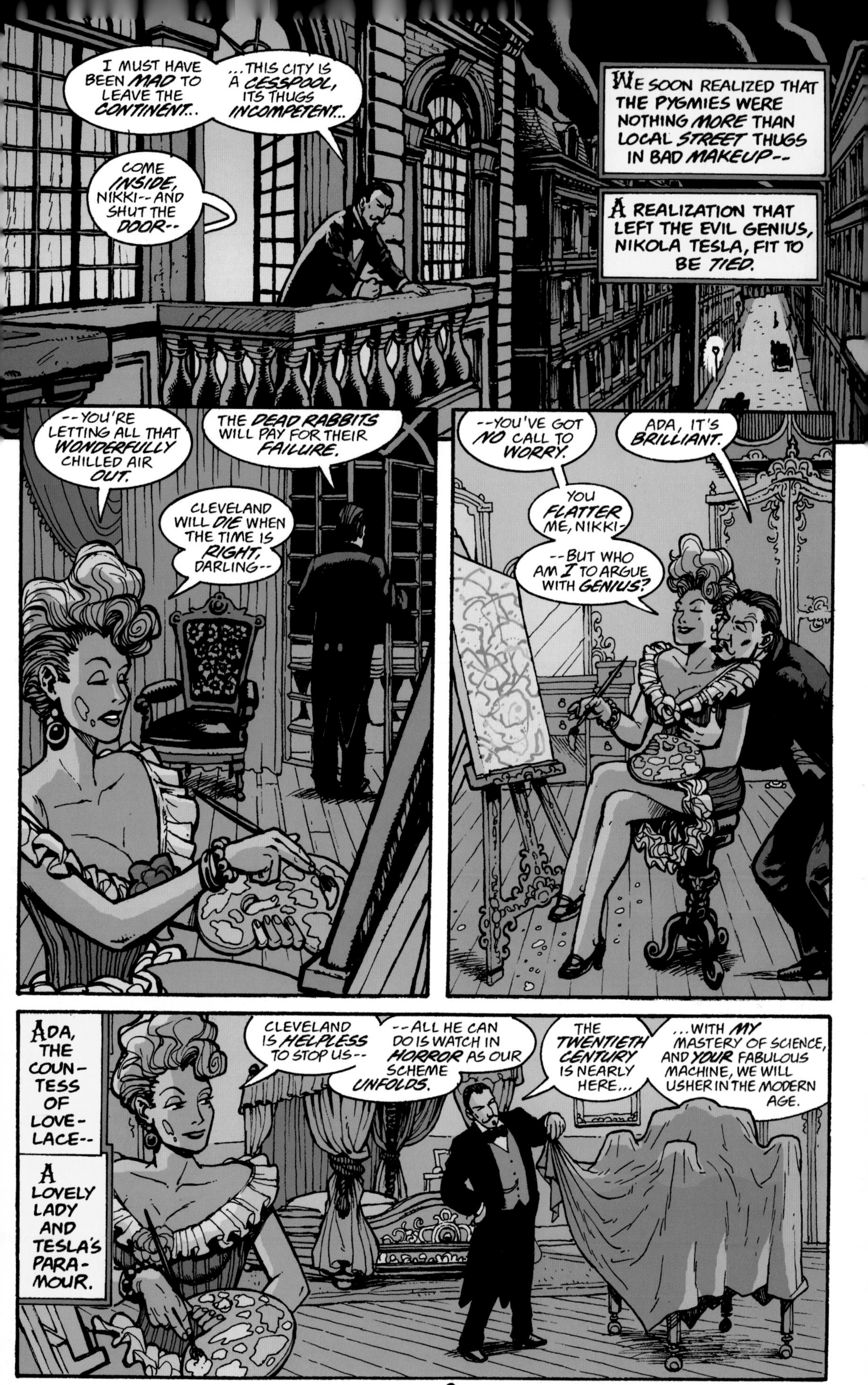
I MUST HAVE BEEN MAD TO LEAVE THE CONTINENT...
...THIS CITY IS A CESSPOOL, ITS THUGS INCOMPETENT...
COME INSIDE, NIKKI--AND SHUT THE DOOR--
WE SOON REALIZED THAT THE PYGMIES WERE NOTHING MORE THAN LOCAL STREET THUGS IN BAD MAKEUP--
A REALIZATION THAT LEFT THE EVIL GENIUS, NIKOLA TESLA, FIT TO BE TIED.
--YOU'RE LETTING ALL THAT WONDERFULLY CHILLED AIR OUT.
THE DEAD RABBITS WILL PAY FOR THEIR FAILURE.
CLEVELAND WILL DIE WHEN THE TIME IS RIGHT, DARLING--
--YOU'VE GOT NO CALL TO WORRY.
ADA, IT'S BRILLIANT.
YOU FLATTER ME, NIKKI-
--BUT WHO AM I TO ARGUE WITH GENIUS?
ADA, THE COUNTESS OF LOVELACE--
A LOVELY LADY AND TESLA'S PARAMOUR.
CLEVELAND IS HELPLESS TO STOP US--
--ALL HE CAN DO IS WATCH IN HORROR AS OUR SCHEME UNFOLDS.
THE TWENTIETH CENTURY IS NEARLY HERE...
...WITH MY MASTERY OF SCIENCE, AND YOUR FABULOUS MACHINE, WE WILL USHER IN THE MODERN AGE.

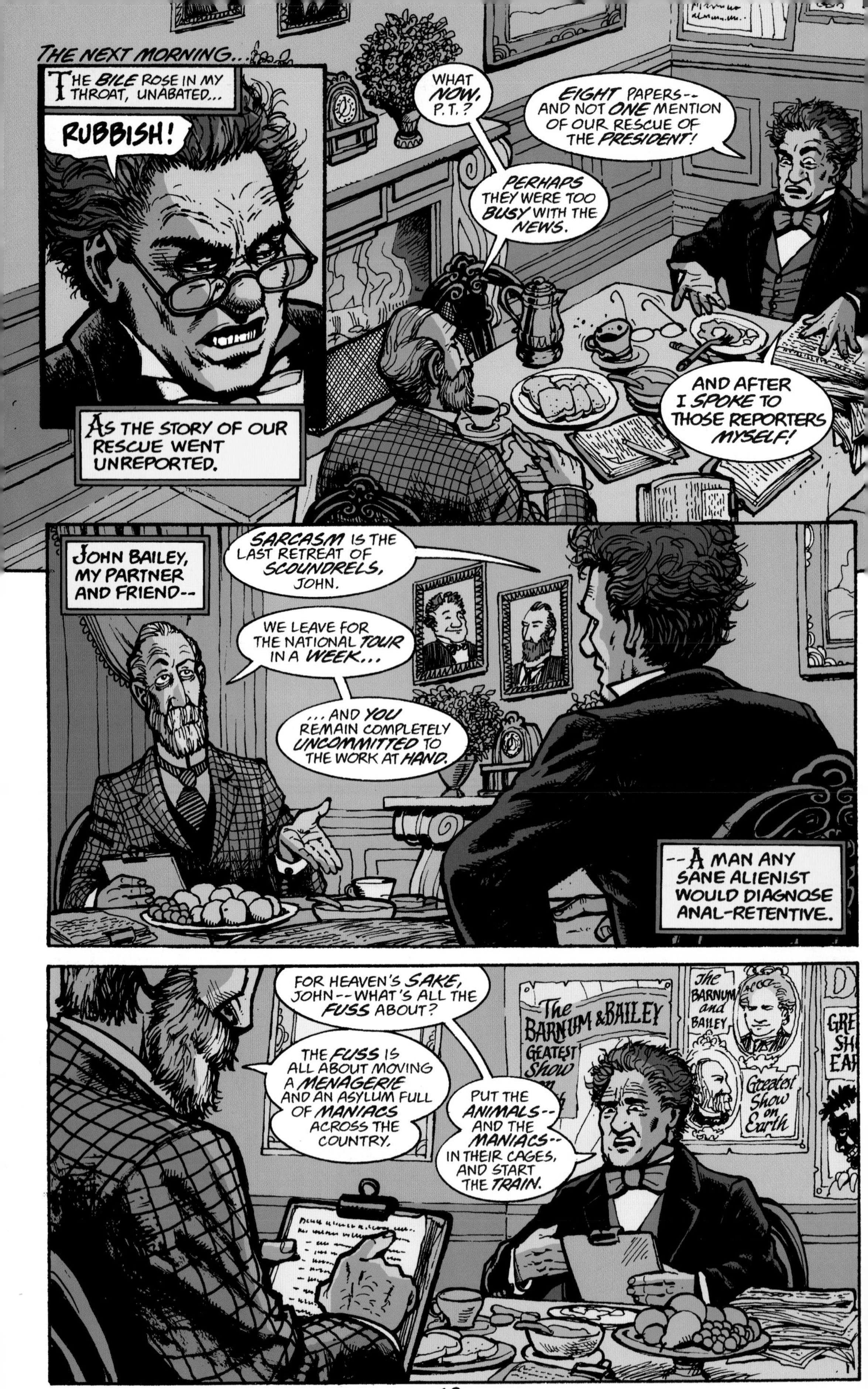
THE NEXT MORNING...
THE BILE ROSE IN MY THROAT, UNABATED...
RUBBISH!
AS THE STORY OF OUR RESCUE WENT UNREPORTED.
WHAT NOW, P.T.?
EIGHT PAPERS--AND NOT ONE MENTION OF OUR RESCUE OF THE PRESIDENT!
PERHAPS THEY WERE TOO BUSY WITH THE NEWS.
AND AFTER I SPOKE TO THOSE REPORTERS MYSELF!
JOHN BAILEY, MY PARTNER AND FRIEND--
SARCASM IS THE LAST RETREAT OF SCOUNDRELS, JOHN.
WE LEAVE FOR THE NATIONAL TOUR IN A WEEK...
...AND YOU REMAIN COMPLETELY UNCOMMITTED TO THE WORK AT HAND.
--A MAN ANY SANE ALIENIST WOULD DIAGNOSE ANAL-RETENTIVE.
FOR HEAVEN'S SAKE, JOHN--WHAT'S ALL THE FUSS ABOUT?
THE FUSS IS ALL ABOUT MOVING A MENAGERIE AND AN ASYLUM FULL OF MANIACS ACROSS THE COUNTRY.
PUT THE ANIMALS--AND THE MANIACS--IN THEIR CAGES, AND START THE TRAIN.
The BARNUM & BAILEY GEATEST Show
The BARNUM and BAILEY Greatest Show on Earth

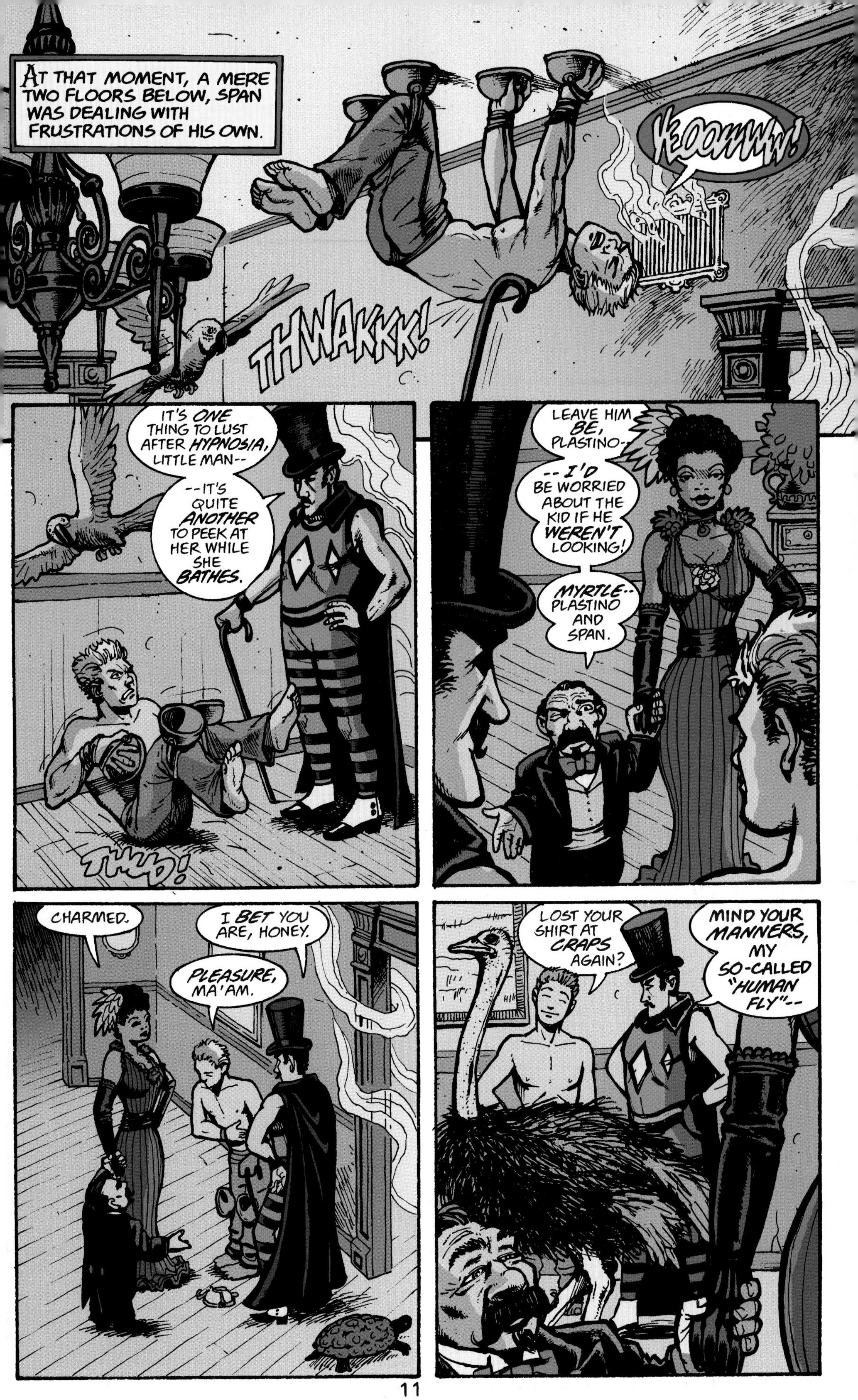

AT THAT MOMENT, A MERE TWO FLOORS BELOW, SPAN WAS DEALING WITH FRUSTRATIONS OF HIS OWN.
YEOOWWW!
THWAKKK!
IT'S ONE THING TO LUST AFTER HYPNOSIA, LITTLE MAN--
--IT'S QUITE ANOTHER TO PEEK AT HER WHILE SHE BATHES.
THUD!
LEAVE HIM BE, PLASTINO--
--I'D BE WORRIED ABOUT THE KID IF HE WEREN'T LOOKING!
MYRTLE-- PLASTINO AND SPAN.
CHARMED.
I BET YOU ARE, HONEY.
PLEASURE, MA'AM.
LOST YOUR SHIRT AT CRAPS AGAIN?
MIND YOUR MANNERS, MY SO-CALLED "HUMAN FLY"--

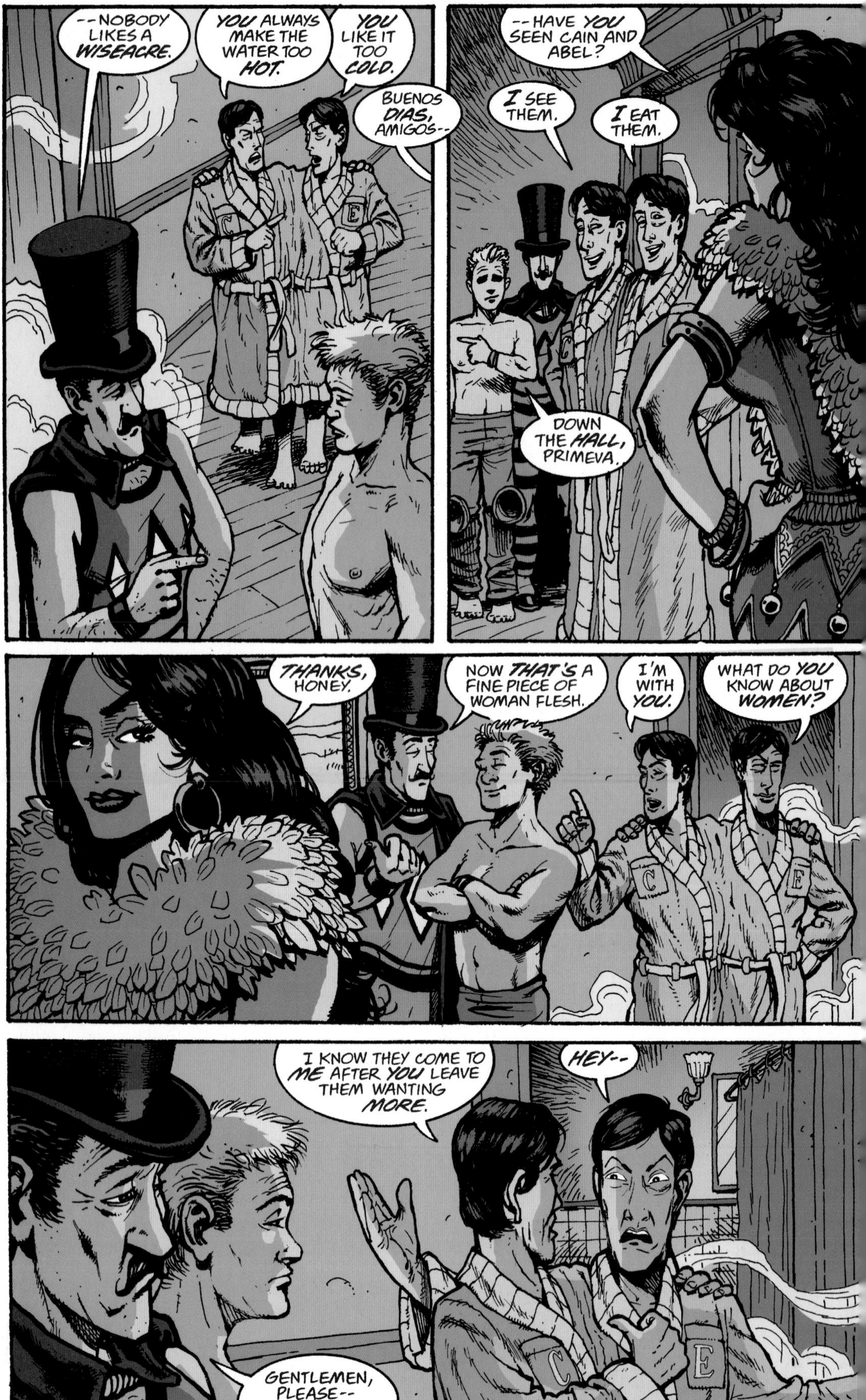
--NOBODY LIKES A WISEACRE.
YOU ALWAYS MAKE THE WATER TOO HOT.
YOU LIKE IT TOO COLD.
BUENOS DIAS, AMIGOS--
--HAVE YOU SEEN CAIN AND ABEL?
I SEE THEM.
I EAT THEM.
DOWN THE HALL, PRIMEVA.
THANKS, HONEY.
NOW THAT'S A FINE PIECE OF WOMAN FLESH.
I'M WITH YOU.
WHAT DO YOU KNOW ABOUT WOMEN?
I KNOW THEY COME TO ME AFTER YOU LEAVE THEM WANTING MORE.
HEY--
GENTLEMEN, PLEASE--

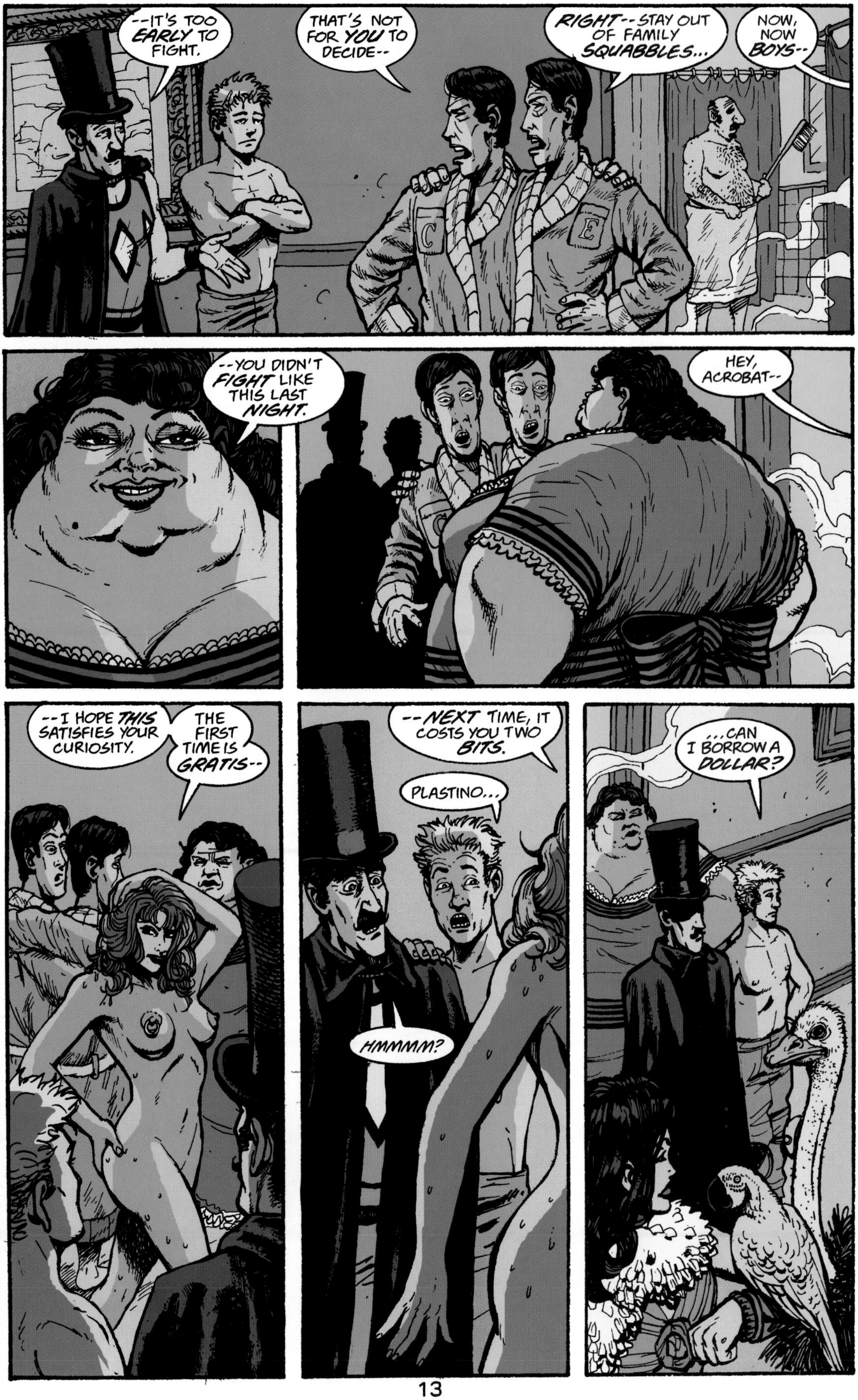
--IT'S TOO EARLY TO FIGHT.
THAT'S NOT FOR YOU TO DECIDE--
RIGHT--STAY OUT OF FAMILY SQUABBLES...
NOW, NOW BOYS--
--YOU DIDN'T FIGHT LIKE THIS LAST NIGHT.
HEY, ACROBAT--
--I HOPE THIS SATISFIES YOUR CURIOSITY.
THE FIRST TIME IS GRATIS--
--NEXT TIME, IT COSTS YOU TWO BITS.
PLASTINO...
HMMMM?
...CAN I BORROW A DOLLAR?

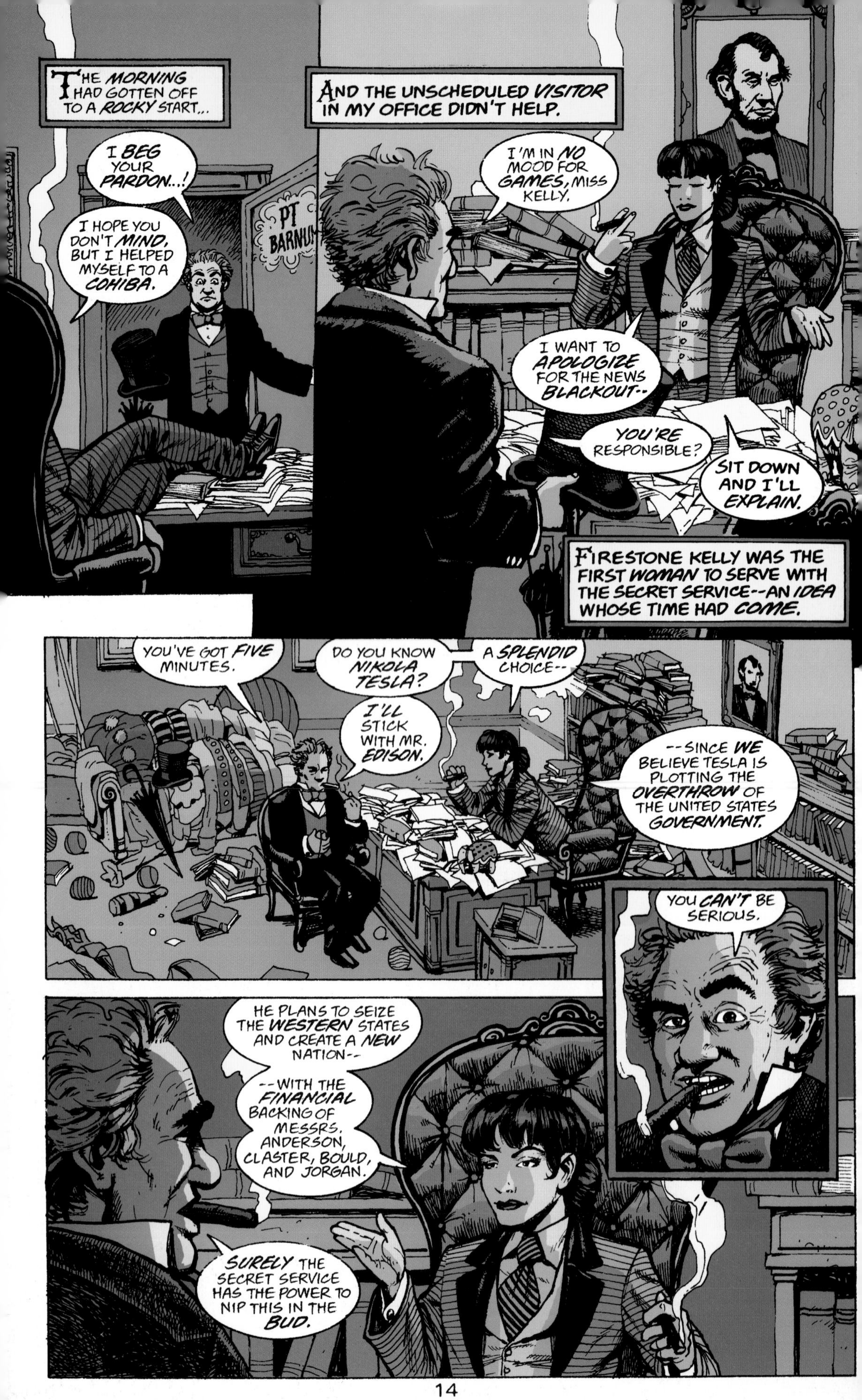
THE MORNING HAD GOTTEN OFF TO A ROCKY START...
I BEG YOUR PARDON...!
I HOPE YOU DON'T MIND, BUT I HELPED MYSELF TO A COHIBA.
PT BARNUM
AND THE UNSCHEDULED VISITOR IN MY OFFICE DIDN'T HELP.
I'M IN NO MOOD FOR GAMES, MISS KELLY.
I WANT TO APOLOGIZE FOR THE NEWS BLACKOUT--
YOU'RE RESPONSIBLE?
SIT DOWN AND I'LL EXPLAIN.
FIRESTONE KELLY WAS THE FIRST WOMAN TO SERVE WITH THE SECRET SERVICE--AN IDEA WHOSE TIME HAD COME.
YOU'VE GOT FIVE MINUTES.
DO YOU KNOW NIKOLA TESLA?
I'LL STICK WITH MR. EDISON.
A SPLENDID CHOICE--
--SINCE WE BELIEVE TESLA IS PLOTTING THE OVERTHROW OF THE UNITED STATES GOVERNMENT.
YOU CAN'T BE SERIOUS.
HE PLANS TO SEIZE THE WESTERN STATES AND CREATE A NEW NATION--
--WITH THE FINANCIAL BACKING OF MESSRS. ANDERSON, CLASTER, BOULD, AND JORGAN.
SURELY THE SECRET SERVICE HAS THE POWER TO NIP THIS IN THE BUD.

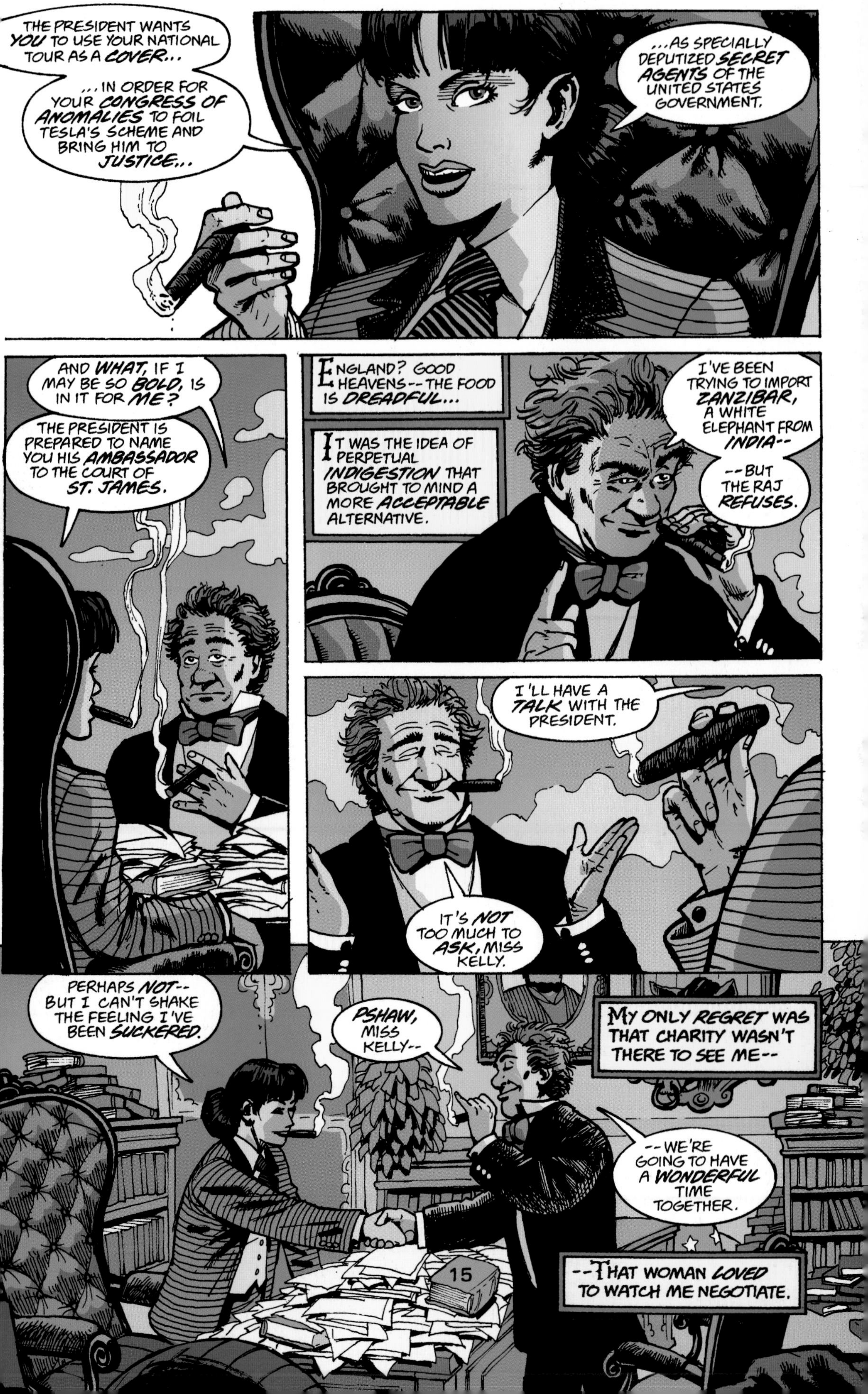
THE PRESIDENT WANTS YOU TO USE YOUR NATIONAL TOUR AS A COVER...
...IN ORDER FOR YOUR CONGRESS OF ANOMALIES TO FOIL TESLA'S SCHEME AND BRING HIM TO JUSTICE...
...AS SPECIALLY DEPUTIZED SECRET AGENTS OF THE UNITED STATES GOVERNMENT.
AND WHAT, IF I MAY BE SO BOLD, IS IN IT FOR ME?
THE PRESIDENT IS PREPARED TO NAME YOU HIS AMBASSADOR TO THE COURT OF ST. JAMES.
ENGLAND? GOOD HEAVENS--THE FOOD IS DREADFUL...
IT WAS THE IDEA OF PERPETUAL INDIGESTION THAT BROUGHT TO MIND A MORE ACCEPTABLE ALTERNATIVE.
I'VE BEEN TRYING TO IMPORT ZANZIBAR, A WHITE ELEPHANT FROM INDIA--
--BUT THE RAJ REFUSES.
I'LL HAVE A TALK WITH THE PRESIDENT.
IT'S NOT TOO MUCH TO ASK, MISS KELLY.
PERHAPS NOT--BUT I CAN'T SHAKE THE FEELING I'VE BEEN SUCKERED.
PSHAW, MISS KELLY--
MY ONLY REGRET WAS THAT CHARITY WASN'T THERE TO SEE ME--
--WE'RE GOING TO HAVE A WONDERFUL TIME TOGETHER.
--THAT WOMAN LOVED TO WATCH ME NEGOTIATE.

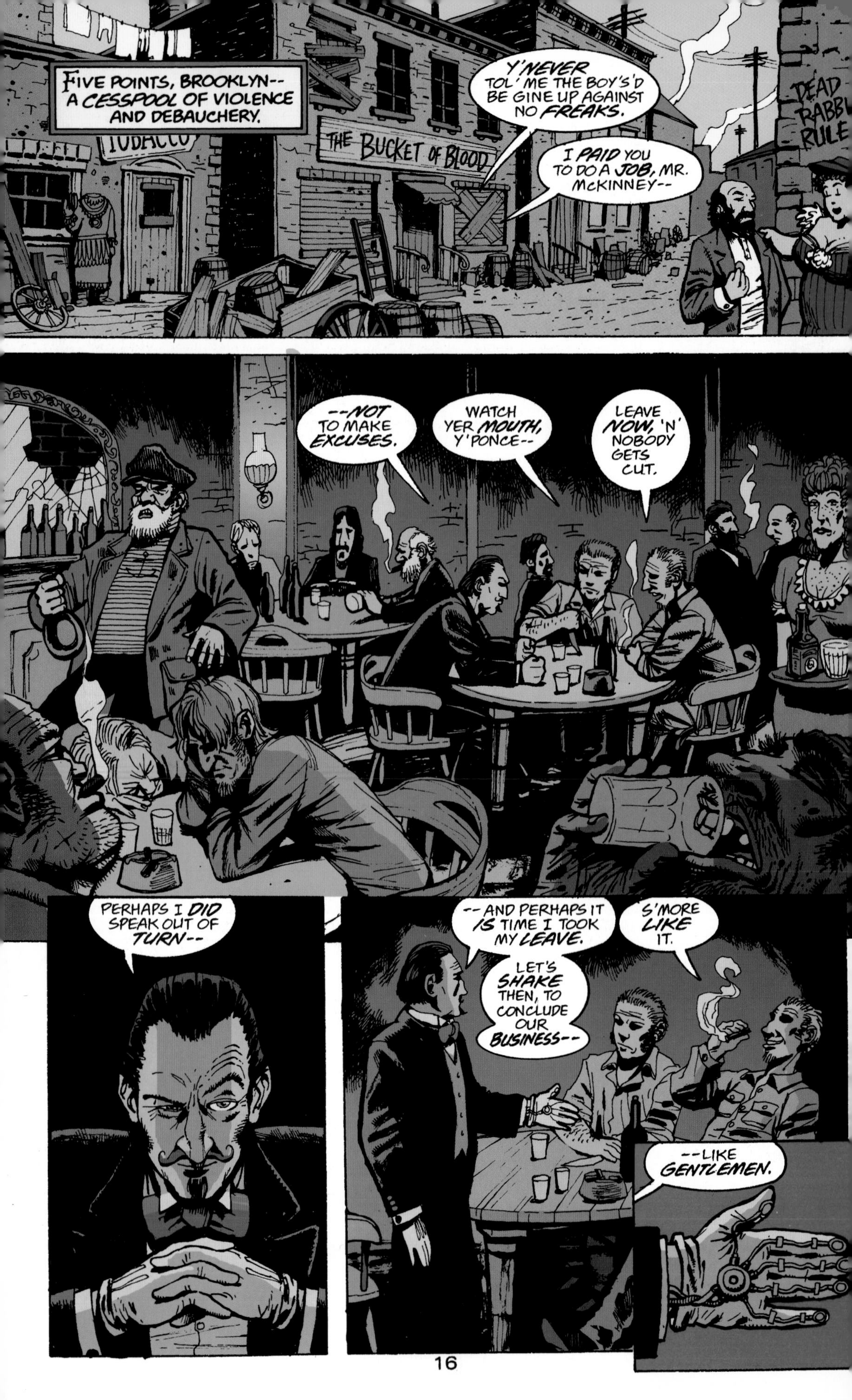
FIVE POINTS, BROOKLYN-- A CESSPOOL OF VIOLENCE AND DEBAUCHERY.
TOBACCO
THE BUCKET OF BLOOD
Y'NEVER TOL' ME THE BOY'S'D BE GINE UP AGAINST NO FREAKS.
I PAID YOU TO DO A JOB, MR. McKINNEY--
--NOT TO MAKE EXCUSES.
WATCH YER MOUTH, Y'PONCE--
LEAVE NOW, 'N' NOBODY GETS CUT.
PERHAPS I DID SPEAK OUT OF TURN--
--AND PERHAPS IT IS TIME I TOOK MY LEAVE.
LET'S SHAKE THEN, TO CONCLUDE OUR BUSINESS--
S'MORE LIKE IT.
--LIKE GENTLEMEN.

IN *MY* WORLD, FAILURE IS *UNACCEPTABLE.*

YAAAAAAAA!

FOR GOD'S *SAKE*-- --Y' *FRIED* POOR MIKE LIKE AN *EGG!*

THIS WILL COVER ANY *INCONVENIENCE.*

COME BACK *ANY* TIME, SIR.

TESLA!

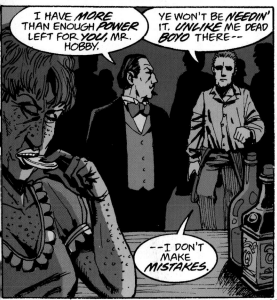

I HAVE *MORE* THAN ENOUGH *POWER* LEFT FOR *YOU,* MR. HOBBY.

YE WON'T BE *NEEDIN'* IT. *UNLIKE* ME DEAD *BOYO* THERE--

--I DON'T MAKE *MISTAKES.*

THEN PERHAPS WE *DO* HAVE BUSINESS TO DISCUSS.

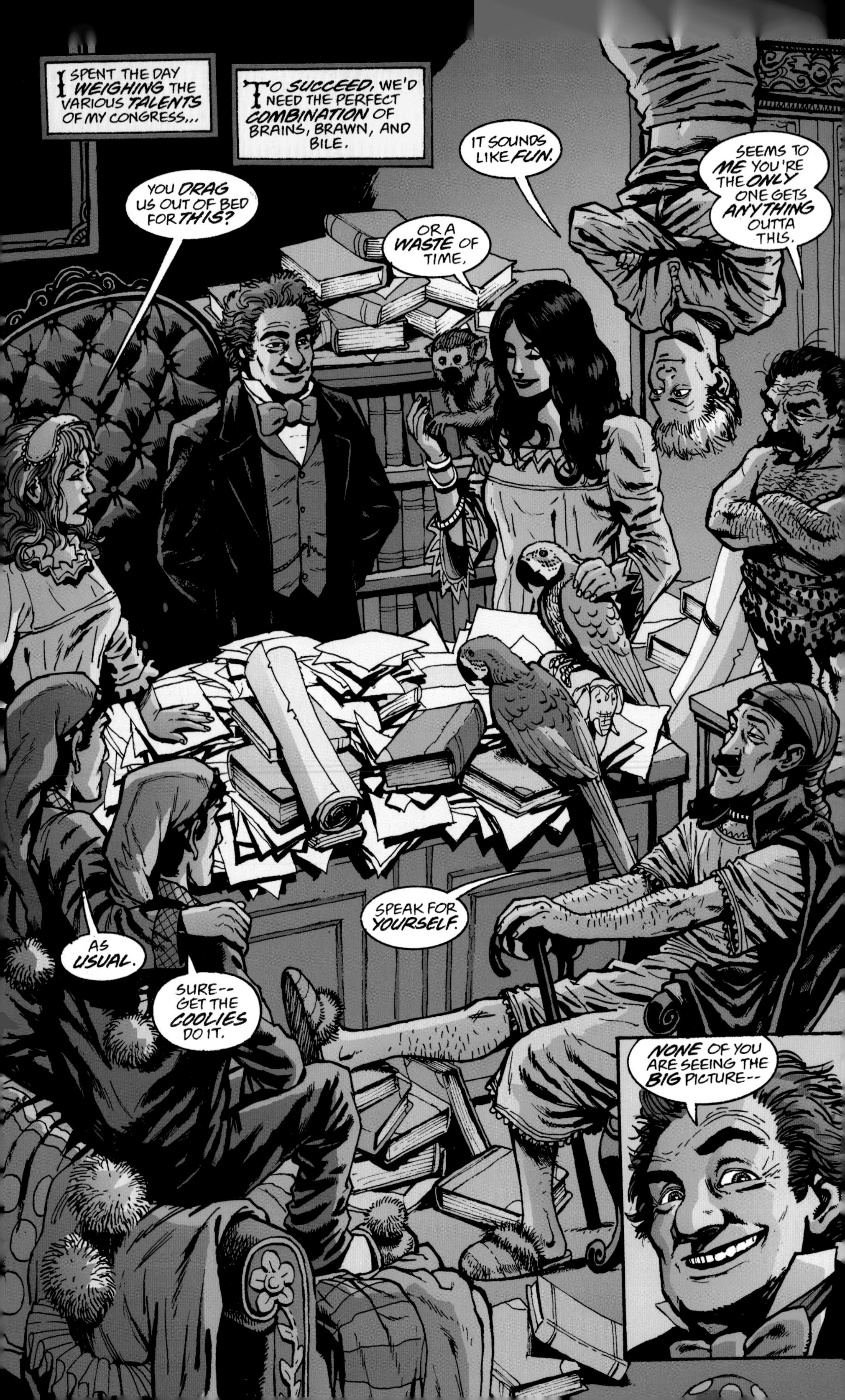
I SPENT THE DAY WEIGHING THE VARIOUS TALENTS OF MY CONGRESS...
TO SUCCEED, WE'D NEED THE PERFECT COMBINATION OF BRAINS, BRAWN, AND BILE.
YOU DRAG US OUT OF BED FOR THIS?
IT SOUNDS LIKE FUN.
OR A WASTE OF TIME.
SEEMS TO ME YOU'RE THE ONLY ONE GETS ANYTHING OUTTA THIS.
SPEAK FOR YOURSELF.
AS USUAL.
SURE-- GET THE COOLIES DO IT.
NONE OF YOU ARE SEEING THE BIG PICTURE--

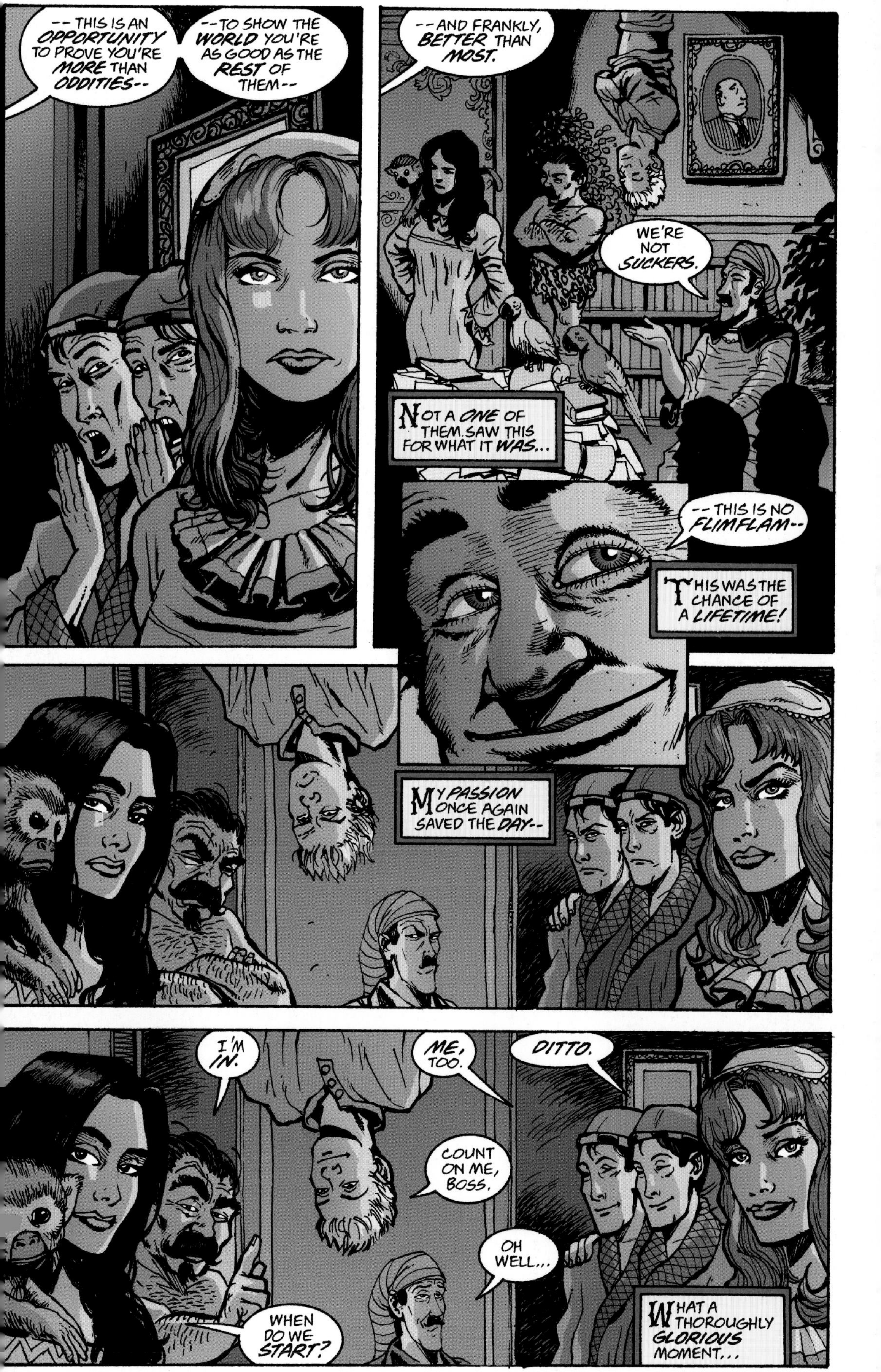
-- THIS IS AN OPPORTUNITY TO PROVE YOU'RE MORE THAN ODDITIES--
--TO SHOW THE WORLD YOU'RE AS GOOD AS THE REST OF THEM--
--AND FRANKLY, BETTER THAN MOST.
WE'RE NOT SUCKERS.
NOT A ONE OF THEM SAW THIS FOR WHAT IT WAS...
-- THIS IS NO FLIMFLAM--
THIS WAS THE CHANCE OF A LIFETIME!
MY PASSION ONCE AGAIN SAVED THE DAY--
I'M IN.
ME, TOO.
DITTO.
COUNT ON ME, BOSS.
OH WELL...
WHEN DO WE START?
WHAT A THOROUGHLY GLORIOUS MOMENT...

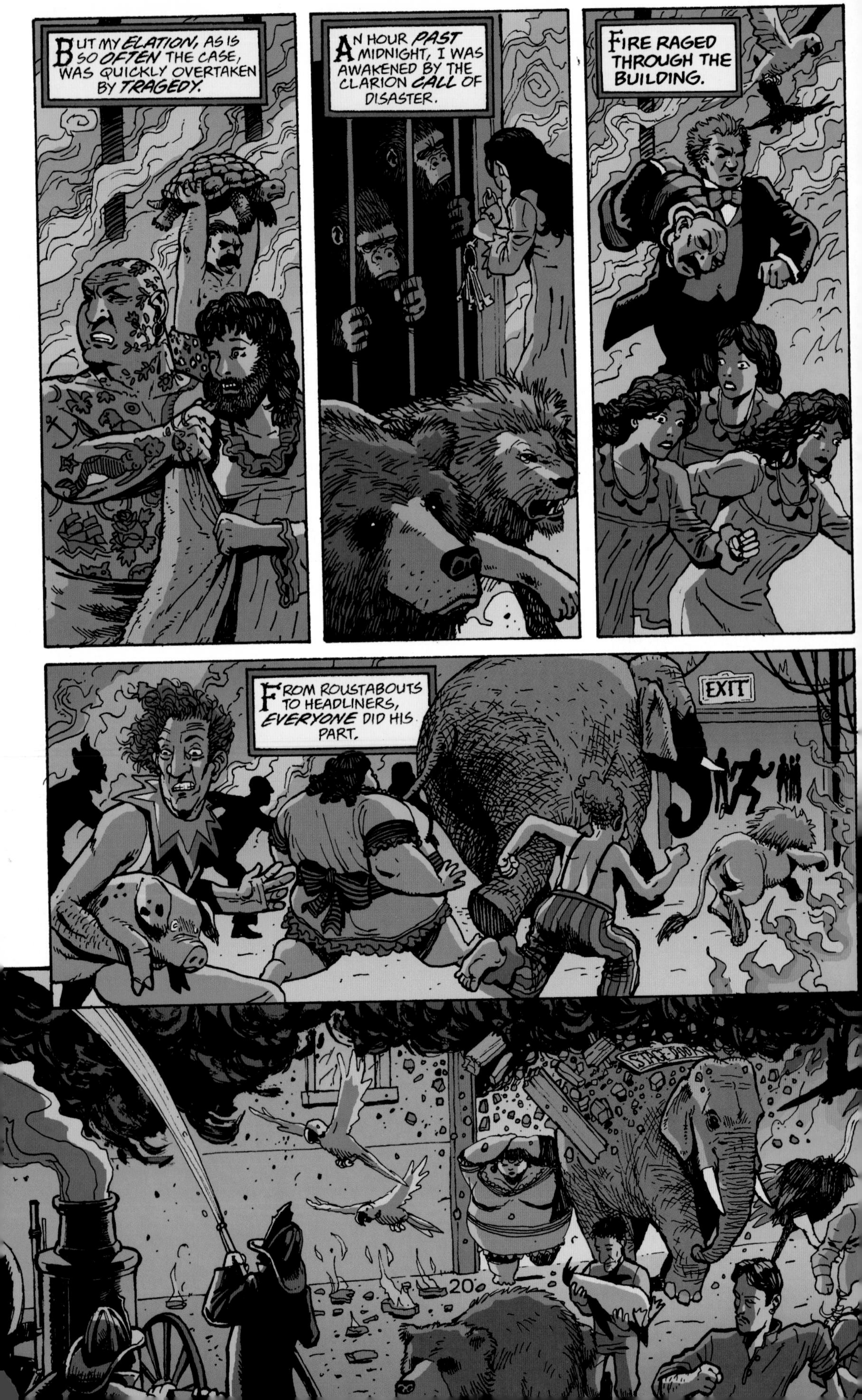
But my elation, as is so often the case, was quickly overtaken by tragedy.
An hour past midnight, I was awakened by the clarion call of disaster.
Fire raged through the building.
From roustabouts to headliners, everyone did his part.
EXIT
STAGE DOOR

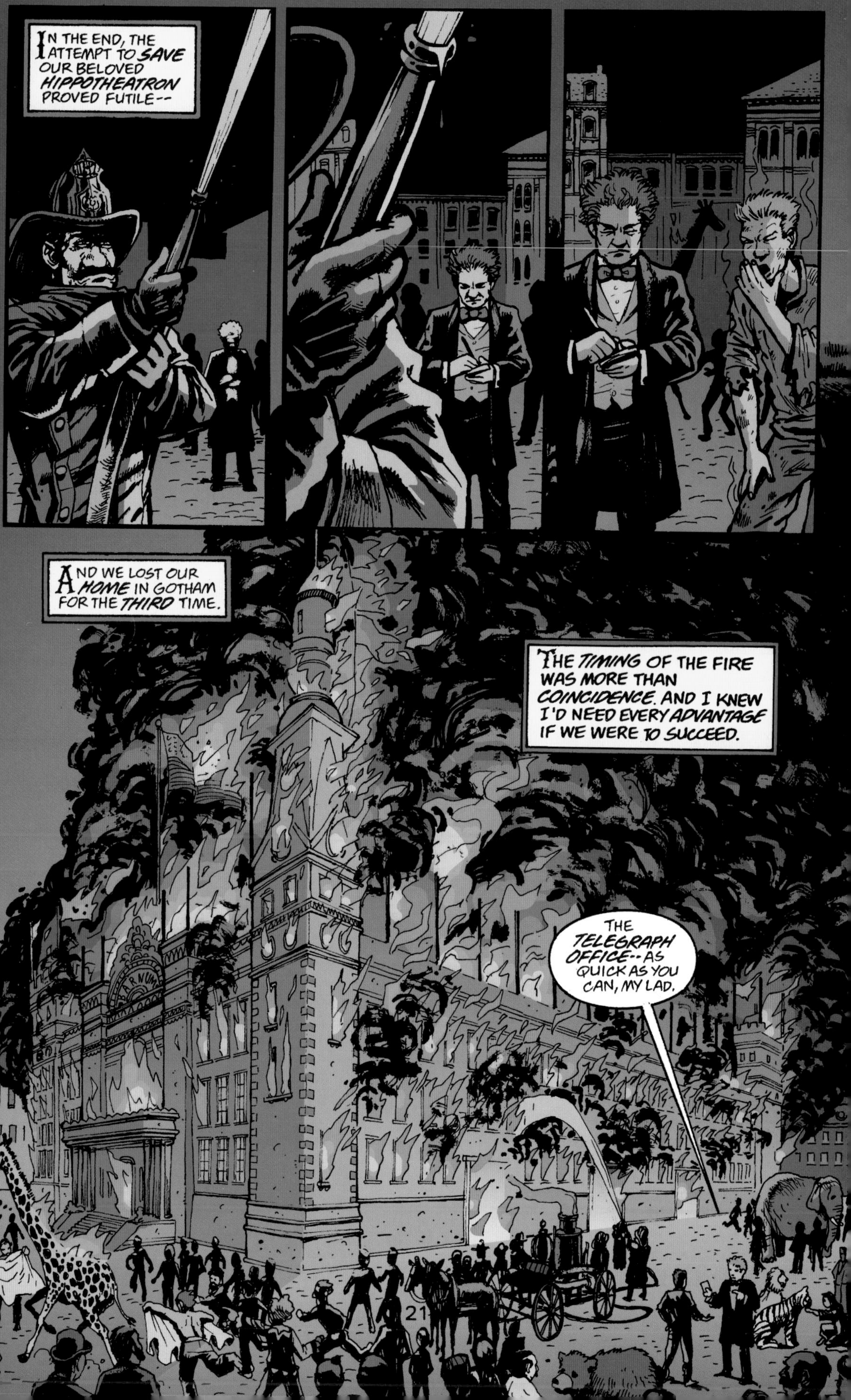
IN THE END, THE ATTEMPT TO SAVE OUR BELOVED HIPPOTHEATRON PROVED FUTILE--
AND WE LOST OUR HOME IN GOTHAM FOR THE THIRD TIME.
THE TIMING OF THE FIRE WAS MORE THAN COINCIDENCE. AND I KNEW I'D NEED EVERY ADVANTAGE IF WE WERE TO SUCCEED.
THE TELEGRAPH OFFICE--AS QUICK AS YOU CAN, MY LAD.
BARNUM

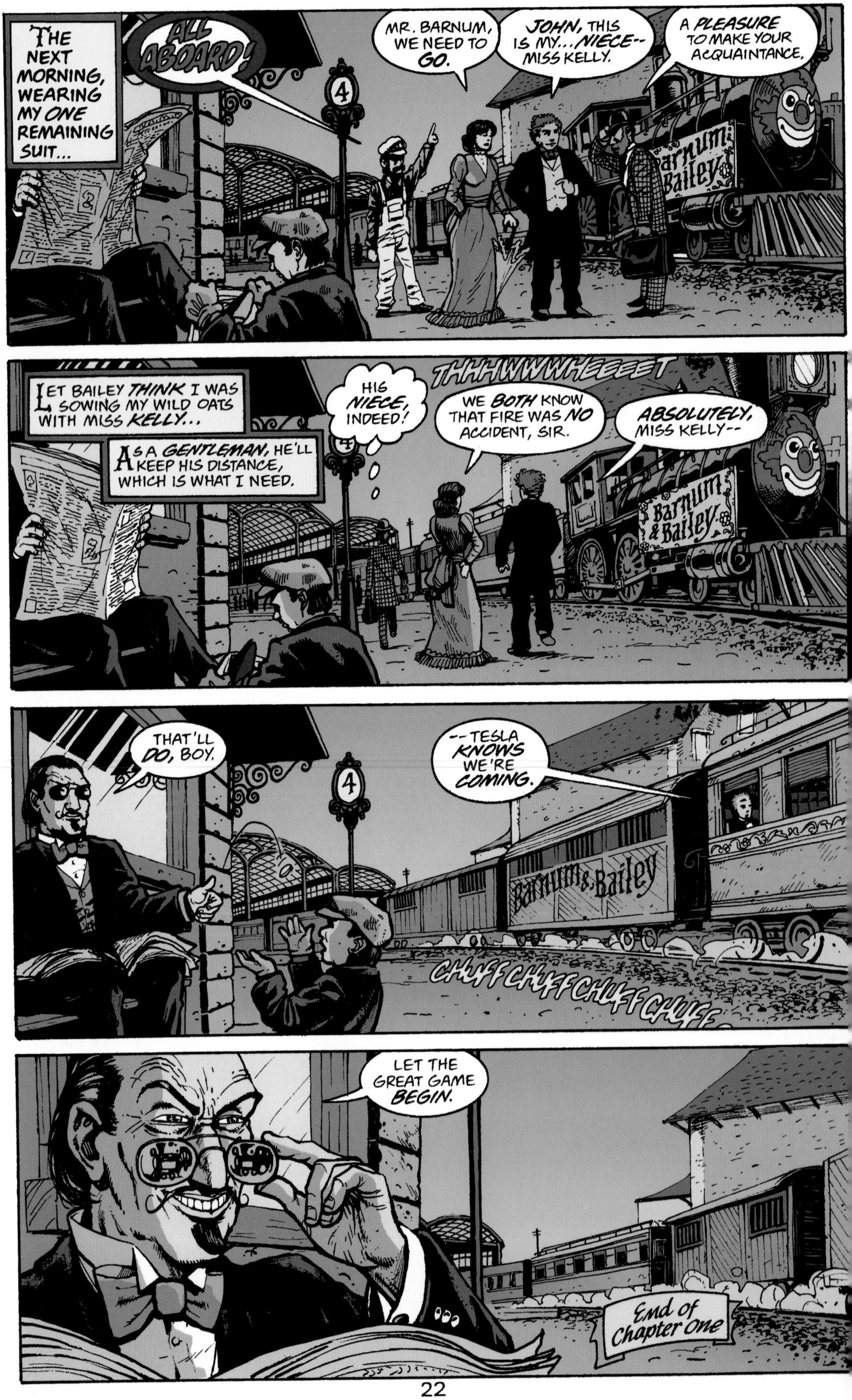
THE NEXT MORNING, WEARING MY ONE REMAINING SUIT...
ALL ABOARD!
MR. BARNUM, WE NEED TO GO.
JOHN, THIS IS MY... NIECE-- MISS KELLY.
A PLEASURE TO MAKE YOUR ACQUAINTANCE.
Barnum & Bailey
LET BAILEY THINK I WAS SOWING MY WILD OATS WITH MISS KELLY...
AS A GENTLEMAN, HE'LL KEEP HIS DISTANCE, WHICH IS WHAT I NEED.
HIS NIECE, INDEED!
THHHWWWHEEEEET
WE BOTH KNOW THAT FIRE WAS NO ACCIDENT, SIR.
ABSOLUTELY, MISS KELLY--
Barnum & Bailey
THAT'LL DO, BOY.
--TESLA KNOWS WE'RE COMING.
Barnum & Bailey
CHUFF CHUFF CHUFF CHUFF
LET THE GREAT GAME BEGIN.
End of Chapter One

CHAPTER 2

CHAPTER 2

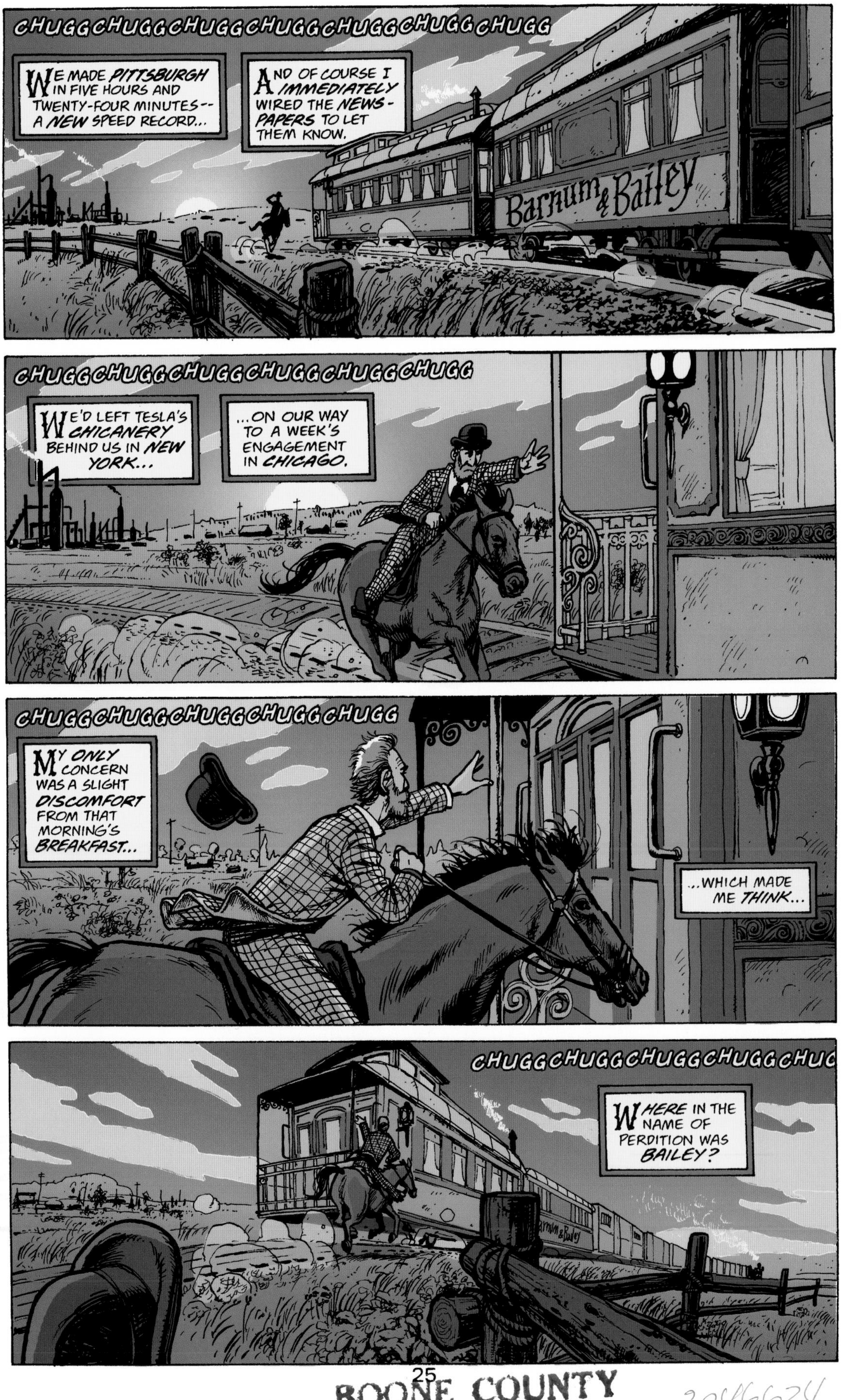
CHUGGCHUGGCHUGGCHUGGCHUGGCHUGGCHUGG
WE MADE PITTSBURGH IN FIVE HOURS AND TWENTY-FOUR MINUTES-- A NEW SPEED RECORD...
AND OF COURSE I IMMEDIATELY WIRED THE NEWS-PAPERS TO LET THEM KNOW.
Barnum & Bailey
CHUGGCHUGGCHUGGCHUGGCHUGGCHUGG
WE'D LEFT TESLA'S CHICANERY BEHIND US IN NEW YORK...
...ON OUR WAY TO A WEEK'S ENGAGEMENT IN CHICAGO.
CHUGGCHUGGCHUGGCHUGGCHUGG
MY ONLY CONCERN WAS A SLIGHT DISCOMFORT FROM THAT MORNING'S BREAKFAST...
...WHICH MADE ME THINK...
CHUGGCHUGGCHUGGCHUGGCHUG
WHERE IN THE NAME OF PERDITION WAS BAILEY?
Barnum & Bailey

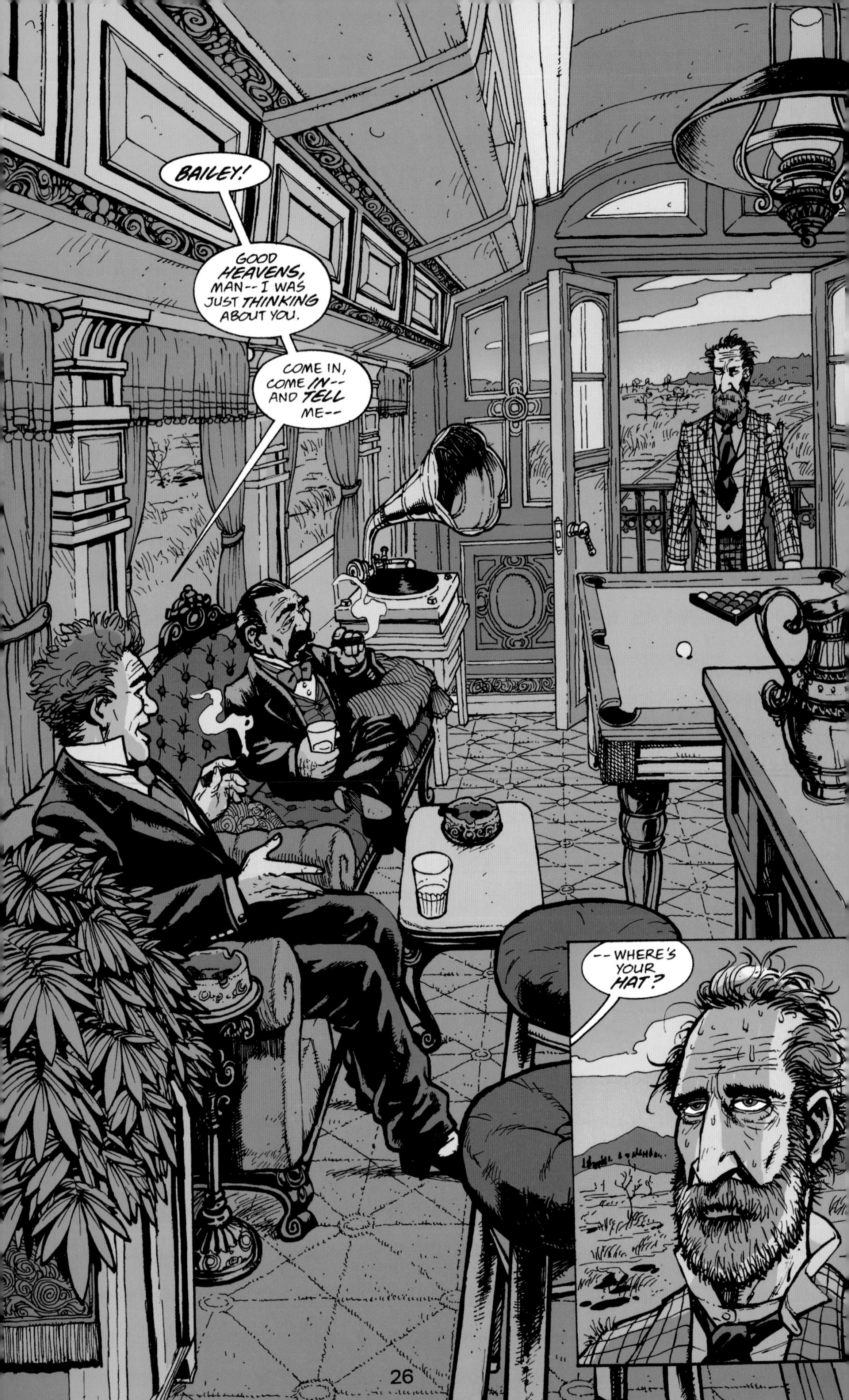
BAILEY!
GOOD HEAVENS, MAN-- I WAS JUST THINKING ABOUT YOU.
COME IN, COME IN-- AND TELL ME--
--WHERE'S YOUR HAT?

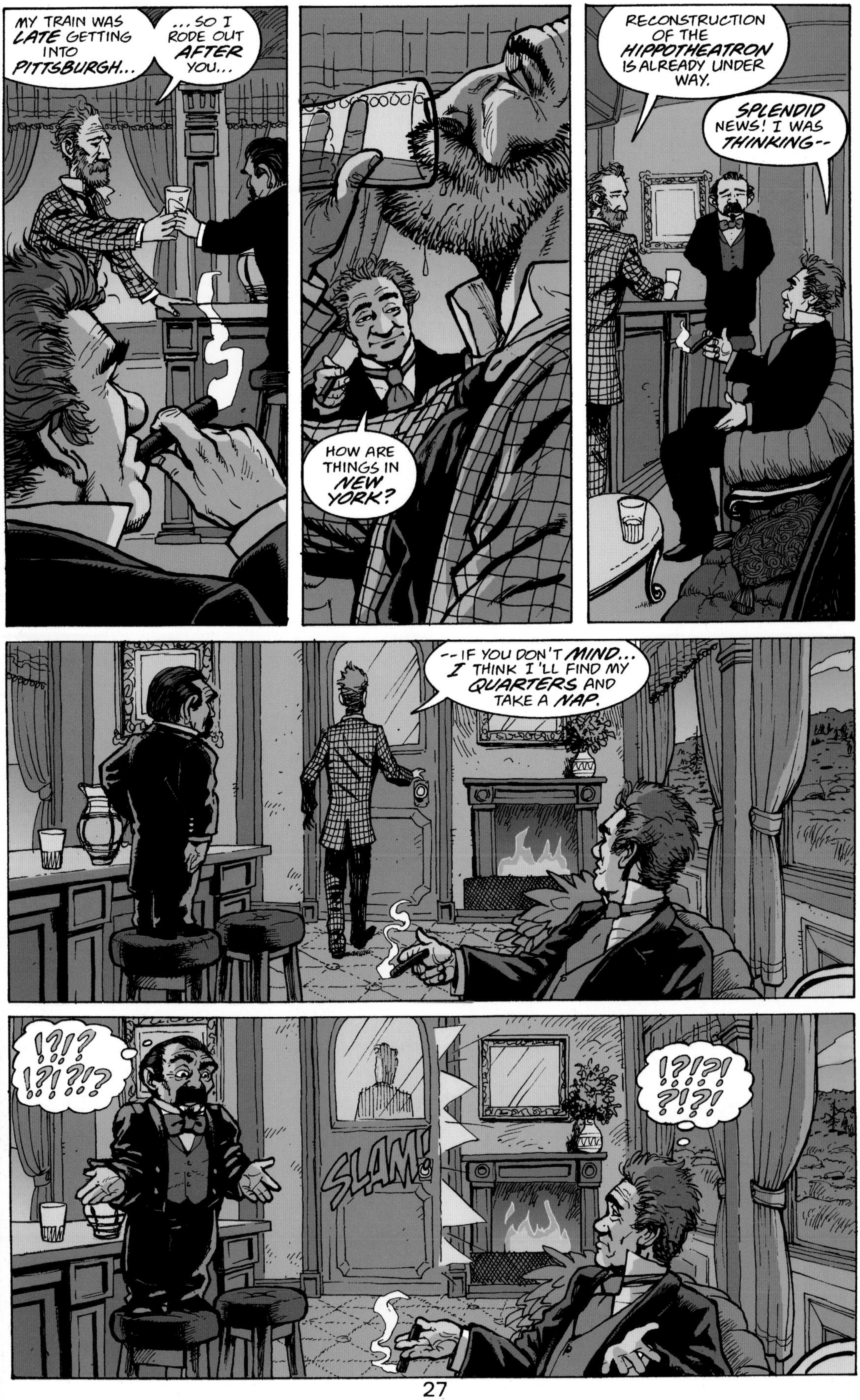
MY TRAIN WAS LATE GETTING INTO PITTSBURGH...
...SO I RODE OUT AFTER YOU...
HOW ARE THINGS IN NEW YORK?
RECONSTRUCTION OF THE HIPPOTHEATRON IS ALREADY UNDER WAY.
SPLENDID NEWS! I WAS THINKING--
--IF YOU DON'T MIND... I THINK I'LL FIND MY QUARTERS AND TAKE A NAP.
!?!?
!?!?!?
SLAM!
!?!?!
?!?!

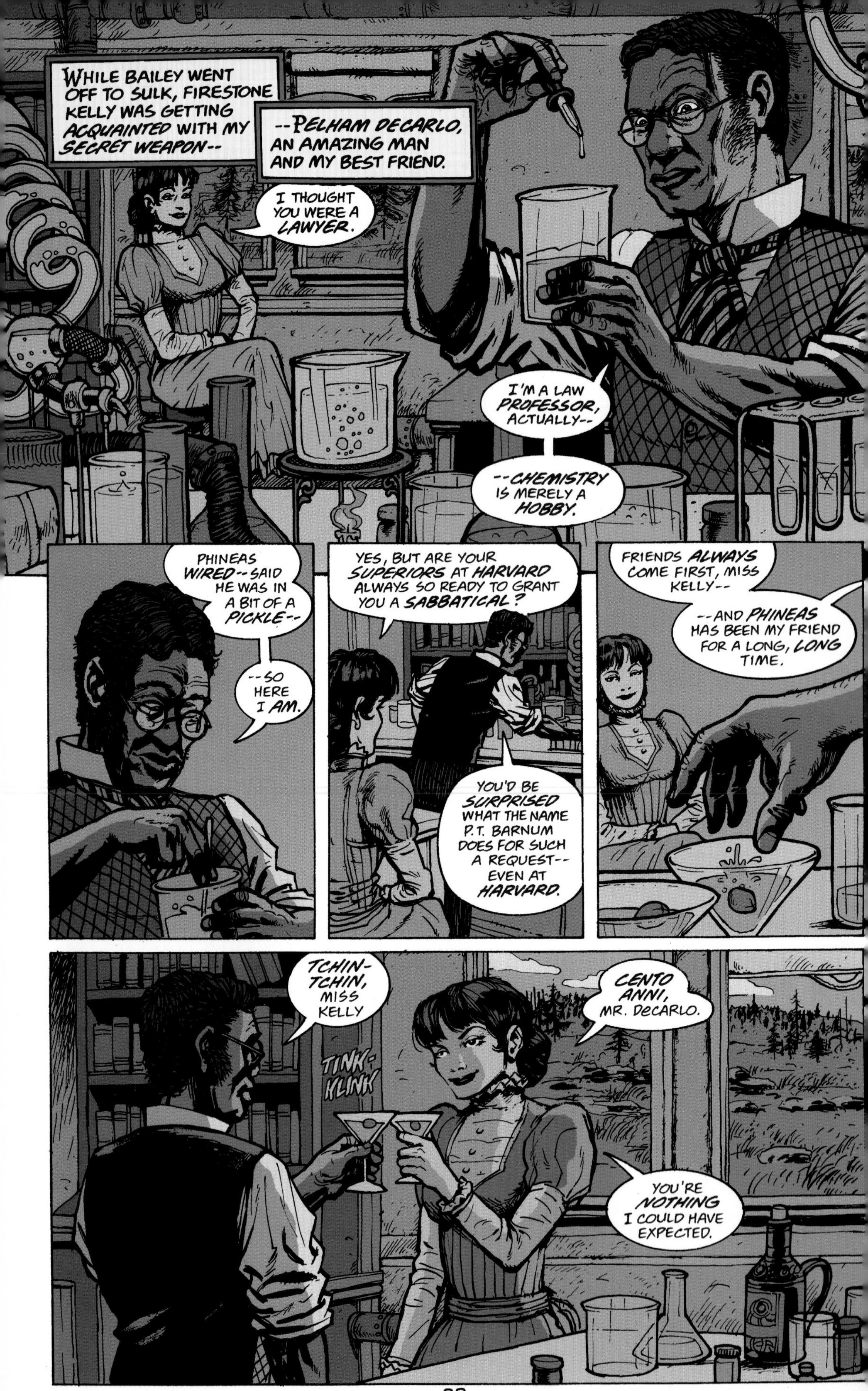

WHILE BAILEY WENT OFF TO SULK, FIRESTONE KELLY WAS GETTING ACQUAINTED WITH MY SECRET WEAPON--
--PELHAM DECARLO, AN AMAZING MAN AND MY BEST FRIEND.
I THOUGHT YOU WERE A LAWYER.
I'M A LAW PROFESSOR, ACTUALLY--
--CHEMISTRY IS MERELY A HOBBY.
PHINEAS WIRED--SAID HE WAS IN A BIT OF A PICKLE--
--SO HERE I AM.
YES, BUT ARE YOUR SUPERIORS AT HARVARD ALWAYS SO READY TO GRANT YOU A SABBATICAL?
YOU'D BE SURPRISED WHAT THE NAME P.T. BARNUM DOES FOR SUCH A REQUEST--EVEN AT HARVARD.
FRIENDS ALWAYS COME FIRST, MISS KELLY--
--AND PHINEAS HAS BEEN MY FRIEND FOR A LONG, LONG TIME.
TCHIN-TCHIN, MISS KELLY
TINK-KLINK
CENTO ANNI, MR. DECARLO.
YOU'RE NOTHING I COULD HAVE EXPECTED.

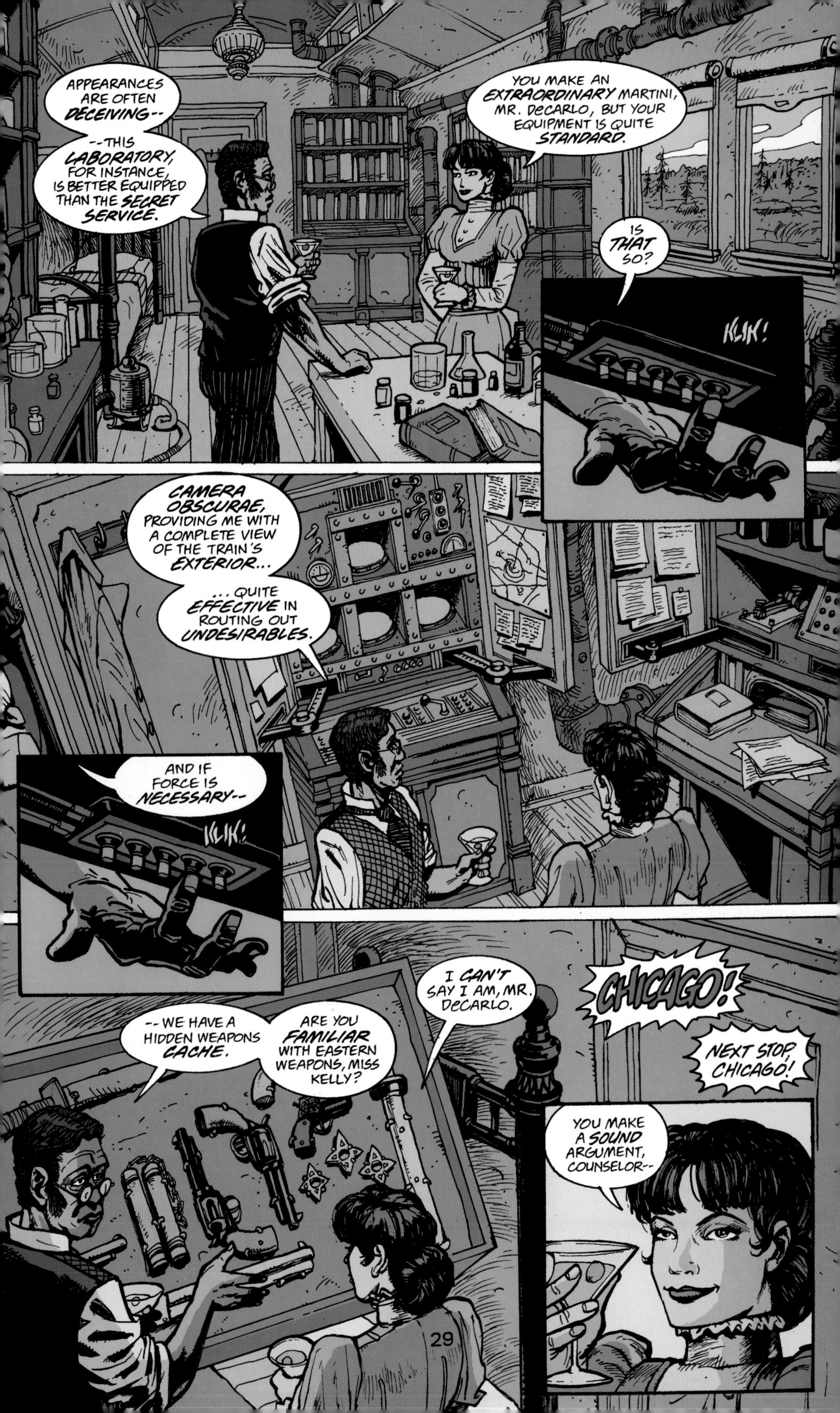
APPEARANCES ARE OFTEN DECEIVING--
--THIS LABORATORY, FOR INSTANCE, IS BETTER EQUIPPED THAN THE SECRET SERVICE.
YOU MAKE AN EXTRAORDINARY MARTINI, MR. DeCARLO, BUT YOUR EQUIPMENT IS QUITE STANDARD.
IS THAT SO?
KLIK!
CAMERA OBSCURAE, PROVIDING ME WITH A COMPLETE VIEW OF THE TRAIN'S EXTERIOR...
...QUITE EFFECTIVE IN ROUTING OUT UNDESIRABLES.
AND IF FORCE IS NECESSARY--
KLIK!
--WE HAVE A HIDDEN WEAPONS CACHE.
ARE YOU FAMILIAR WITH EASTERN WEAPONS, MISS KELLY?
I CAN'T SAY I AM, MR. DeCARLO.
CHICAGO!
NEXT STOP, CHICAGO!
YOU MAKE A SOUND ARGUMENT, COUNSELOR--

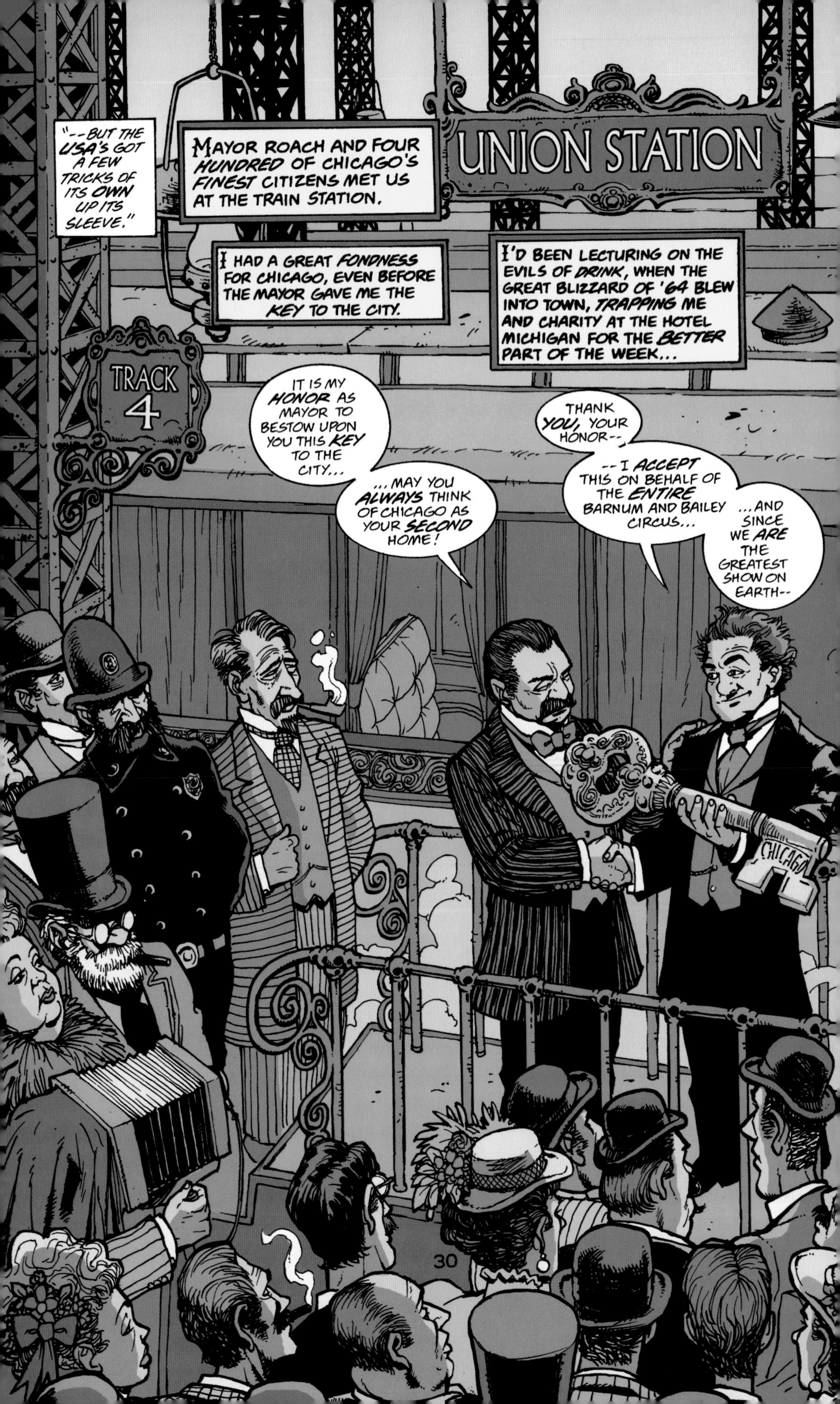
"--BUT THE USA'S GOT A FEW TRICKS OF ITS OWN UP ITS SLEEVE."
MAYOR ROACH AND FOUR HUNDRED OF CHICAGO'S FINEST CITIZENS MET US AT THE TRAIN STATION.
UNION STATION
I HAD A GREAT FONDNESS FOR CHICAGO, EVEN BEFORE THE MAYOR GAVE ME THE KEY TO THE CITY.
I'D BEEN LECTURING ON THE EVILS OF DRINK, WHEN THE GREAT BLIZZARD OF '64 BLEW INTO TOWN, TRAPPING ME AND CHARITY AT THE HOTEL MICHIGAN FOR THE BETTER PART OF THE WEEK...
TRACK 4
IT IS MY HONOR AS MAYOR TO BESTOW UPON YOU THIS KEY TO THE CITY...
...MAY YOU ALWAYS THINK OF CHICAGO AS YOUR SECOND HOME!
THANK YOU, YOUR HONOR--
--I ACCEPT THIS ON BEHALF OF THE ENTIRE BARNUM AND BAILEY CIRCUS...
...AND SINCE WE ARE THE GREATEST SHOW ON EARTH--
CHICAGO

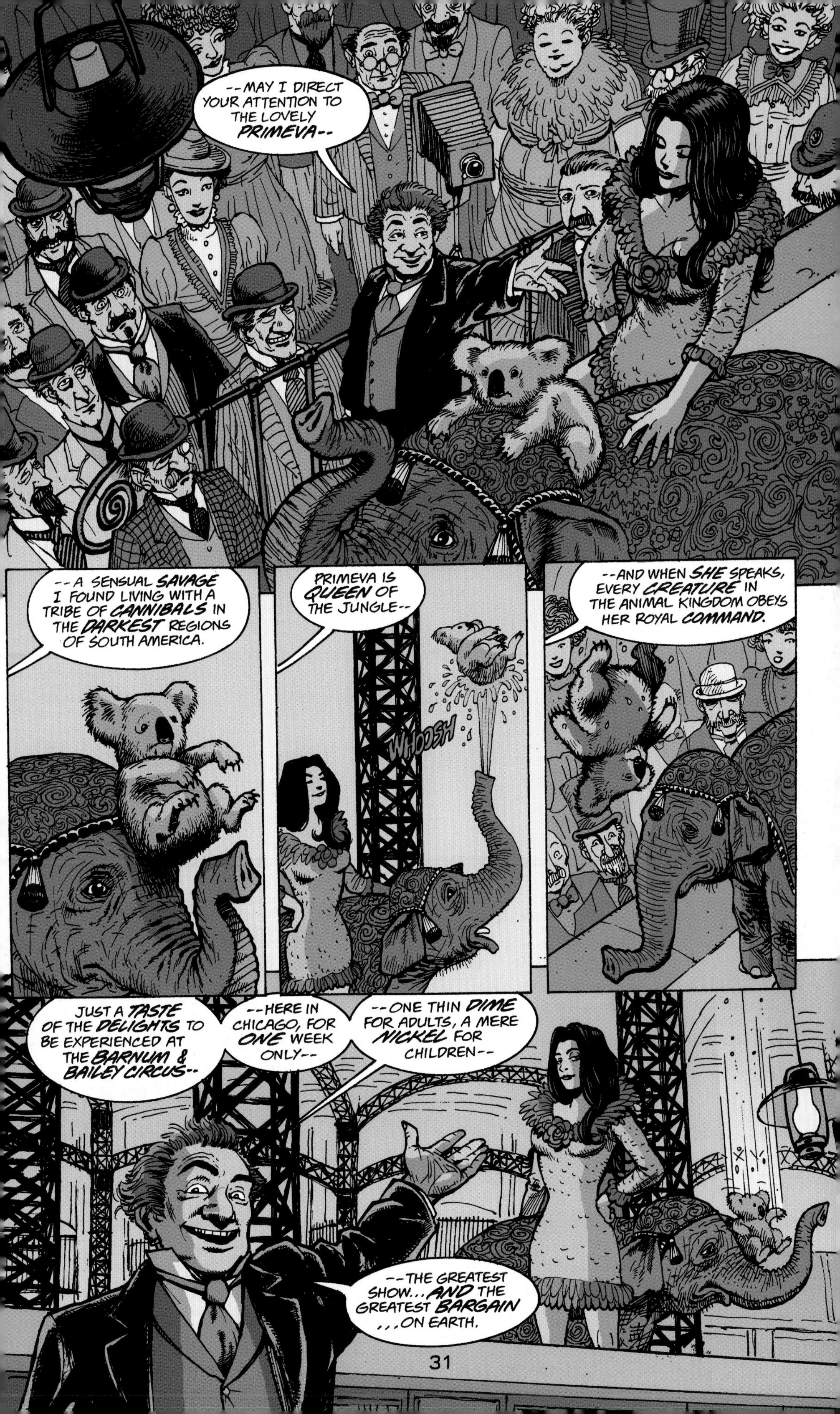

--MAY I DIRECT YOUR ATTENTION TO THE LOVELY PRIMEVA--
--A SENSUAL SAVAGE I FOUND LIVING WITH A TRIBE OF CANNIBALS IN THE DARKEST REGIONS OF SOUTH AMERICA.
PRIMEVA IS QUEEN OF THE JUNGLE--
WHOOSH
--AND WHEN SHE SPEAKS, EVERY CREATURE IN THE ANIMAL KINGDOM OBEYS HER ROYAL COMMAND.
JUST A TASTE OF THE DELIGHTS TO BE EXPERIENCED AT THE BARNUM & BAILEY CIRCUS--
--HERE IN CHICAGO, FOR ONE WEEK ONLY--
--ONE THIN DIME FOR ADULTS, A MERE NICKEL FOR CHILDREN--
--THE GREATEST SHOW...AND THE GREATEST BARGAIN ...ON EARTH.

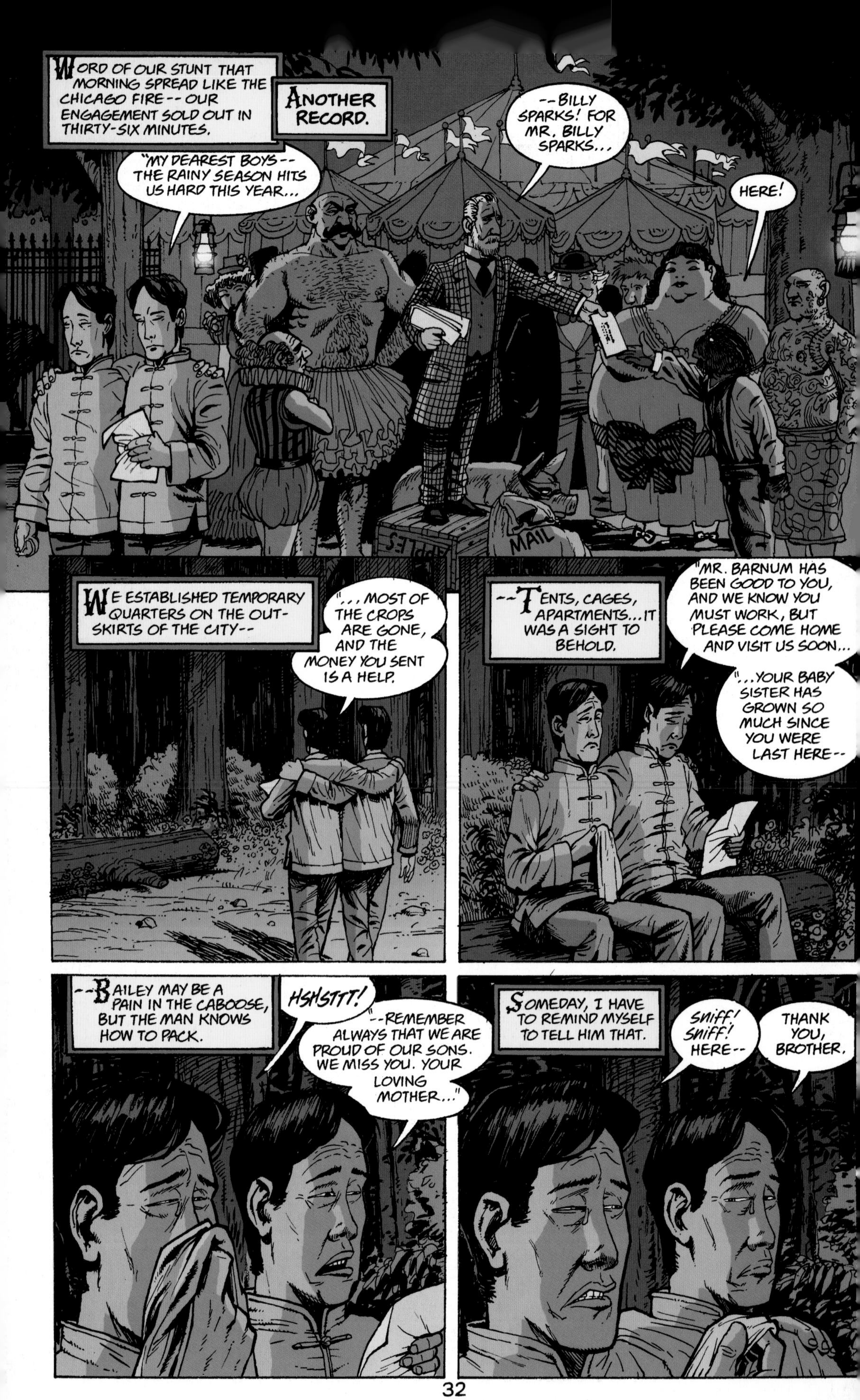

WORD OF OUR STUNT THAT MORNING SPREAD LIKE THE CHICAGO FIRE -- OUR ENGAGEMENT SOLD OUT IN THIRTY-SIX MINUTES.
ANOTHER RECORD.
--BILLY SPARKS! FOR MR. BILLY SPARKS...
"MY DEAREST BOYS -- THE RAINY SEASON HITS US HARD THIS YEAR...
HERE!
APPLES
MAIL
WE ESTABLISHED TEMPORARY QUARTERS ON THE OUT-SKIRTS OF THE CITY--
"...MOST OF THE CROPS ARE GONE, AND THE MONEY YOU SENT IS A HELP.
--TENTS, CAGES, APARTMENTS...IT WAS A SIGHT TO BEHOLD.
"MR. BARNUM HAS BEEN GOOD TO YOU, AND WE KNOW YOU MUST WORK, BUT PLEASE COME HOME AND VISIT US SOON...
"...YOUR BABY SISTER HAS GROWN SO MUCH SINCE YOU WERE LAST HERE--
--BAILEY MAY BE A PAIN IN THE CABOOSE, BUT THE MAN KNOWS HOW TO PACK.
HSHSTTT!
"--REMEMBER ALWAYS THAT WE ARE PROUD OF OUR SONS. WE MISS YOU. YOUR LOVING MOTHER..."
SOMEDAY, I HAVE TO REMIND MYSELF TO TELL HIM THAT.
SNIFF! SNIFF! HERE--
THANK YOU, BROTHER.

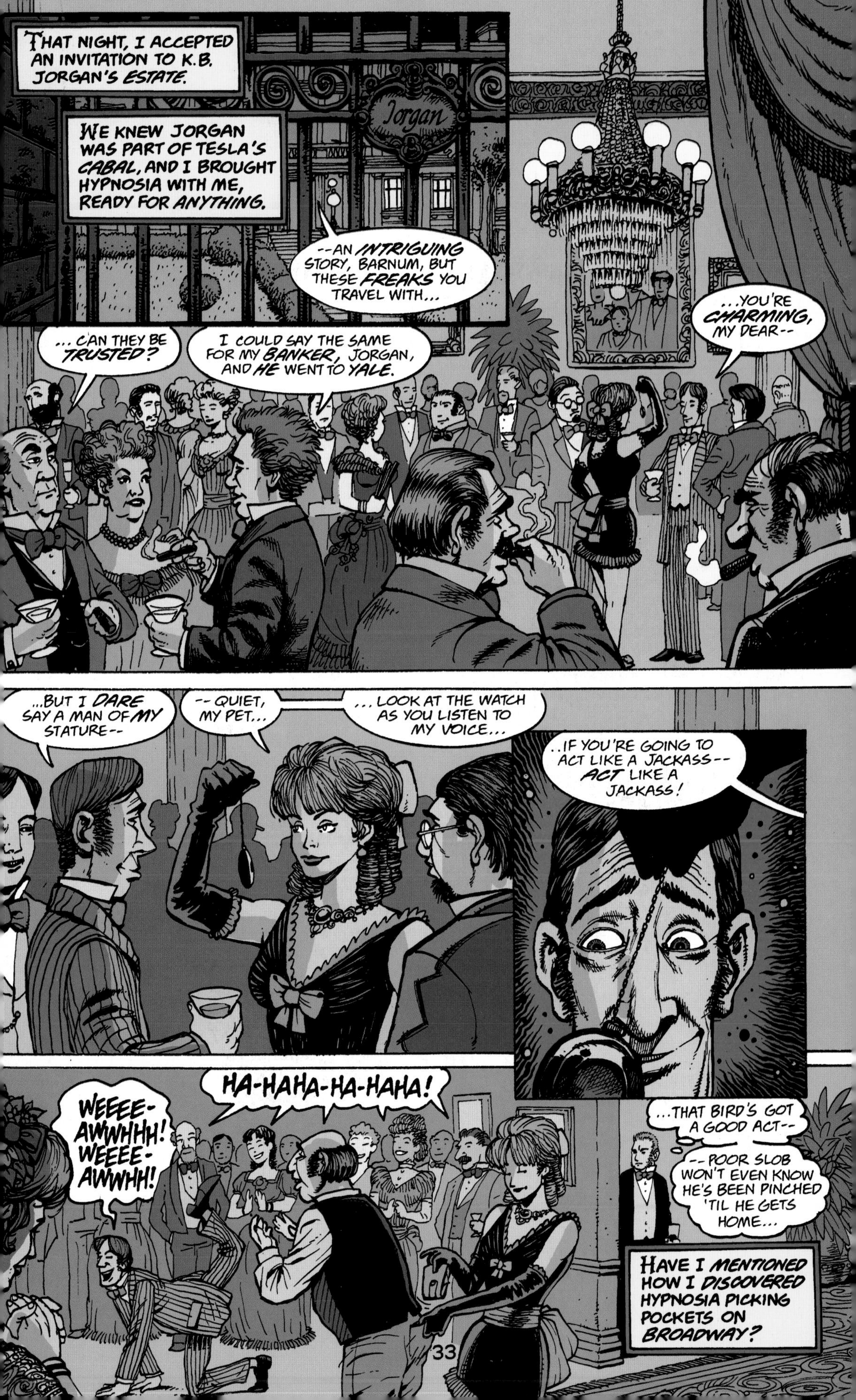

THAT NIGHT, I ACCEPTED AN INVITATION TO K.B. JORGAN'S *ESTATE*.
WE KNEW JORGAN WAS PART OF TESLA'S *CABAL*, AND I BROUGHT HYPNOSIA WITH ME, READY FOR *ANYTHING*.
Jorgan
--AN *INTRIGUING* STORY, BARNUM, BUT THESE *FREAKS* YOU TRAVEL WITH...
...CAN THEY BE *TRUSTED*?
I COULD SAY THE SAME FOR MY *BANKER*, JORGAN, AND *HE* WENT TO *YALE*.
...YOU'RE *CHARMING*, MY DEAR--
...BUT I *DARE* SAY A MAN OF *MY* STATURE--
--QUIET, MY PET...
...LOOK AT THE WATCH AS YOU LISTEN TO MY VOICE...
..IF YOU'RE GOING TO ACT LIKE A JACKASS-- *ACT* LIKE A JACKASS!
HA-HAHA-HA-HAHA!
WEEEE-AWWHHH! WEEEE-AWWHH!
...THAT BIRD'S GOT A GOOD ACT--
--POOR SLOB WON'T EVEN KNOW HE'S BEEN PINCHED 'TIL HE GETS HOME...
HAVE I *MENTIONED* HOW I *DISCOVERED* HYPNOSIA PICKING POCKETS ON *BROADWAY*?

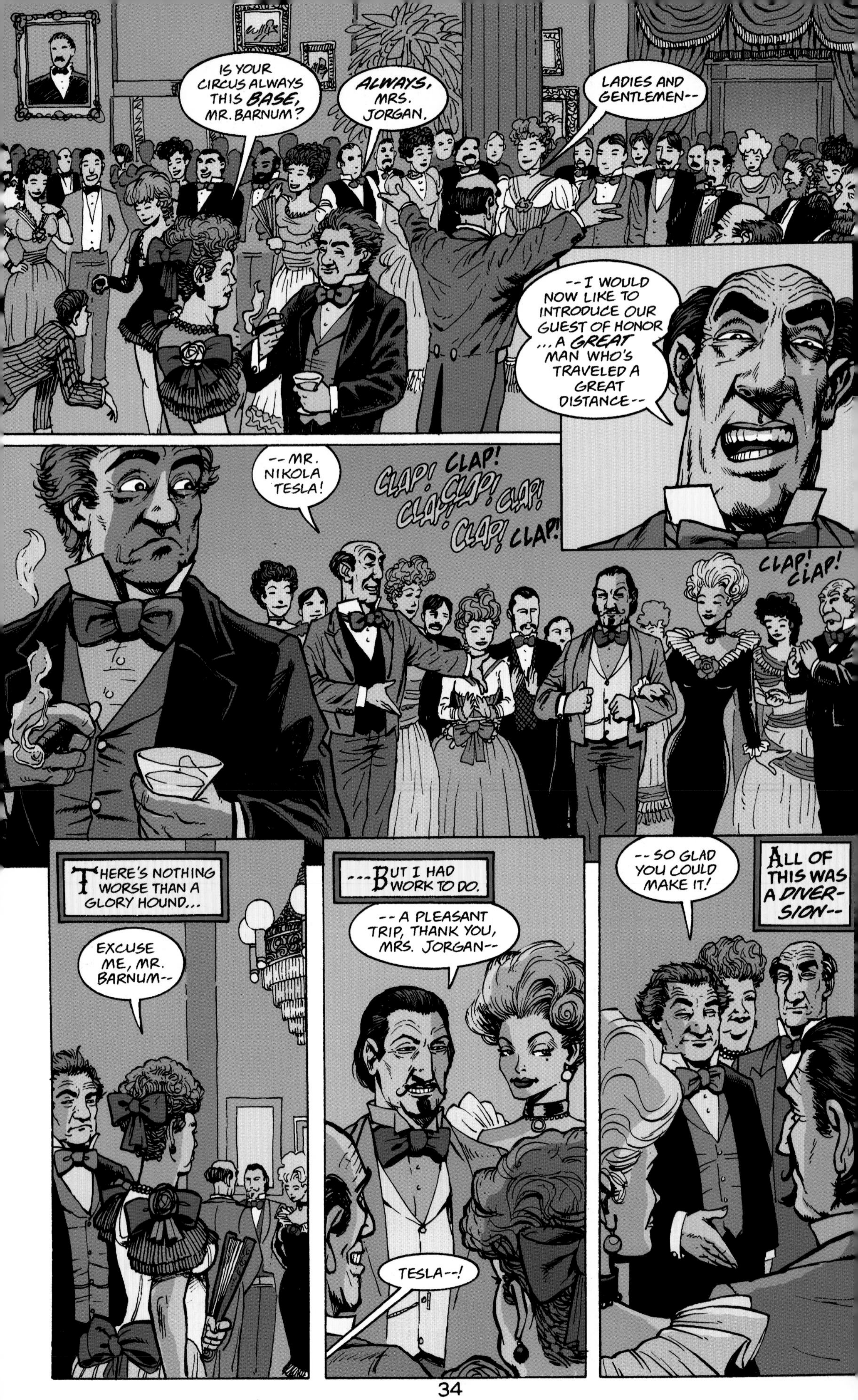
IS YOUR CIRCUS ALWAYS THIS BASE, MR. BARNUM?
ALWAYS, MRS. JORGAN.
LADIES AND GENTLEMEN--
--I WOULD NOW LIKE TO INTRODUCE OUR GUEST OF HONOR ...A GREAT MAN WHO'S TRAVELED A GREAT DISTANCE--
--MR. NIKOLA TESLA!
CLAP! CLAP! CLAP! CLAP! CLAP! CLAP! CLAP!
CLAP! CLAP!
THERE'S NOTHING WORSE THAN A GLORY HOUND...
EXCUSE ME, MR. BARNUM--
...BUT I HAD WORK TO DO.
--A PLEASANT TRIP, THANK YOU, MRS. JORGAN--
TESLA--!
--SO GLAD YOU COULD MAKE IT!
ALL OF THIS WAS A DIVERSION--

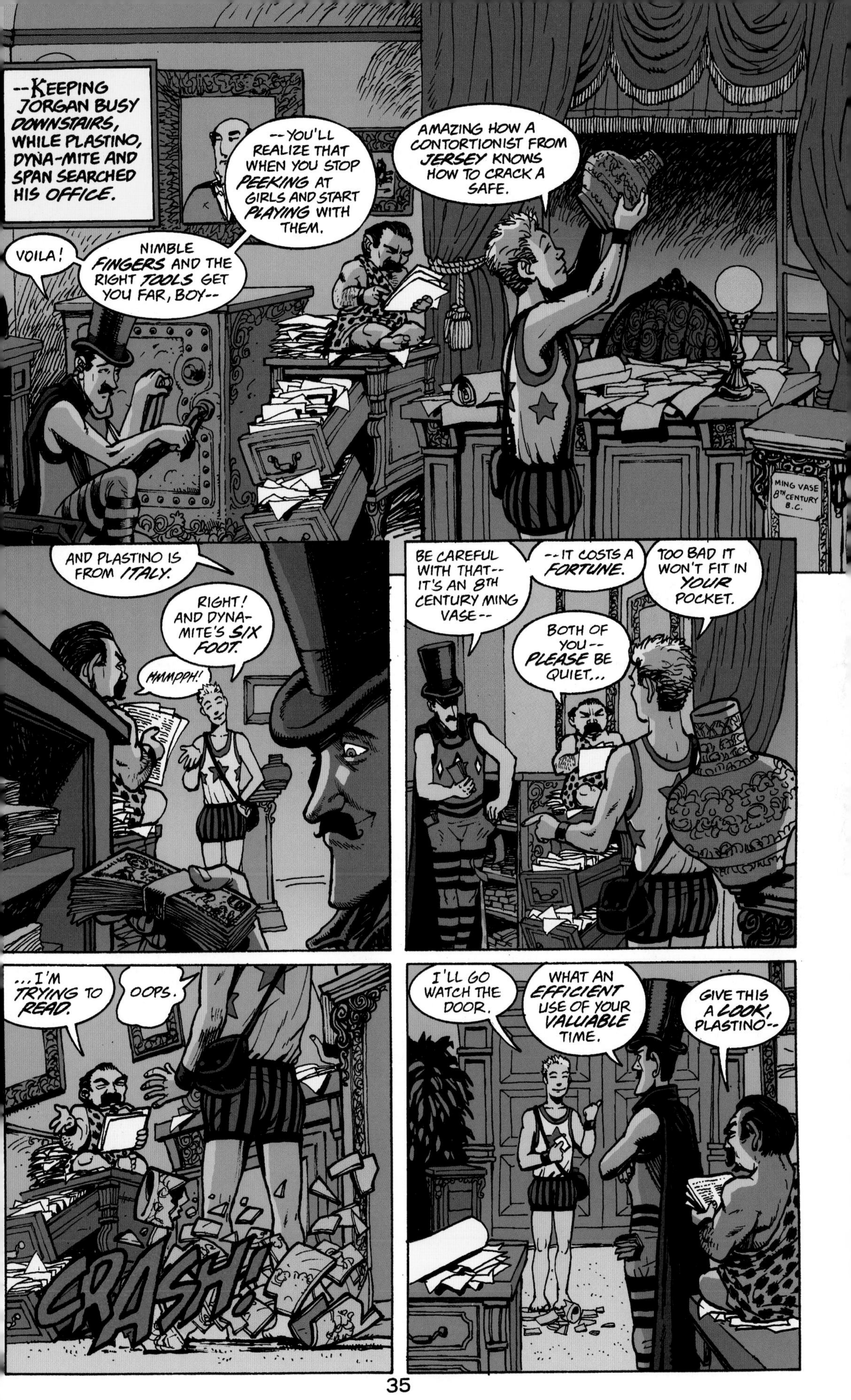

--KEEPING JORGAN BUSY DOWNSTAIRS, WHILE PLASTINO, DYNA-MITE AND SPAN SEARCHED HIS OFFICE.
VOILA!
NIMBLE FINGERS AND THE RIGHT TOOLS GET YOU FAR, BOY--
--YOU'LL REALIZE THAT WHEN YOU STOP PEEKING AT GIRLS AND START PLAYING WITH THEM.
AMAZING HOW A CONTORTIONIST FROM JERSEY KNOWS HOW TO CRACK A SAFE.
MING VASE 8TH CENTURY B.C.
AND PLASTINO IS FROM ITALY.
RIGHT! AND DYNA-MITE'S SIX FOOT.
HMMPPH!
BE CAREFUL WITH THAT-- IT'S AN 8TH CENTURY MING VASE--
--IT COSTS A FORTUNE.
TOO BAD IT WON'T FIT IN YOUR POCKET.
BOTH OF YOU-- PLEASE BE QUIET...
...I'M TRYING TO READ.
OOPS.
CRASH!
I'LL GO WATCH THE DOOR.
WHAT AN EFFICIENT USE OF YOUR VALUABLE TIME.
GIVE THIS A LOOK, PLASTINO--

-- I THINK I *FOUND* SOMETHING.

THESE ARE JORGAN'S *WIRE TRANSFERS* FOR THE PAST SIX MONTHS.

FINALLY... AN *ANSWER* TO THIS ASININE *INQUIRY.*

IF WE LEAVE NOW, I CAN STILL MAKE THAT *POKER* GAME ON THE EAST SIDE.

HE'S BEEN TRANSFERRING A *MILLION* DOLLARS EACH *MONTH* TO BANKS ACROSS CALIFORNIA--

First Bank of San Francisco
April 12, 1888–K.B. Jorgan–
Transfer $1,000,000.

Los Angeles Savings Bank
May 17, 1888–K.B. Jorgan–
Transfer $1,000,000.

-- HIS ENTIRE *FORTUNE'S* BEEN MOVED OUT WEST.

AND HERE ANDERSON'S *TRIPLED* RAILROAD CONSTRUCTION WEST OF THE ROCKIES--

--THE TRACKS HAVE A SPECIFIC *PATTERN,* EVEN WHERE THERE AREN'T ANY TOWNS.

WHAT DO YOU THINK IT *MEANS?*

SPAN -- AREN'T YOU SUPPOSED TO BE WATCHING THE--

WHAMM

--DOOR?

...NOT AGAIN...

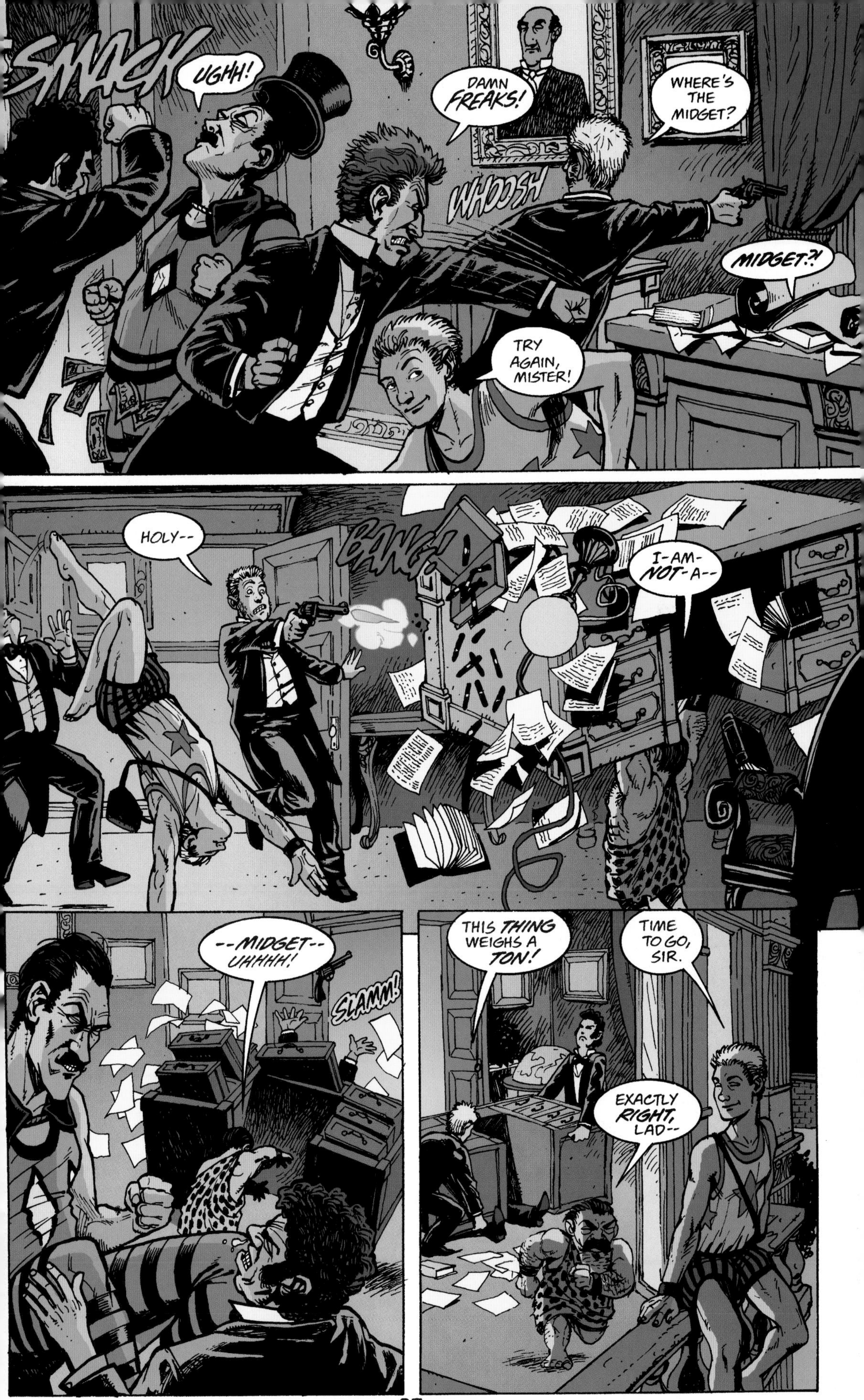
SMACK
UGHH!
DAMN FREAKS!
WHERE'S THE MIDGET?
WHOOSH
MIDGET?!
TRY AGAIN, MISTER!
HOLY--
BANG!
I-AM-NOT-A--
--MIDGET--
UHHHH!
SLAMM!
THIS THING WEIGHS A TON!
TIME TO GO, SIR.
EXACTLY RIGHT, LAD--

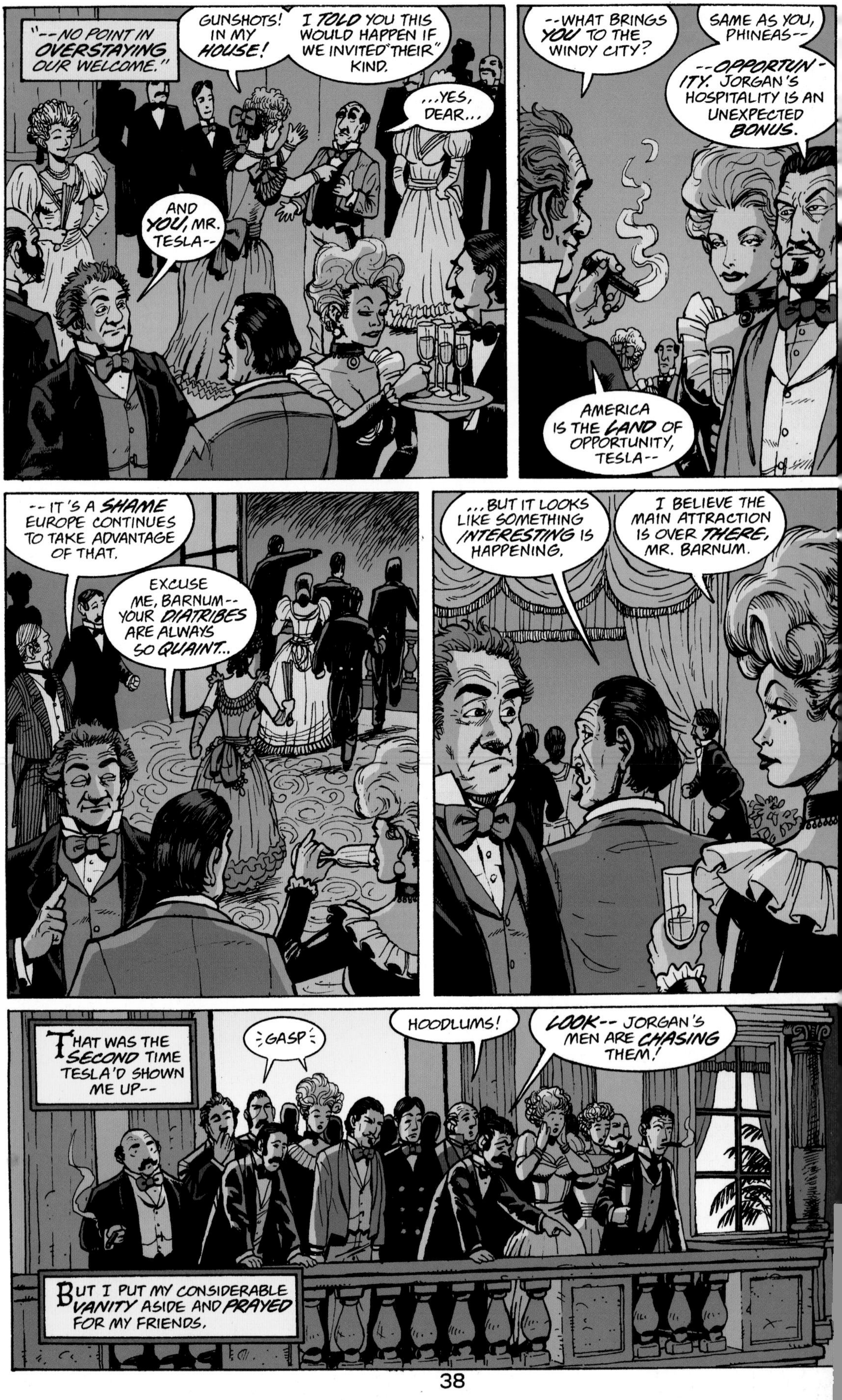
"--NO POINT IN OVERSTAYING OUR WELCOME."
GUNSHOTS! IN MY HOUSE!
I TOLD YOU THIS WOULD HAPPEN IF WE INVITED "THEIR" KIND.
...YES, DEAR...
AND YOU, MR. TESLA--
--WHAT BRINGS YOU TO THE WINDY CITY?
SAME AS YOU, PHINEAS--
--OPPORTUNITY. JORGAN'S HOSPITALITY IS AN UNEXPECTED BONUS.
AMERICA IS THE LAND OF OPPORTUNITY, TESLA--
--IT'S A SHAME EUROPE CONTINUES TO TAKE ADVANTAGE OF THAT.
EXCUSE ME, BARNUM--YOUR DIATRIBES ARE ALWAYS SO QUAINT...
...BUT IT LOOKS LIKE SOMETHING INTERESTING IS HAPPENING.
I BELIEVE THE MAIN ATTRACTION IS OVER THERE, MR. BARNUM.
THAT WAS THE SECOND TIME TESLA'D SHOWN ME UP--
GASP
HOODLUMS!
LOOK-- JORGAN'S MEN ARE CHASING THEM!
BUT I PUT MY CONSIDERABLE VANITY ASIDE AND PRAYED FOR MY FRIENDS.

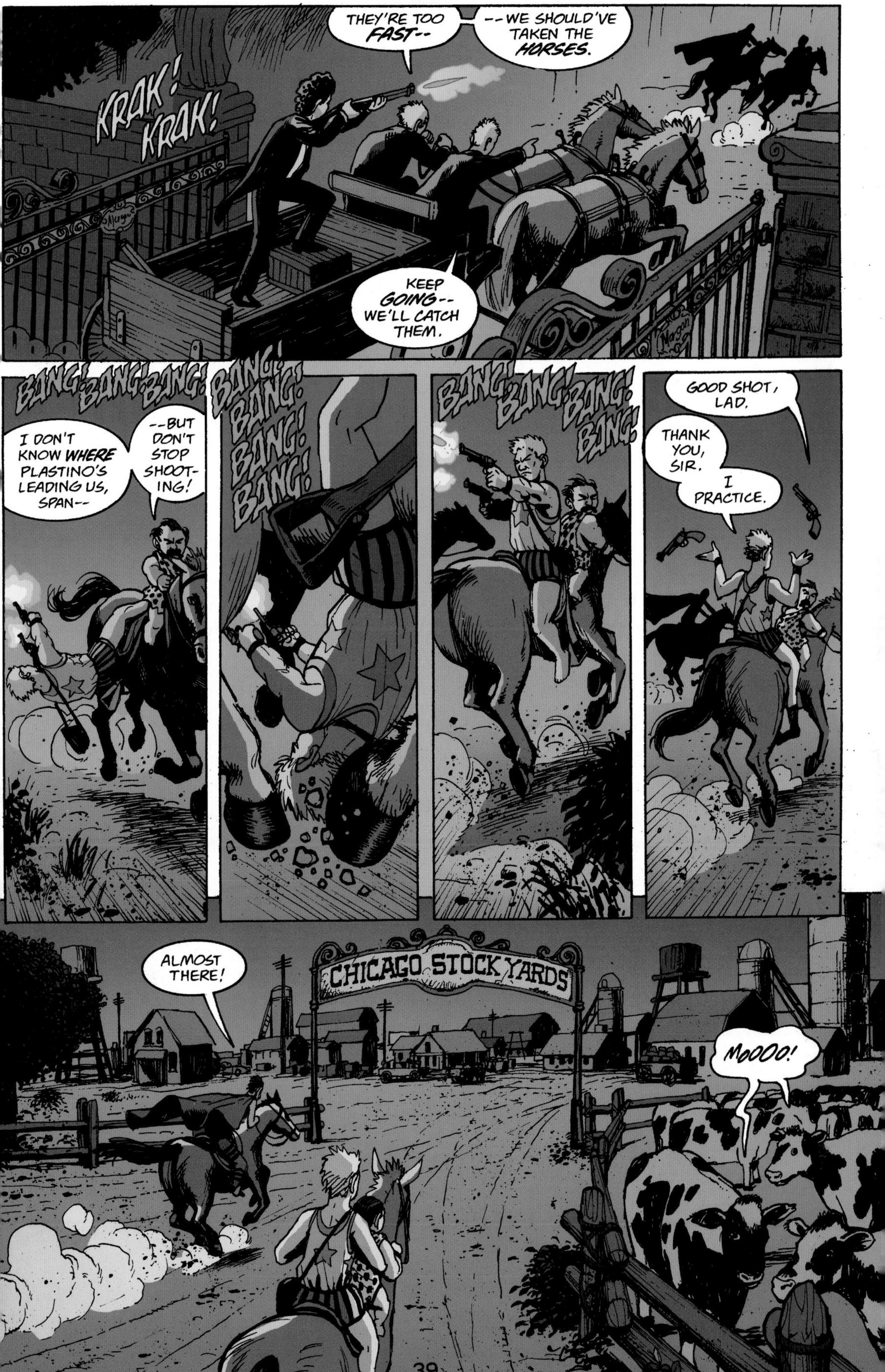
KRAK! KRAK!
THEY'RE TOO FAST--
--WE SHOULD'VE TAKEN THE HORSES.
KEEP GOING-- WE'LL CATCH THEM.
BANG! BANG! BANG!
I DON'T KNOW WHERE PLASTINO'S LEADING US, SPAN--
--BUT DON'T STOP SHOOTING!
BANG! BANG! BANG! BANG! BANG!
BANG! BANG! BANG! BANG!
GOOD SHOT, LAD.
THANK YOU, SIR.
I PRACTICE.
ALMOST THERE!
CHICAGO STOCK YARDS
MoOOO!

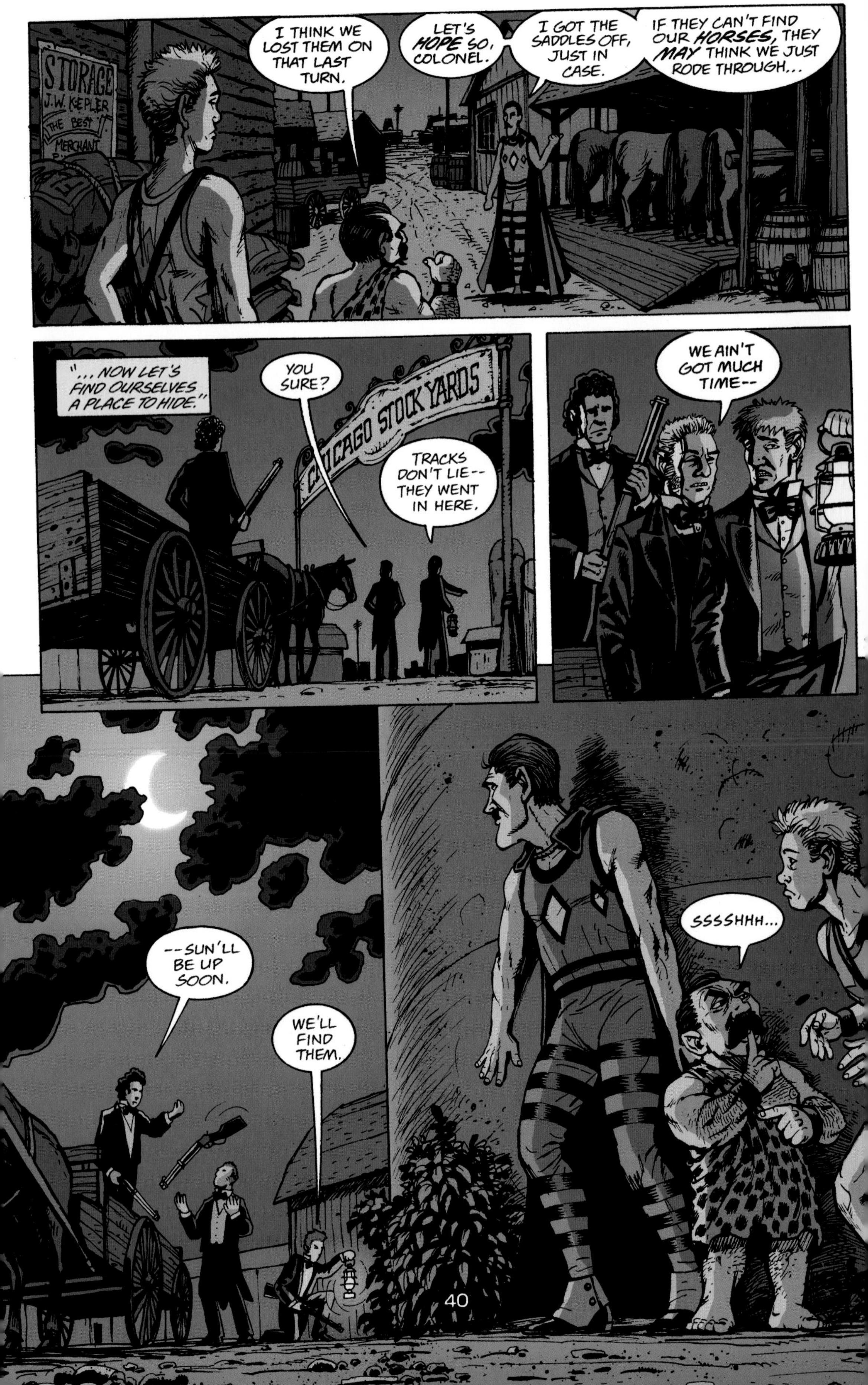
STORAGE
J.W. KEPLER
THE BEST
MERCHANT
I THINK WE LOST THEM ON THAT LAST TURN.
LET'S HOPE SO, COLONEL.
I GOT THE SADDLES OFF, JUST IN CASE.
IF THEY CAN'T FIND OUR HORSES, THEY MAY THINK WE JUST RODE THROUGH...
"...NOW LET'S FIND OURSELVES A PLACE TO HIDE."
YOU SURE?
CHICAGO STOCK YARDS
TRACKS DON'T LIE-- THEY WENT IN HERE.
WE AIN'T GOT MUCH TIME--
--SUN'LL BE UP SOON.
WE'LL FIND THEM.
SSSSHHH...

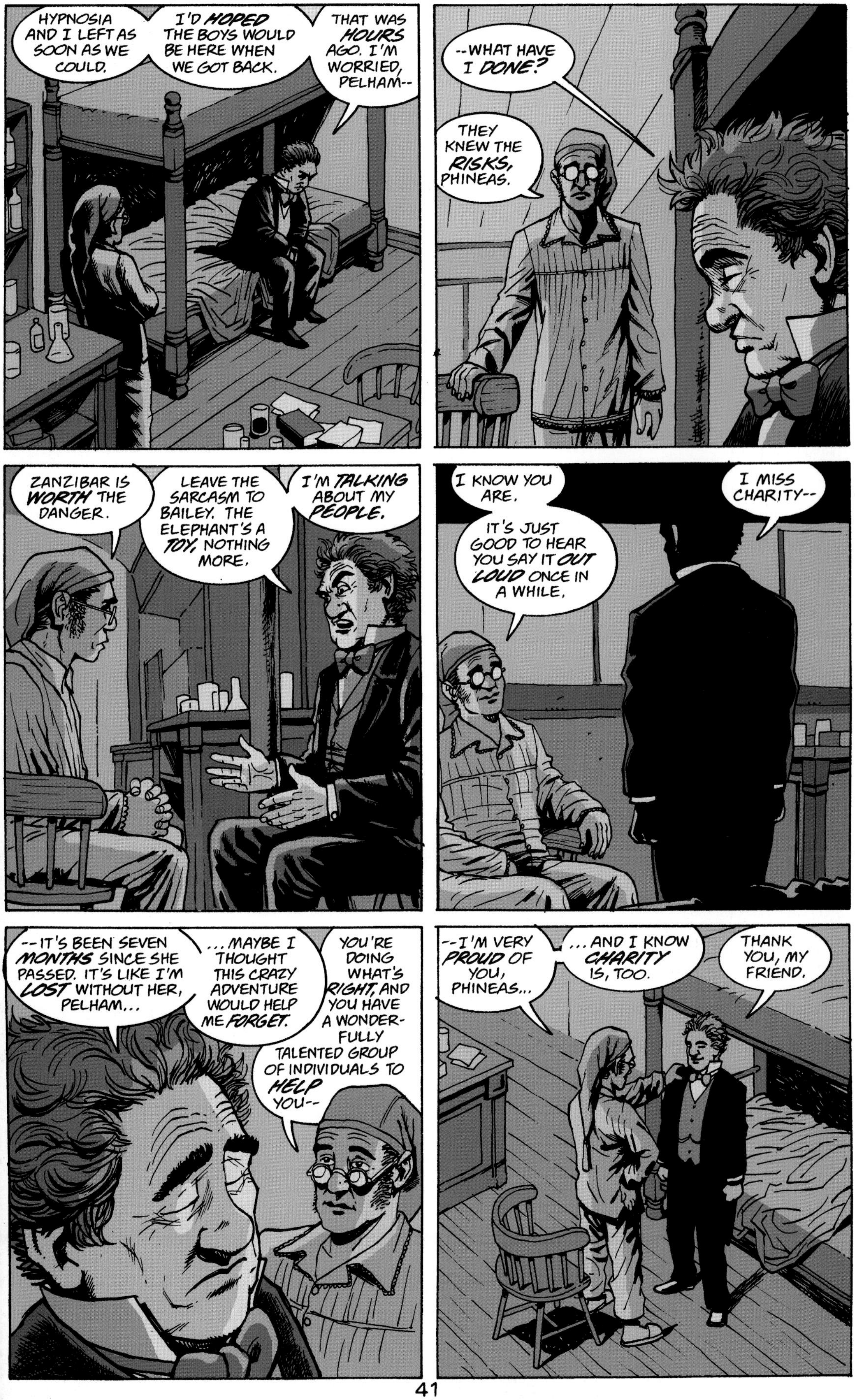
HYPNOSIA AND I LEFT AS SOON AS WE COULD.
I'D HOPED THE BOYS WOULD BE HERE WHEN WE GOT BACK.
THAT WAS HOURS AGO. I'M WORRIED, PELHAM--
--WHAT HAVE I DONE?
THEY KNEW THE RISKS, PHINEAS.
ZANZIBAR IS WORTH THE DANGER.
LEAVE THE SARCASM TO BAILEY. THE ELEPHANT'S A TOY, NOTHING MORE.
I'M TALKING ABOUT MY PEOPLE.
I KNOW YOU ARE.
IT'S JUST GOOD TO HEAR YOU SAY IT OUT LOUD ONCE IN A WHILE.
I MISS CHARITY--
--IT'S BEEN SEVEN MONTHS SINCE SHE PASSED. IT'S LIKE I'M LOST WITHOUT HER, PELHAM...
...MAYBE I THOUGHT THIS CRAZY ADVENTURE WOULD HELP ME FORGET.
YOU'RE DOING WHAT'S RIGHT, AND YOU HAVE A WONDERFULLY TALENTED GROUP OF INDIVIDUALS TO HELP YOU--
--I'M VERY PROUD OF YOU, PHINEAS...
...AND I KNOW CHARITY IS, TOO.
THANK YOU, MY FRIEND.

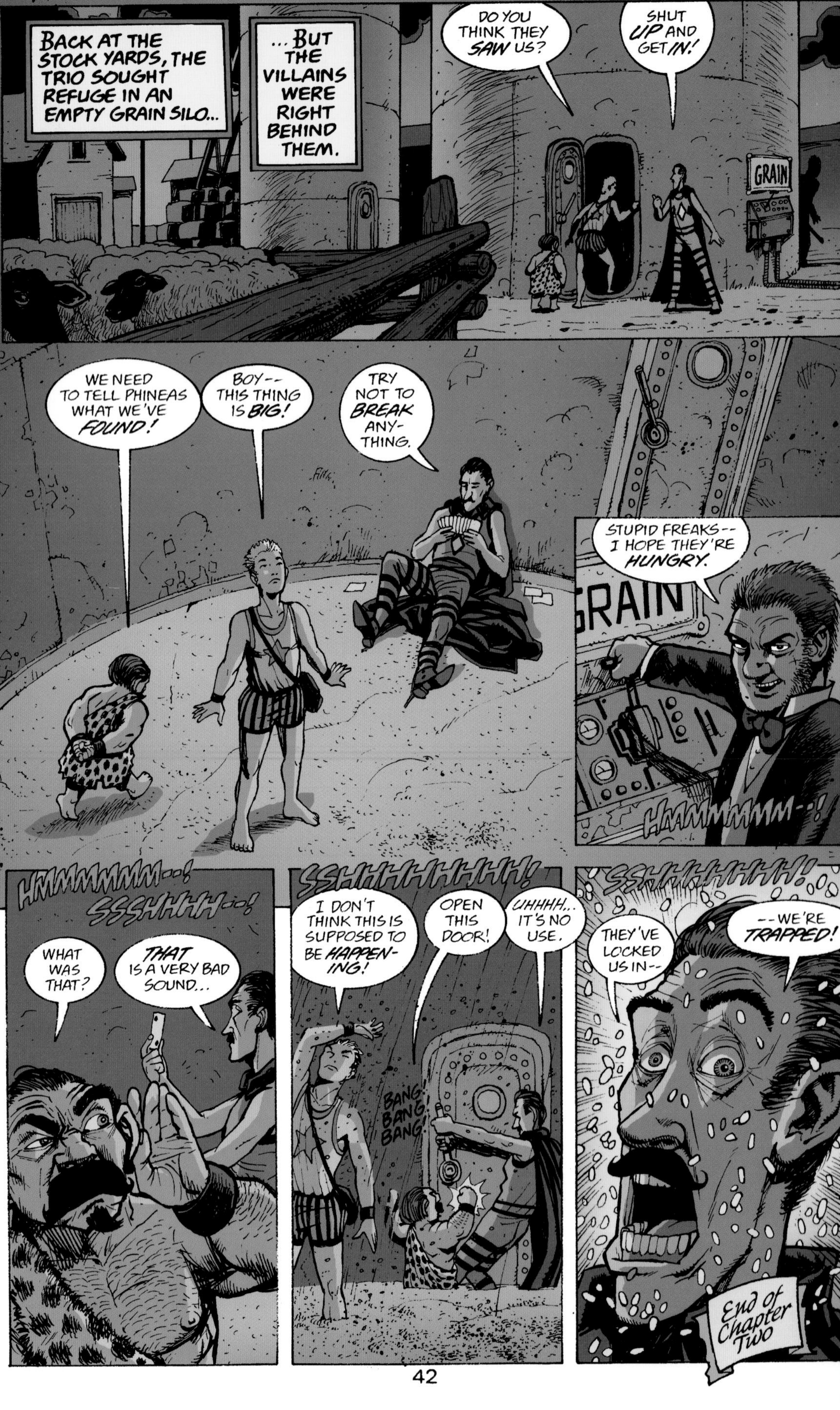
BACK AT THE STOCK YARDS, THE TRIO SOUGHT REFUGE IN AN EMPTY GRAIN SILO...
...BUT THE VILLAINS WERE RIGHT BEHIND THEM.
DO YOU THINK THEY SAW US?
SHUT UP AND GET IN!
GRAIN
WE NEED TO TELL PHINEAS WHAT WE'VE FOUND!
BOY-- THIS THING IS BIG!
TRY NOT TO BREAK ANY-THING.
STUPID FREAKS-- I HOPE THEY'RE HUNGRY.
GRAIN
HMMMMMM--!
HMMMMMM--!
SSSHHHH--!
WHAT WAS THAT?
THAT IS A VERY BAD SOUND...
SSHHHHHHHHH!
I DON'T THINK THIS IS SUPPOSED TO BE HAPPEN-ING!
OPEN THIS DOOR!
UHHHH... IT'S NO USE.
BANG BANG BANG
SSHHHHHHHH!
THEY'VE LOCKED US IN--
--WE'RE TRAPPED!
End of Chapter Two

CHAPTER 3

CHAPTER 3

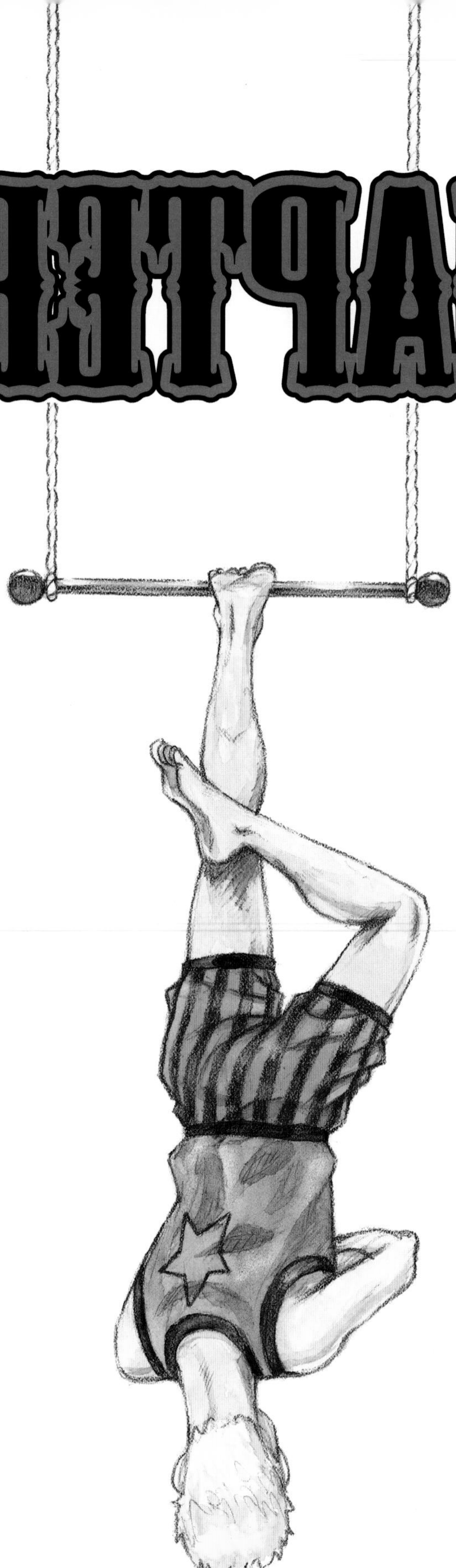

MY FRIENDS WERE TRAPPED!

TONG! TONG!

GIVE IT A REST, PLASTINO--!

SSHOOOOOOSHHH!!

--NOBODY'S LISTENING!

BANG! BANG!

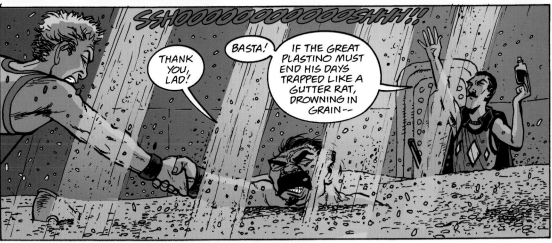

SSHOOOOOOOOOOOOSHHH!!

THANK YOU, LAD!

BASTA!

IF THE GREAT PLASTINO MUST END HIS DAYS TRAPPED LIKE A GUTTER RAT, DROWNING IN GRAIN--

ONLY A MIRACLE COULD SAVE THE TRIO FROM CERTAIN DOOM--

SSHOOOOOOOOOOOOOOOOSHH

--AT LEAST HE WON'T HAVE TO DO IT SOBER.

GULP!

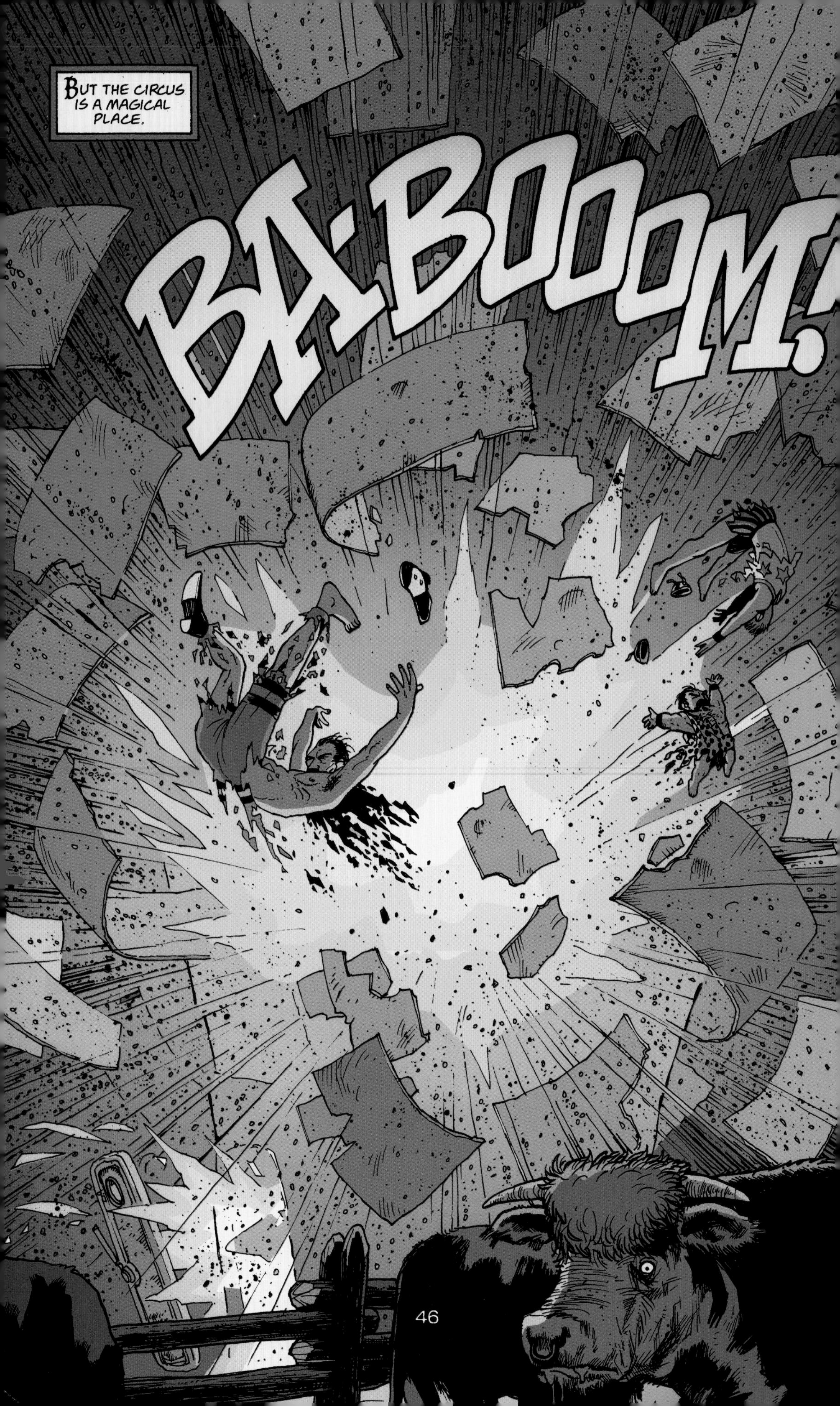
BUT THE CIRCUS IS A MAGICAL PLACE.
BA-BOOOM!

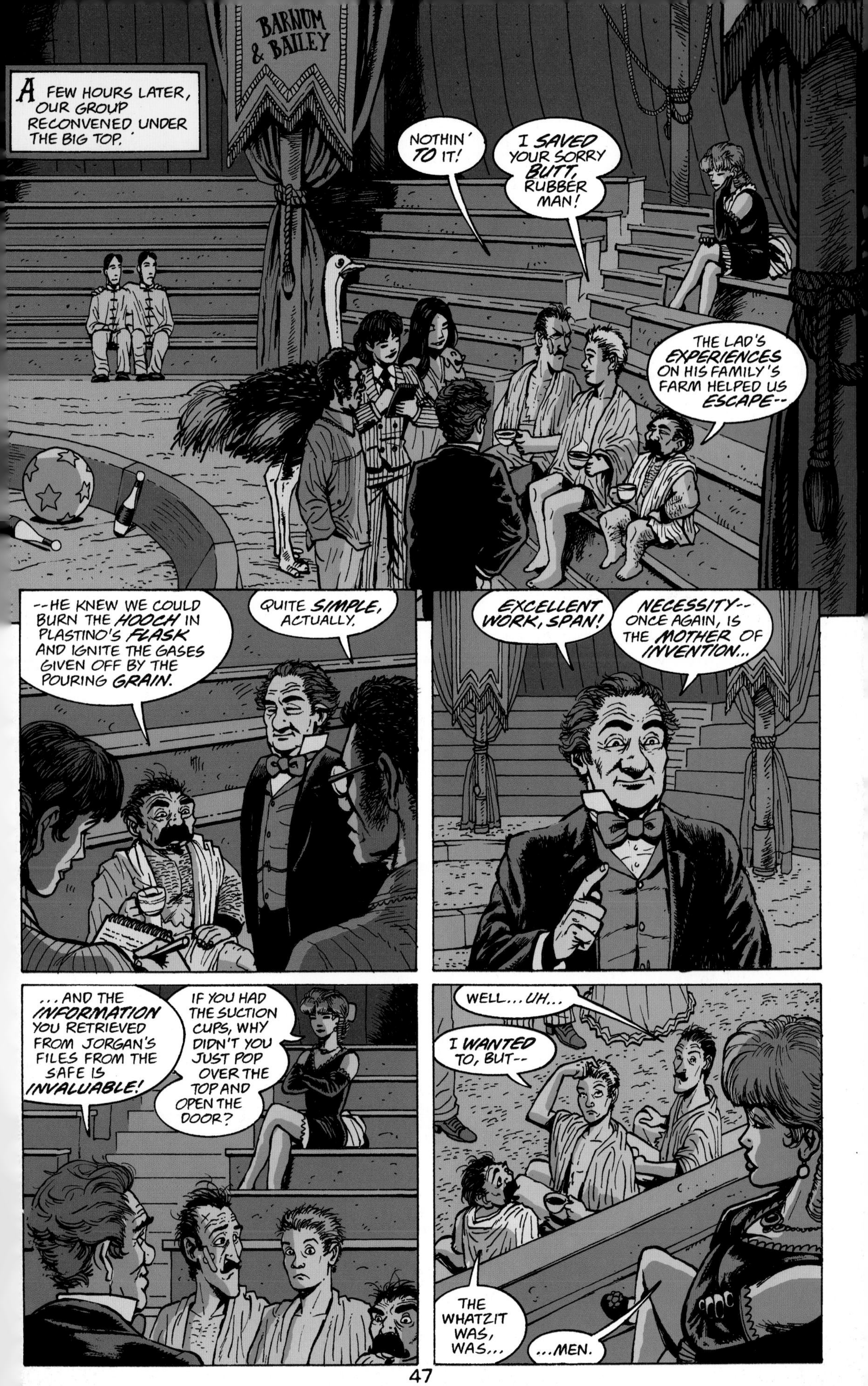
A FEW HOURS LATER, OUR GROUP RECONVENED UNDER THE BIG TOP.
BARNUM & BAILEY
NOTHIN' TO IT!
I SAVED YOUR SORRY BUTT, RUBBER MAN!
THE LAD'S EXPERIENCES ON HIS FAMILY'S FARM HELPED US ESCAPE--
--HE KNEW WE COULD BURN THE HOOCH IN PLASTINO'S FLASK AND IGNITE THE GASES GIVEN OFF BY THE POURING GRAIN.
QUITE SIMPLE, ACTUALLY.
EXCELLENT WORK, SPAN!
NECESSITY-- ONCE AGAIN, IS THE MOTHER OF INVENTION...
...AND THE INFORMATION YOU RETRIEVED FROM JORGAN'S FILES FROM THE SAFE IS INVALUABLE!
IF YOU HAD THE SUCTION CUPS, WHY DIDN'T YOU JUST POP OVER THE TOP AND OPEN THE DOOR?
WELL...UH...
I WANTED TO, BUT--
THE WHATZIT WAS, WAS...
...MEN.

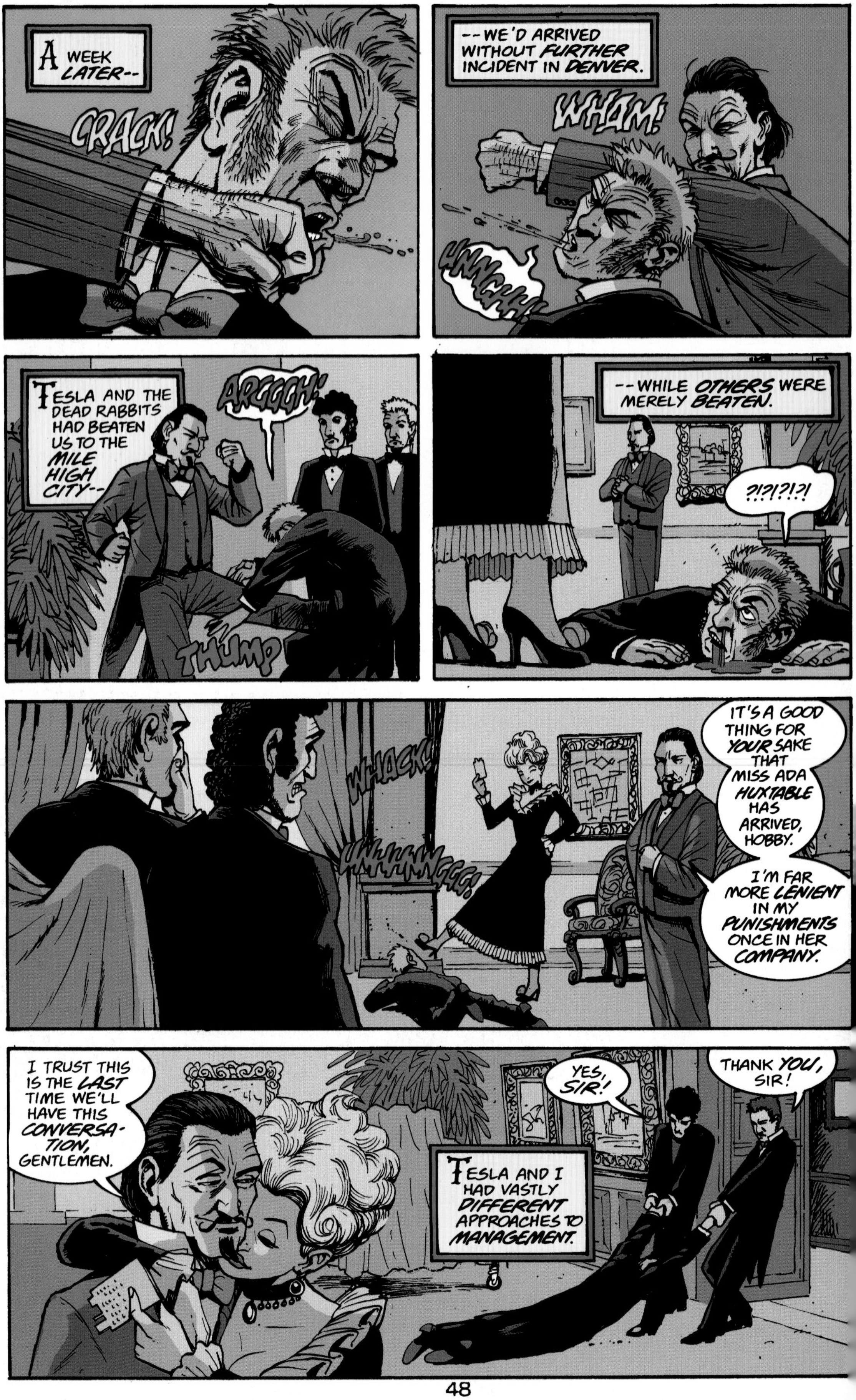
A WEEK LATER--
CRACK!
--WE'D ARRIVED WITHOUT FURTHER INCIDENT IN DENVER.
WHAM!
UNNGHH!
TESLA AND THE DEAD RABBITS HAD BEATEN US TO THE MILE HIGH CITY--
ARGGGH!
THUMP
--WHILE OTHERS WERE MERELY BEATEN.
?!?!?!?!
WHACK!
UNHHNNGGG!
IT'S A GOOD THING FOR YOUR SAKE THAT MISS ADA HUXTABLE HAS ARRIVED, HOBBY.
I'M FAR MORE LENIENT IN MY PUNISHMENTS ONCE IN HER COMPANY.
I TRUST THIS IS THE LAST TIME WE'LL HAVE THIS CONVERSATION, GENTLEMEN.
YES, SIR!
THANK YOU, SIR!
TESLA AND I HAD VASTLY DIFFERENT APPROACHES TO MANAGEMENT.

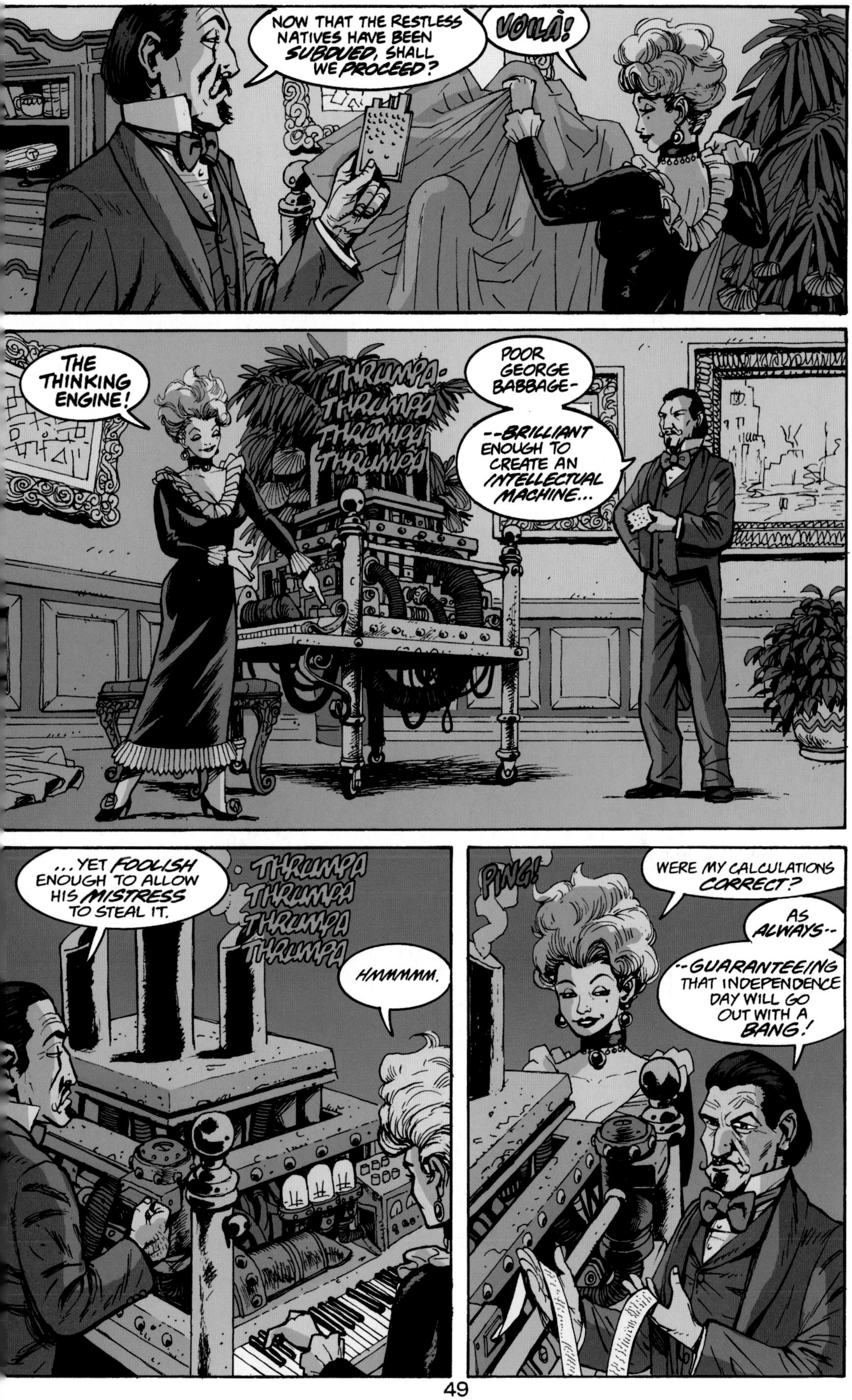
NOW THAT THE RESTLESS NATIVES HAVE BEEN SUBDUED, SHALL WE PROCEED?
VOILÀ!
THE THINKING ENGINE!
THRUMPA- THRUMPA THRUMPA THRUMPA
POOR GEORGE BABBAGE-
--BRILLIANT ENOUGH TO CREATE AN INTELLECTUAL MACHINE...
...YET FOOLISH ENOUGH TO ALLOW HIS MISTRESS TO STEAL IT.
THRUMPA THRUMPA THRUMPA THRUMPA
HMMMMM.
PING!
WERE MY CALCULATIONS CORRECT?
AS ALWAYS--
--GUARANTEEING THAT INDEPENDENCE DAY WILL GO OUT WITH A BANG!

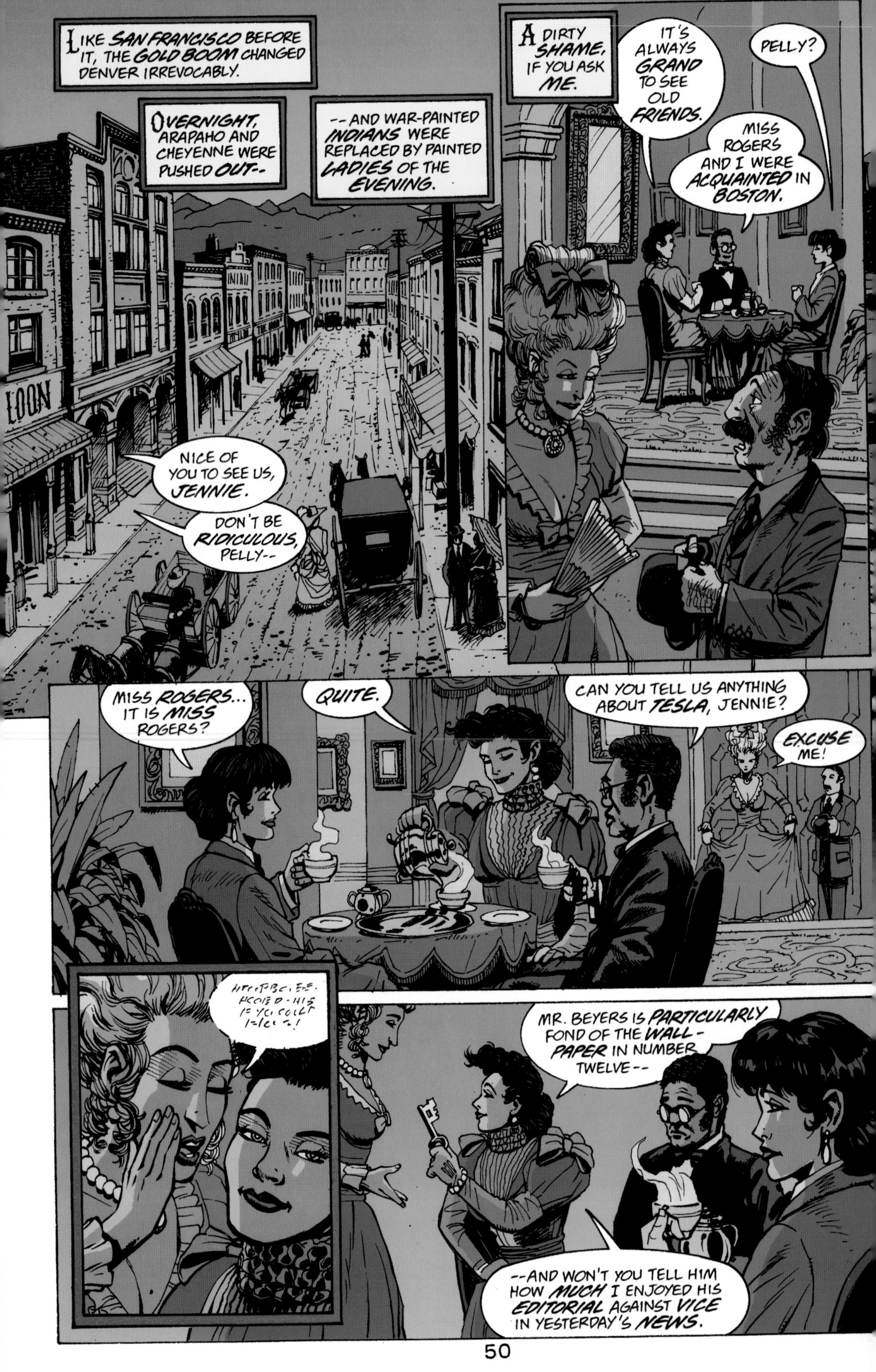
LIKE SAN FRANCISCO BEFORE IT, THE GOLD BOOM CHANGED DENVER IRREVOCABLY.
OVERNIGHT, ARAPAHO AND CHEYENNE WERE PUSHED OUT--
--AND WAR-PAINTED INDIANS WERE REPLACED BY PAINTED LADIES OF THE EVENING.
LOON
NICE OF YOU TO SEE US, JENNIE.
DON'T BE RIDICULOUS, PELLY--
A DIRTY SHAME, IF YOU ASK ME.
IT'S ALWAYS GRAND TO SEE OLD FRIENDS.
PELLY?
MISS ROGERS AND I WERE ACQUAINTED IN BOSTON.
MISS ROGERS... IT IS MISS ROGERS?
QUITE.
CAN YOU TELL US ANYTHING ABOUT TESLA, JENNIE?
EXCUSE ME!
MR. BEYERS IS PARTICULARLY FOND OF THE WALL-PAPER IN NUMBER TWELVE--
--AND WON'T YOU TELL HIM HOW MUCH I ENJOYED HIS EDITORIAL AGAINST VICE IN YESTERDAY'S NEWS.

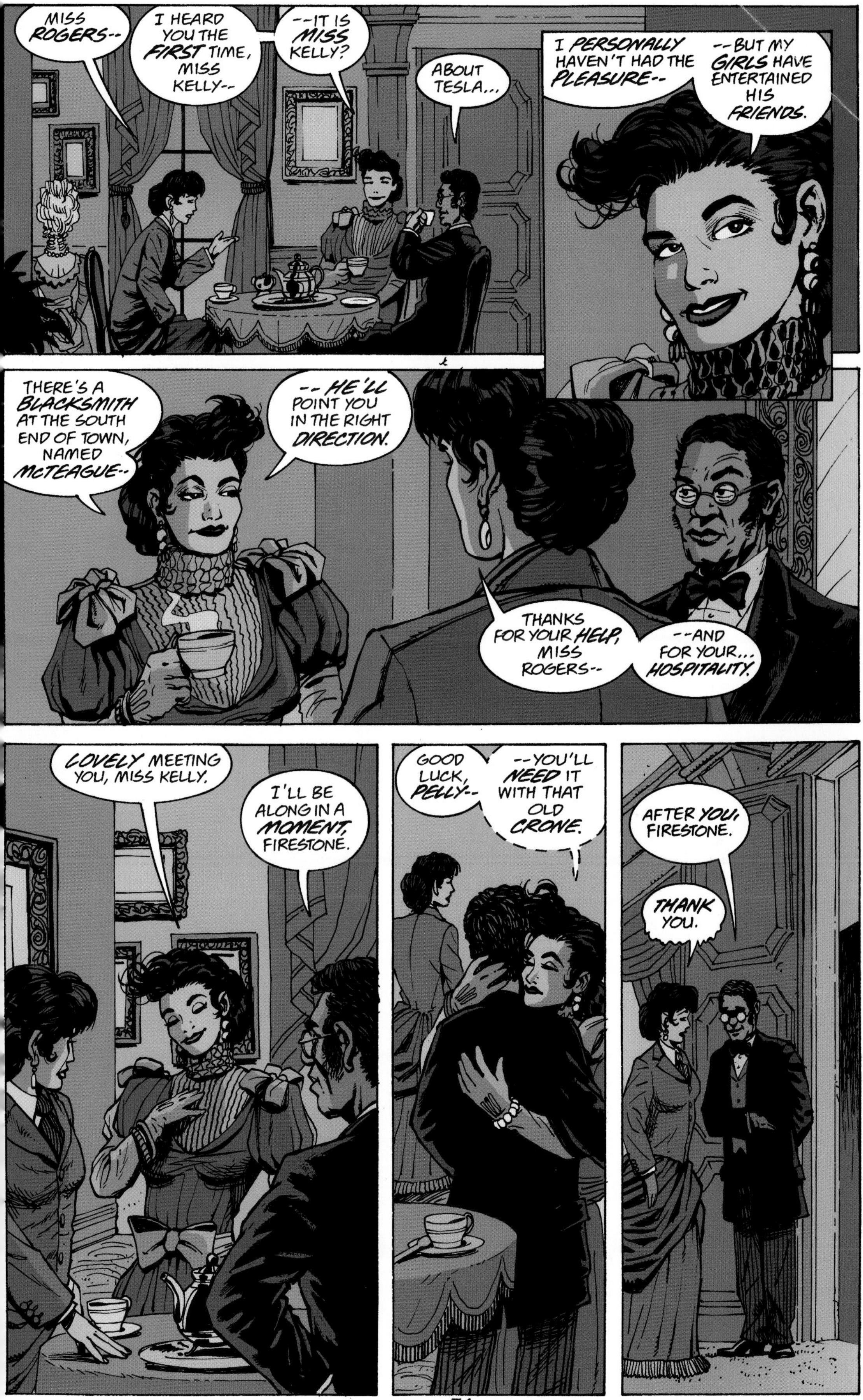
MISS ROGERS--
I HEARD YOU THE FIRST TIME, MISS KELLY--
--IT IS MISS KELLY?
ABOUT TESLA...
I PERSONALLY HAVEN'T HAD THE PLEASURE--
--BUT MY GIRLS HAVE ENTERTAINED HIS FRIENDS.
THERE'S A BLACKSMITH AT THE SOUTH END OF TOWN, NAMED MCTEAGUE--
--HE'LL POINT YOU IN THE RIGHT DIRECTION.
THANKS FOR YOUR HELP, MISS ROGERS--
--AND FOR YOUR... HOSPITALITY.
LOVELY MEETING YOU, MISS KELLY.
I'LL BE ALONG IN A MOMENT, FIRESTONE.
GOOD LUCK, PELLY--
--YOU'LL NEED IT WITH THAT OLD CRONE.
AFTER YOU, FIRESTONE.
THANK YOU.

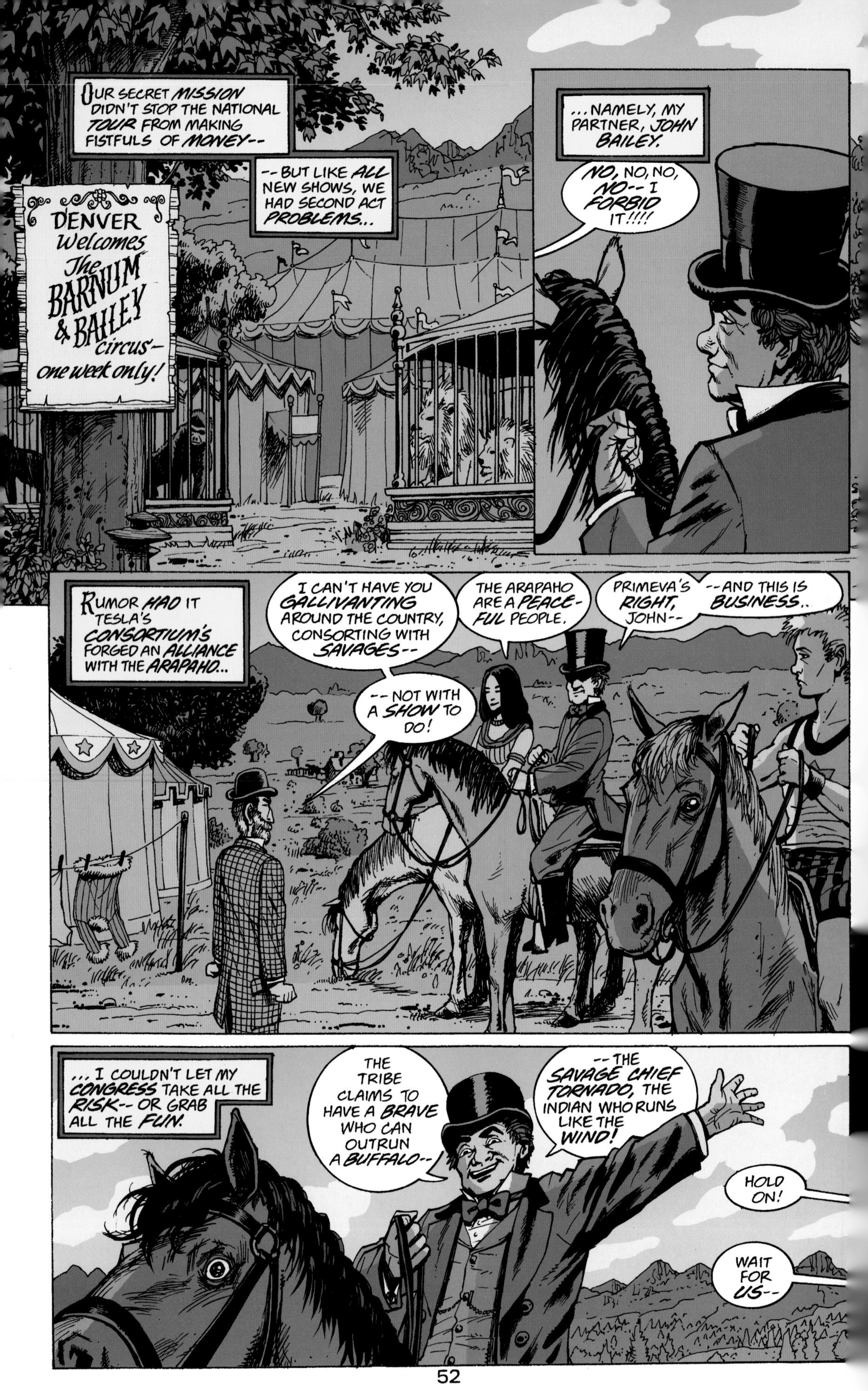
OUR SECRET MISSION DIDN'T STOP THE NATIONAL TOUR FROM MAKING FISTFULS OF MONEY--
DENVER Welcomes The BARNUM & BAILEY circus-- one week only!
--BUT LIKE ALL NEW SHOWS, WE HAD SECOND ACT PROBLEMS...
...NAMELY, MY PARTNER, JOHN BAILEY.
NO, NO, NO, NO-- I FORBID IT!!!!
RUMOR HAD IT TESLA'S CONSORTIUM'S FORGED AN ALLIANCE WITH THE ARAPAHO...
I CAN'T HAVE YOU GALLIVANTING AROUND THE COUNTRY, CONSORTING WITH SAVAGES--
--NOT WITH A SHOW TO DO!
THE ARAPAHO ARE A PEACEFUL PEOPLE.
PRIMEVA'S RIGHT, JOHN--
--AND THIS IS BUSINESS..
...I COULDN'T LET MY CONGRESS TAKE ALL THE RISK-- OR GRAB ALL THE FUN.
THE TRIBE CLAIMS TO HAVE A BRAVE WHO CAN OUTRUN A BUFFALO--
--THE SAVAGE CHIEF TORNADO, THE INDIAN WHO RUNS LIKE THE WIND!
HOLD ON!
WAIT FOR US--

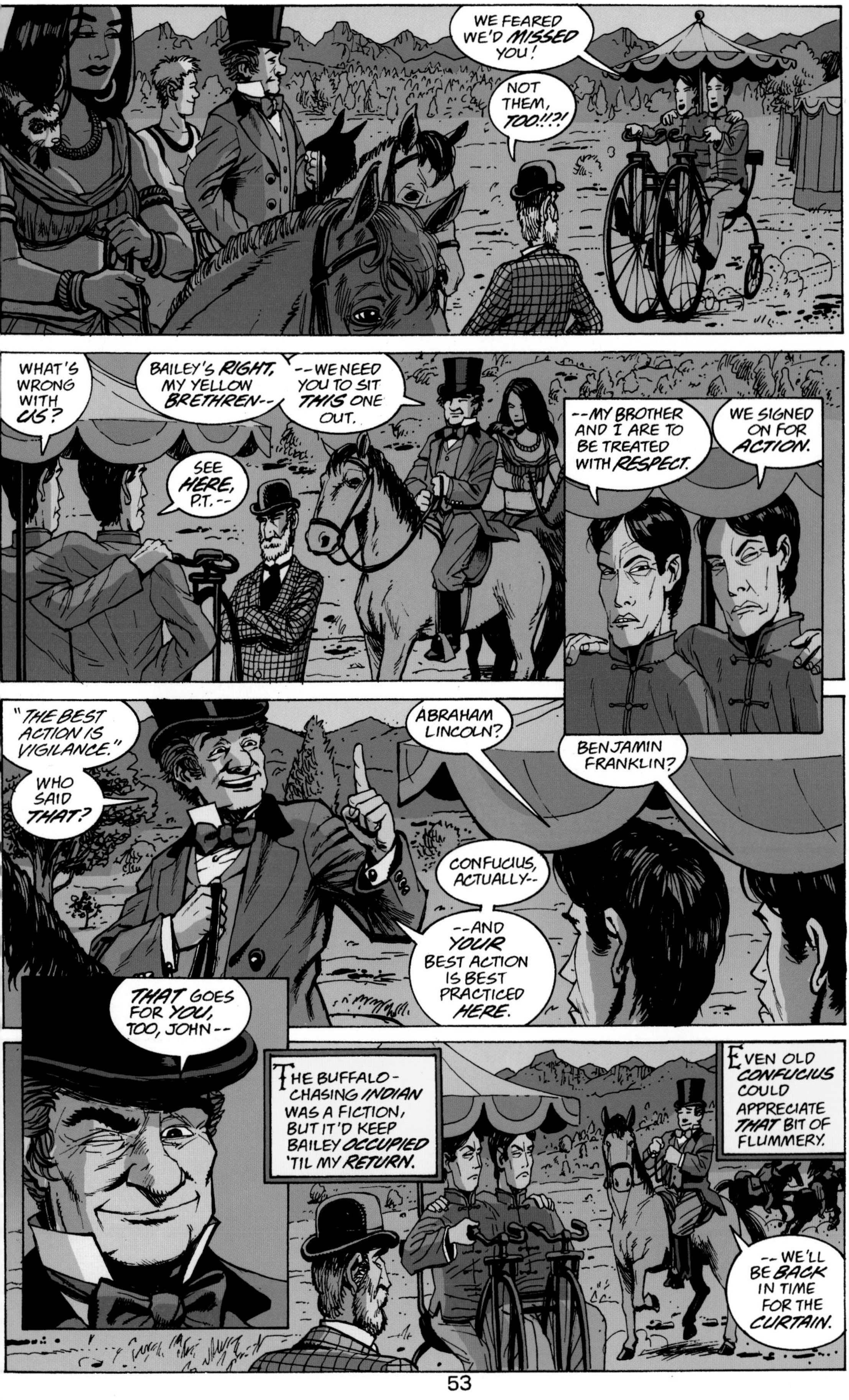
WE FEARED WE'D MISSED YOU!
NOT THEM, TOO!!?!
WHAT'S WRONG WITH US?
BAILEY'S RIGHT, MY YELLOW BRETHREN--
--WE NEED YOU TO SIT THIS ONE OUT.
SEE HERE, P.T.--
--MY BROTHER AND I ARE TO BE TREATED WITH RESPECT.
WE SIGNED ON FOR ACTION.
"THE BEST ACTION IS VIGILANCE."
WHO SAID THAT?
ABRAHAM LINCOLN?
BENJAMIN FRANKLIN?
CONFUCIUS, ACTUALLY--
--AND YOUR BEST ACTION IS BEST PRACTICED HERE.
THAT GOES FOR YOU, TOO, JOHN--
THE BUFFALO-CHASING INDIAN WAS A FICTION, BUT IT'D KEEP BAILEY OCCUPIED 'TIL MY RETURN.
EVEN OLD CONFUCIUS COULD APPRECIATE THAT BIT OF FLUMMERY.
--WE'LL BE BACK IN TIME FOR THE CURTAIN.

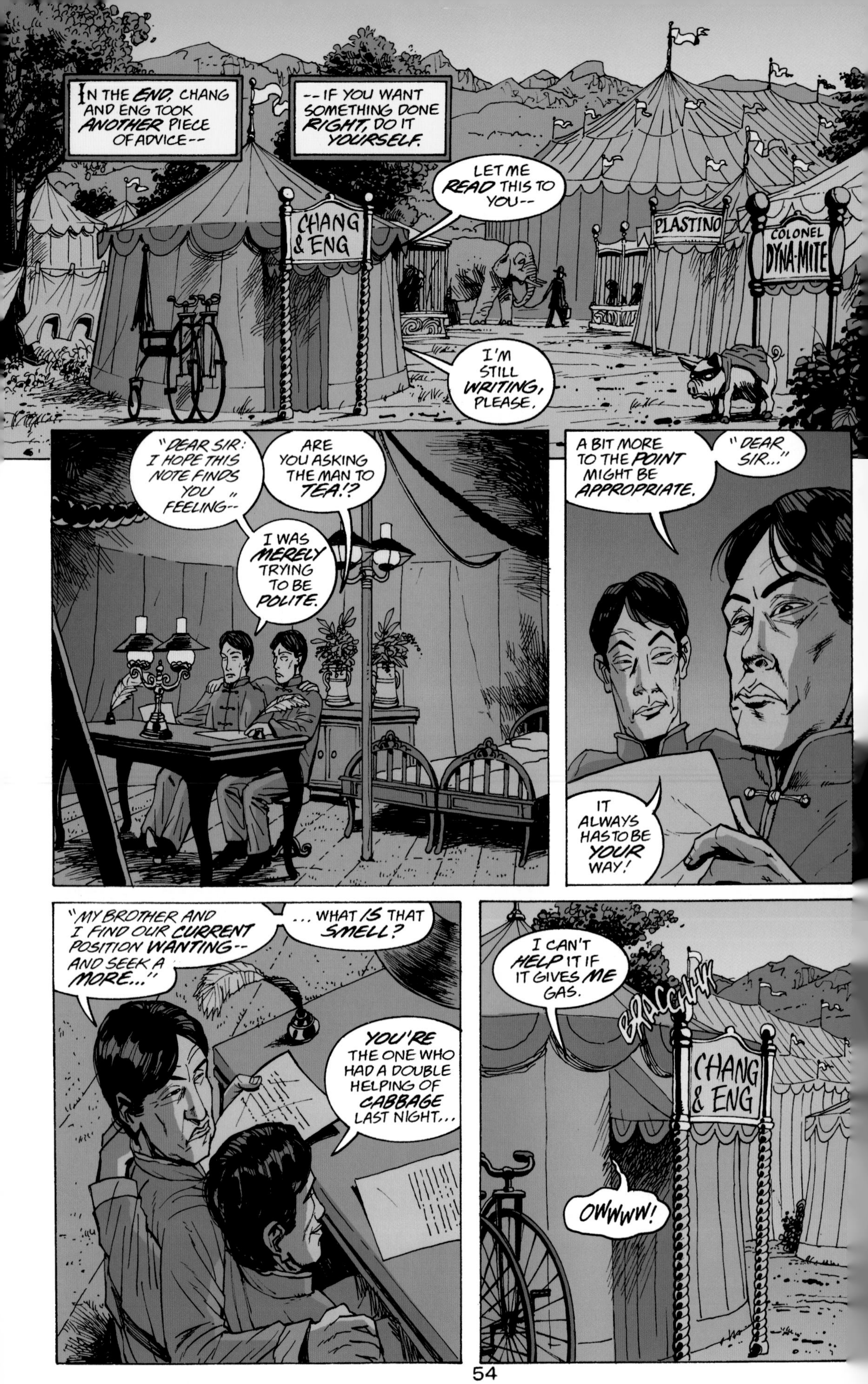
IN THE END, CHANG AND ENG TOOK ANOTHER PIECE OF ADVICE--
--IF YOU WANT SOMETHING DONE RIGHT, DO IT YOURSELF.
LET ME READ THIS TO YOU--
CHANG & ENG
PLASTINO
COLONEL DYNA-MITE
I'M STILL WRITING, PLEASE.
"DEAR SIR: I HOPE THIS NOTE FINDS YOU FEELING--"
ARE YOU ASKING THE MAN TO TEA!?
I WAS MERELY TRYING TO BE POLITE.
A BIT MORE TO THE POINT MIGHT BE APPROPRIATE.
"DEAR SIR..."
IT ALWAYS HAS TO BE YOUR WAY!
"MY BROTHER AND I FIND OUR CURRENT POSITION WANTING--AND SEEK A MORE..."
...WHAT IS THAT SMELL?
YOU'RE THE ONE WHO HAD A DOUBLE HELPING OF CABBAGE LAST NIGHT...
I CAN'T HELP IT IF IT GIVES ME GAS.
BRAACHHK
CHANG & ENG
OWWWW!

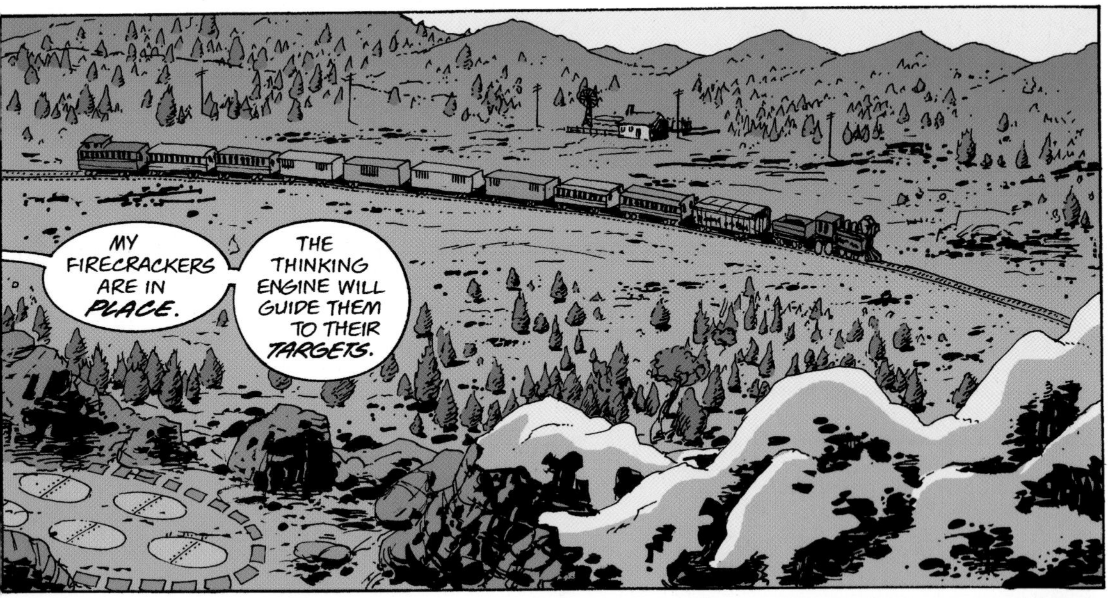
MY FIRECRACKERS ARE IN PLACE.
THE THINKING ENGINE WILL GUIDE THEM TO THEIR TARGETS.

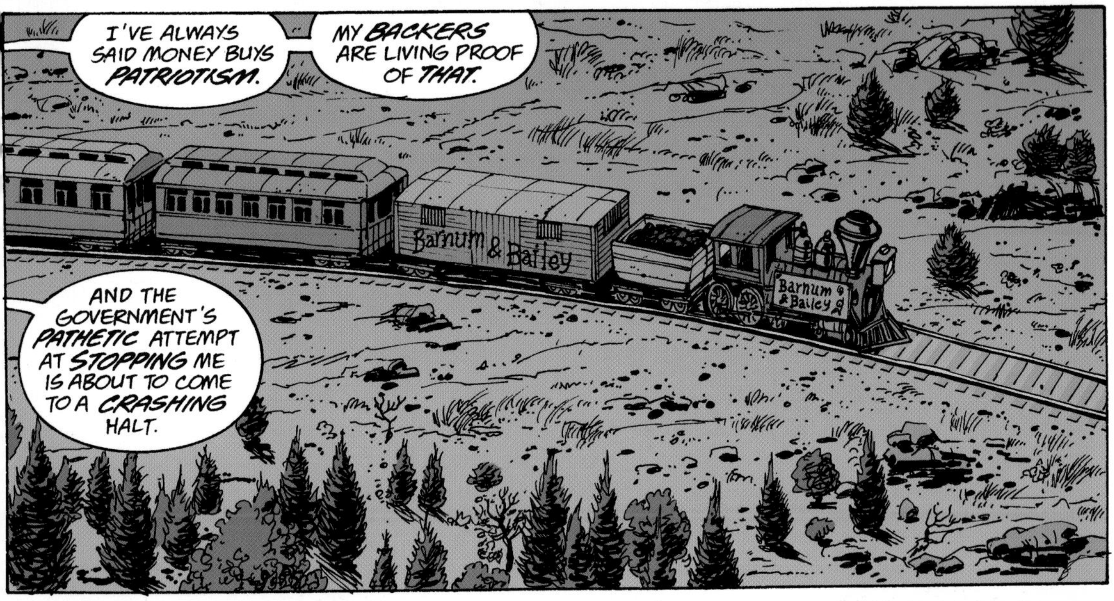
I'VE ALWAYS SAID MONEY BUYS PATRIOTISM.
MY BACKERS ARE LIVING PROOF OF THAT.
Barnum & Bailey
Barnum & Bailey
AND THE GOVERNMENT'S PATHETIC ATTEMPT AT STOPPING ME IS ABOUT TO COME TO A CRASHING HALT.

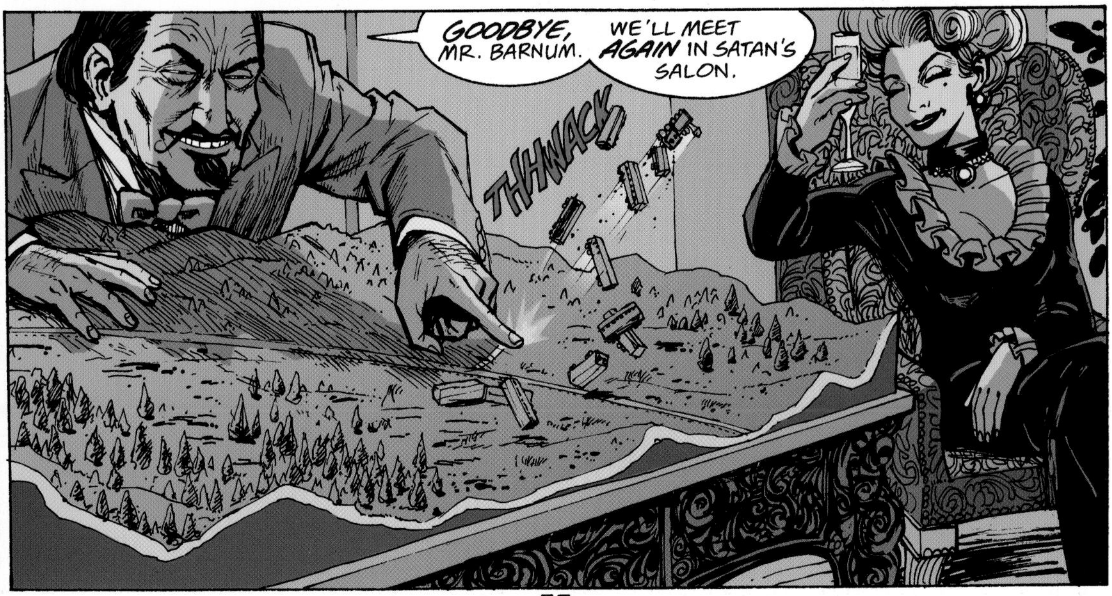
GOODBYE, MR. BARNUM.
WE'LL MEET AGAIN IN SATAN'S SALON.
THHWACK

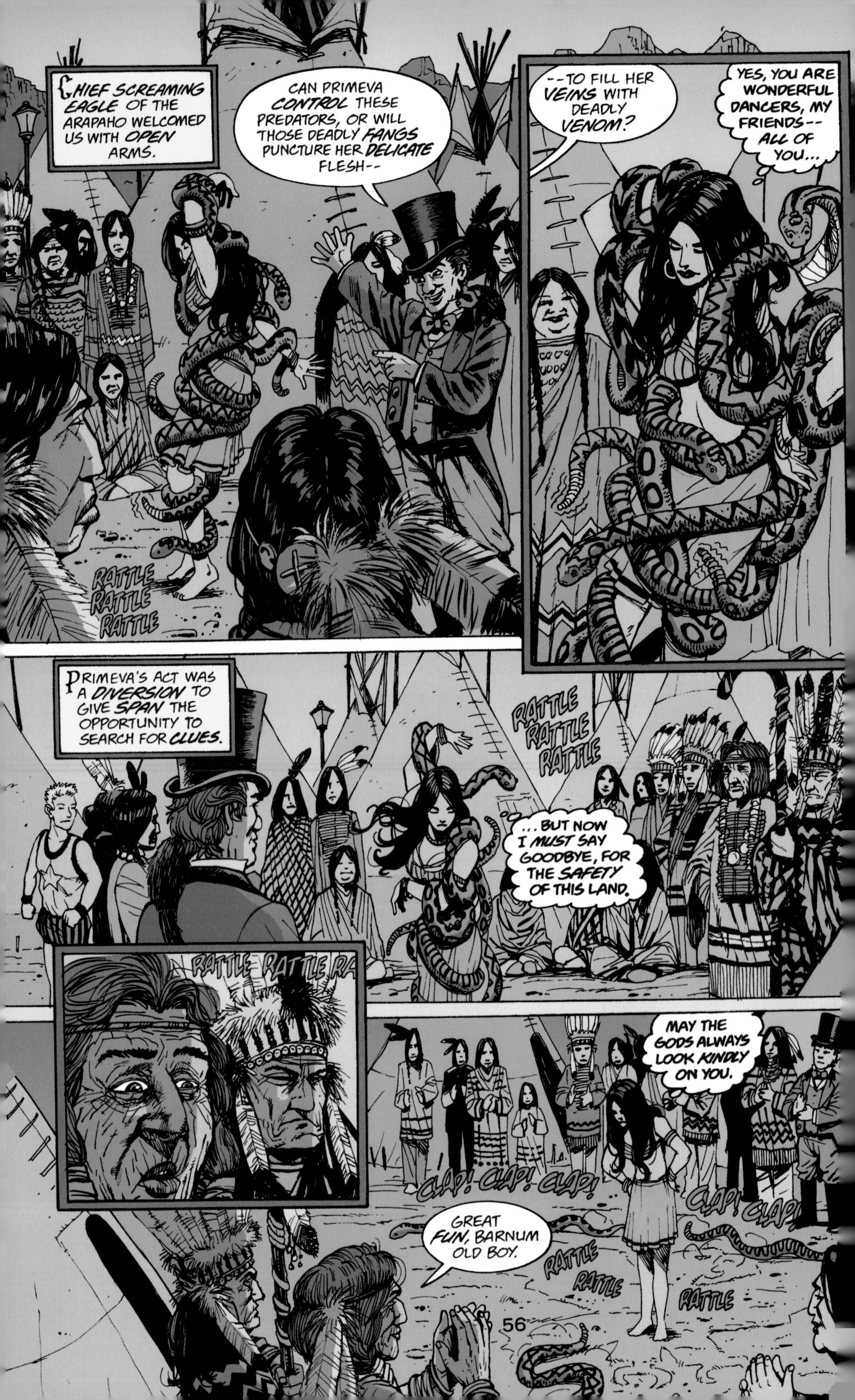

CHIEF SCREAMING EAGLE OF THE ARAPAHO WELCOMED US WITH OPEN ARMS.
CAN PRIMEVA CONTROL THESE PREDATORS, OR WILL THOSE DEADLY FANGS PUNCTURE HER DELICATE FLESH--
RATTLE RATTLE RATTLE
--TO FILL HER VEINS WITH DEADLY VENOM?
YES, YOU ARE WONDERFUL DANCERS, MY FRIENDS-- ALL OF YOU...
PRIMEVA'S ACT WAS A DIVERSION TO GIVE SPAN THE OPPORTUNITY TO SEARCH FOR CLUES.
RATTLE RATTLE RATTLE
...BUT NOW I MUST SAY GOODBYE, FOR THE SAFETY OF THIS LAND.
RATTLE RATTLE
MAY THE GODS ALWAYS LOOK KINDLY ON YOU.
CLAP! CLAP! CLAP!
CLAP! CLAP!
GREAT FUN, BARNUM OLD BOY.
RATTLE RATTLE RATTLE

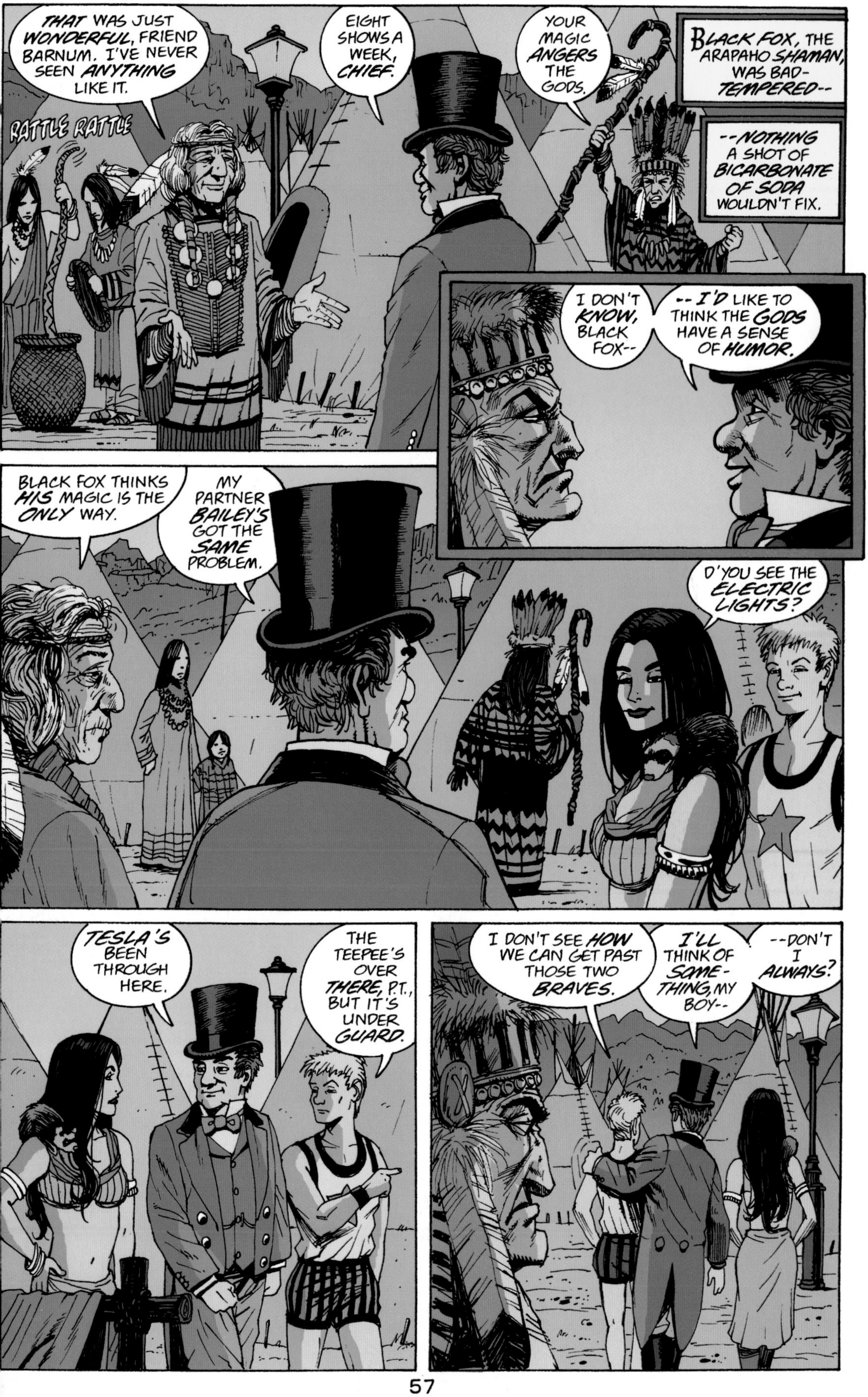
THAT WAS JUST WONDERFUL, FRIEND BARNUM. I'VE NEVER SEEN ANYTHING LIKE IT.
RATTLE RATTLE
EIGHT SHOWS A WEEK, CHIEF.
YOUR MAGIC ANGERS THE GODS.
BLACK FOX, THE ARAPAHO SHAMAN, WAS BAD-TEMPERED--
--NOTHING A SHOT OF BICARBONATE OF SODA WOULDN'T FIX.
I DON'T KNOW, BLACK FOX--
--I'D LIKE TO THINK THE GODS HAVE A SENSE OF HUMOR.
BLACK FOX THINKS HIS MAGIC IS THE ONLY WAY.
MY PARTNER BAILEY'S GOT THE SAME PROBLEM.
D'YOU SEE THE ELECTRIC LIGHTS?
TESLA'S BEEN THROUGH HERE.
THE TEEPEE'S OVER THERE, P.T., BUT IT'S UNDER GUARD.
I DON'T SEE HOW WE CAN GET PAST THOSE TWO BRAVES.
I'LL THINK OF SOME-THING, MY BOY--
--DON'T I ALWAYS?

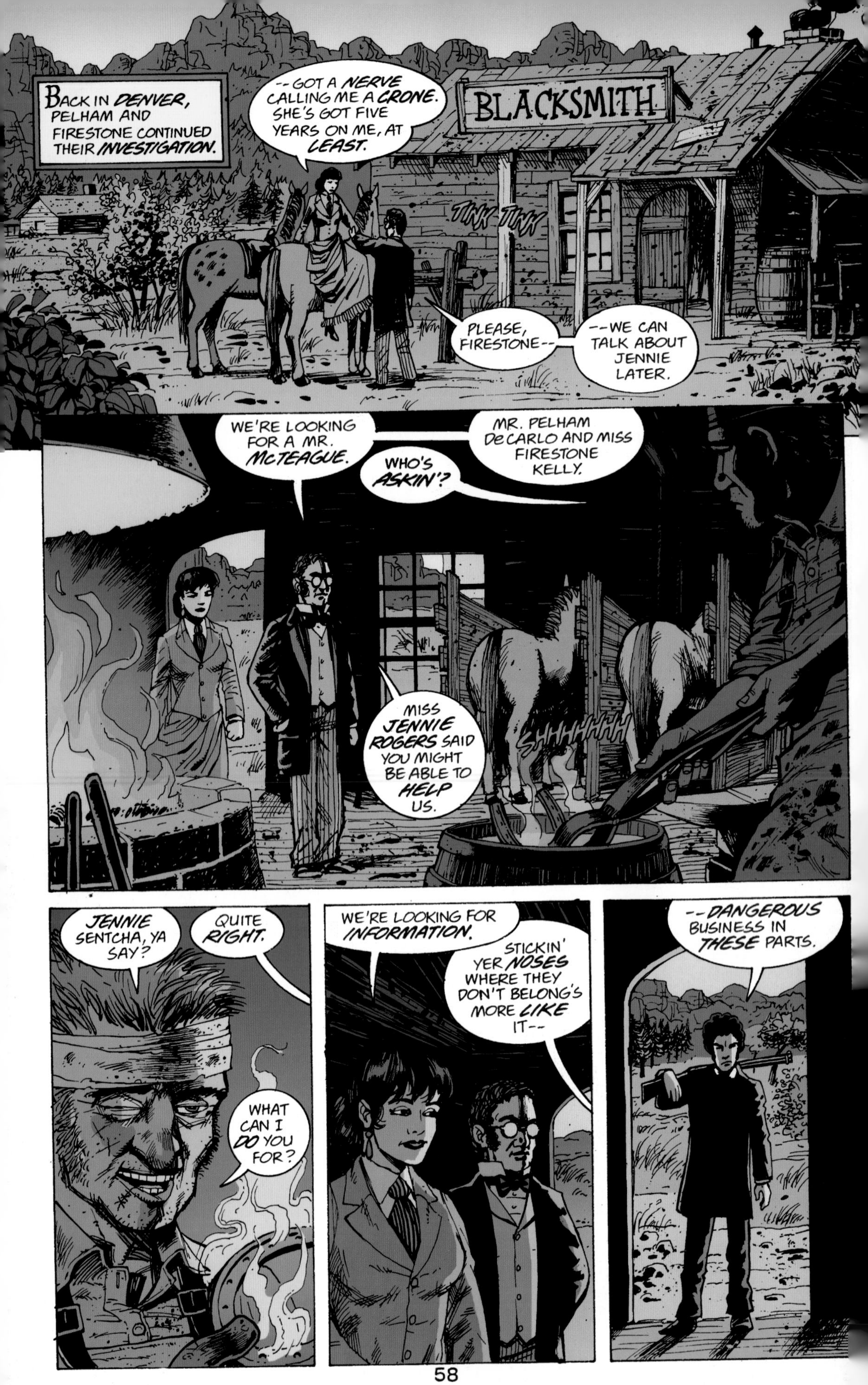
BACK IN DENVER, PELHAM AND FIRESTONE CONTINUED THEIR INVESTIGATION.
--GOT A NERVE CALLING ME A CRONE. SHE'S GOT FIVE YEARS ON ME, AT LEAST.
BLACKSMITH
TINK TINK
PLEASE, FIRESTONE--
--WE CAN TALK ABOUT JENNIE LATER.
WE'RE LOOKING FOR A MR. McTEAGUE.
WHO'S ASKIN'?
MR. PELHAM DeCARLO AND MISS FIRESTONE KELLY.
MISS JENNIE ROGERS SAID YOU MIGHT BE ABLE TO HELP US.
SHHHHHH
JENNIE SENTCHA, YA SAY?
QUITE RIGHT.
WHAT CAN I DO YOU FOR?
WE'RE LOOKING FOR INFORMATION.
STICKIN' YER NOSES WHERE THEY DON'T BELONG'S MORE LIKE IT--
--DANGEROUS BUSINESS IN THESE PARTS.

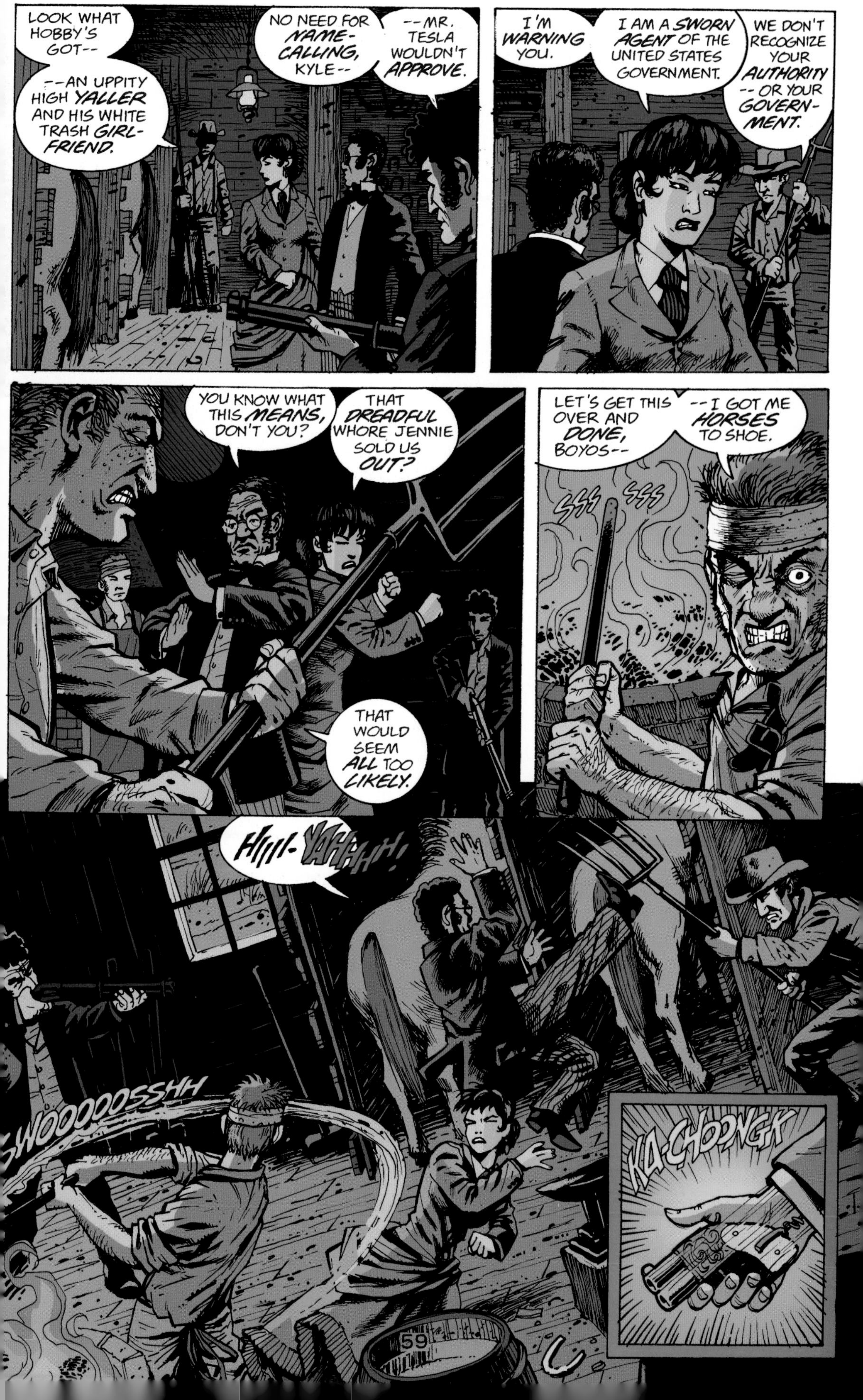

LOOK WHAT HOBBY'S GOT--
--AN UPPITY HIGH YALLER AND HIS WHITE TRASH GIRLFRIEND.
NO NEED FOR NAME-CALLING, KYLE--
--MR. TESLA WOULDN'T APPROVE.
I'M WARNING YOU.
I AM A SWORN AGENT OF THE UNITED STATES GOVERNMENT.
WE DON'T RECOGNIZE YOUR AUTHORITY --OR YOUR GOVERNMENT.
YOU KNOW WHAT THIS MEANS, DON'T YOU?
THAT DREADFUL WHORE JENNIE SOLD US OUT?
THAT WOULD SEEM ALL TOO LIKELY.
LET'S GET THIS OVER AND DONE, BOYOS--
--I GOT ME HORSES TO SHOE.
SSS SSS
HIII-YAHHHH!
SWOOOOOSSHH
KA-CHOONGK

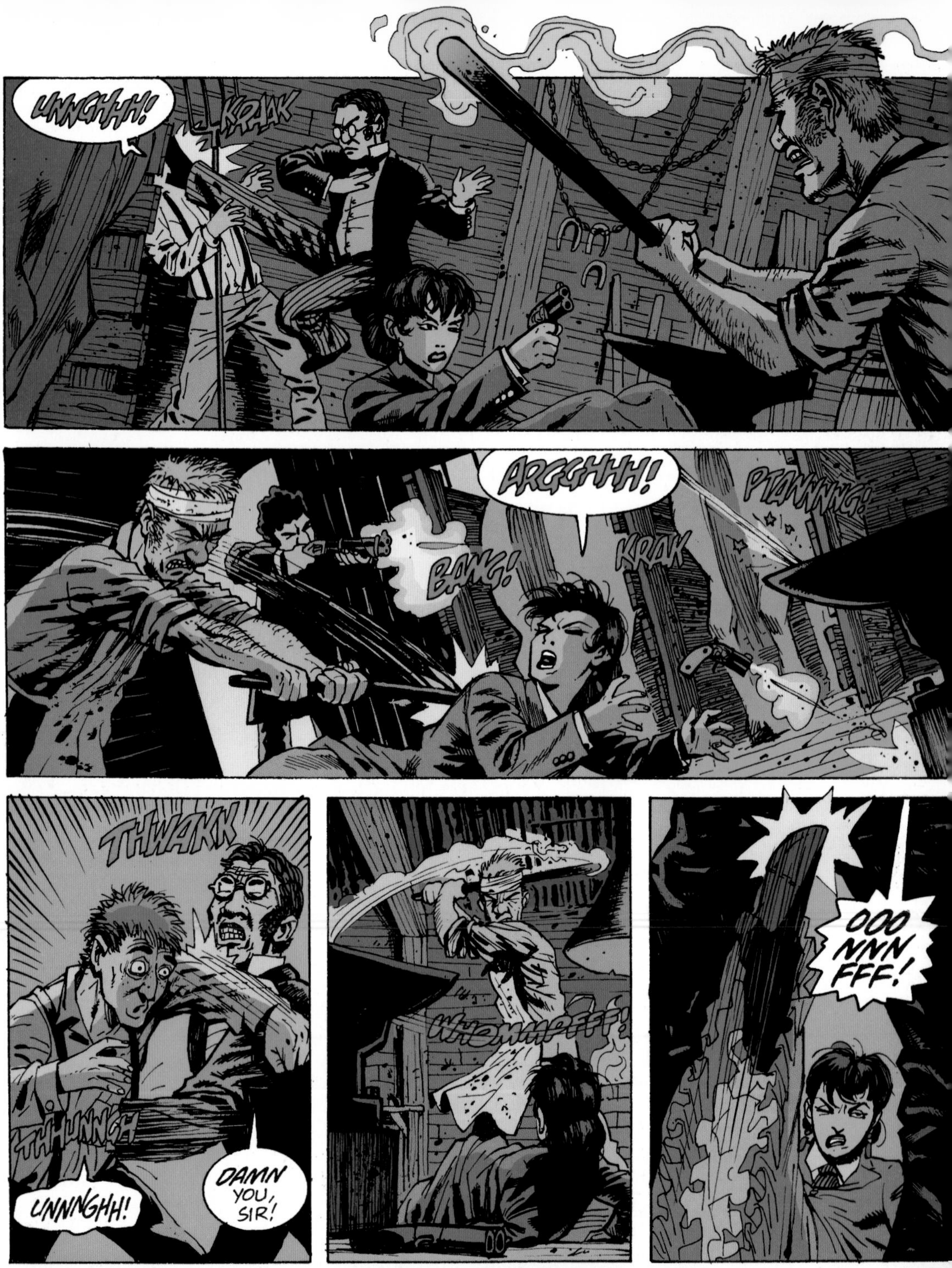
UNNGHHH!
KRAAK
ARGGHHH!
PTANNNNG!
BANG!
KRAK
THWAKK
THHUNNCH
UNNNGHH!
DAMN YOU, SIR!
OOO NNN FFF!
PELHAM!

MEANWHILE...

IS *BARNUM* THE EVIL YOU SPEAK OF, O *SPIRIT?*

WE MUST TELL *BLACK FOX!*

TAKE ME TO HIM. *QUICKLY--*

--WHILE THERE IS STILL *TIME!*

--WHILE THERE IS STILL *TIME!*

--WHILE THERE IS STILL *TIME!*

*D*ID I MENTION I STUDIED *VENTRILOQUISM* IN *INDIA?*

THE *FERRET* WON'T FOOL 'EM FOR *LONG.*

THIS IS *NOTHING* BUT A TIN CAN.

A *PNEUMATIC* TUBE--

--IN WHICH *COMPRESSED AIR* DRIVES THE *CAPSULE* FROM ONE PLACE TO *ANOTHER.*

WHERE DOES IT GO?

CLIK

SSSSSSS

*W*E WOULDN'T KNOW *THAT* UNTIL WE GOT THERE.

LADIES AND GENTLEMEN--

--AFTER *YOU.*

61

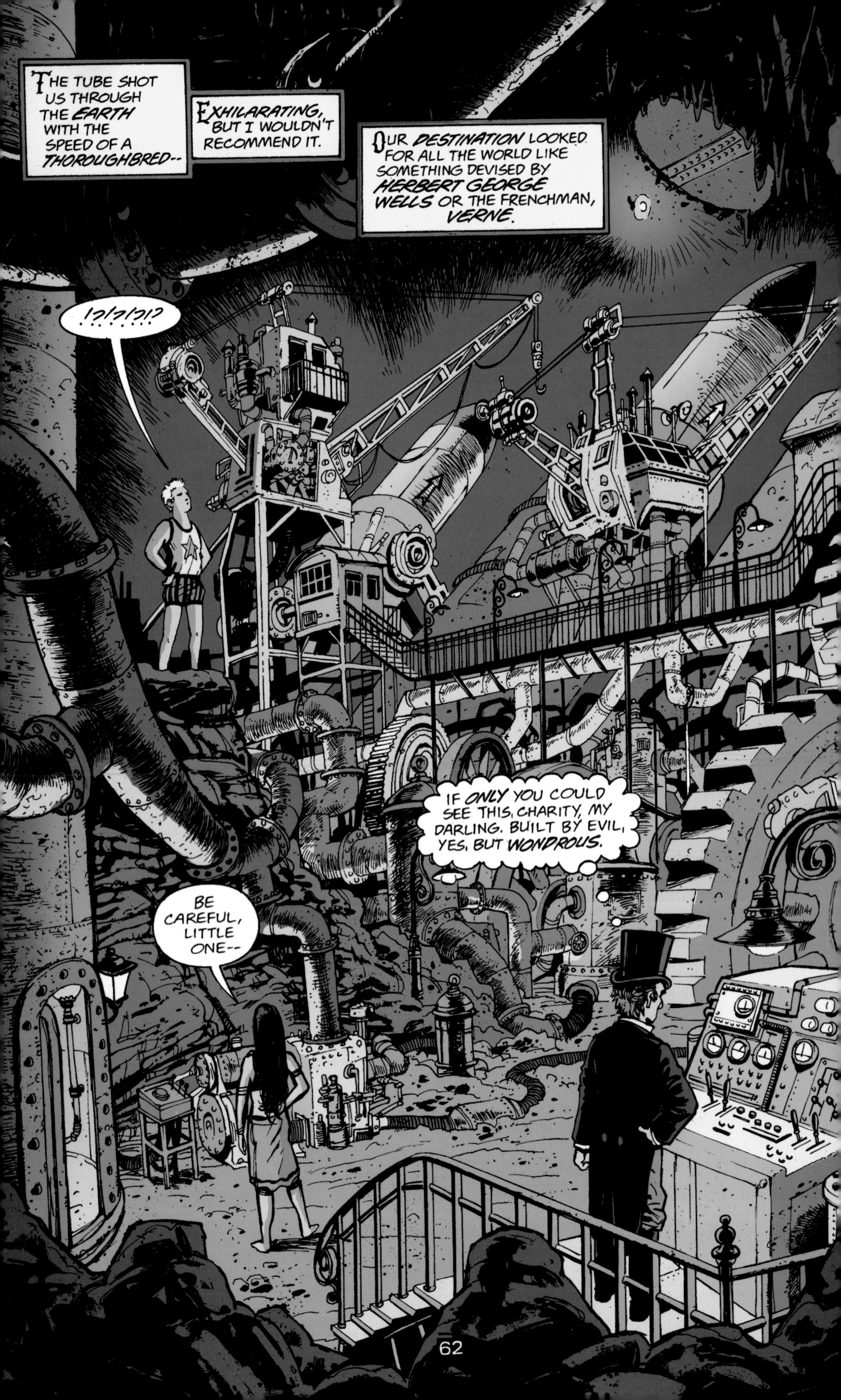

THE TUBE SHOT US THROUGH THE EARTH WITH THE SPEED OF A THOROUGHBRED--
EXHILARATING, BUT I WOULDN'T RECOMMEND IT.
OUR DESTINATION LOOKED FOR ALL THE WORLD LIKE SOMETHING DEVISED BY HERBERT GEORGE WELLS OR THE FRENCHMAN, VERNE.
!?!?!?!?
IF ONLY YOU COULD SEE THIS, CHARITY, MY DARLING. BUILT BY EVIL, YES, BUT WONDROUS.
BE CAREFUL, LITTLE ONE--

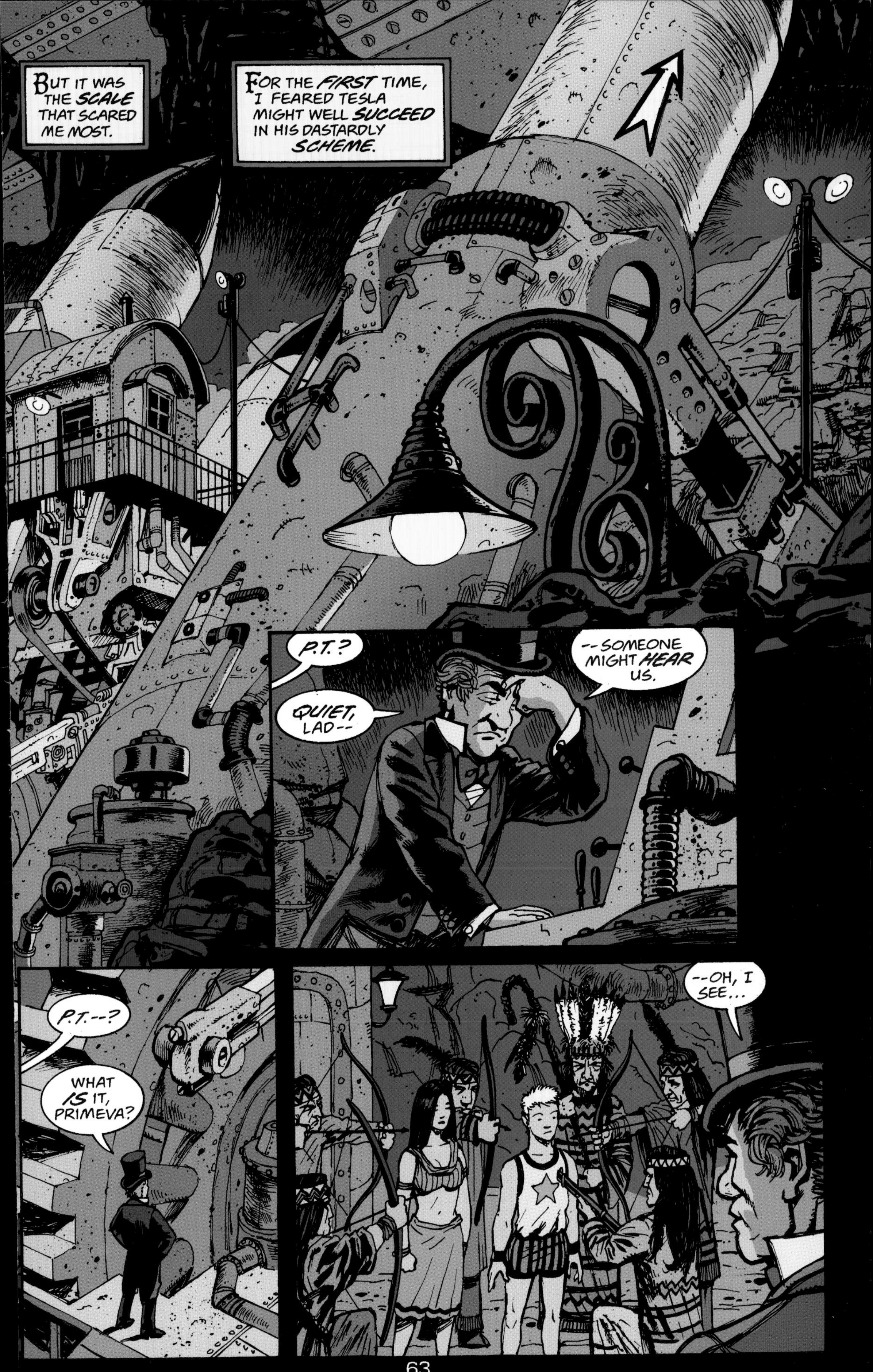
BUT IT WAS THE SCALE THAT SCARED ME MOST.
FOR THE FIRST TIME, I FEARED TESLA MIGHT WELL SUCCEED IN HIS DASTARDLY SCHEME.
P.T.?
QUIET, LAD--
--SOMEONE MIGHT HEAR US.
P.T.--?
WHAT IS IT, PRIMEVA?
--OH, I SEE...

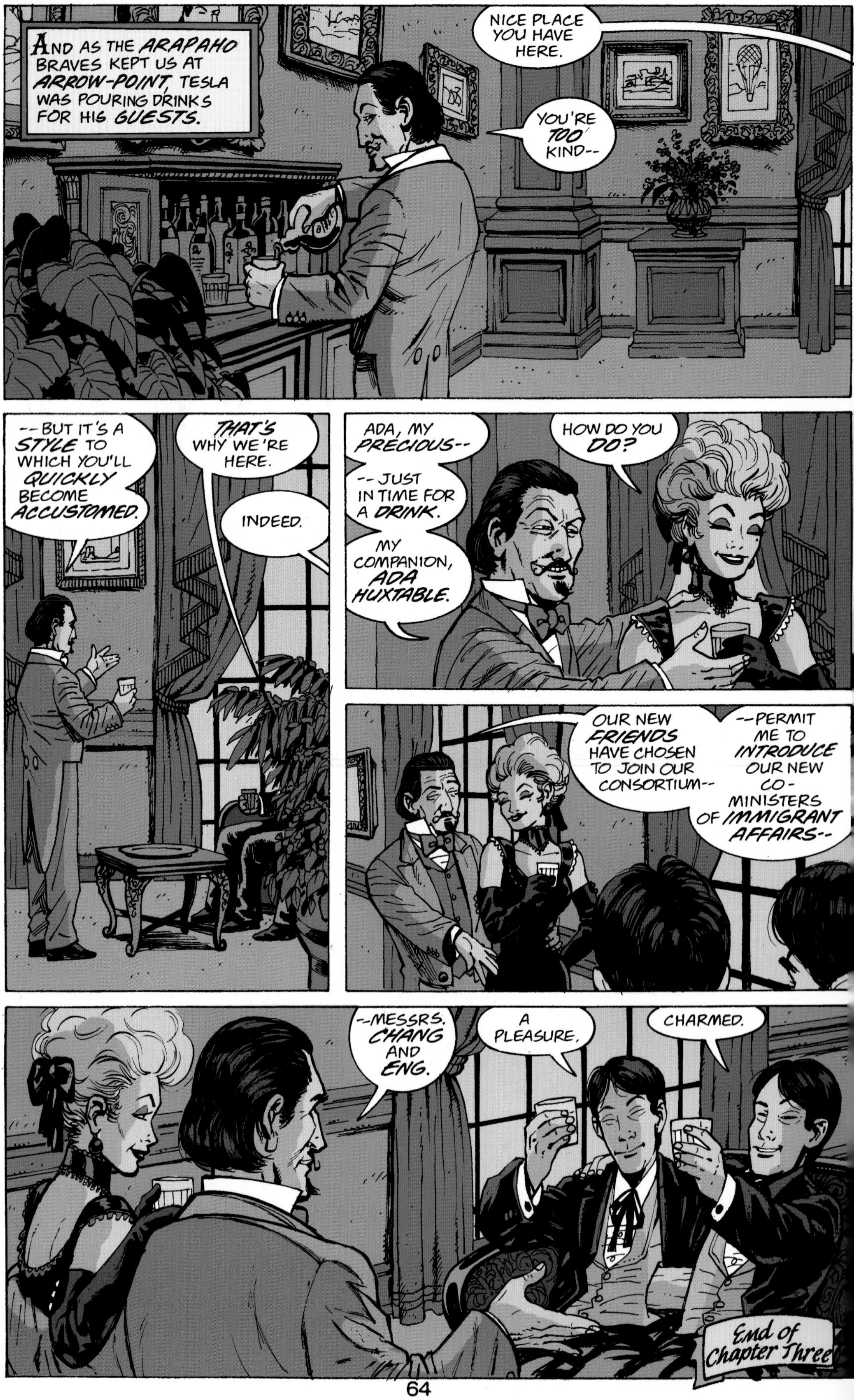
AND AS THE ARAPAHO BRAVES KEPT US AT ARROW-POINT, TESLA WAS POURING DRINKS FOR HIS GUESTS.
NICE PLACE YOU HAVE HERE.
YOU'RE TOO KIND--
--BUT IT'S A STYLE TO WHICH YOU'LL QUICKLY BECOME ACCUSTOMED.
THAT'S WHY WE'RE HERE.
INDEED.
ADA, MY PRECIOUS--
--JUST IN TIME FOR A DRINK.
MY COMPANION, ADA HUXTABLE.
HOW DO YOU DO?
OUR NEW FRIENDS HAVE CHOSEN TO JOIN OUR CONSORTIUM--
--PERMIT ME TO INTRODUCE OUR NEW CO-MINISTERS OF IMMIGRANT AFFAIRS--
--MESSRS. CHANG AND ENG.
A PLEASURE.
CHARMED.
End of Chapter Three

CHAPTER 4

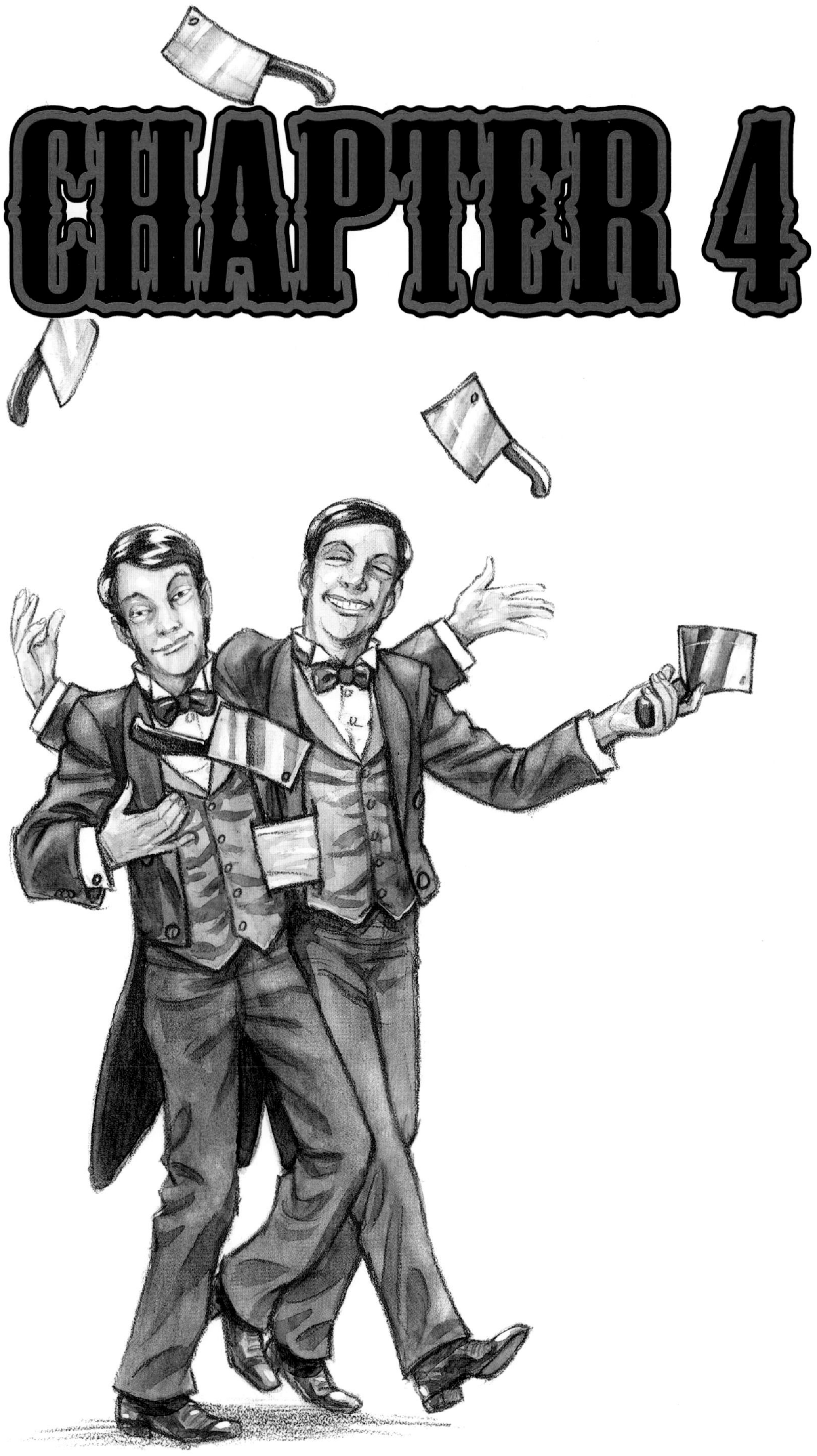

CHAPTER 4

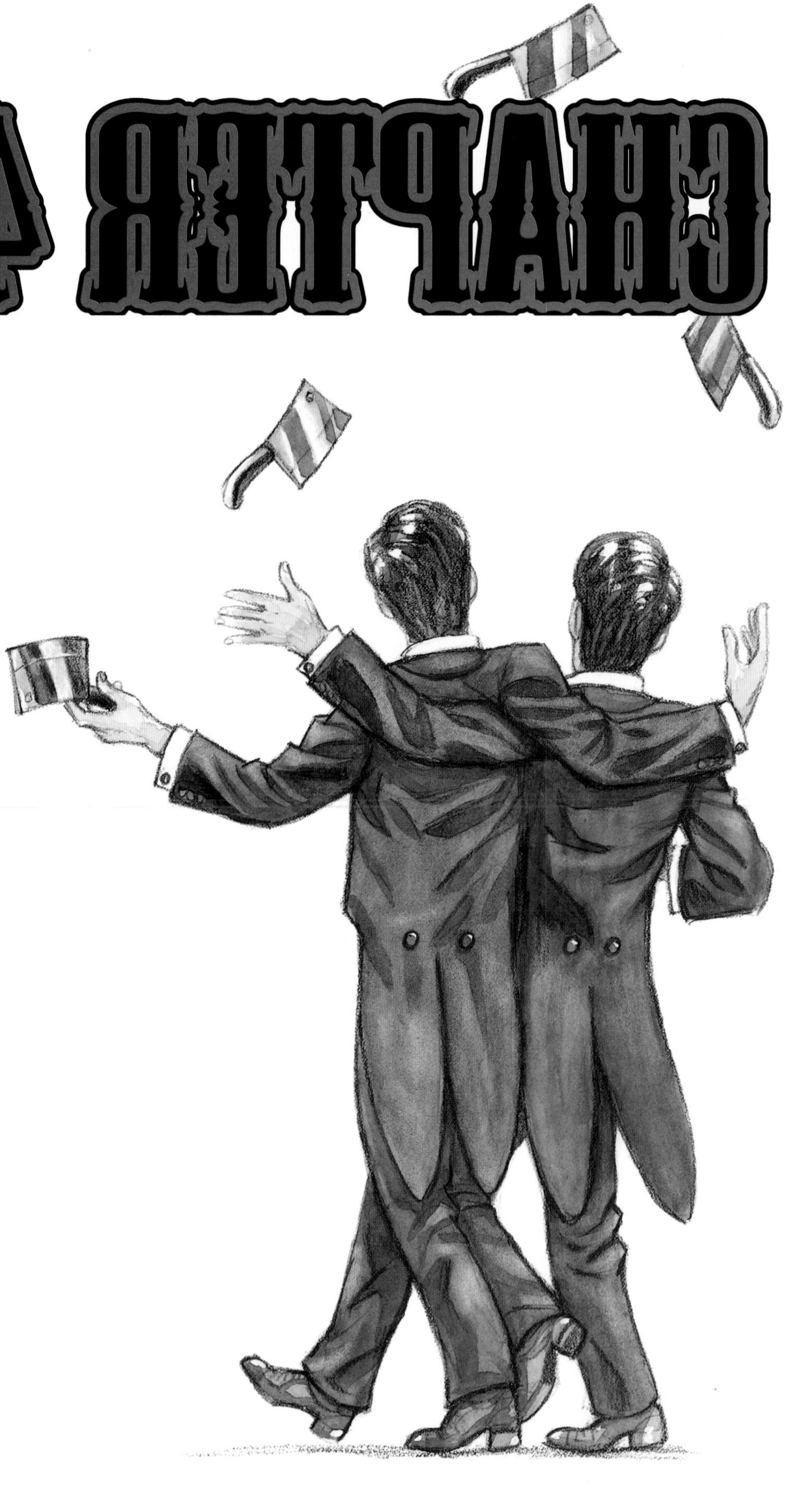

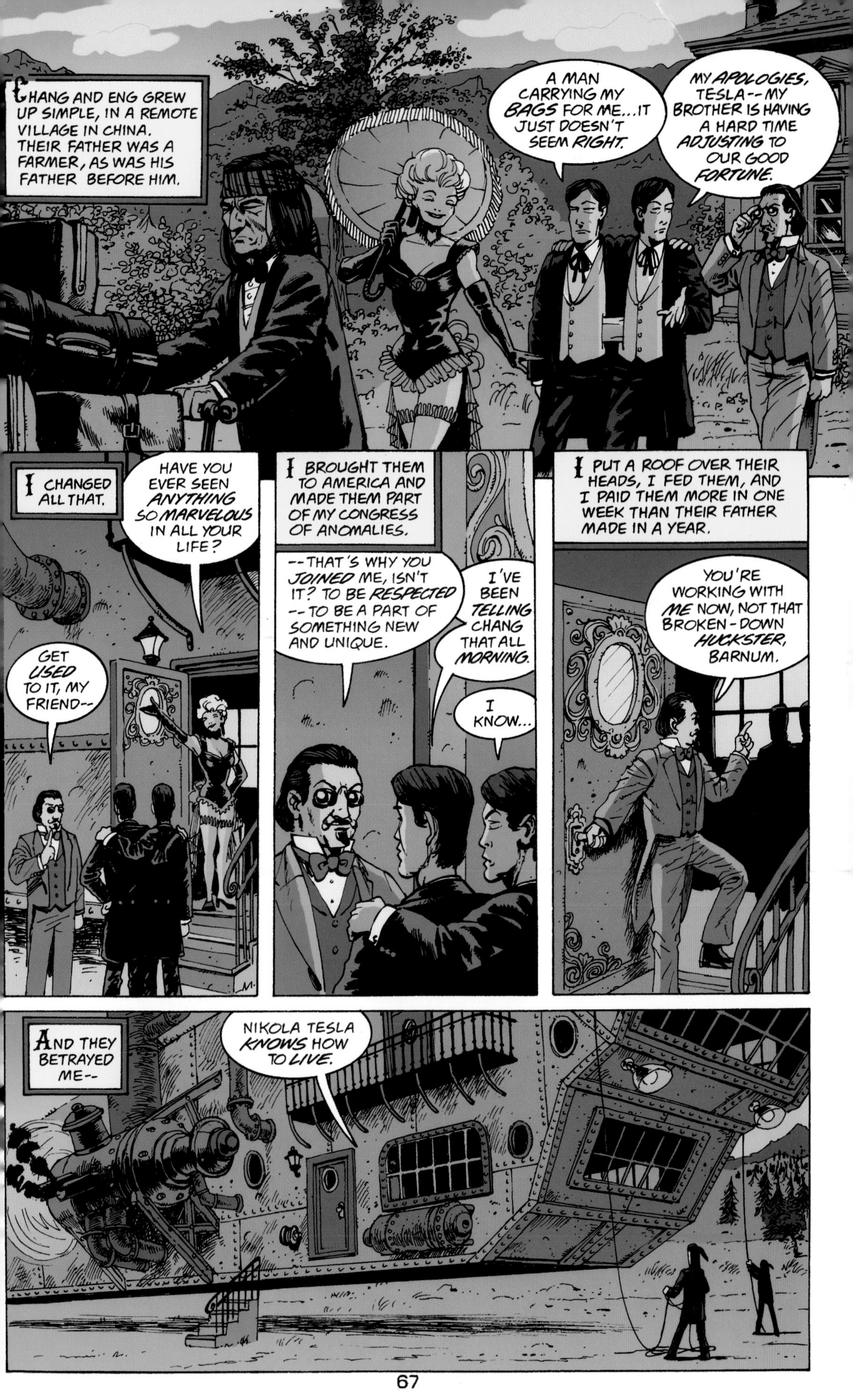
CHANG AND ENG GREW UP SIMPLE, IN A REMOTE VILLAGE IN CHINA. THEIR FATHER WAS A FARMER, AS WAS HIS FATHER BEFORE HIM.
A MAN CARRYING MY BAGS FOR ME... IT JUST DOESN'T SEEM RIGHT.
MY APOLOGIES, TESLA-- MY BROTHER IS HAVING A HARD TIME ADJUSTING TO OUR GOOD FORTUNE.
I CHANGED ALL THAT.
HAVE YOU EVER SEEN ANYTHING SO MARVELOUS IN ALL YOUR LIFE?
GET USED TO IT, MY FRIEND--
I BROUGHT THEM TO AMERICA AND MADE THEM PART OF MY CONGRESS OF ANOMALIES.
--THAT'S WHY YOU JOINED ME, ISN'T IT? TO BE RESPECTED --TO BE A PART OF SOMETHING NEW AND UNIQUE.
I'VE BEEN TELLING CHANG THAT ALL MORNING.
I KNOW...
I PUT A ROOF OVER THEIR HEADS, I FED THEM, AND I PAID THEM MORE IN ONE WEEK THAN THEIR FATHER MADE IN A YEAR.
YOU'RE WORKING WITH ME NOW, NOT THAT BROKEN-DOWN HUCKSTER, BARNUM.
AND THEY BETRAYED ME--
NIKOLA TESLA KNOWS HOW TO LIVE.

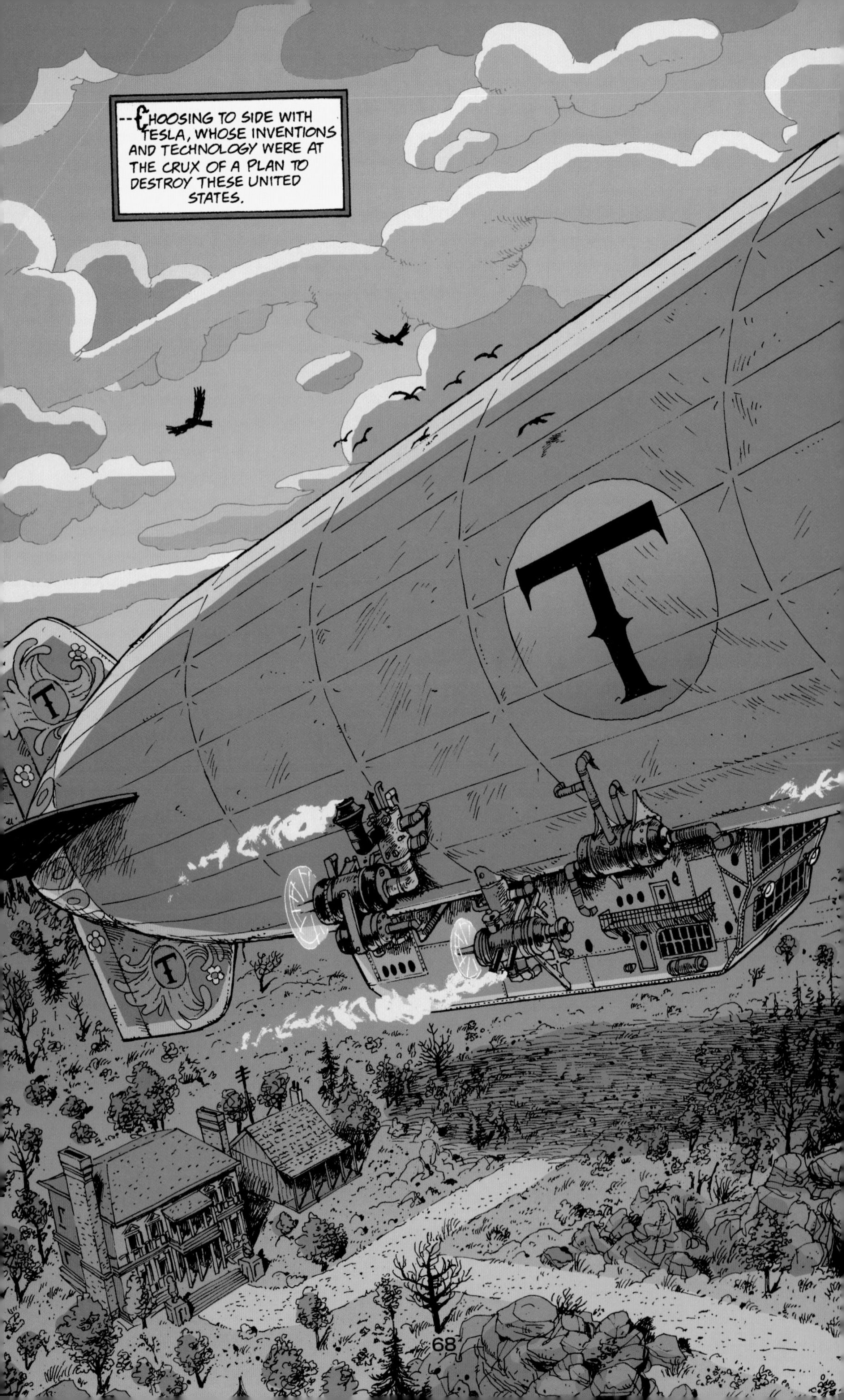
--CHOOSING TO SIDE WITH TESLA, WHOSE INVENTIONS AND TECHNOLOGY WERE AT THE CRUX OF A PLAN TO DESTROY THESE UNITED STATES.

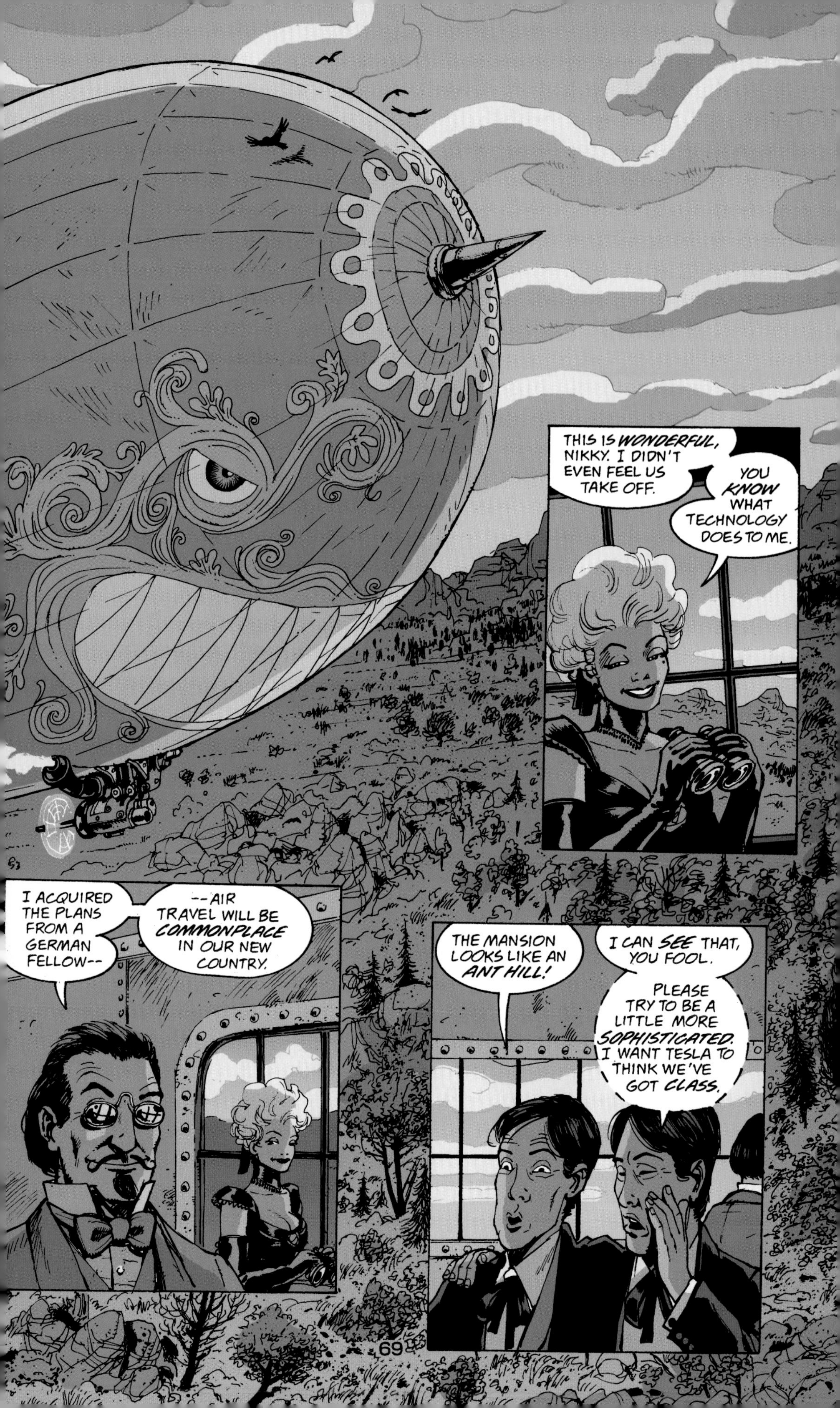
THIS IS WONDERFUL, NIKKY. I DIDN'T EVEN FEEL US TAKE OFF.
YOU KNOW WHAT TECHNOLOGY DOES TO ME.
I ACQUIRED THE PLANS FROM A GERMAN FELLOW--
--AIR TRAVEL WILL BE COMMONPLACE IN OUR NEW COUNTRY.
THE MANSION LOOKS LIKE AN ANT HILL!
I CAN SEE THAT, YOU FOOL.
PLEASE TRY TO BE A LITTLE MORE SOPHISTICATED. I WANT TESLA TO THINK WE'VE GOT CLASS.

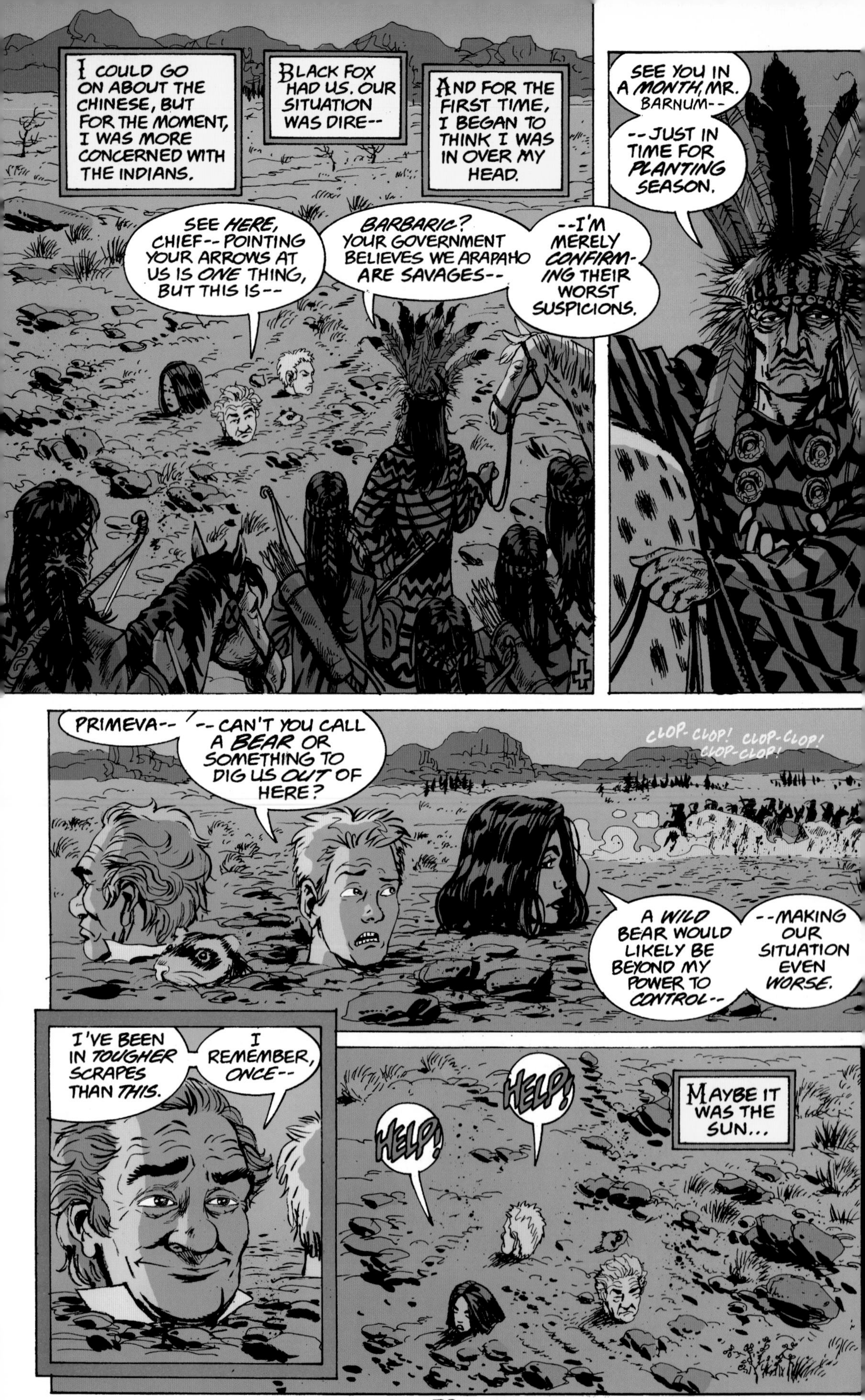
I COULD GO ON ABOUT THE CHINESE, BUT FOR THE MOMENT, I WAS MORE CONCERNED WITH THE INDIANS.
BLACK FOX HAD US. OUR SITUATION WAS DIRE--
AND FOR THE FIRST TIME, I BEGAN TO THINK I WAS IN OVER MY HEAD.
SEE HERE, CHIEF-- POINTING YOUR ARROWS AT US IS ONE THING, BUT THIS IS--
BARBARIC? YOUR GOVERNMENT BELIEVES WE ARAPAHO ARE SAVAGES--
--I'M MERELY CONFIRMING THEIR WORST SUSPICIONS.
SEE YOU IN A MONTH, MR. BARNUM--
--JUST IN TIME FOR PLANTING SEASON.
PRIMEVA--
--CAN'T YOU CALL A BEAR OR SOMETHING TO DIG US OUT OF HERE?
CLOP-CLOP! CLOP-CLOP! CLOP-CLOP!
A WILD BEAR WOULD LIKELY BE BEYOND MY POWER TO CONTROL--
--MAKING OUR SITUATION EVEN WORSE.
I'VE BEEN IN TOUGHER SCRAPES THAN THIS.
I REMEMBER, ONCE--
HELP!
HELP!
MAYBE IT WAS THE SUN...

BUT MY EARS WERE BURNING.

...PHINEAS TAYLOR BARNUM IS A *DEAD* MAN!

GIVE IT A *REST*, BAILEY-- YOU'VE BEEN SQUAWKING FOR OVER AN *HOUR*.

I'M *SURE* P.T. AND THE OTHERS HAVE A GOOD *REASON* FOR MISSING THE PERFORMANCE.

EXCUSES!

THEY *COULD* BE *HURT*...

NOT PHINEAS. THAT MAN HAS MORE *LIVES* THAN A *CAT* -- AND MORE *LUCK* THAN THREE *IRISHMEN*.

I *TOLD* HIM NOT TO GO, BUT DOES HE LISTEN TO *ME*? OF *COURSE* NOT!

WHO DO YOU THINK KEEPS THIS PLACE *RUNNING*, PLASTINO? HMMM?

ME, *THAT'S* WHO!

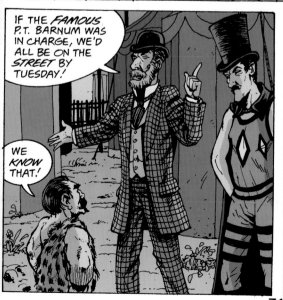

IF THE *FAMOUS* P.T. BARNUM WAS IN CHARGE, WE'D ALL BE ON THE *STREET* BY TUESDAY!

WE *KNOW* THAT!

P.T. GETS 'EM *IN* THE DOOR, BUT *YOU* KEEP THE DOORS *OPEN*.

NOBODY ELSE KNOWS HOW TO WORK ALL THOSE NUMBERS.

JUST THE OTHER DAY, THE DOG-FACED BOY WAS SAYING HOW HE LOOKS *UP* TO YOU--

...HE *DOES*?

71

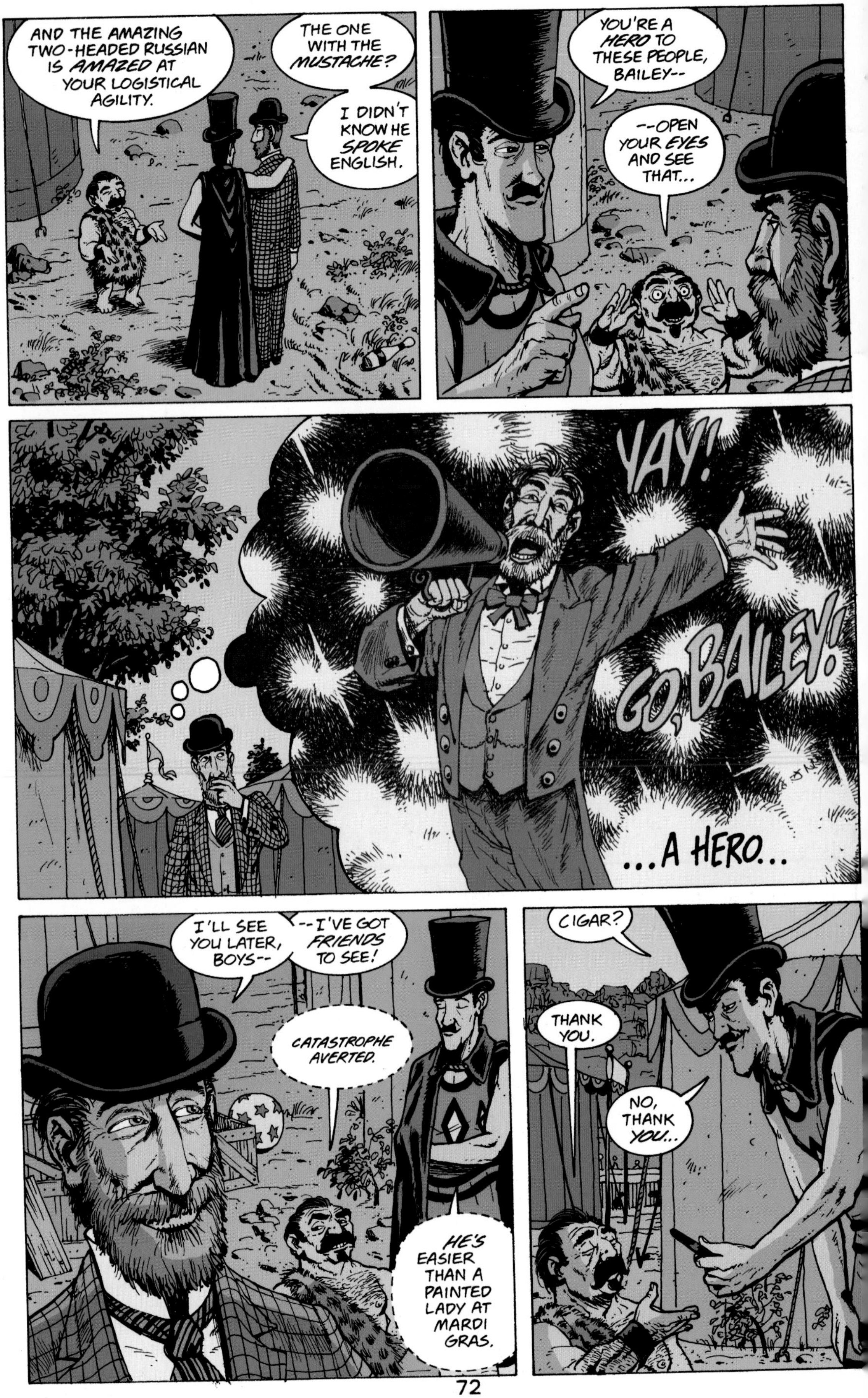

AND THE AMAZING TWO-HEADED RUSSIAN IS AMAZED AT YOUR LOGISTICAL AGILITY.
THE ONE WITH THE MUSTACHE?
I DIDN'T KNOW HE SPOKE ENGLISH.
YOU'RE A HERO TO THESE PEOPLE, BAILEY--
--OPEN YOUR EYES AND SEE THAT...
YAY!
GO, BAILEY!
...A HERO...
I'LL SEE YOU LATER, BOYS--
--I'VE GOT FRIENDS TO SEE!
CATASTROPHE AVERTED.
HE'S EASIER THAN A PAINTED LADY AT MARDI GRAS.
CIGAR?
THANK YOU.
NO, THANK YOU...

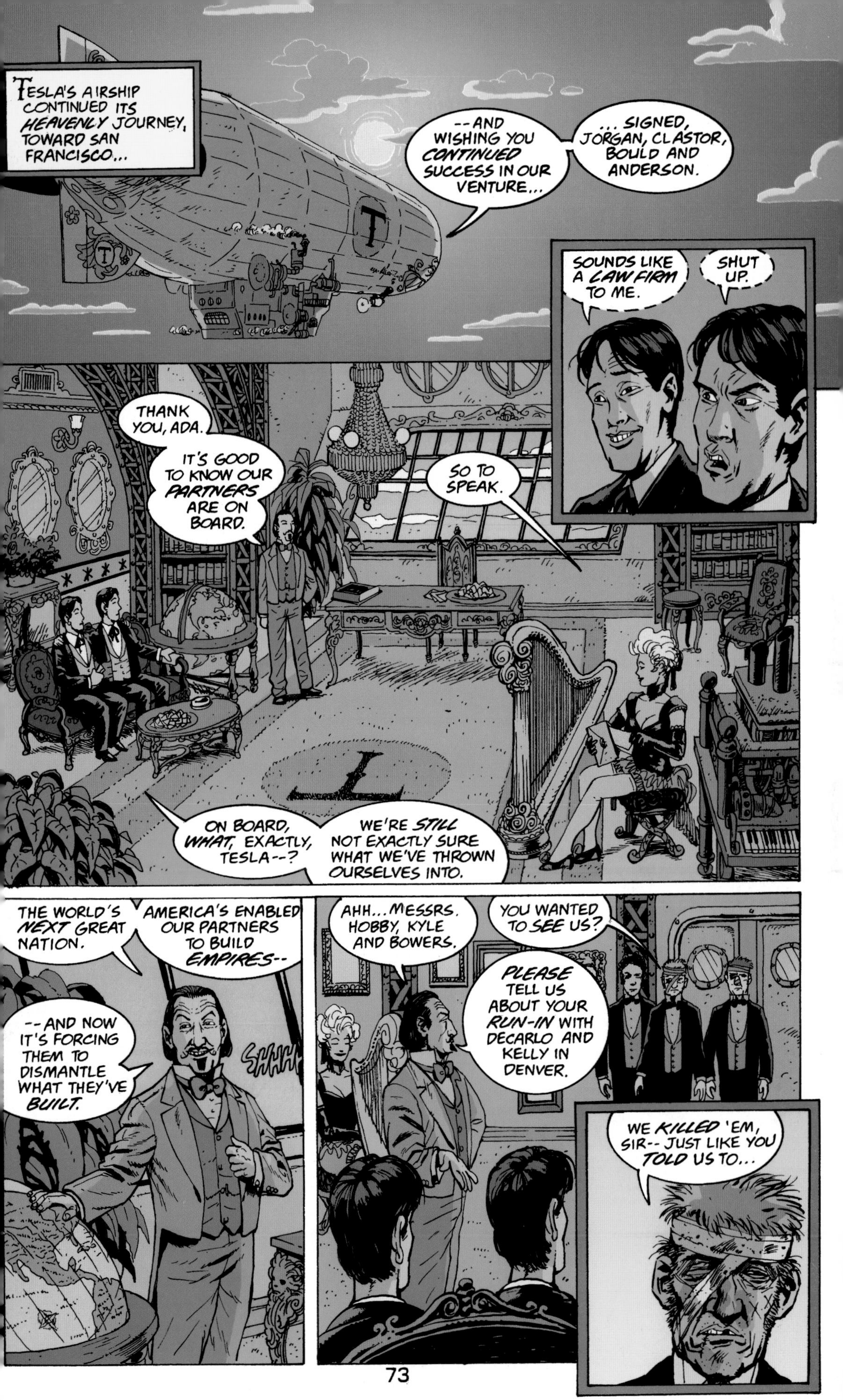
TESLA'S AIRSHIP CONTINUED ITS HEAVENLY JOURNEY, TOWARD SAN FRANCISCO...
--AND WISHING YOU CONTINUED SUCCESS IN OUR VENTURE...
...SIGNED, JORGAN, CLASTOR, BOULD AND ANDERSON.
SOUNDS LIKE A LAW FIRM TO ME.
SHUT UP.
THANK YOU, ADA.
IT'S GOOD TO KNOW OUR PARTNERS ARE ON BOARD.
SO TO SPEAK.
ON BOARD, WHAT, EXACTLY, TESLA--?
WE'RE STILL NOT EXACTLY SURE WHAT WE'VE THROWN OURSELVES INTO.
THE WORLD'S NEXT GREAT NATION.
AMERICA'S ENABLED OUR PARTNERS TO BUILD EMPIRES--
--AND NOW IT'S FORCING THEM TO DISMANTLE WHAT THEY'VE BUILT.
AHH... MESSRS. HOBBY, KYLE AND BOWERS.
YOU WANTED TO SEE US?
PLEASE TELL US ABOUT YOUR RUN-IN WITH DECARLO AND KELLY IN DENVER.
WE KILLED 'EM, SIR-- JUST LIKE YOU TOLD US TO...

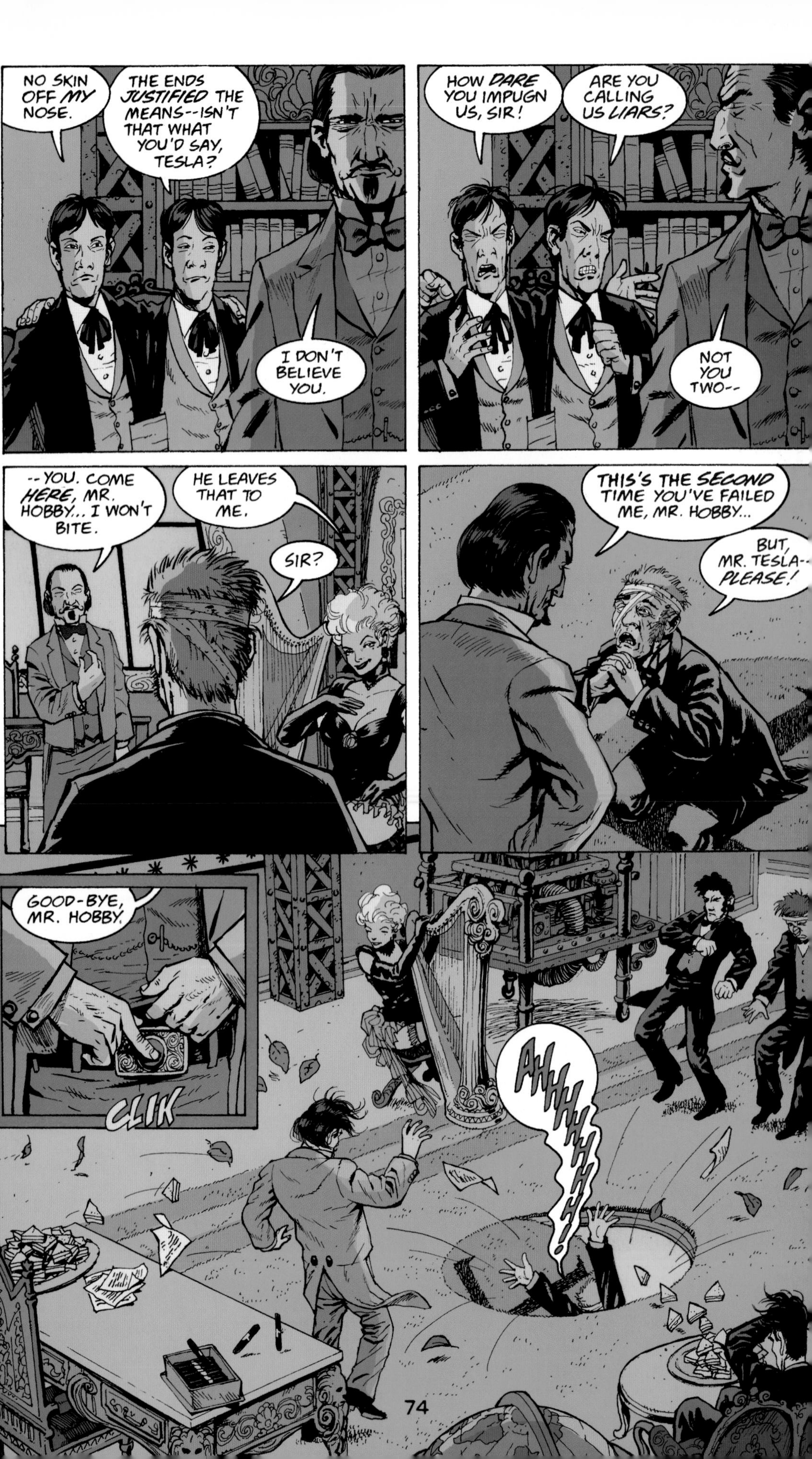
NO SKIN OFF MY NOSE.
THE ENDS JUSTIFIED THE MEANS--ISN'T THAT WHAT YOU'D SAY, TESLA?
I DON'T BELIEVE YOU.
HOW DARE YOU IMPUGN US, SIR!
ARE YOU CALLING US LIARS?
NOT YOU TWO--
--YOU. COME HERE, MR. HOBBY... I WON'T BITE.
HE LEAVES THAT TO ME.
SIR?
THIS'S THE SECOND TIME YOU'VE FAILED ME, MR. HOBBY...
BUT, MR. TESLA-- PLEASE!
GOOD-BYE, MR. HOBBY.
CLIK
AHHHHHHHH!

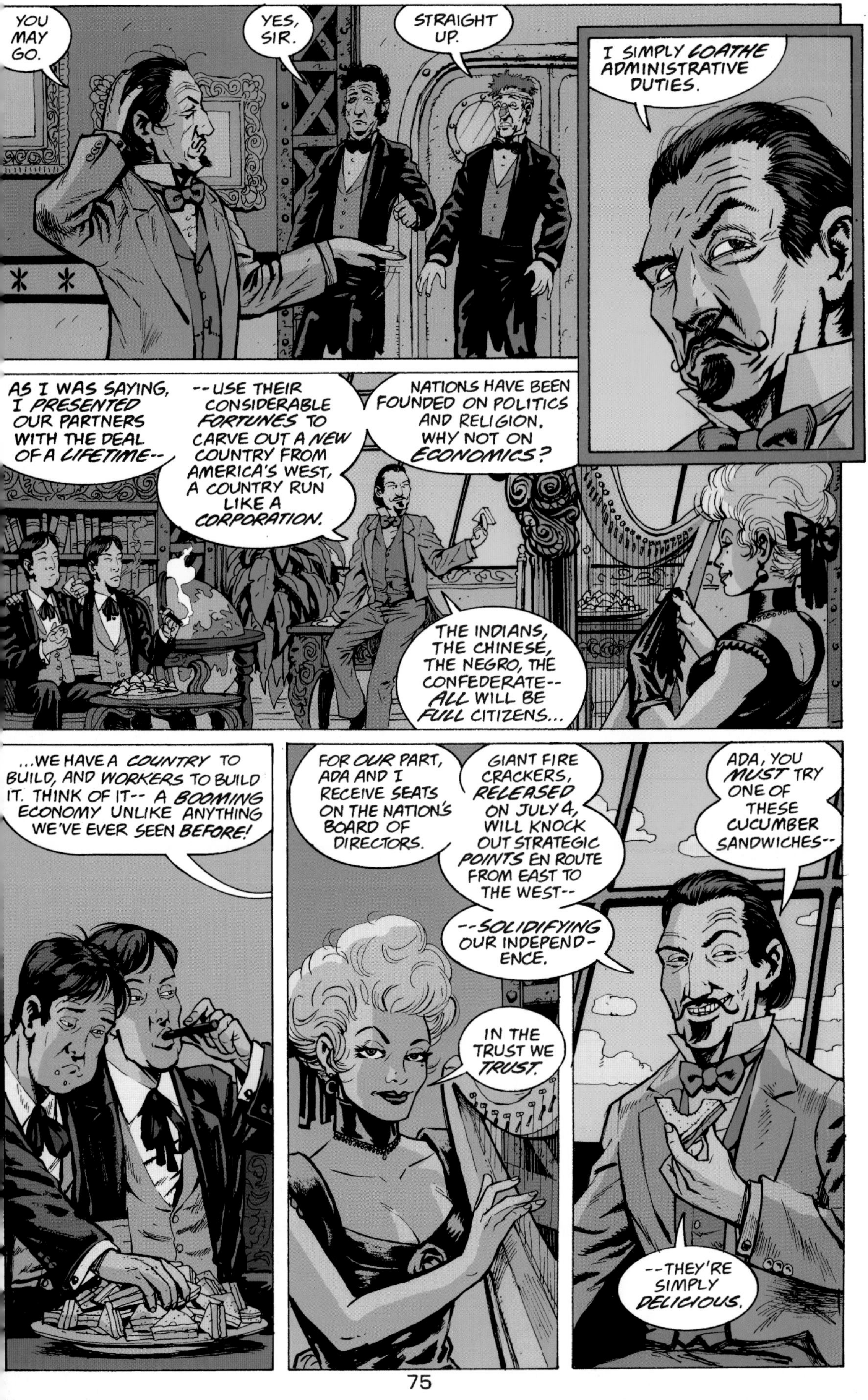
YOU MAY GO.
YES, SIR.
STRAIGHT UP.
I SIMPLY LOATHE ADMINISTRATIVE DUTIES.
AS I WAS SAYING, I PRESENTED OUR PARTNERS WITH THE DEAL OF A LIFETIME--
--USE THEIR CONSIDERABLE FORTUNES TO CARVE OUT A NEW COUNTRY FROM AMERICA'S WEST, A COUNTRY RUN LIKE A CORPORATION.
NATIONS HAVE BEEN FOUNDED ON POLITICS AND RELIGION, WHY NOT ON ECONOMICS?
THE INDIANS, THE CHINESE, THE NEGRO, THE CONFEDERATE-- ALL WILL BE FULL CITIZENS...
...WE HAVE A COUNTRY TO BUILD, AND WORKERS TO BUILD IT. THINK OF IT-- A BOOMING ECONOMY UNLIKE ANYTHING WE'VE EVER SEEN BEFORE!
FOR OUR PART, ADA AND I RECEIVE SEATS ON THE NATION'S BOARD OF DIRECTORS.
GIANT FIRE CRACKERS, RELEASED ON JULY 4, WILL KNOCK OUT STRATEGIC POINTS EN ROUTE FROM EAST TO THE WEST--
--SOLIDIFYING OUR INDEPEND-ENCE.
IN THE TRUST WE TRUST.
ADA, YOU MUST TRY ONE OF THESE CUCUMBER SANDWICHES--
--THEY'RE SIMPLY DELICIOUS.

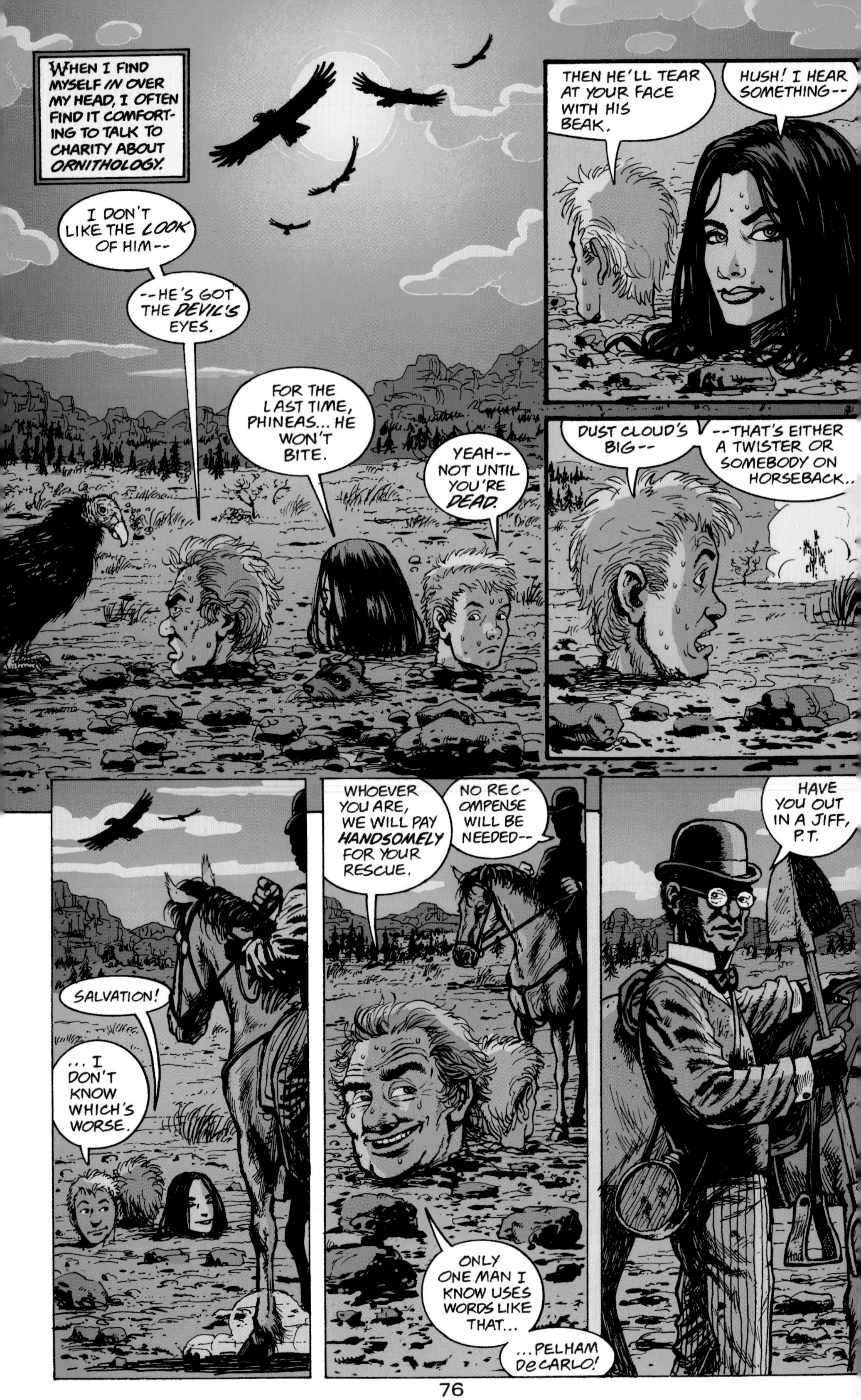

WHEN I FIND MYSELF IN OVER MY HEAD, I OFTEN FIND IT COMFORTING TO TALK TO CHARITY ABOUT ORNITHOLOGY.
I DON'T LIKE THE LOOK OF HIM--
--HE'S GOT THE DEVIL'S EYES.
FOR THE LAST TIME, PHINEAS... HE WON'T BITE.
YEAH-- NOT UNTIL YOU'RE DEAD.
THEN HE'LL TEAR AT YOUR FACE WITH HIS BEAK.
HUSH! I HEAR SOMETHING--
DUST CLOUD'S BIG--
--THAT'S EITHER A TWISTER OR SOMEBODY ON HORSEBACK..
SALVATION!
... I DON'T KNOW WHICH'S WORSE.
WHOEVER YOU ARE, WE WILL PAY HANDSOMELY FOR YOUR RESCUE.
NO RECOMPENSE WILL BE NEEDED--
ONLY ONE MAN I KNOW USES WORDS LIKE THAT...
...PELHAM DeCARLO!
HAVE YOU OUT IN A JIFF, P.T.

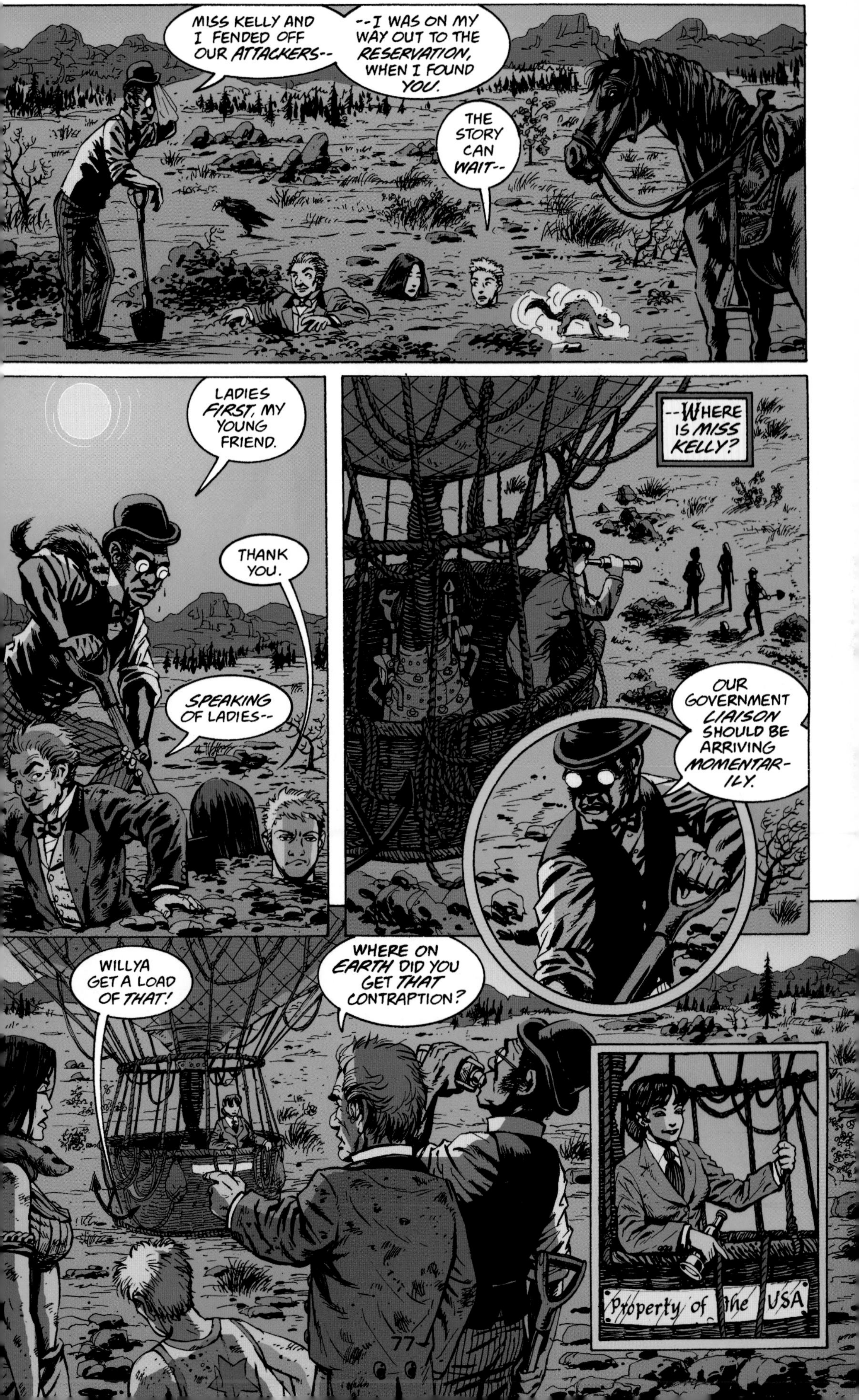
MISS KELLY AND I FENDED OFF OUR ATTACKERS--
--I WAS ON MY WAY OUT TO THE RESERVATION, WHEN I FOUND YOU.
THE STORY CAN WAIT--
LADIES FIRST, MY YOUNG FRIEND.
THANK YOU.
SPEAKING OF LADIES--
--WHERE IS MISS KELLY?
OUR GOVERNMENT LIAISON SHOULD BE ARRIVING MOMENTARILY.
WILLYA GET A LOAD OF THAT!
WHERE ON EARTH DID YOU GET THAT CONTRAPTION?
Property of the USA
77

THE BALLOON RIDE WAS *EXHILARATING*. I DECIDED THE CIRCUS NEEDED A DOZEN...

EVEN IF I HAD TO *TRICK* BAILEY INTO *BUYING* THEM.

OFFICE

-- JUST ANOTHER OF PHINEAS' *INFERNAL* TRICKS!

I DON'T *LOOK UP* TO NOBODY!

I SHOULD *FIRE* THE *LOT* OF YOU. I *CAN*, YOU KNOW!

EXCUSE ME, MR. BAILEY--

--MAY I SEE YOU IN *PRIVATE?*

I DON'T SEE WHAT'S SO IMPORTANT, HYPNOSIA--

THAT WASN'T A *REQUEST.*

VA-VA-VOOM!

INCREDIBLE...

...AMAZING.

THIS *SHOULD* ONLY TAKE A *FEW MINUTES.*

YES, WE I GUESS CAN SPAR A *FEW* MINUTES.

WHAT A *PEACH!*

SHOULDN'T YOU BE IN *BED*, LAD?

I'M *OLD* ENOUGH TO--

COME ON-- *BEAT IT.* GO DO WHATEVER IT IS YOU DOG-FACED PEOPLE DO--

--WE'RE *BUSY.*

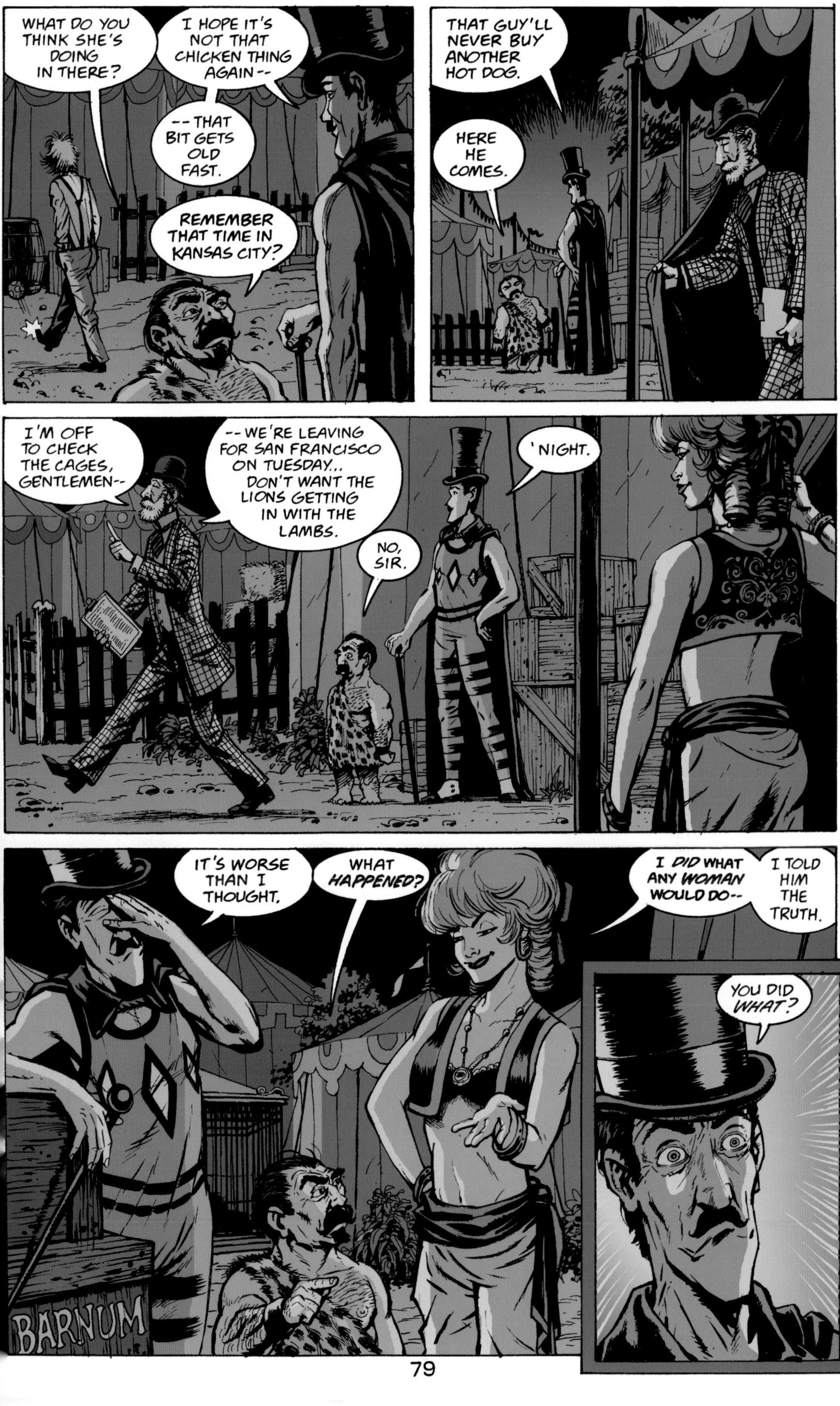

WHAT DO YOU THINK SHE'S DOING IN THERE?
I HOPE IT'S NOT THAT CHICKEN THING AGAIN--
--THAT BIT GETS OLD FAST.
REMEMBER THAT TIME IN KANSAS CITY?
THAT GUY'LL NEVER BUY ANOTHER HOT DOG.
HERE HE COMES.
I'M OFF TO CHECK THE CAGES, GENTLEMEN--
--WE'RE LEAVING FOR SAN FRANCISCO ON TUESDAY... DON'T WANT THE LIONS GETTING IN WITH THE LAMBS.
NO, SIR.
'NIGHT.
IT'S WORSE THAN I THOUGHT.
WHAT HAPPENED?
I DID WHAT ANY WOMAN WOULD DO--
I TOLD HIM THE TRUTH.
BARNUM
YOU DID WHAT?

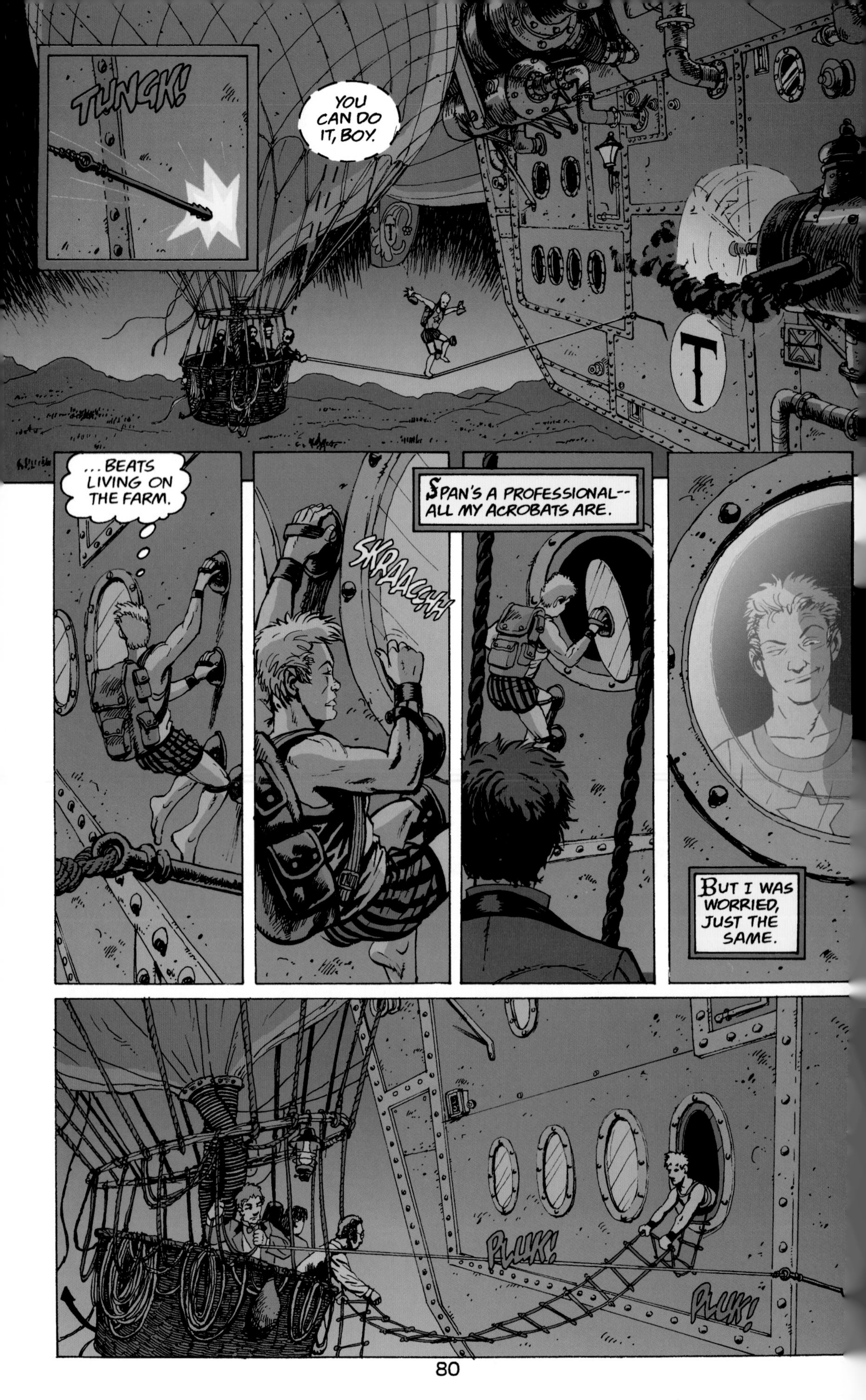
TUNCK!
YOU CAN DO IT, BOY.
...BEATS LIVING ON THE FARM.
SKRAACHH
SPAN'S A PROFESSIONAL-- ALL MY ACROBATS ARE.
BUT I WAS WORRIED, JUST THE SAME.
PLUK!
PLUK!

OUR LITTLE PACK *CLAMBERED* UP THE LADDER INTO THE DARKENED *AIRSHIP--*

PRAYING TO DEAR *HEAVEN* FOR A LIGHT AT THE END OF THE *TUNNEL.*

IT SAYS, "NO ADMITTANCE."

WE'VE *TRIED EVERYWHERE ELSE!*

NO ADMITTANCE

IN CASE OF EMERGENCY BREAK GLASS

IF TESLA'S SUCH A *GENIUS,* HOW COME HE *FORGOT* TO PUT A *FLUSH TOILET* ON THIS TUB?

WE'VE *BEEN DOWN* THIS WAY *THREE* TIMES!

WILL YOU *PLEASE* CEASE COMPLAINING--

--WHY DOES YOUR GLASS *ALWAYS* HAVE TO BE HALF *EMPTY?*

IT CAN BE HALF *FULL--* JUST SO LONG AS I CAN UNLOAD MY *BLADDER.*

IN CASE OF EMERGENCY BREAK GLASS

NEXT TIME YOU NEED TO CREATE *WATER,* I'LL BRING BREAD CRUMBS.

ENTER

HERE GOES--

--NOTHING?!

?!?!?!?

?!?!?!?

OF NCY SS

EAK GLASS

CRASH

AA-OOOGGAAA

81

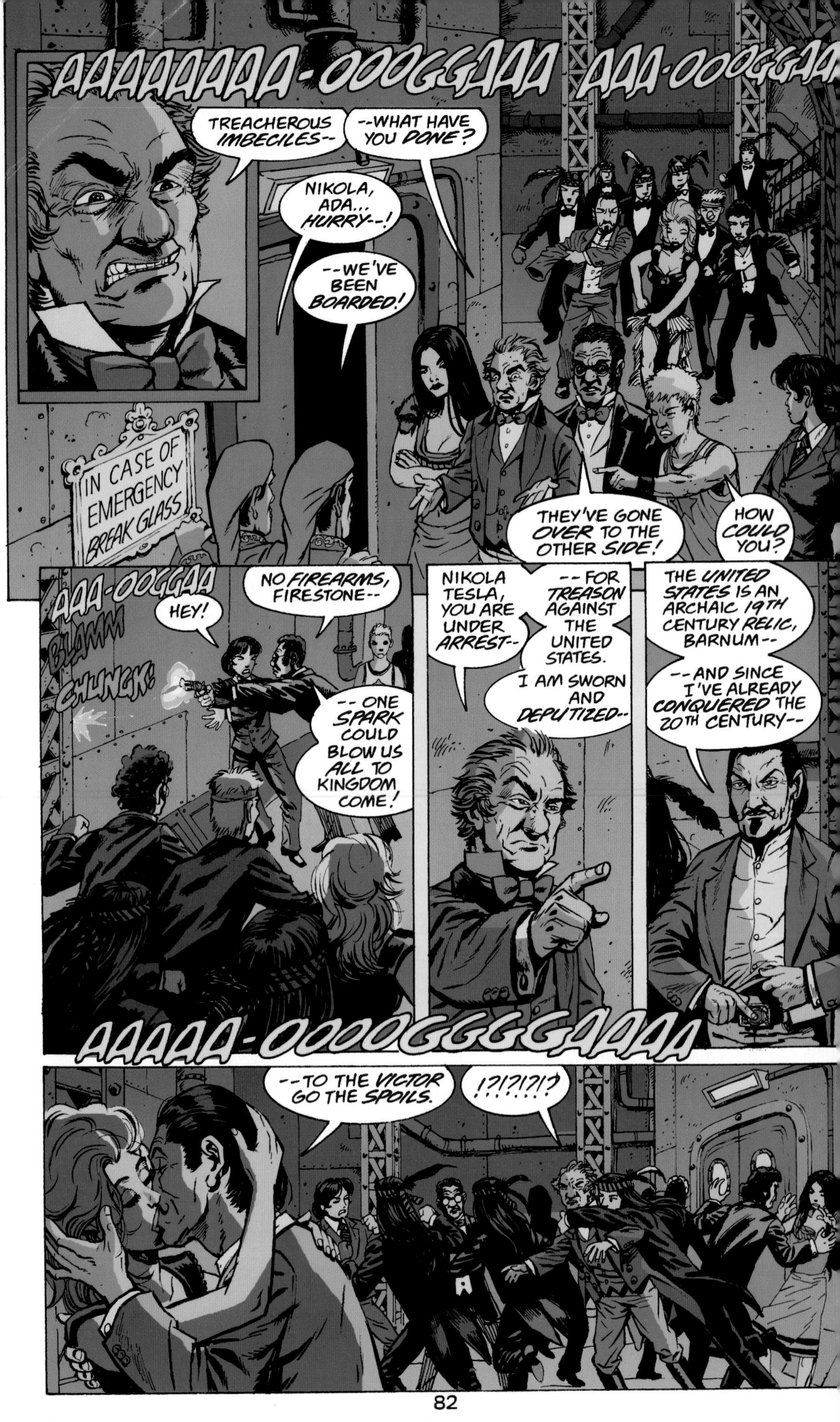
AAAAAAAA-OOOGGAAA AAA-OOOGGAA
TREACHEROUS IMBECILES--
--WHAT HAVE YOU DONE?
NIKOLA, ADA... HURRY--!
--WE'VE BEEN BOARDED!
IN CASE OF EMERGENCY BREAK GLASS
THEY'VE GONE OVER TO THE OTHER SIDE!
HOW COULD YOU?
AAA-OOGGAA
HEY!
NO FIREARMS, FIRESTONE--
BLAMM
CHUNGK!
--ONE SPARK COULD BLOW US ALL TO KINGDOM COME!
NIKOLA TESLA, YOU ARE UNDER ARREST--
--FOR TREASON AGAINST THE UNITED STATES.
I AM SWORN AND DEPUTIZED--
THE UNITED STATES IS AN ARCHAIC 19TH CENTURY RELIC, BARNUM--
--AND SINCE I'VE ALREADY CONQUERED THE 20TH CENTURY--
AAAAA-OOOOGGGGAAAA
--TO THE VICTOR GO THE SPOILS.
!?!?!?!?

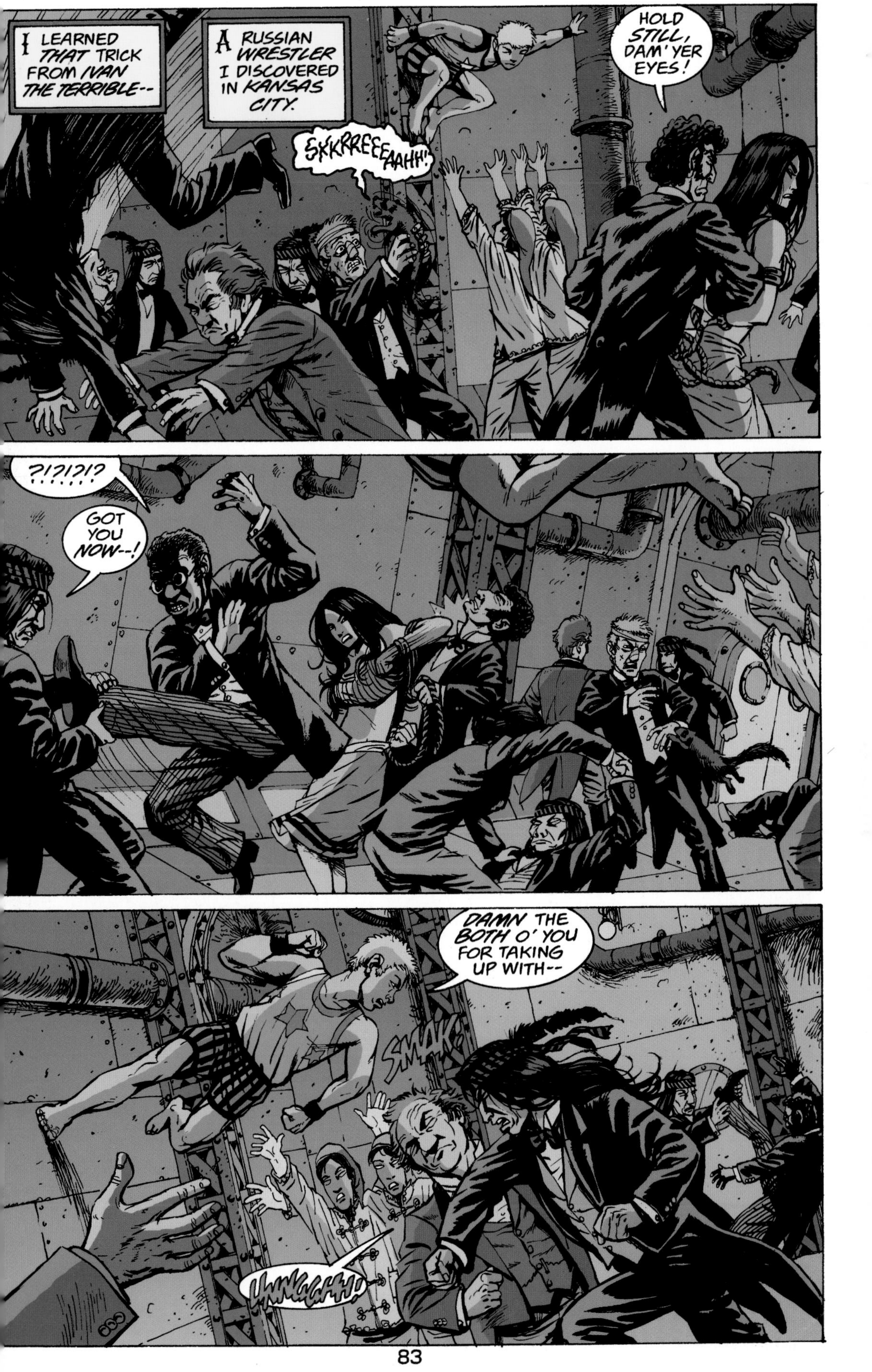

I LEARNED THAT TRICK FROM IVAN THE TERRIBLE--
A RUSSIAN WRESTLER I DISCOVERED IN KANSAS CITY.
HOLD STILL, DAM' YER EYES!
SKKRREEEAAHH!
?!?!?!?
GOT YOU NOW--!
DAMN THE BOTH O' YOU FOR TAKING UP WITH--
SMAK!
UNNGGHH!

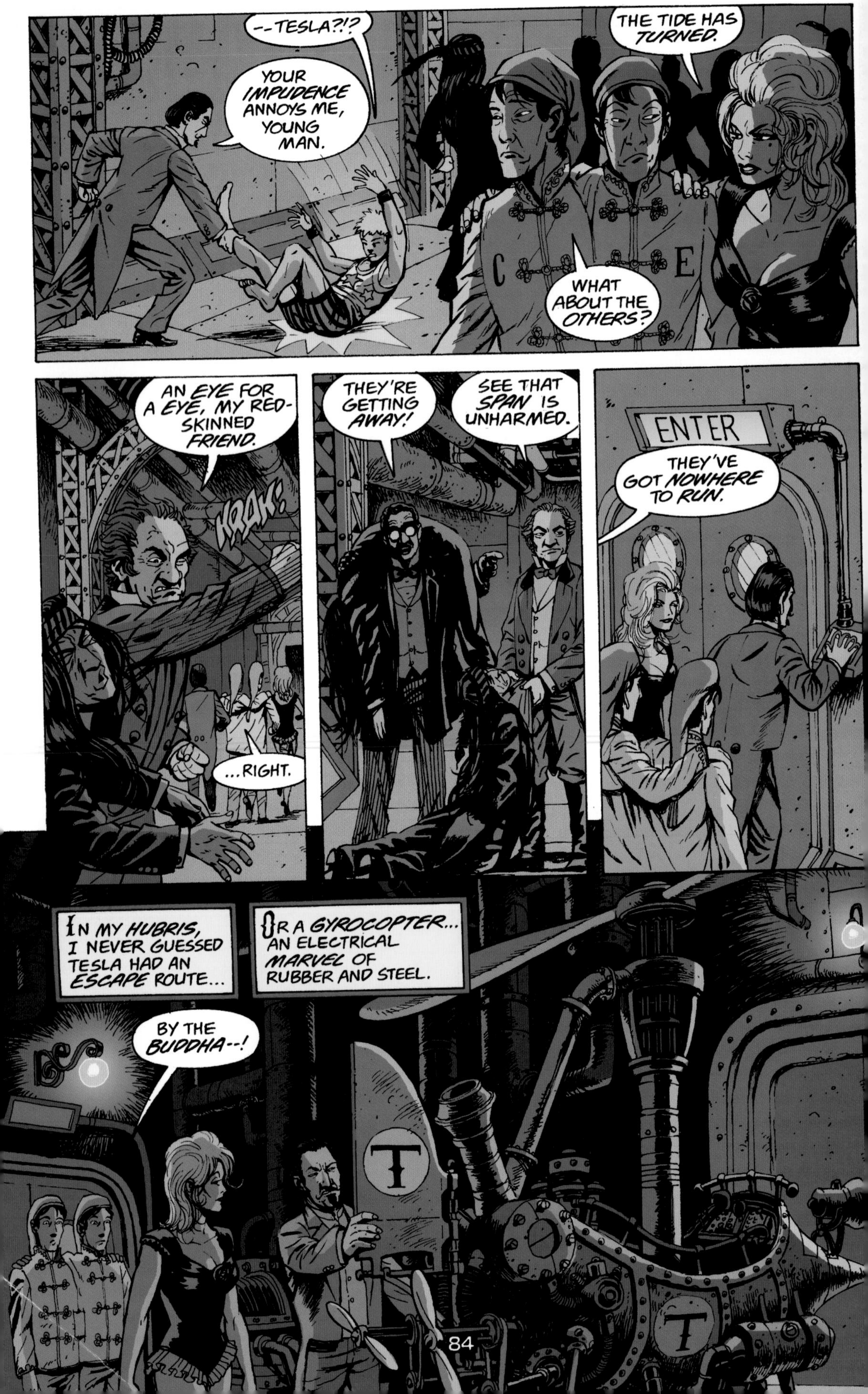

YOUR IMPUDENCE ANNOYS ME, YOUNG MAN.
--TESLA?!?
THE TIDE HAS TURNED.
WHAT ABOUT THE OTHERS?
AN EYE FOR A EYE, MY RED-SKINNED FRIEND.
KRAK!
...RIGHT.
THEY'RE GETTING AWAY!
SEE THAT SPAN IS UNHARMED.
ENTER
THEY'VE GOT NOWHERE TO RUN.
IN MY HUBRIS, I NEVER GUESSED TESLA HAD AN ESCAPE ROUTE...
OR A GYROCOPTER... AN ELECTRICAL MARVEL OF RUBBER AND STEEL.
BY THE BUDDHA--!

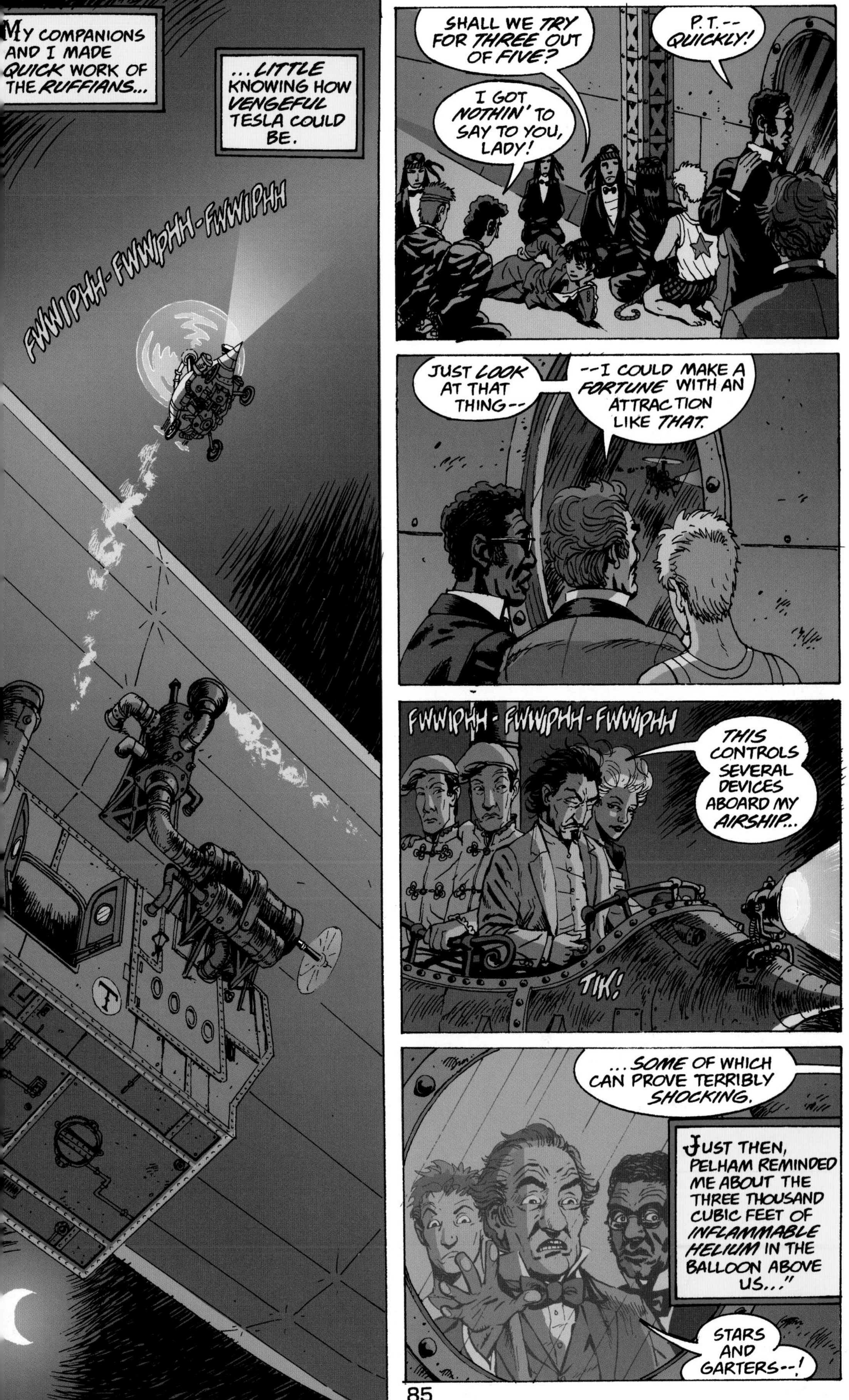
MY COMPANIONS AND I MADE QUICK WORK OF THE RUFFIANS...
...LITTLE KNOWING HOW VENGEFUL TESLA COULD BE.
FWWIPHH-FWWIPHH-FWWIPHH
SHALL WE TRY FOR THREE OUT OF FIVE?
I GOT NOTHIN' TO SAY TO YOU, LADY!
P.T.-- QUICKLY!
JUST LOOK AT THAT THING--
--I COULD MAKE A FORTUNE WITH AN ATTRACTION LIKE THAT.
FWWIPHH-FWWIPHH-FWWIPHH
THIS CONTROLS SEVERAL DEVICES ABOARD MY AIRSHIP...
TIK!
...SOME OF WHICH CAN PROVE TERRIBLY SHOCKING.
JUST THEN, PELHAM REMINDED ME ABOUT THE THREE THOUSAND CUBIC FEET OF INFLAMMABLE HELIUM IN THE BALLOON ABOVE US..."
STARS AND GARTERS--!

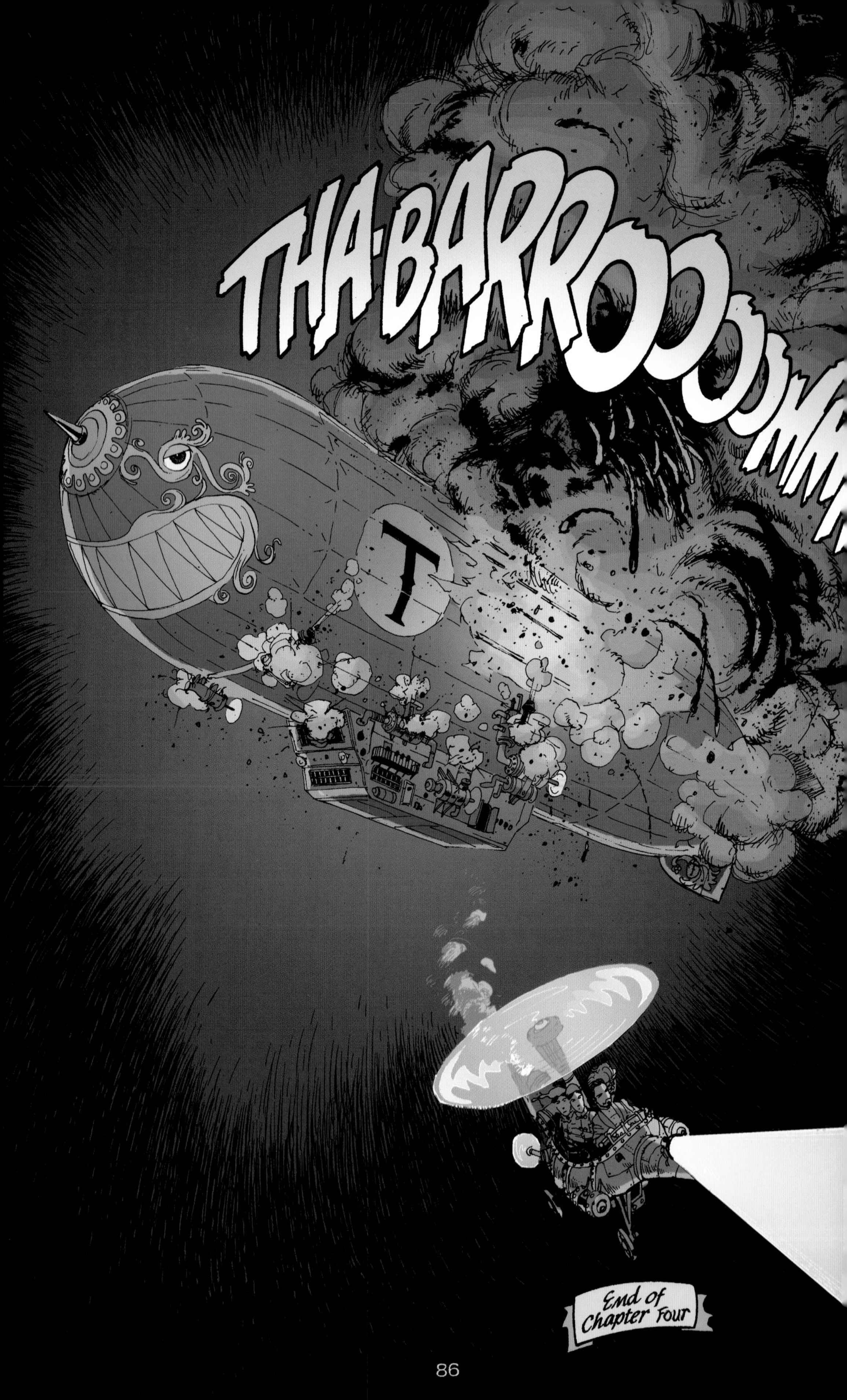
THA-BARROOOOMM
T
End of Chapter Four

CHAPTER 5

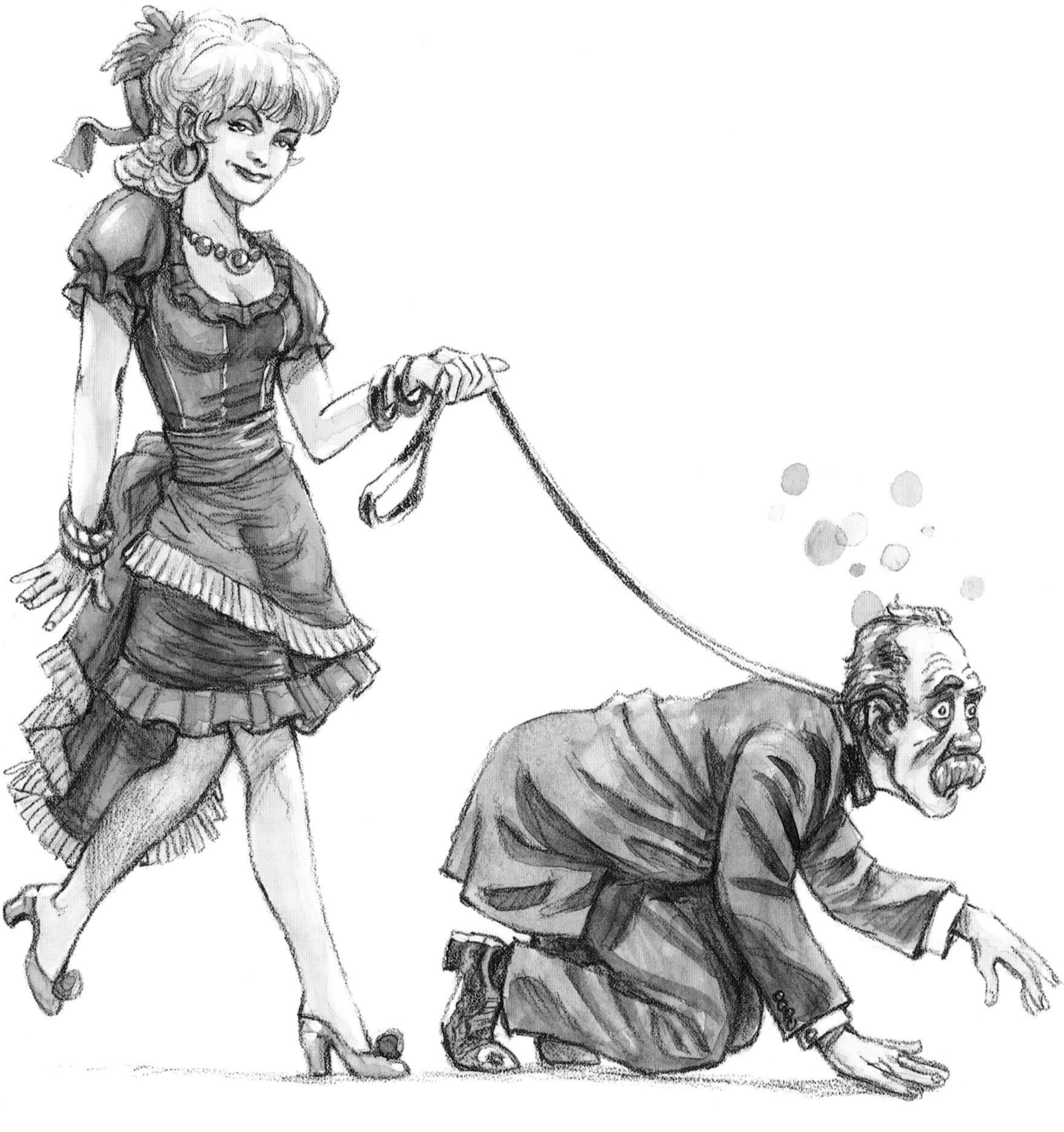

CHAPTER 5

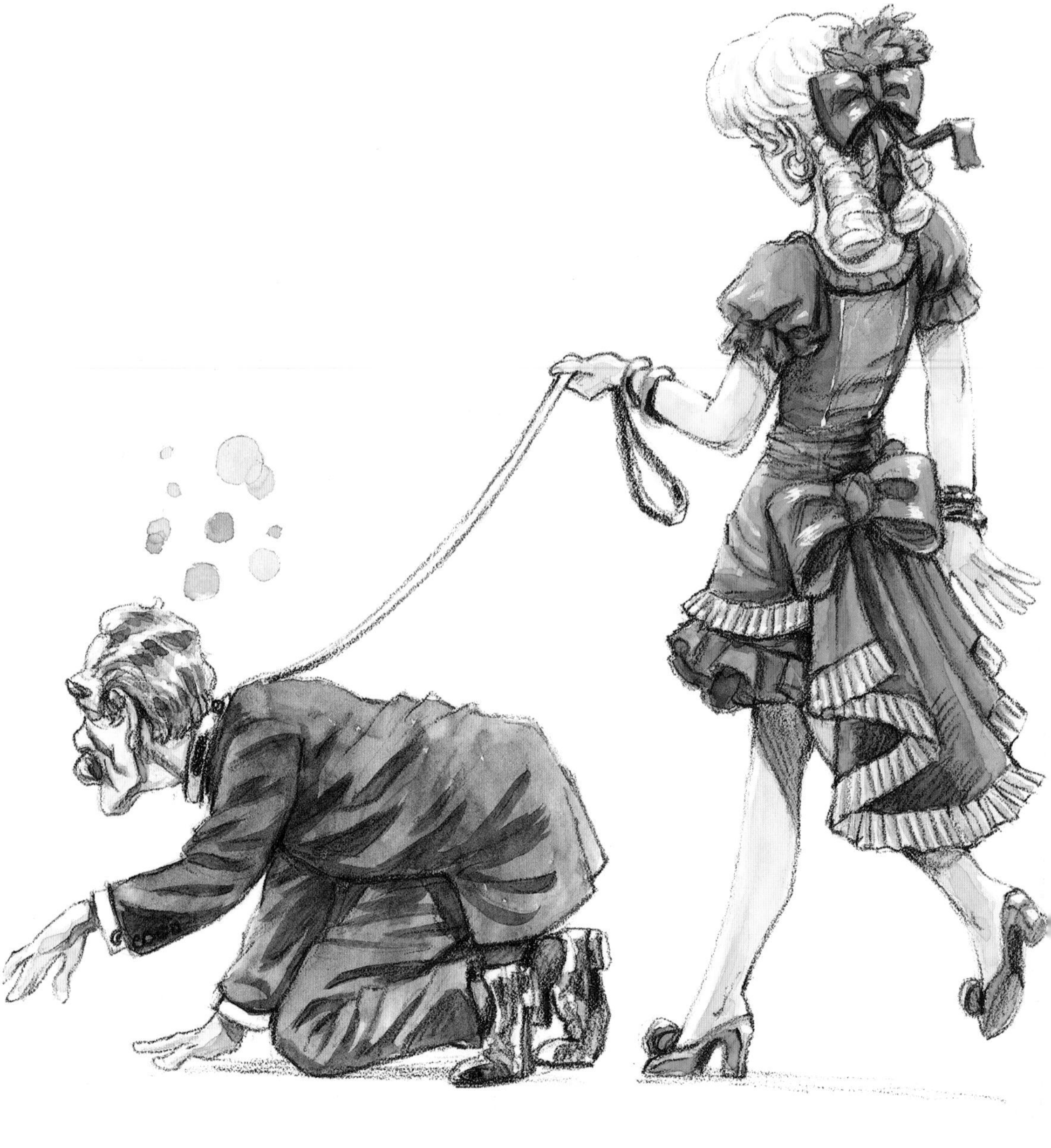

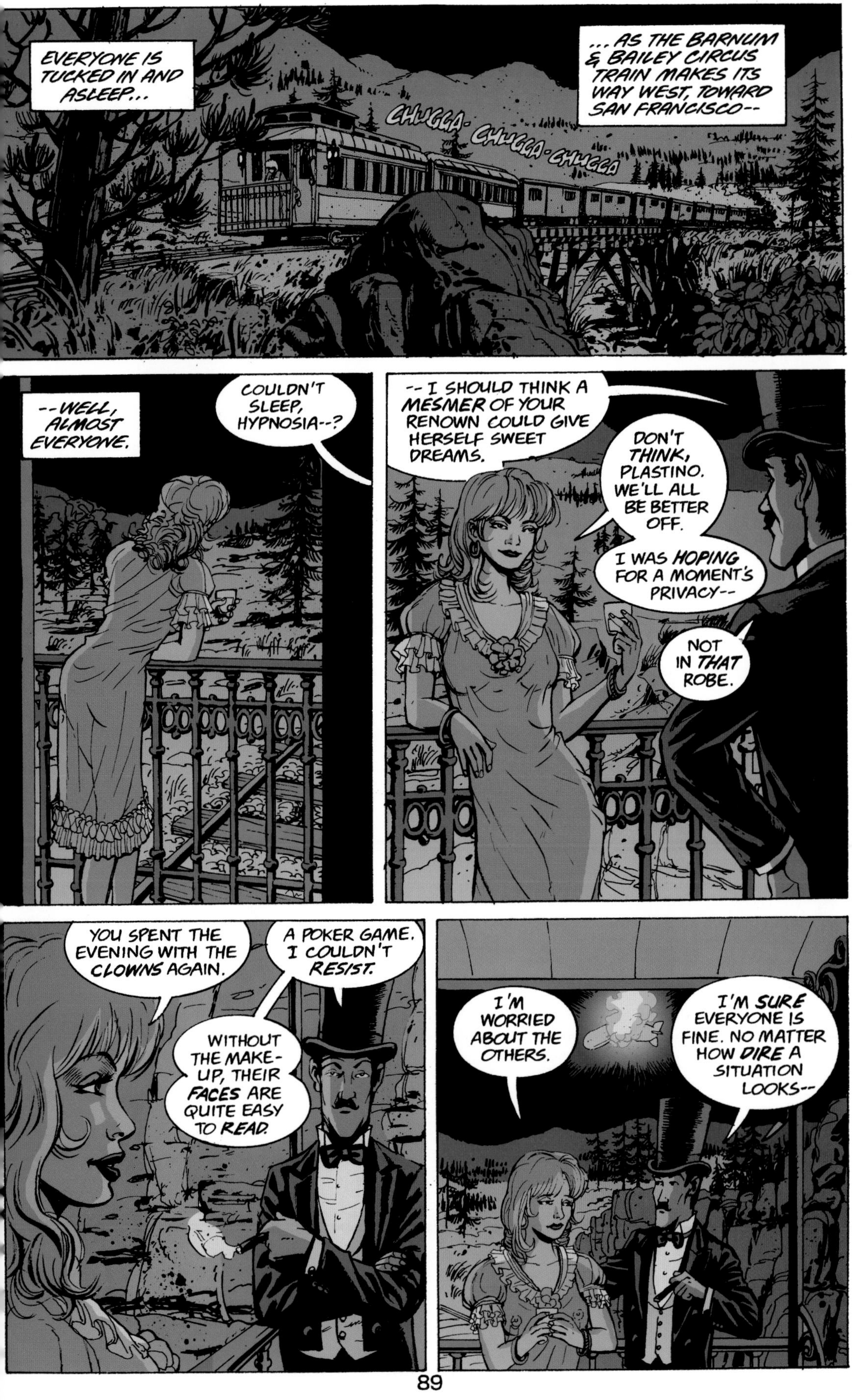

EVERYONE IS TUCKED IN AND ASLEEP...
...AS THE BARNUM & BAILEY CIRCUS TRAIN MAKES ITS WAY WEST, TOWARD SAN FRANCISCO--
CHUGGA-CHUGGA-CHUGGA
--WELL, ALMOST EVERYONE.
COULDN'T SLEEP, HYPNOSIA--?
--I SHOULD THINK A MESMER OF YOUR RENOWN COULD GIVE HERSELF SWEET DREAMS.
DON'T THINK, PLASTINO. WE'LL ALL BE BETTER OFF.
I WAS HOPING FOR A MOMENT'S PRIVACY--
NOT IN THAT ROBE.
YOU SPENT THE EVENING WITH THE CLOWNS AGAIN.
A POKER GAME. I COULDN'T RESIST.
WITHOUT THE MAKE-UP, THEIR FACES ARE QUITE EASY TO READ.
I'M WORRIED ABOUT THE OTHERS.
I'M SURE EVERYONE IS FINE. NO MATTER HOW DIRE A SITUATION LOOKS--

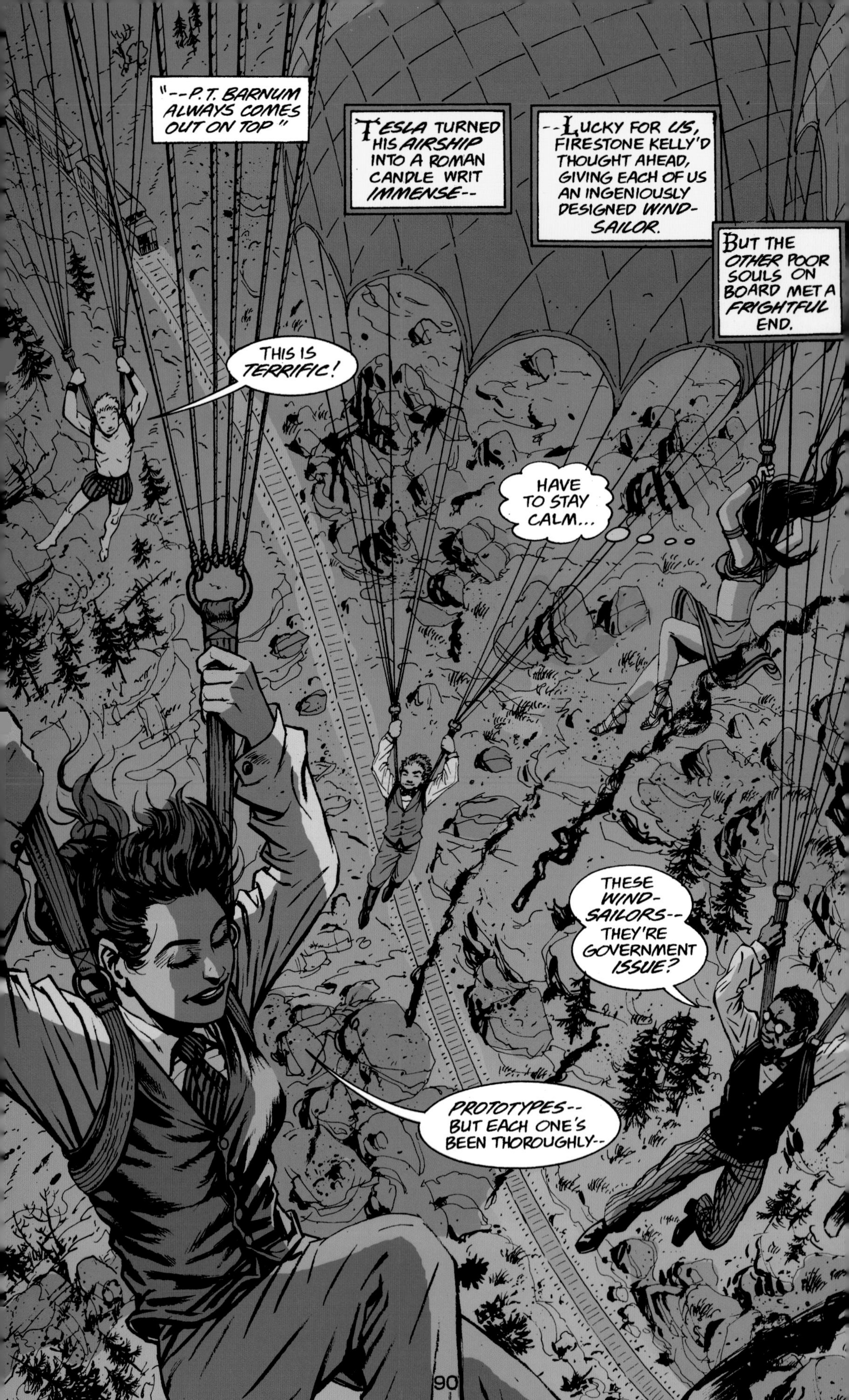
"--P.T. BARNUM ALWAYS COMES OUT ON TOP"
TESLA TURNED HIS AIRSHIP INTO A ROMAN CANDLE WRIT IMMENSE--
--LUCKY FOR US, FIRESTONE KELLY'D THOUGHT AHEAD, GIVING EACH OF US AN INGENIOUSLY DESIGNED WIND-SAILOR.
BUT THE OTHER POOR SOULS ON BOARD MET A FRIGHTFUL END.
THIS IS TERRIFIC!
HAVE TO STAY CALM...
THESE WIND-SAILORS-- THEY'RE GOVERNMENT ISSUE?
PROTOTYPES-- BUT EACH ONE'S BEEN THOROUGHLY--

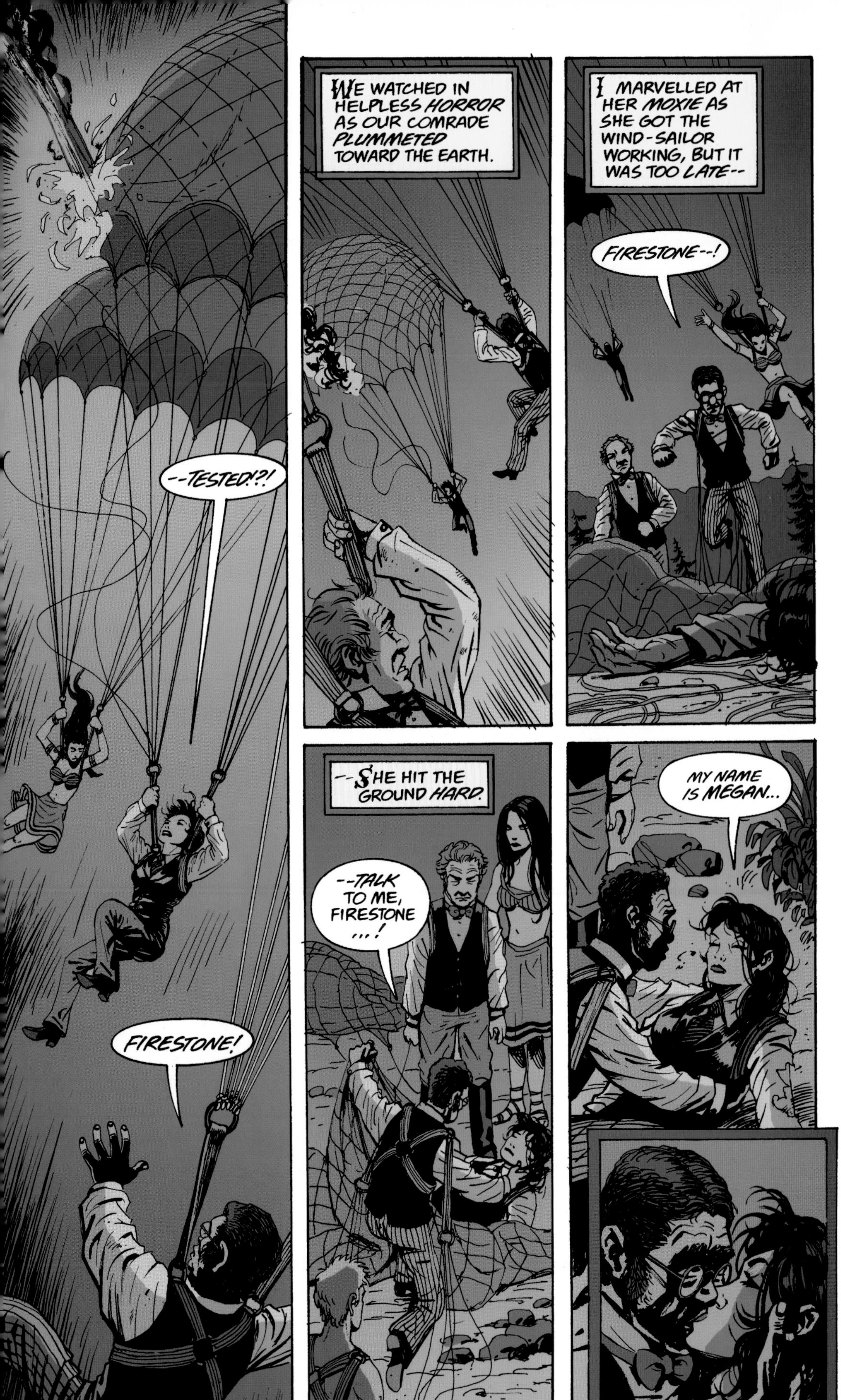
--TESTED!?!
FIRESTONE!
WE WATCHED IN HELPLESS HORROR AS OUR COMRADE PLUMMETED TOWARD THE EARTH.
I MARVELLED AT HER MOXIE AS SHE GOT THE WIND-SAILOR WORKING, BUT IT WAS TOO LATE--
FIRESTONE--!
--SHE HIT THE GROUND HARD.
--TALK TO ME, FIRESTONE ...!
MY NAME IS MEGAN...

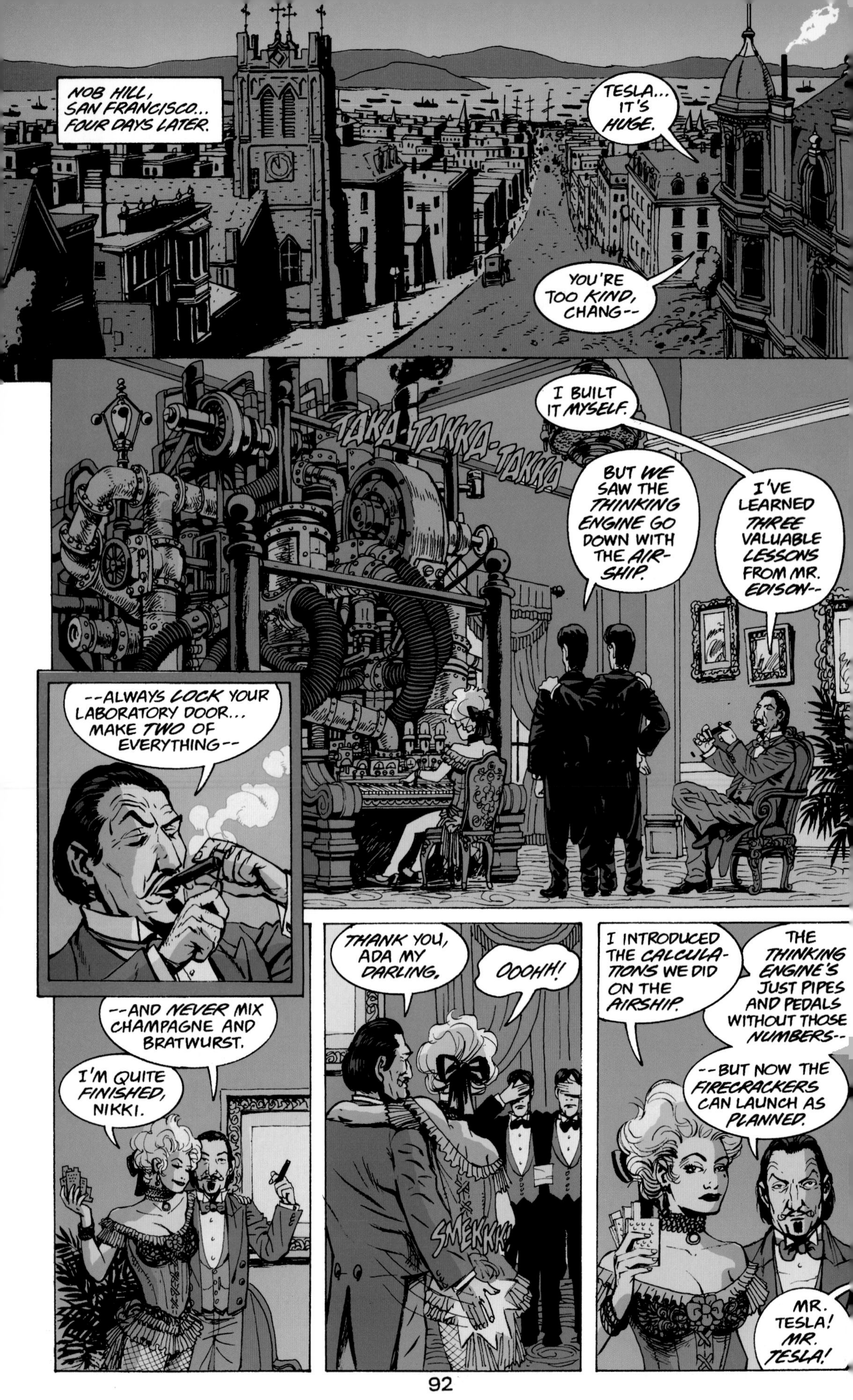

NOB HILL, SAN FRANCISCO... FOUR DAYS LATER.
TESLA... IT'S HUGE.
YOU'RE TOO KIND, CHANG--
I BUILT IT MYSELF.
TAKA-TAKKA-TAKKA
BUT WE SAW THE THINKING ENGINE GO DOWN WITH THE AIR-SHIP.
I'VE LEARNED THREE VALUABLE LESSONS FROM MR. EDISON--
--ALWAYS LOCK YOUR LABORATORY DOOR... MAKE TWO OF EVERYTHING--
--AND NEVER MIX CHAMPAGNE AND BRATWURST.
I'M QUITE FINISHED, NIKKI.
THANK YOU, ADA MY DARLING.
OOOHH!
SMEKKK!
I INTRODUCED THE CALCULA-TIONS WE DID ON THE AIRSHIP.
THE THINKING ENGINE'S JUST PIPES AND PEDALS WITHOUT THOSE NUMBERS--
--BUT NOW THE FIRECRACKERS CAN LAUNCH AS PLANNED.
MR. TESLA! MR. TESLA!

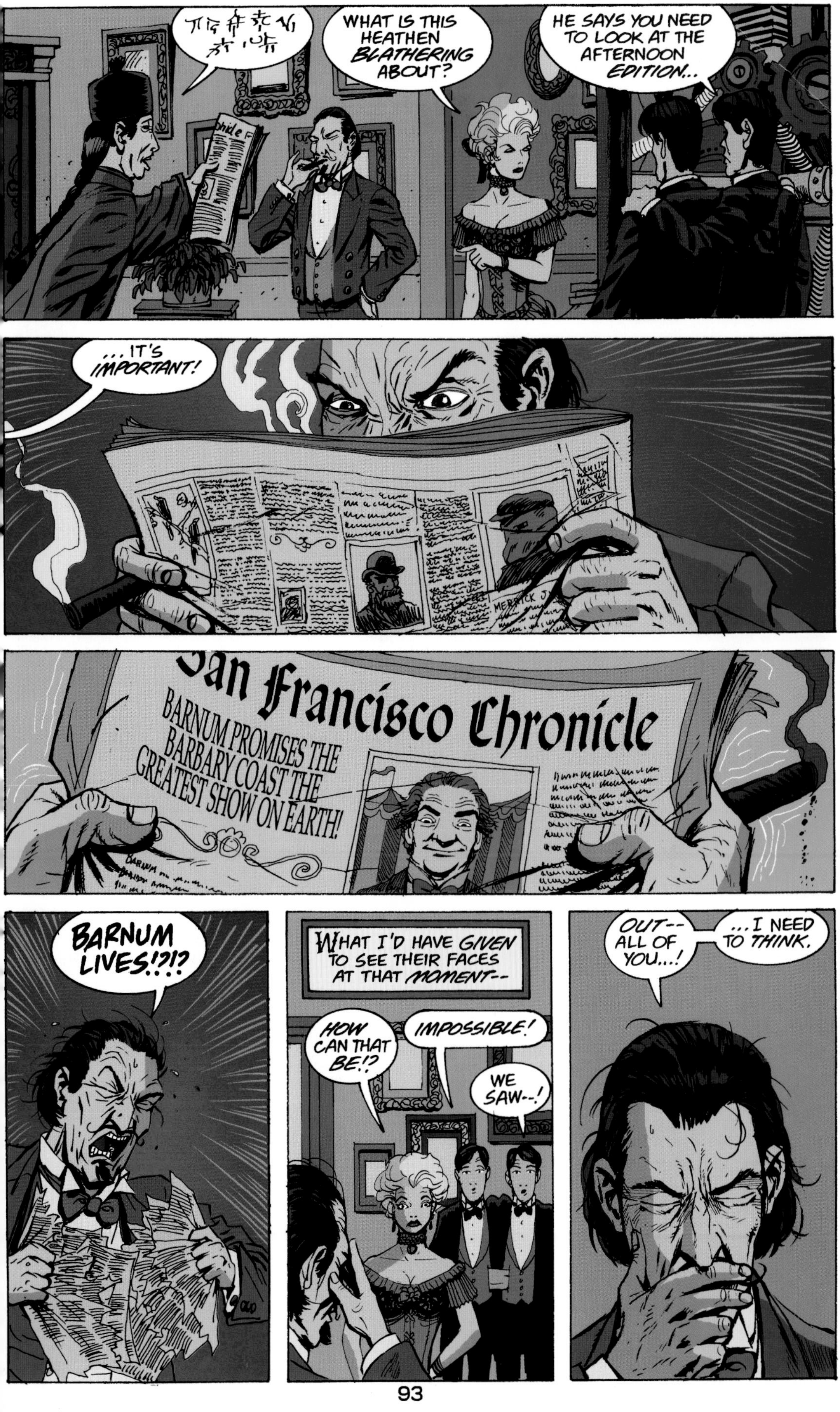
WHAT IS THIS HEATHEN BLATHERING ABOUT?
HE SAYS YOU NEED TO LOOK AT THE AFTERNOON EDITION...
...IT'S IMPORTANT!
San Francisco Chronicle
BARNUM PROMISES THE BARBARY COAST THE GREATEST SHOW ON EARTH!
BARNUM LIVES!?!?
WHAT I'D HAVE GIVEN TO SEE THEIR FACES AT THAT MOMENT--
HOW CAN THAT BE!?
IMPOSSIBLE!
WE SAW--!
OUT-- ALL OF YOU...!
...I NEED TO THINK.

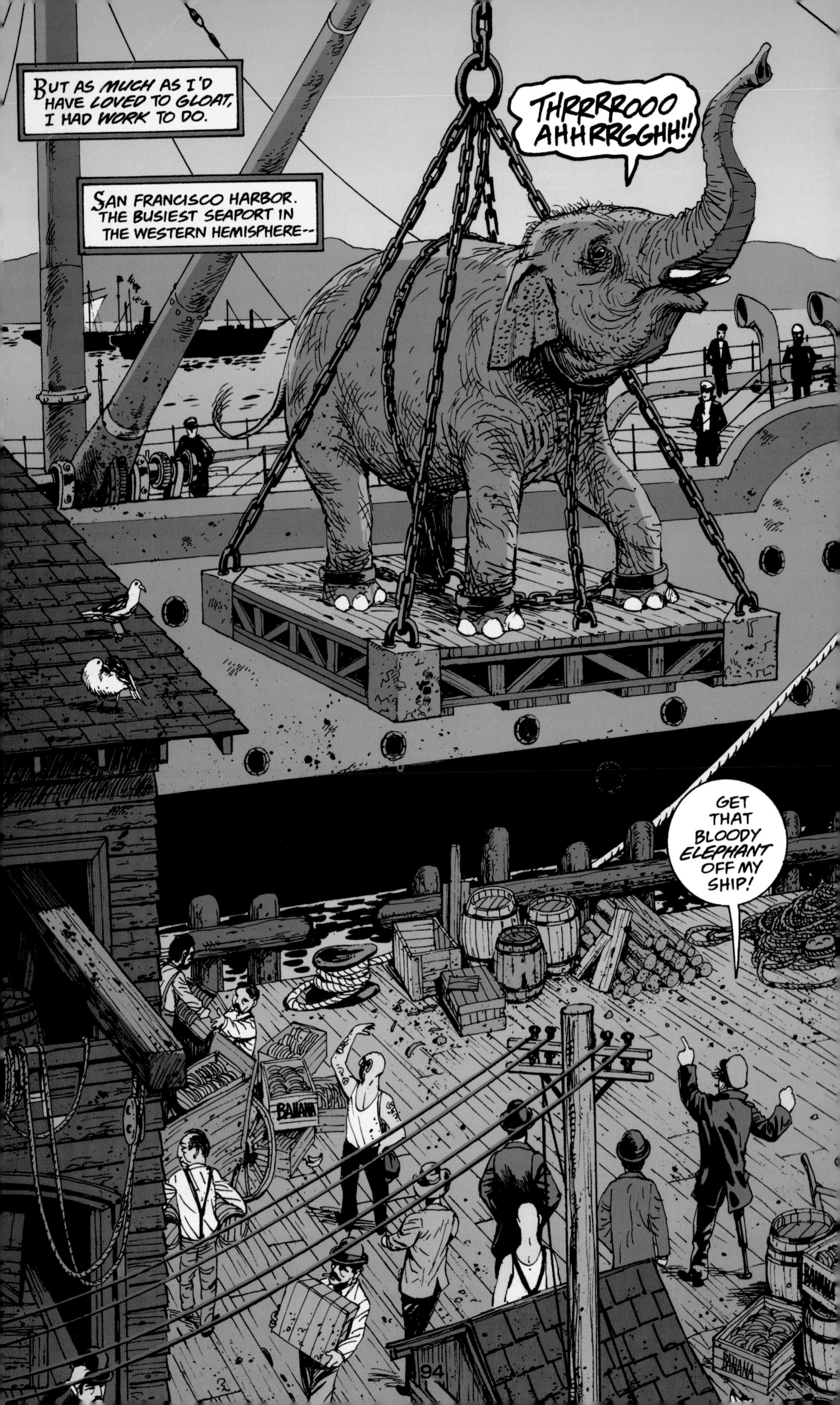
BUT AS MUCH AS I'D HAVE LOVED TO GLOAT, I HAD WORK TO DO.
SAN FRANCISCO HARBOR. THE BUSIEST SEAPORT IN THE WESTERN HEMISPHERE--
THRRRROOO AHHRRGGHH!!
GET THAT BLOODY ELEPHANT OFF MY SHIP!
BANANA
BANANA
BANANA

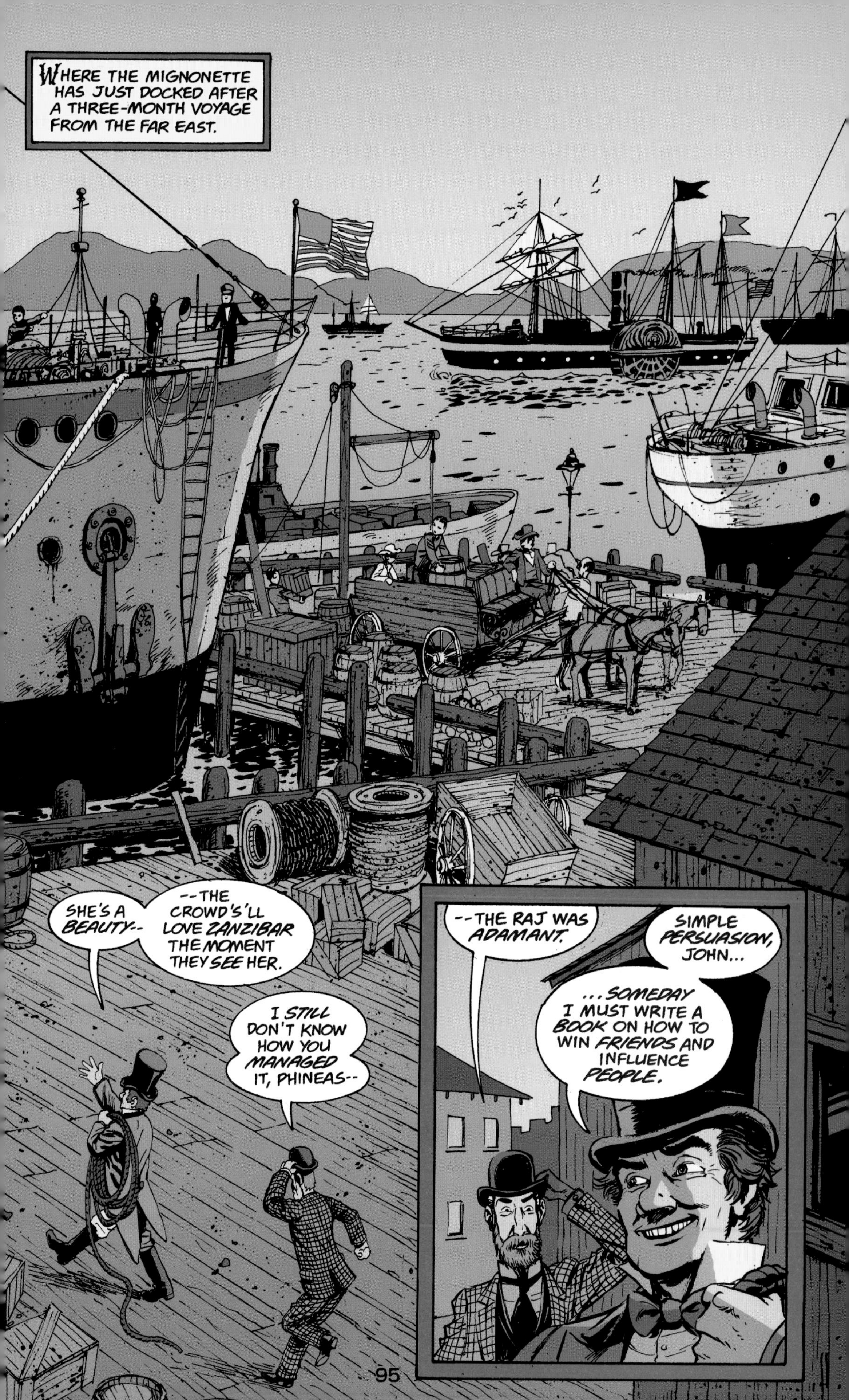
WHERE THE MIGNONETTE HAS JUST DOCKED AFTER A THREE-MONTH VOYAGE FROM THE FAR EAST.
SHE'S A BEAUTY--
--THE CROWD'S'LL LOVE ZANZIBAR THE MOMENT THEY SEE HER.
I STILL DON'T KNOW HOW YOU MANAGED IT, PHINEAS--
--THE RAJ WAS ADAMANT.
SIMPLE PERSUASION, JOHN...
...SOMEDAY I MUST WRITE A BOOK ON HOW TO WIN FRIENDS AND INFLUENCE PEOPLE.

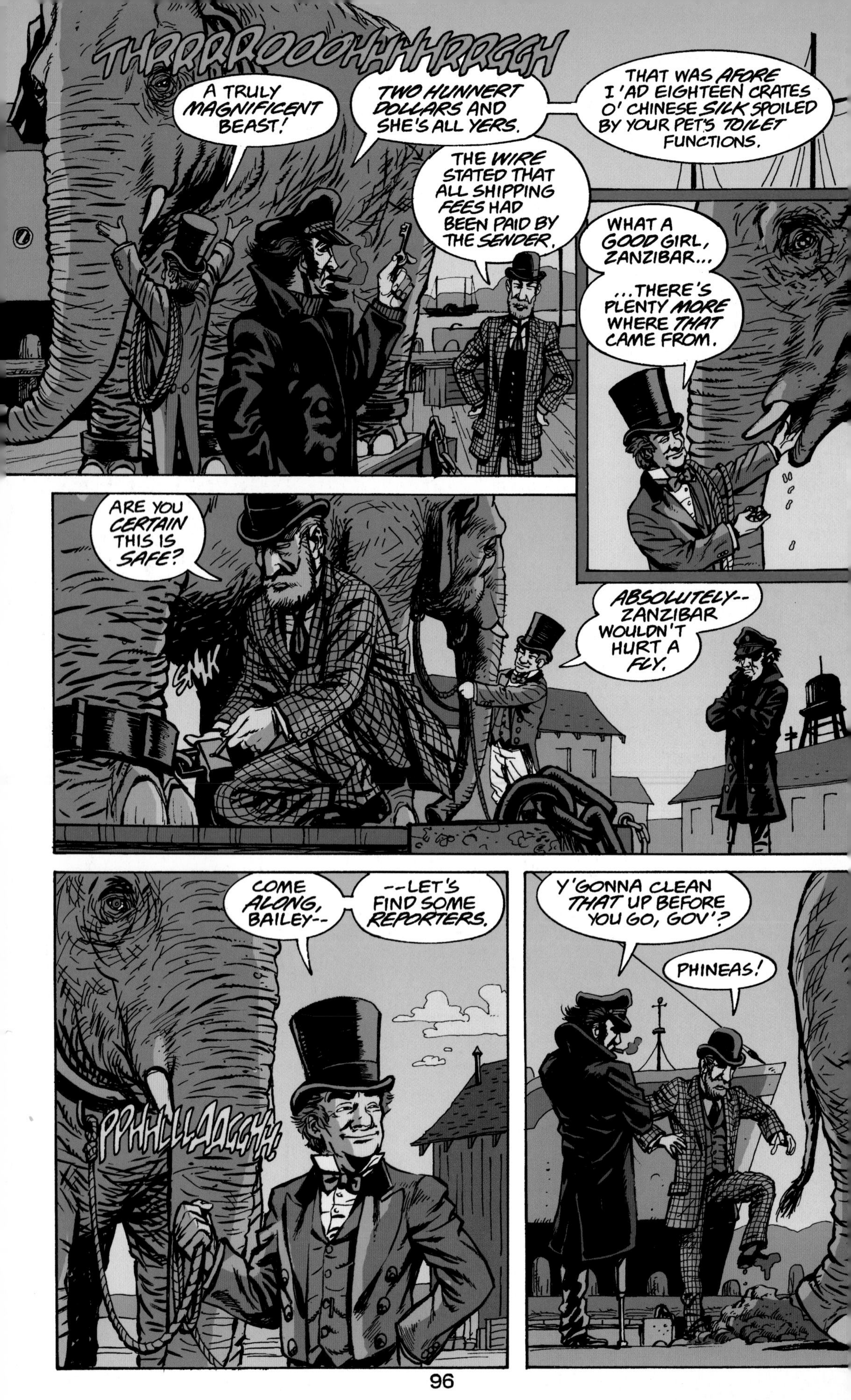
THRRRROOOHHHHRRGGH
A TRULY MAGNIFICENT BEAST!
TWO HUNNERT DOLLARS AND SHE'S ALL YERS.
THAT WAS AFORE I'AD EIGHTEEN CRATES O' CHINESE SILK SPOILED BY YOUR PET'S TOILET FUNCTIONS.
THE WIRE STATED THAT ALL SHIPPING FEES HAD BEEN PAID BY THE SENDER.
WHAT A GOOD GIRL, ZANZIBAR...
...THERE'S PLENTY MORE WHERE THAT CAME FROM.
ARE YOU CERTAIN THIS IS SAFE?
SNIK
ABSOLUTELY-- ZANZIBAR WOULDN'T HURT A FLY.
COME ALONG, BAILEY--
--LET'S FIND SOME REPORTERS.
PPHHLLAAGGHH!
Y'GONNA CLEAN THAT UP BEFORE YOU GO, GOV'?
PHINEAS!

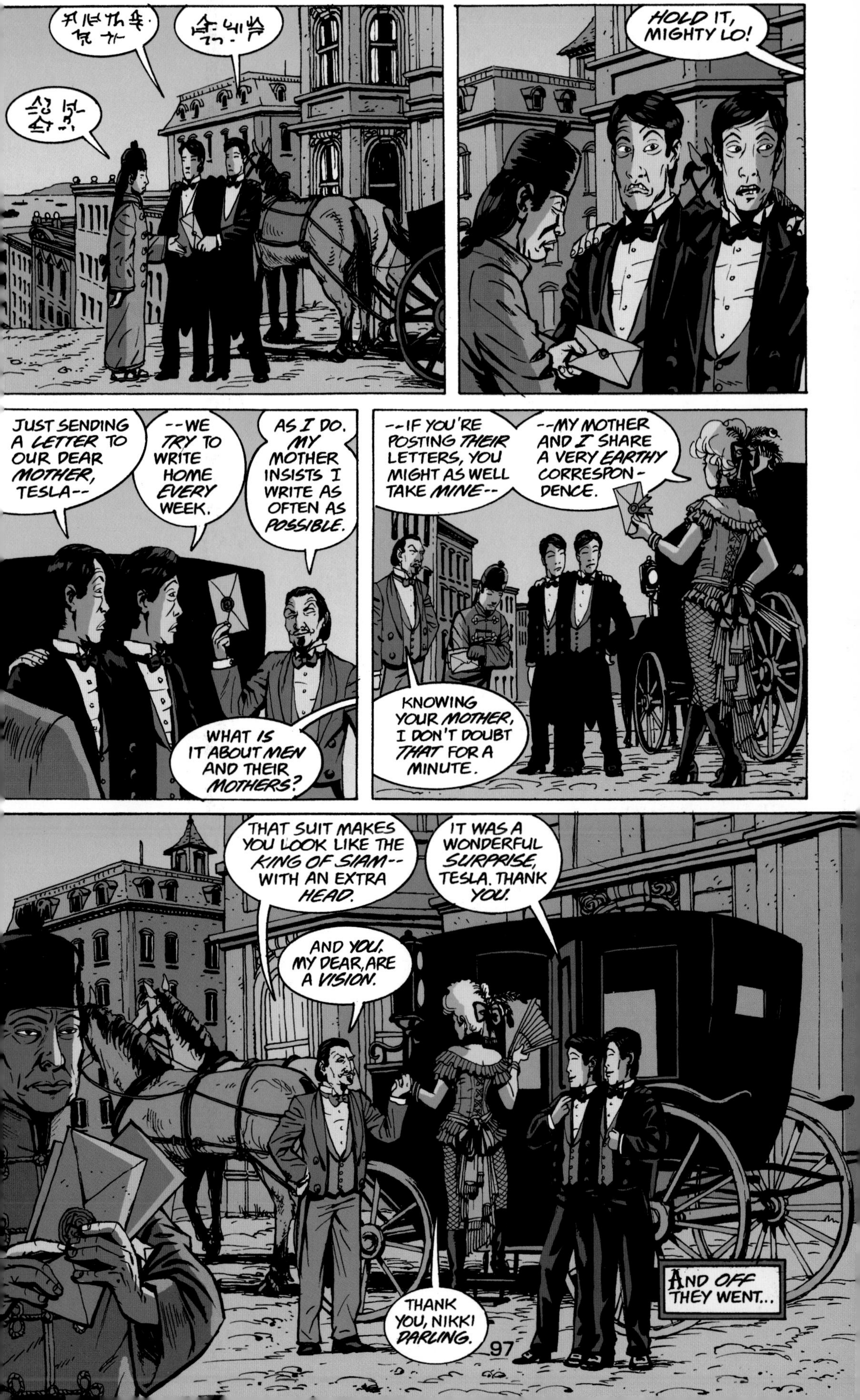
HOLD IT, MIGHTY LO!
JUST SENDING A LETTER TO OUR DEAR MOTHER, TESLA--
--WE TRY TO WRITE HOME EVERY WEEK.
AS I DO. MY MOTHER INSISTS I WRITE AS OFTEN AS POSSIBLE.
WHAT IS IT ABOUT MEN AND THEIR MOTHERS?
--IF YOU'RE POSTING THEIR LETTERS, YOU MIGHT AS WELL TAKE MINE--
--MY MOTHER AND I SHARE A VERY EARTHY CORRESPON-DENCE.
KNOWING YOUR MOTHER, I DON'T DOUBT THAT FOR A MINUTE.
THAT SUIT MAKES YOU LOOK LIKE THE KING OF SIAM--WITH AN EXTRA HEAD.
IT WAS A WONDERFUL SURPRISE, TESLA. THANK YOU.
AND YOU, MY DEAR, ARE A VISION.
THANK YOU, NIKKI DARLING.
AND OFF THEY WENT...

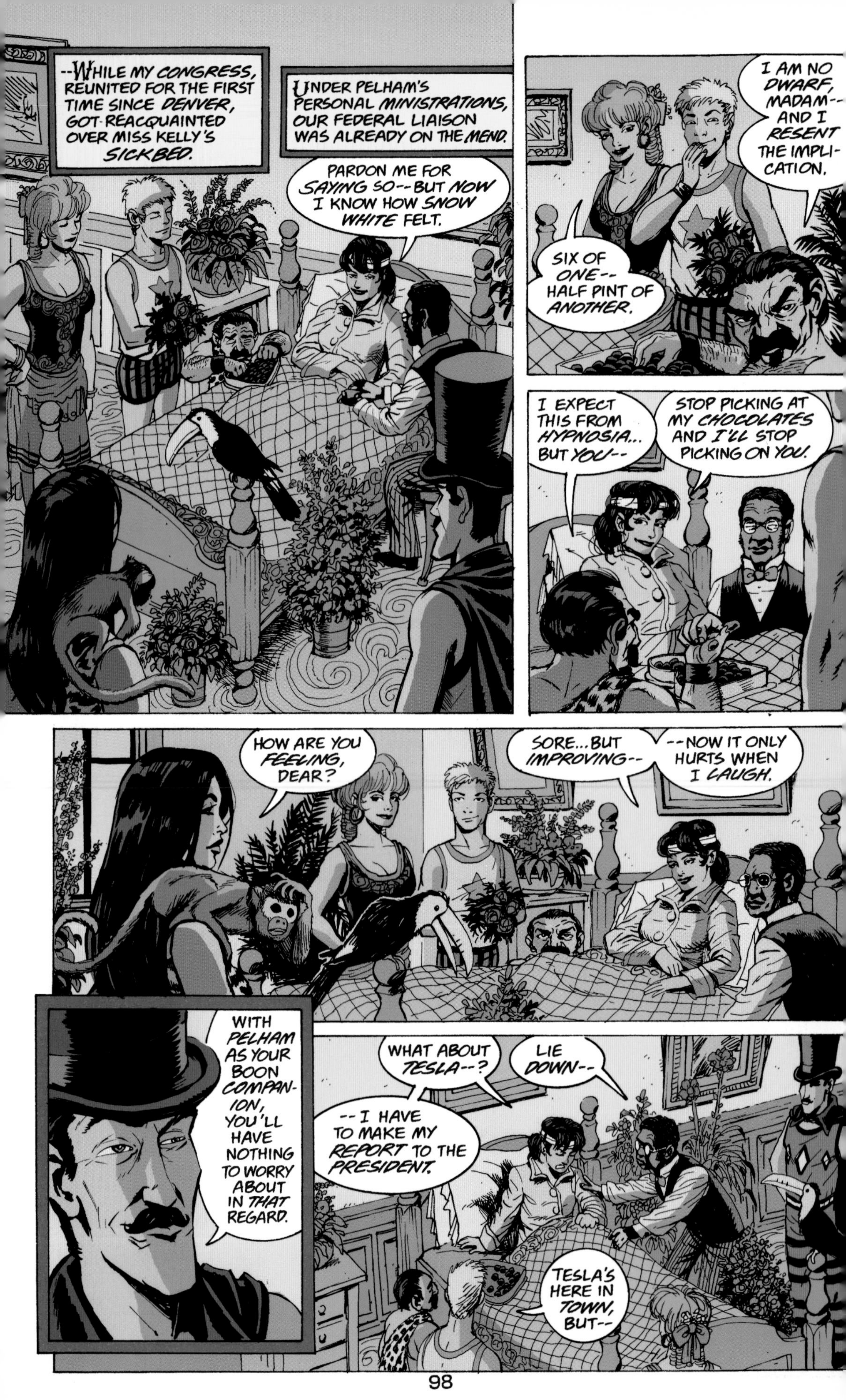
--WHILE MY CONGRESS, REUNITED FOR THE FIRST TIME SINCE DENVER, GOT REACQUAINTED OVER MISS KELLY'S SICKBED.
UNDER PELHAM'S PERSONAL MINISTRATIONS, OUR FEDERAL LIAISON WAS ALREADY ON THE MEND.
PARDON ME FOR SAYING SO--BUT NOW I KNOW HOW SNOW WHITE FELT.
I AM NO DWARF, MADAM--AND I RESENT THE IMPLICATION.
SIX OF ONE--HALF PINT OF ANOTHER.
I EXPECT THIS FROM HYPNOSIA... BUT YOU--
STOP PICKING AT MY CHOCOLATES AND I'LL STOP PICKING ON YOU.
HOW ARE YOU FEELING, DEAR?
SORE... BUT IMPROVING--
--NOW IT ONLY HURTS WHEN I LAUGH.
WITH PELHAM AS YOUR BOON COMPANION, YOU'LL HAVE NOTHING TO WORRY ABOUT IN THAT REGARD.
WHAT ABOUT TESLA--?
LIE DOWN--
--I HAVE TO MAKE MY REPORT TO THE PRESIDENT.
TESLA'S HERE IN TOWN, BUT--

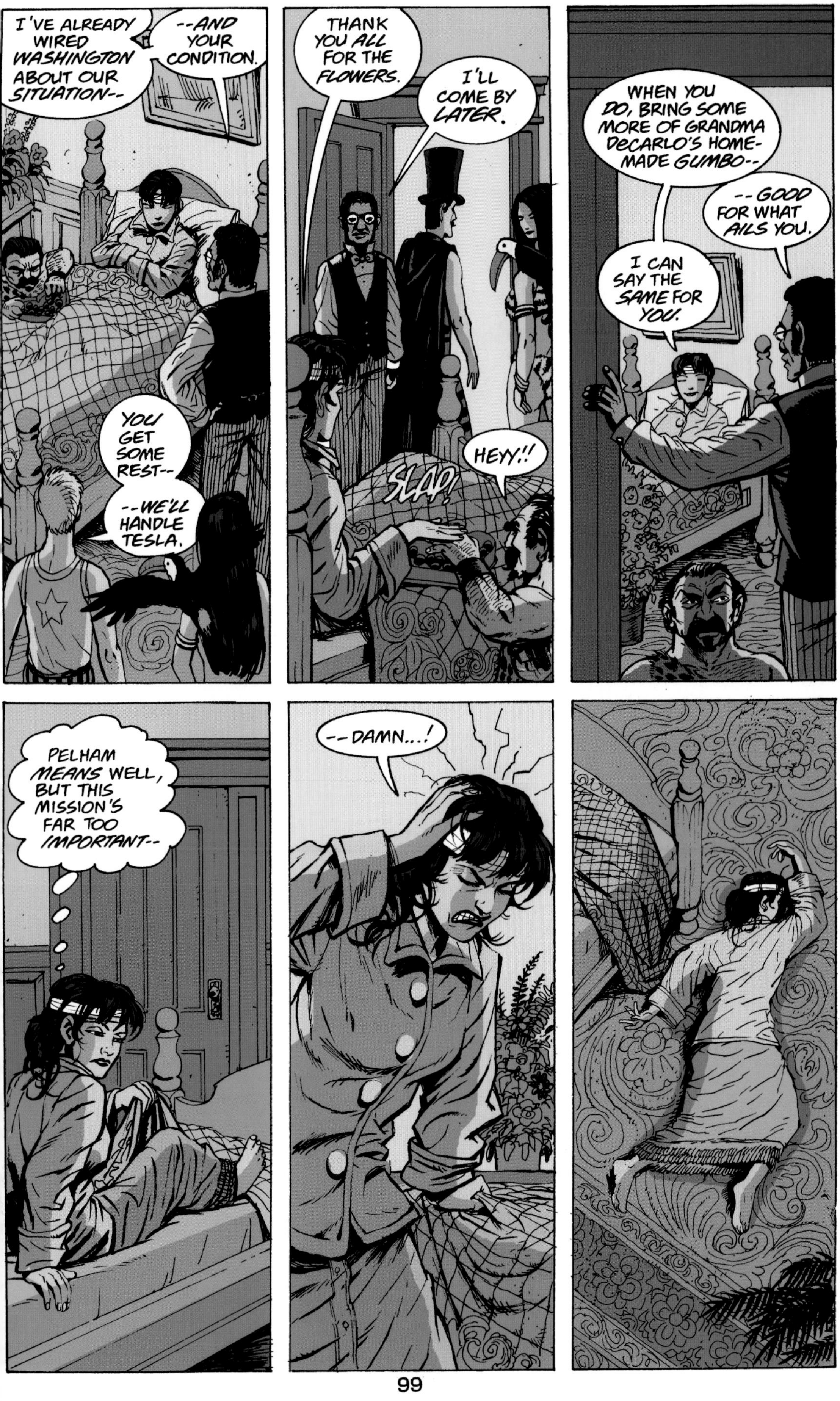
I'VE ALREADY WIRED WASHINGTON ABOUT OUR SITUATION--
--AND YOUR CONDITION.
YOU GET SOME REST--
--WE'LL HANDLE TESLA.
THANK YOU ALL FOR THE FLOWERS.
I'LL COME BY LATER.
SLAP!
HEYY!!
WHEN YOU DO, BRING SOME MORE OF GRANDMA DeCARLO'S HOME-MADE GUMBO--
--GOOD FOR WHAT AILS YOU.
I CAN SAY THE SAME FOR YOU.
PELHAM MEANS WELL, BUT THIS MISSION'S FAR TOO IMPORTANT--
--DAMN...!

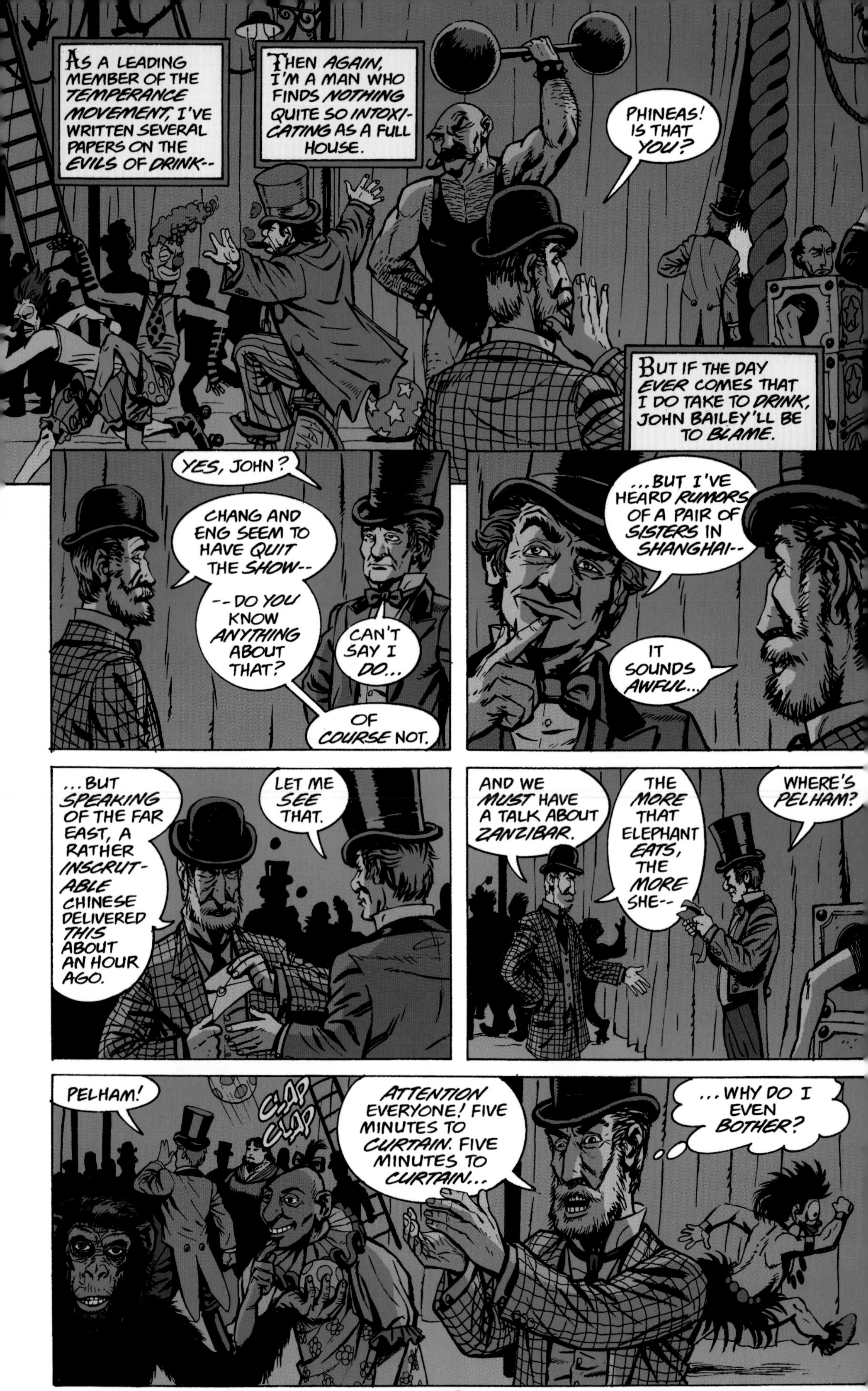
AS A LEADING MEMBER OF THE TEMPERANCE MOVEMENT, I'VE WRITTEN SEVERAL PAPERS ON THE EVILS OF DRINK--
THEN AGAIN, I'M A MAN WHO FINDS NOTHING QUITE SO INTOXICATING AS A FULL HOUSE.
PHINEAS! IS THAT YOU?
BUT IF THE DAY EVER COMES THAT I DO TAKE TO DRINK, JOHN BAILEY'LL BE TO BLAME.
YES, JOHN?
CHANG AND ENG SEEM TO HAVE QUIT THE SHOW--
--DO YOU KNOW ANYTHING ABOUT THAT?
CAN'T SAY I DO...
OF COURSE NOT.
...BUT I'VE HEARD RUMORS OF A PAIR OF SISTERS IN SHANGHAI--
IT SOUNDS AWFUL...
...BUT SPEAKING OF THE FAR EAST, A RATHER INSCRUTABLE CHINESE DELIVERED THIS ABOUT AN HOUR AGO.
LET ME SEE THAT.
AND WE MUST HAVE A TALK ABOUT ZANZIBAR.
THE MORE THAT ELEPHANT EATS, THE MORE SHE--
WHERE'S PELHAM?
PELHAM!
CLAP CLAP
ATTENTION EVERYONE! FIVE MINUTES TO CURTAIN. FIVE MINUTES TO CURTAIN...
...WHY DO I EVEN BOTHER?

WOULD YOU *LOOK* AT THAT *CROWD!*

THAT'S WHAT *I'LL* MISS ABOUT THE *CIRCUS.*

COMMONERS, SIMPLETONS AND WRETCHES.

BARNUM *KNOWS* WE'VE SWITCHED ALLEGIANCES--

AREN'T WE A BIT-- CONSPIC-UOUS?

NONSENSE. YOU'RE TWO OF *US* NOW--

--AND I'M *AFRAID* I MUST *INSIST* YOU ACCOMPANY US.

!!?!??!

WHAT A *BEAUTIFUL* WEAPON, NIKKI.

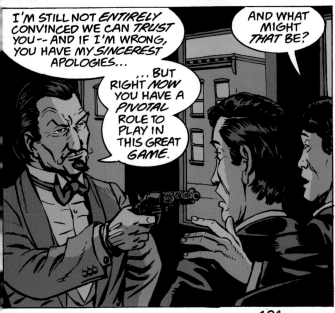

I'M STILL NOT *ENTIRELY* CONVINCED WE CAN *TRUST* YOU -- AND IF I'M WRONG, YOU HAVE MY *SINCEREST* APOLOGIES...

...BUT RIGHT *NOW* YOU HAVE A *PIVOTAL* ROLE TO PLAY IN THIS GREAT *GAME.*

AND WHAT MIGHT *THAT* BE?

YOU'RE GOING TO ASSASSINATE *P.T. BARNUM.*

101

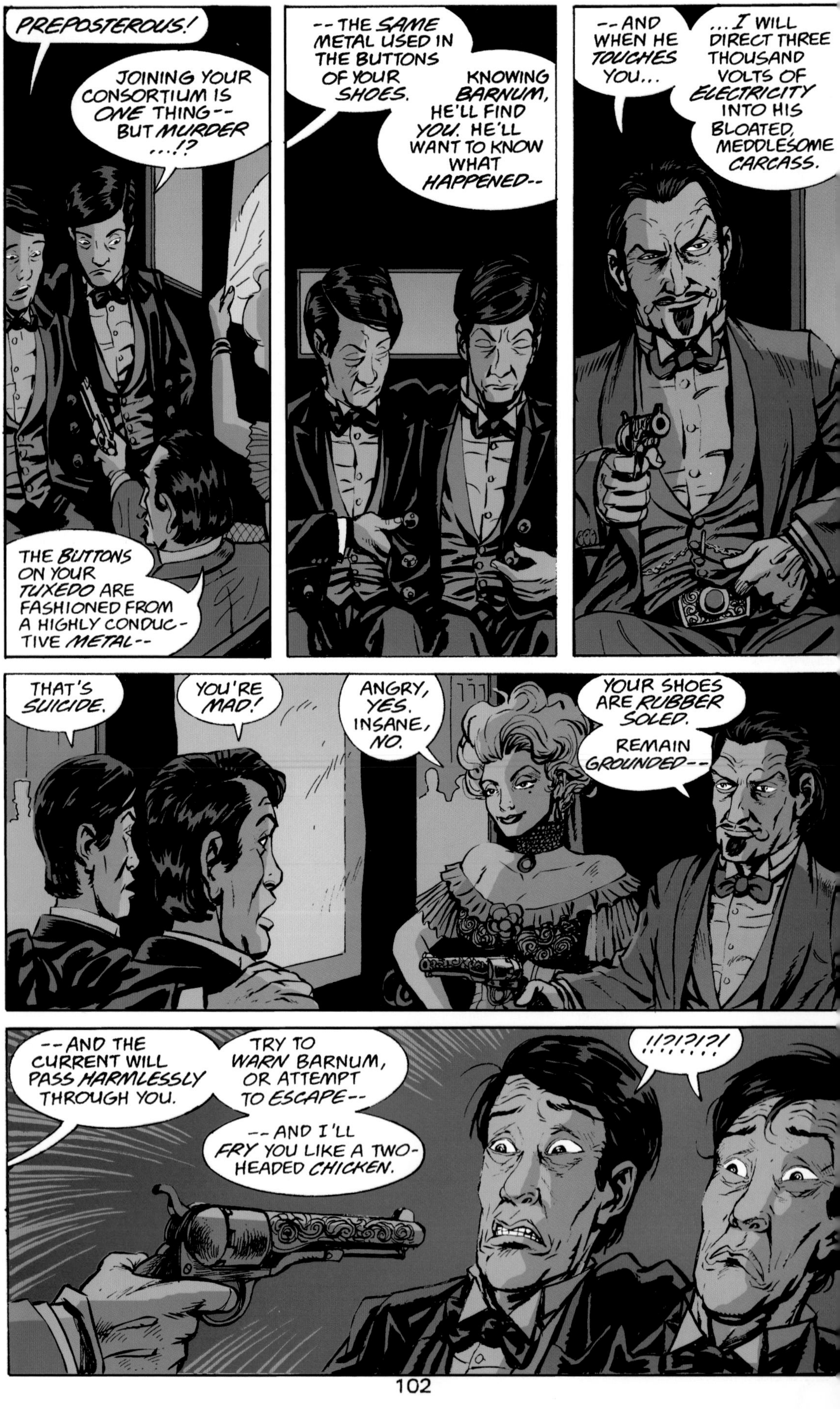
PREPOSTEROUS!
JOINING YOUR CONSORTIUM IS ONE THING-- BUT MURDER ...!?
THE BUTTONS ON YOUR TUXEDO ARE FASHIONED FROM A HIGHLY CONDUCTIVE METAL--
--THE SAME METAL USED IN THE BUTTONS OF YOUR SHOES.
KNOWING BARNUM, HE'LL FIND YOU. HE'LL WANT TO KNOW WHAT HAPPENED--
--AND WHEN HE TOUCHES YOU...
...I WILL DIRECT THREE THOUSAND VOLTS OF ELECTRICITY INTO HIS BLOATED, MEDDLESOME CARCASS.
THAT'S SUICIDE.
YOU'RE MAD!
ANGRY, YES. INSANE, NO.
YOUR SHOES ARE RUBBER SOLED.
REMAIN GROUNDED--
--AND THE CURRENT WILL PASS HARMLESSLY THROUGH YOU.
TRY TO WARN BARNUM, OR ATTEMPT TO ESCAPE--
--AND I'LL FRY YOU LIKE A TWO-HEADED CHICKEN.
!!?!?!?!

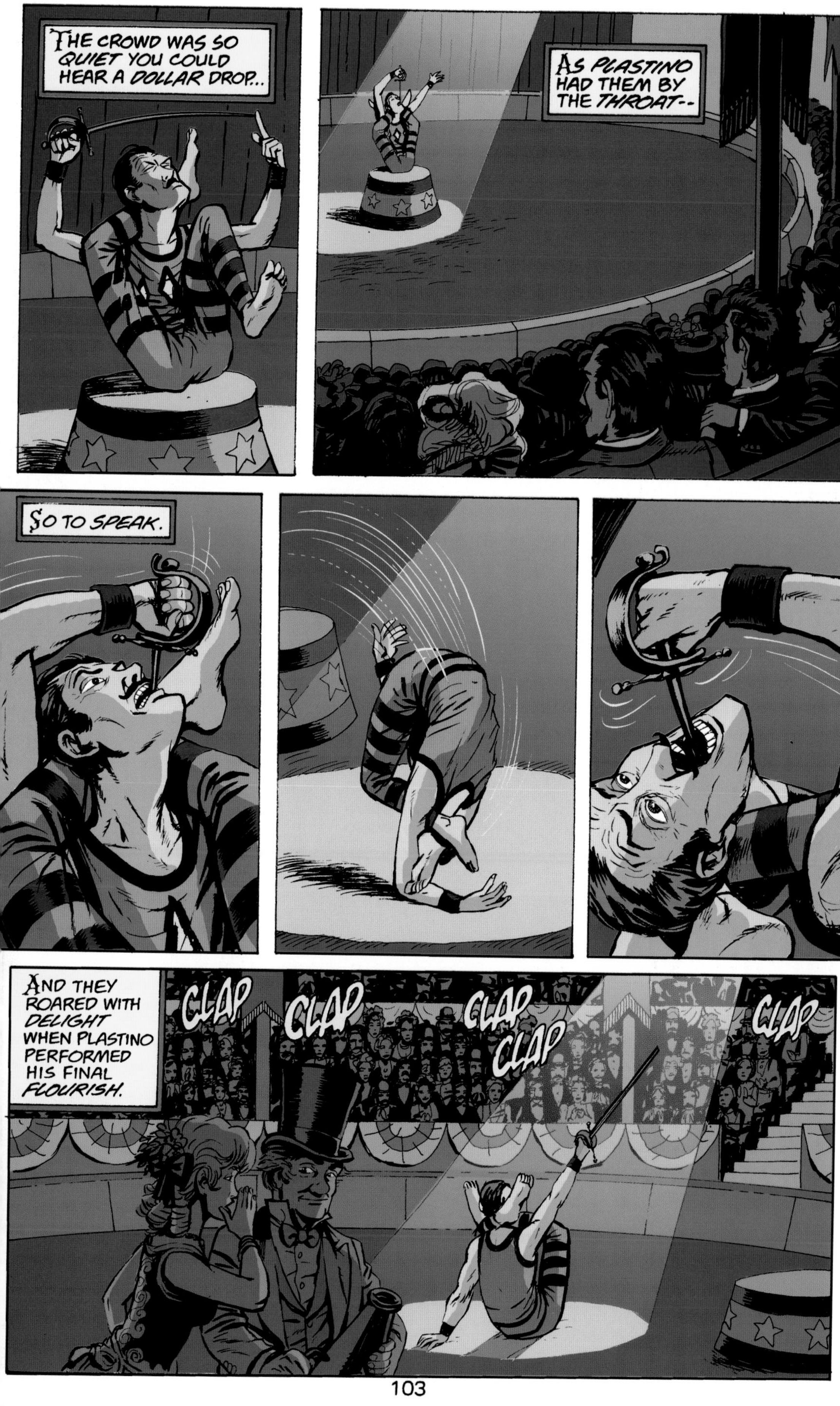
THE CROWD WAS SO QUIET YOU COULD HEAR A DOLLAR DROP...
AS PLASTINO HAD THEM BY THE THROAT--
SO TO SPEAK.
AND THEY ROARED WITH DELIGHT WHEN PLASTINO PERFORMED HIS FINAL FLOURISH.
CLAP
CLAP
CLAP
CLAP
CLAP

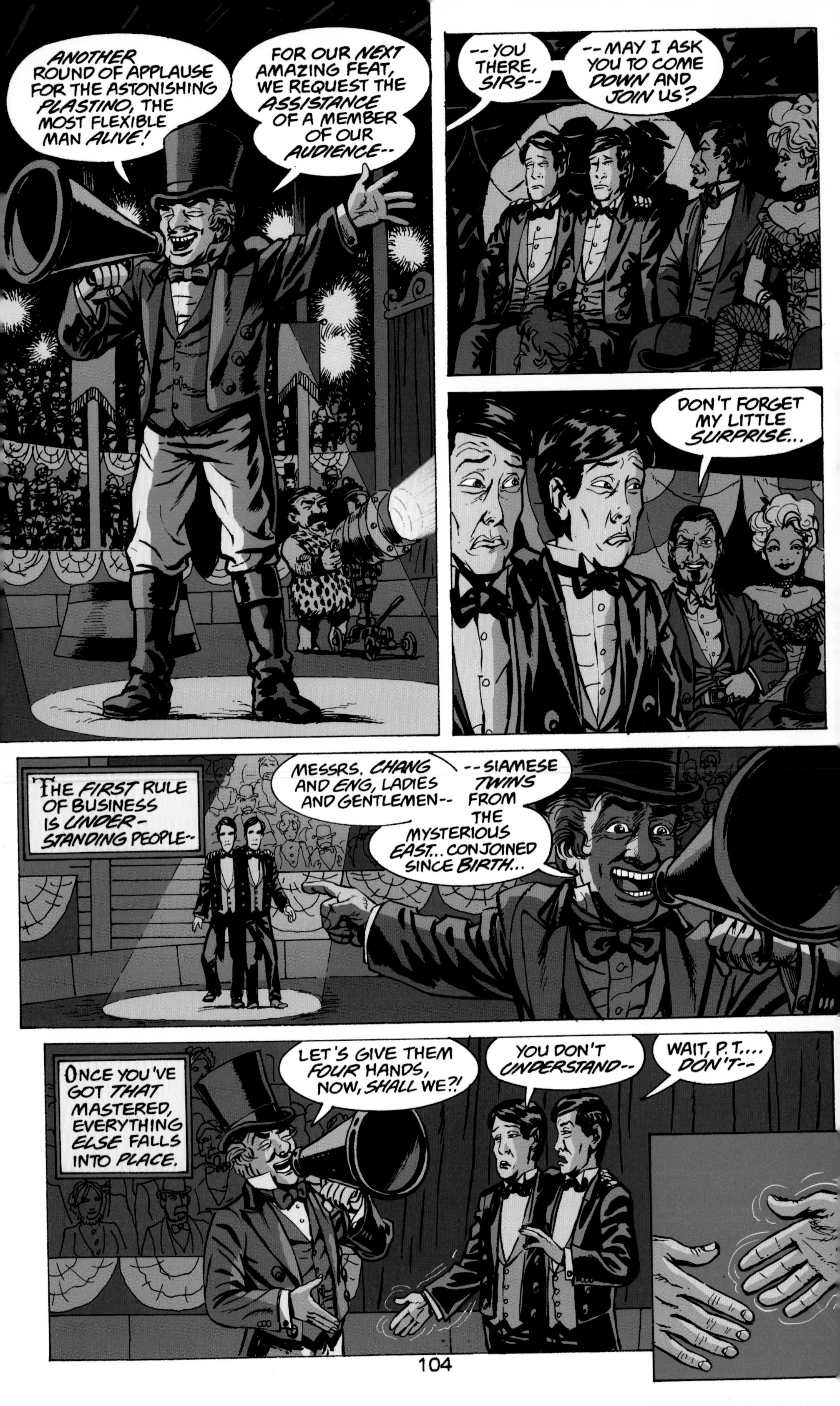
ANOTHER ROUND OF APPLAUSE FOR THE ASTONISHING PLASTINO, THE MOST FLEXIBLE MAN ALIVE!
FOR OUR NEXT AMAZING FEAT, WE REQUEST THE ASSISTANCE OF A MEMBER OF OUR AUDIENCE--
--YOU THERE, SIRS--
--MAY I ASK YOU TO COME DOWN AND JOIN US?
DON'T FORGET MY LITTLE SURPRISE...
THE FIRST RULE OF BUSINESS IS UNDER-STANDING PEOPLE--
MESSRS. CHANG AND ENG, LADIES AND GENTLEMEN--
--SIAMESE TWINS FROM THE MYSTERIOUS EAST... CONJOINED SINCE BIRTH...
ONCE YOU'VE GOT THAT MASTERED, EVERYTHING ELSE FALLS INTO PLACE.
LET'S GIVE THEM FOUR HANDS, NOW, SHALL WE?!
YOU DON'T UNDERSTAND--
WAIT, P.T.... DON'T--

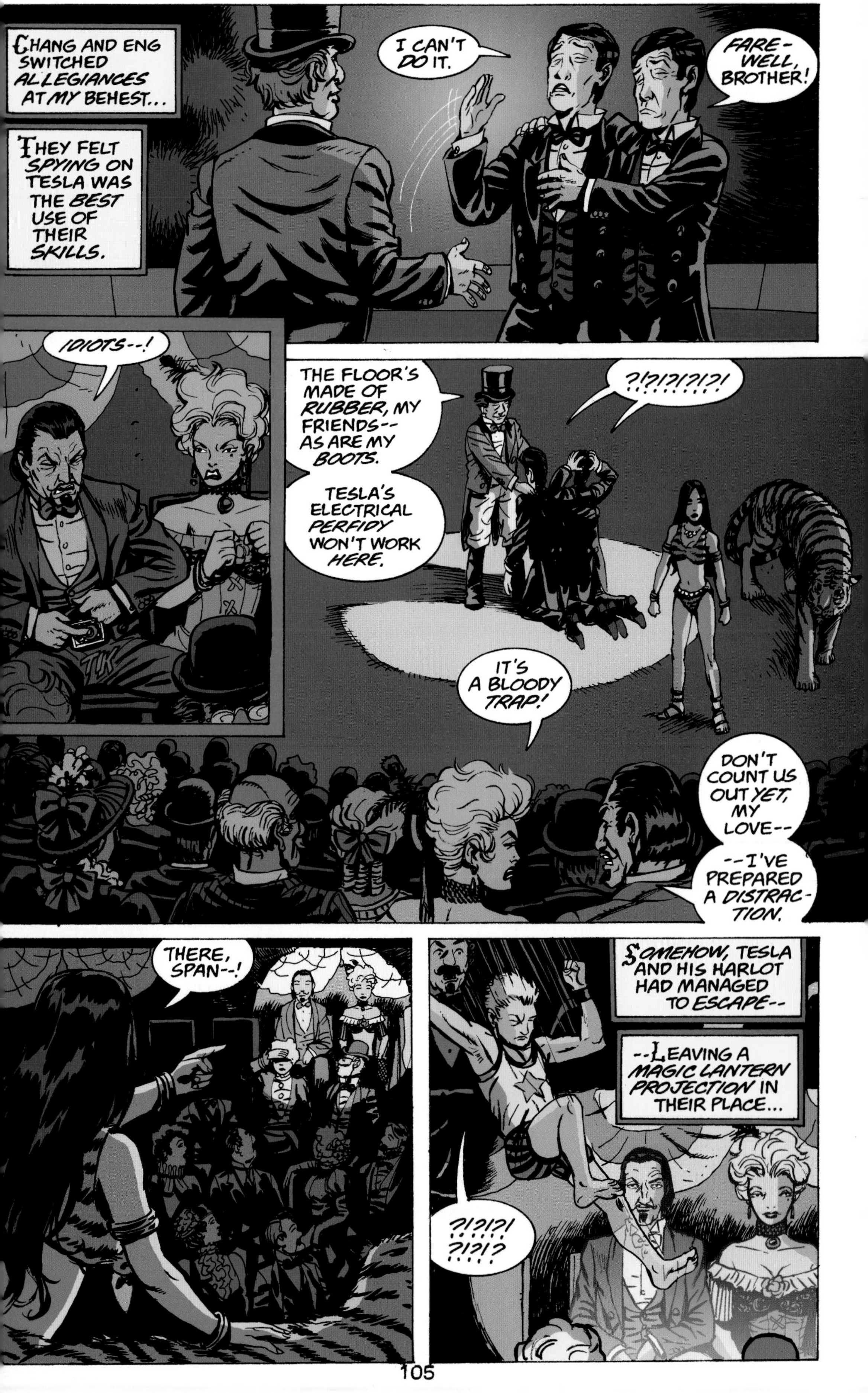
CHANG AND ENG SWITCHED ALLEGIANCES AT MY BEHEST...
THEY FELT SPYING ON TESLA WAS THE BEST USE OF THEIR SKILLS.
I CAN'T DO IT.
FARE-WELL, BROTHER!
IDIOTS--!
THE FLOOR'S MADE OF RUBBER, MY FRIENDS-- AS ARE MY BOOTS.
TESLA'S ELECTRICAL PERFIDY WON'T WORK HERE.
?!?!?!?!?!
IT'S A BLOODY TRAP!
DON'T COUNT US OUT YET, MY LOVE--
--I'VE PREPARED A DISTRACTION.
THERE, SPAN--!
SOMEHOW, TESLA AND HIS HARLOT HAD MANAGED TO ESCAPE--
--LEAVING A MAGIC LANTERN PROJECTION IN THEIR PLACE...
?!?!?!
?!?!?

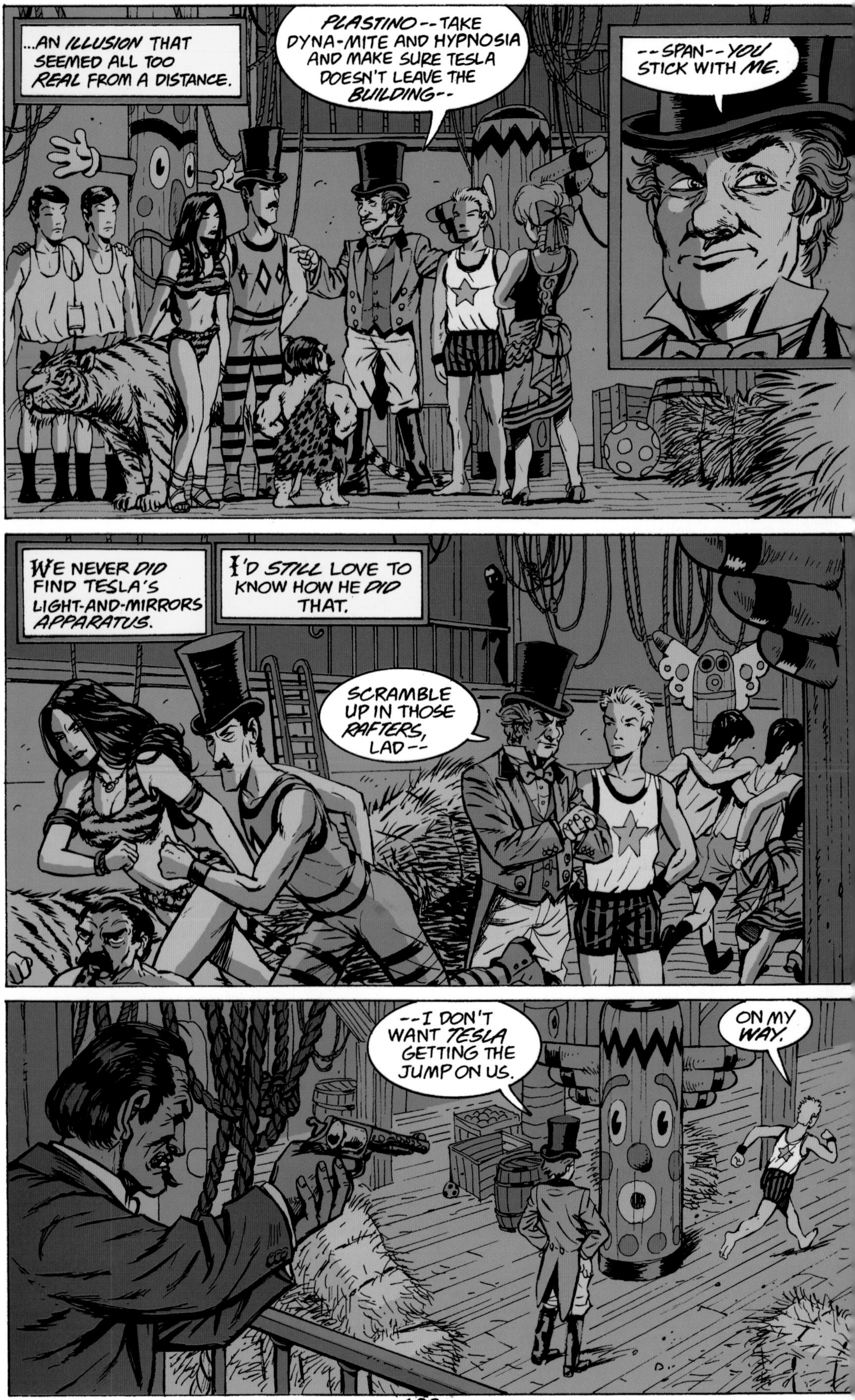
...AN ILLUSION THAT SEEMED ALL TOO REAL FROM A DISTANCE.
PLASTINO--TAKE DYNA-MITE AND HYPNOSIA AND MAKE SURE TESLA DOESN'T LEAVE THE BUILDING--
--SPAN--YOU STICK WITH ME.
WE NEVER DID FIND TESLA'S LIGHT-AND-MIRRORS APPARATUS.
I'D STILL LOVE TO KNOW HOW HE DID THAT.
SCRAMBLE UP IN THOSE RAFTERS, LAD--
--I DON'T WANT TESLA GETTING THE JUMP ON US.
ON MY WAY.

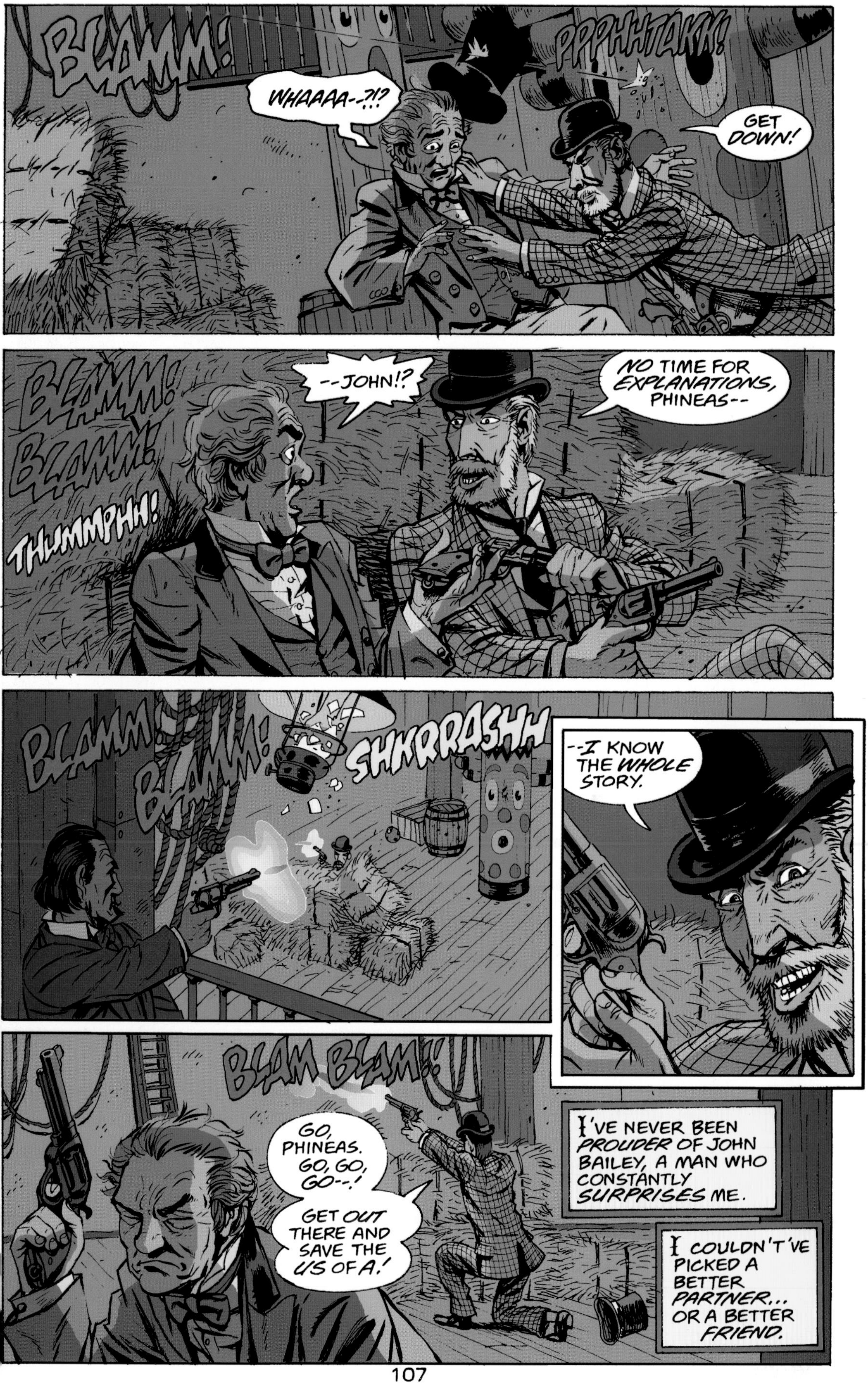
BLAMM!
PPPHHTAKK!
WHAAAA--?!?
GET DOWN!
BLAMM! BLAMM!
THUMMPHH!
--JOHN!?
NO TIME FOR EXPLANATIONS, PHINEAS--
BLAMM! BLAMM!
SHKRRASHH
--I KNOW THE WHOLE STORY.
BLAM BLAM!
GO, PHINEAS. GO, GO, GO--!
GET OUT THERE AND SAVE THE US OF A!
I'VE NEVER BEEN PROUDER OF JOHN BAILEY, A MAN WHO CONSTANTLY SURPRISES ME.
I COULDN'T'VE PICKED A BETTER PARTNER... OR A BETTER FRIEND.

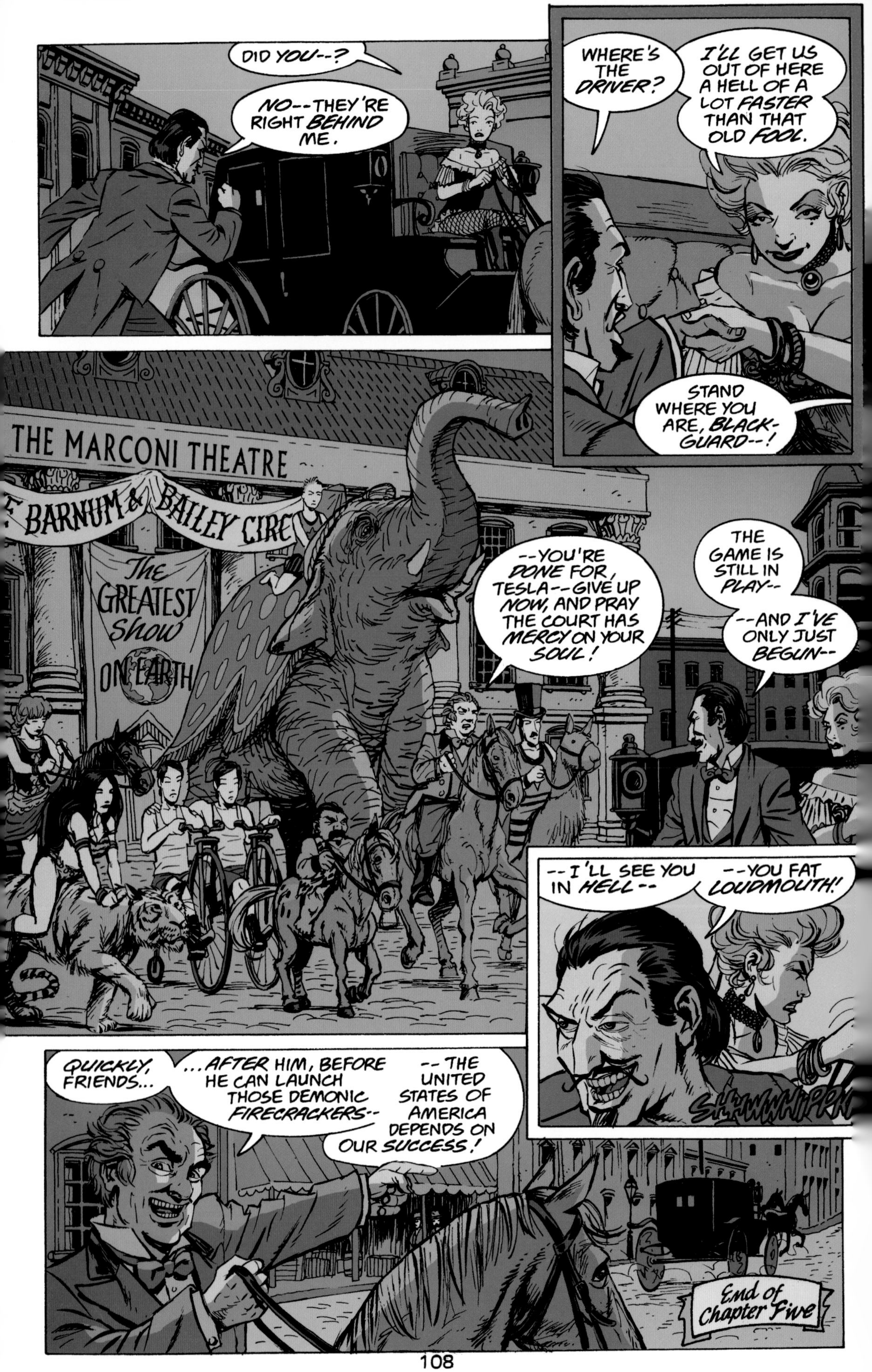
DID YOU--?
NO--THEY'RE RIGHT BEHIND ME.
WHERE'S THE DRIVER?
I'LL GET US OUT OF HERE A HELL OF A LOT FASTER THAN THAT OLD FOOL.
STAND WHERE YOU ARE, BLACK-GUARD--!
THE MARCONI THEATRE
BARNUM & BAILEY CIRC
The GREATEST Show ON EARTH
--YOU'RE DONE FOR, TESLA--GIVE UP NOW, AND PRAY THE COURT HAS MERCY ON YOUR SOUL!
THE GAME IS STILL IN PLAY--
--AND I'VE ONLY JUST BEGUN--
--I'LL SEE YOU IN HELL--
--YOU FAT LOUDMOUTH!
QUICKLY, FRIENDS...
...AFTER HIM, BEFORE HE CAN LAUNCH THOSE DEMONIC FIRECRACKERS--
--THE UNITED STATES OF AMERICA DEPENDS ON OUR SUCCESS!
End of Chapter Five

CHAPTER 6

CHAPTER 6

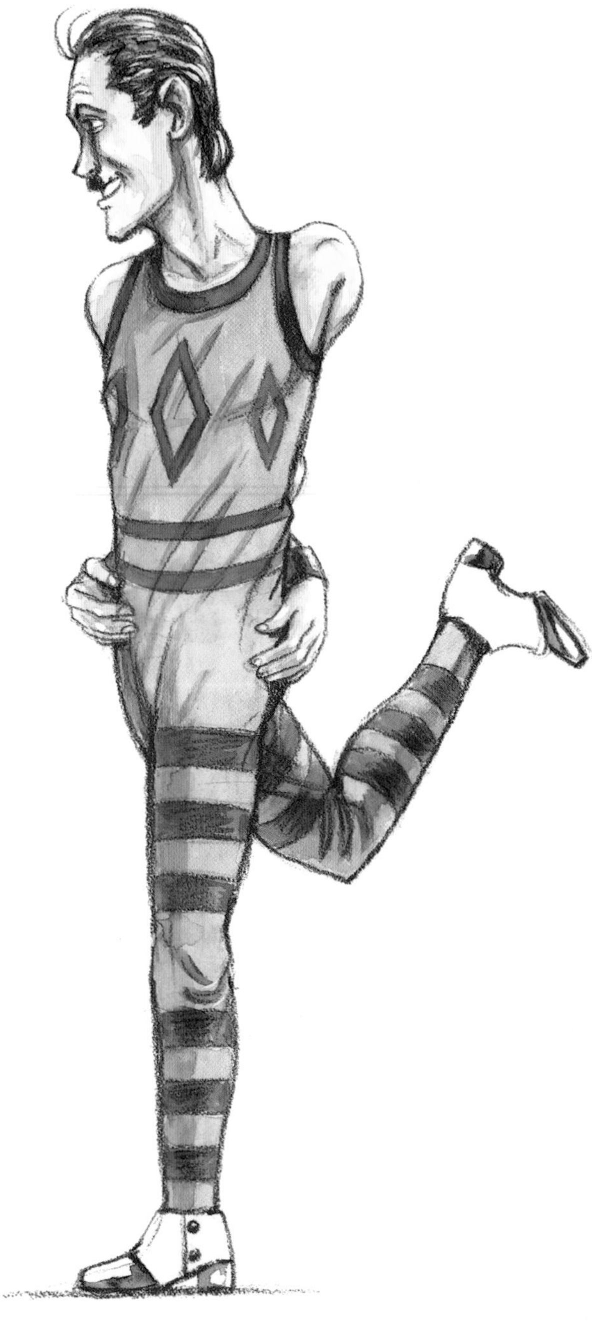

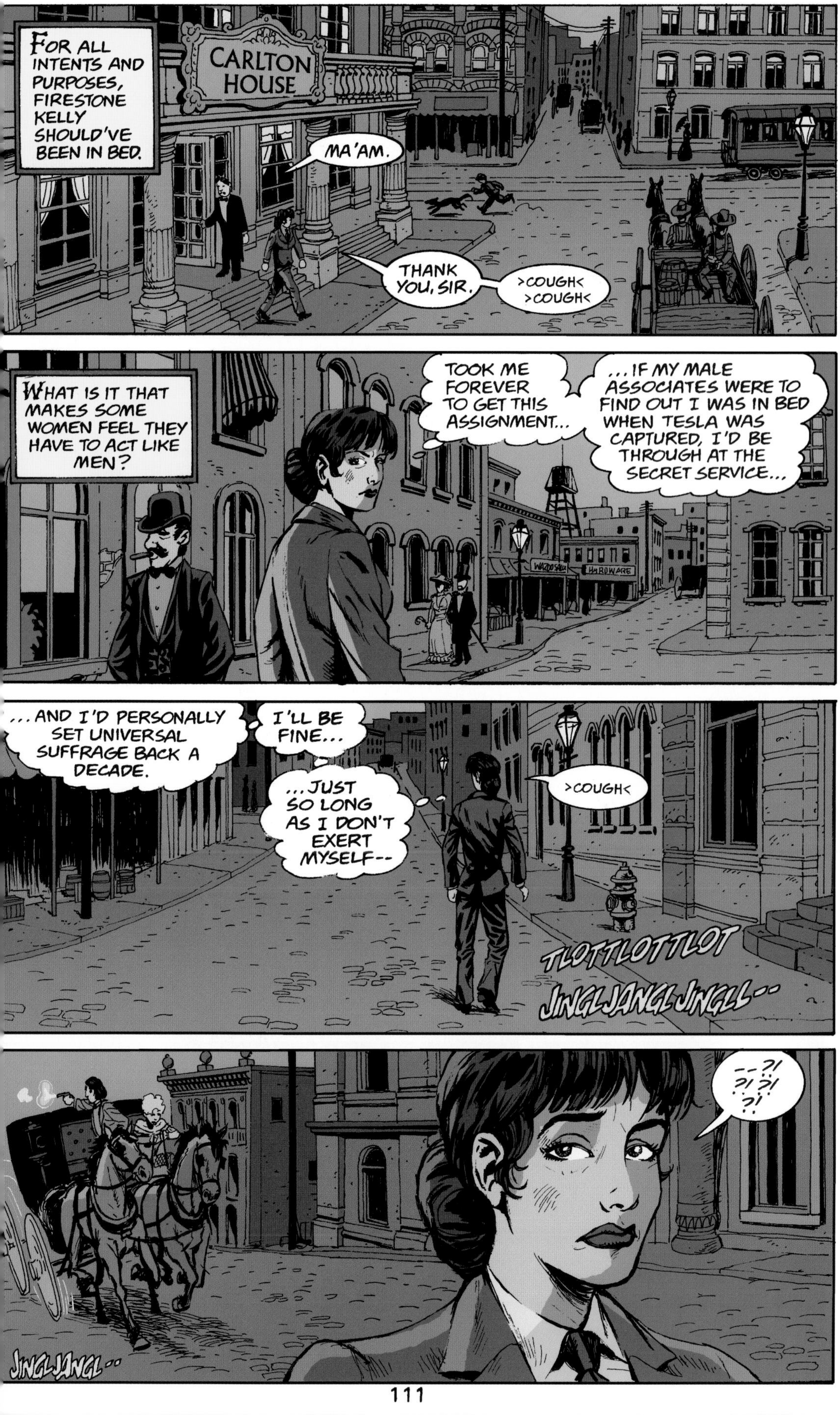
CARLTON HOUSE
FOR ALL INTENTS AND PURPOSES, FIRESTONE KELLY SHOULD'VE BEEN IN BED.
MA'AM.
THANK YOU, SIR.
>COUGH< >COUGH<
WHAT IS IT THAT MAKES SOME WOMEN FEEL THEY HAVE TO ACT LIKE MEN?
TOOK ME FOREVER TO GET THIS ASSIGNMENT...
...IF MY MALE ASSOCIATES WERE TO FIND OUT I WAS IN BED WHEN TESLA WAS CAPTURED, I'D BE THROUGH AT THE SECRET SERVICE...
HARDWARE
...AND I'D PERSONALLY SET UNIVERSAL SUFFRAGE BACK A DECADE.
I'LL BE FINE...
...JUST SO LONG AS I DON'T EXERT MYSELF--
>COUGH<
TLOTTLOTTLOT
JINGLJANGLJINGLL--
--?! ?! ?! ?!
JINGLJANGL--

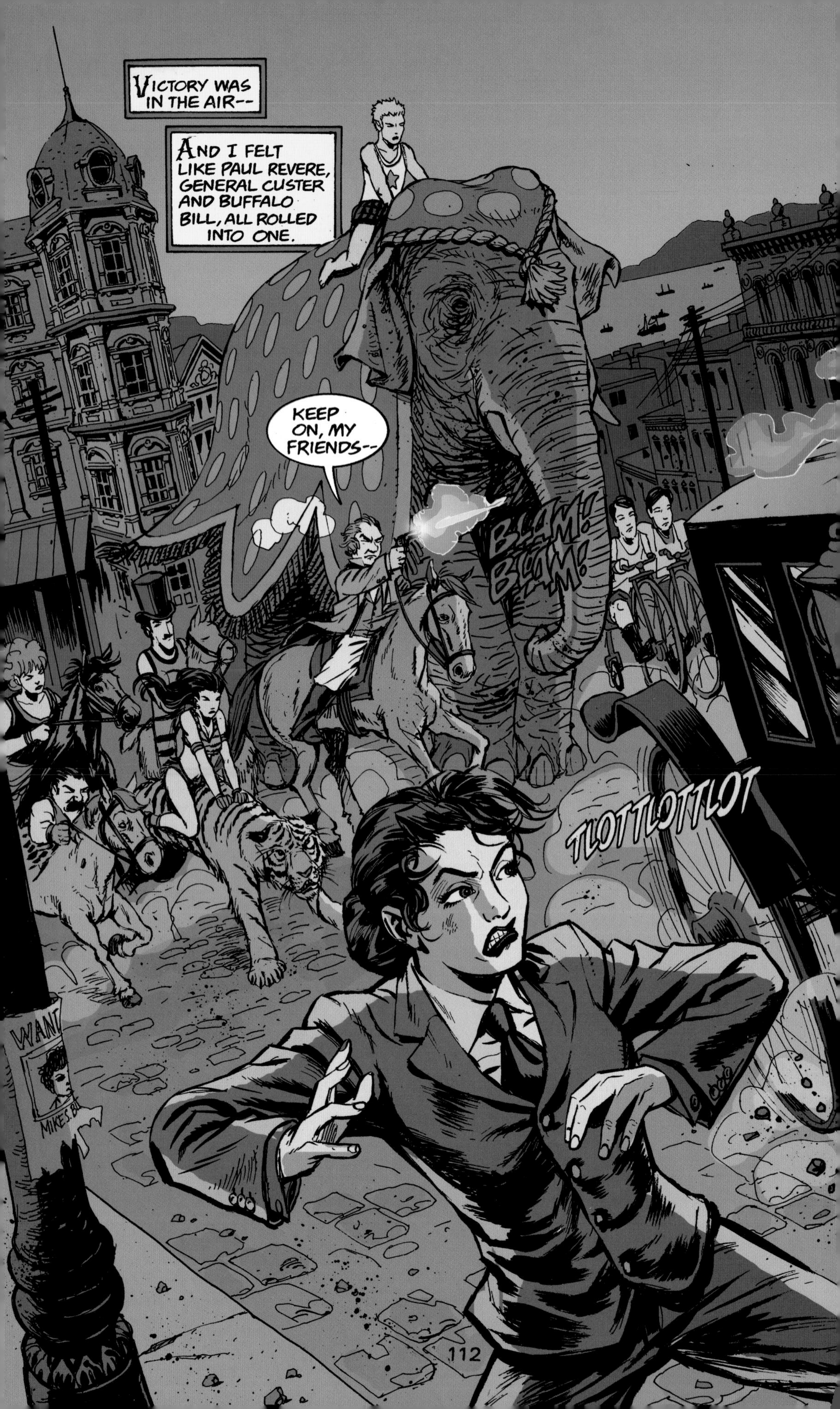
VICTORY WAS IN THE AIR--
AND I FELT LIKE PAUL REVERE, GENERAL CUSTER AND BUFFALO BILL, ALL ROLLED INTO ONE.
KEEP ON, MY FRIENDS--
BLAM! BLAM!
TLOTTLOTTLOT

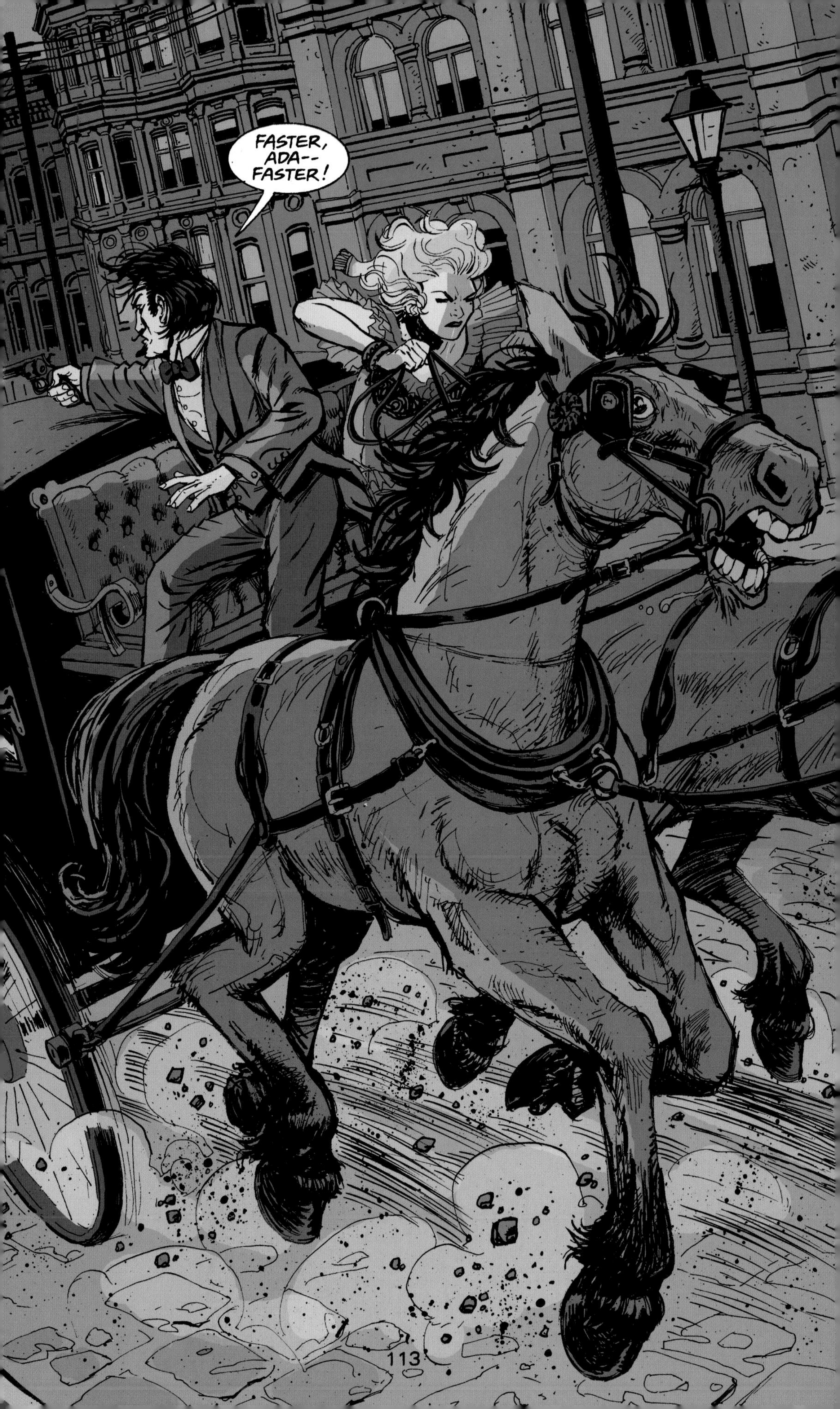
FASTER, ADA-- FASTER!

NIKKI--!

FIRESTONE'S *SHOT* NICKED THE COUNTESS' *SHOULDER*--

*E*NOUGH TO MAKE ADA LOSE CONTROL OF THE *RIG*--

BLAM!

BLAM!

AND *MORE* THAN ENOUGH TO BRING THE HOUSE *DOWN*.

CHAKKRAKSHA

NOT BAD...   ...FOR A GIRL.

BLAM!

*M*ISS KELLY'D GIVEN US THE *UPPER* HAND--

--BUT RESCUING YOU WOULD PUT ME AT RISK.

I SIMPLY CAN'T BE APPREHENDED BY THESE YAHOOS...

NOW IT'S TIME FOR US TO LOWER THE *BOOM*.

HELP ME, NIKKI! MY SHOULDER!

I *SHARE* YOUR PAIN, ADA DARLING.

...NOT WHEN I CAN ALMOST *TASTE* SUCCESS... OURS WILL BE A FREE COUNTRY--

--AND I NEED TO BE FREE TO RULE IT.

YOU MEGALOMANIAC--

-- I HANDED YOU THE THINKING ENGINE, YOU *BASTARD!*

YOU'LL *PAY* FOR THIS--

LOOK OUT--

THRRROOAHHRGH!

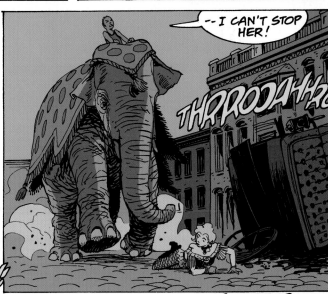

-- I CAN'T STOP HER!

THRROOAHH

OH DEAR...

SPPHHLLAATT!

SAN FRANCISCO HAS SINCE OUTLAWED PACHYDERMS WITHIN CITY LIMITS.

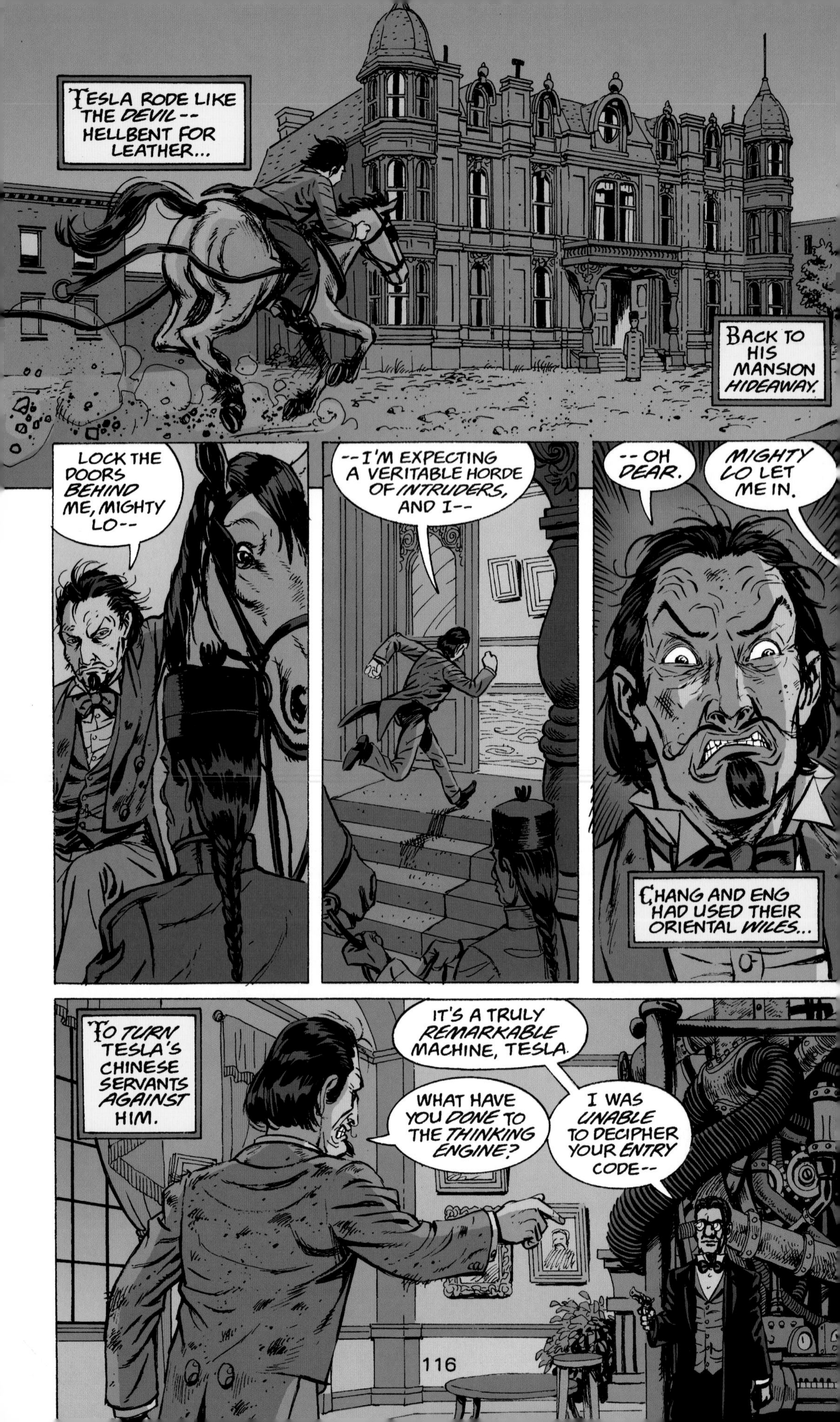
TESLA RODE LIKE THE DEVIL-- HELLBENT FOR LEATHER...
BACK TO HIS MANSION HIDEAWAY.
LOCK THE DOORS BEHIND ME, MIGHTY LO--
--I'M EXPECTING A VERITABLE HORDE OF INTRUDERS, AND I--
--OH DEAR.
MIGHTY LO LET ME IN.
CHANG AND ENG HAD USED THEIR ORIENTAL WILES...
TO TURN TESLA'S CHINESE SERVANTS AGAINST HIM.
IT'S A TRULY REMARKABLE MACHINE, TESLA.
WHAT HAVE YOU DONE TO THE THINKING ENGINE?
I WAS UNABLE TO DECIPHER YOUR ENTRY CODE--

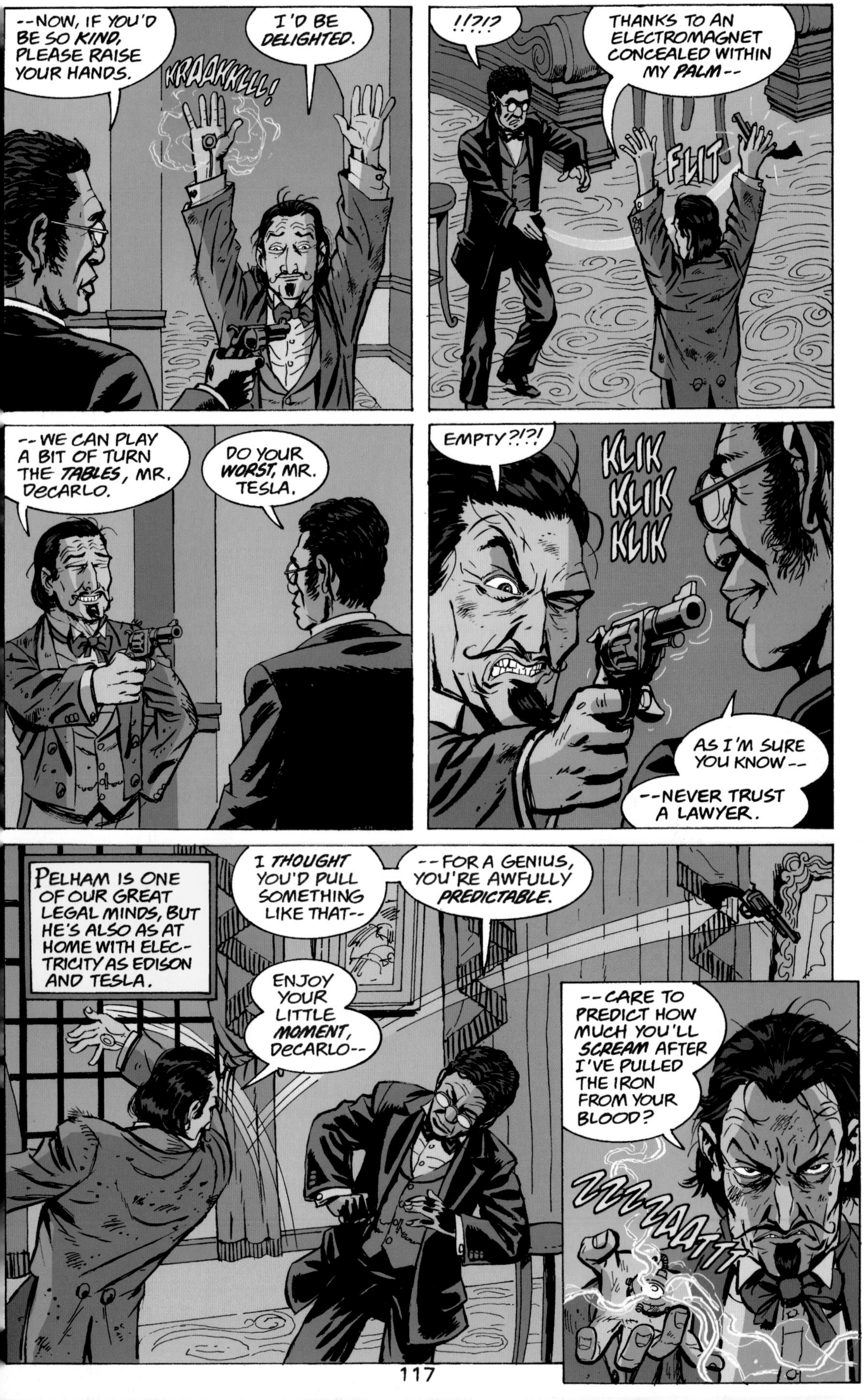
--NOW, IF YOU'D BE SO KIND, PLEASE RAISE YOUR HANDS.
I'D BE DELIGHTED.
KRAAKKLLL!
!!?!?
THANKS TO AN ELECTROMAGNET CONCEALED WITHIN MY PALM--
FLIT
--WE CAN PLAY A BIT OF TURN THE TABLES, MR. DeCARLO.
DO YOUR WORST, MR. TESLA.
EMPTY?!?!
KLIK KLIK KLIK
AS I'M SURE YOU KNOW--
--NEVER TRUST A LAWYER.
PELHAM IS ONE OF OUR GREAT LEGAL MINDS, BUT HE'S ALSO AS AT HOME WITH ELEC-TRICITY AS EDISON AND TESLA.
I THOUGHT YOU'D PULL SOMETHING LIKE THAT--
--FOR A GENIUS, YOU'RE AWFULLY PREDICTABLE.
ENJOY YOUR LITTLE MOMENT, DeCARLO--
--CARE TO PREDICT HOW MUCH YOU'LL SCREAM AFTER I'VE PULLED THE IRON FROM YOUR BLOOD?
ZZZZAATTT

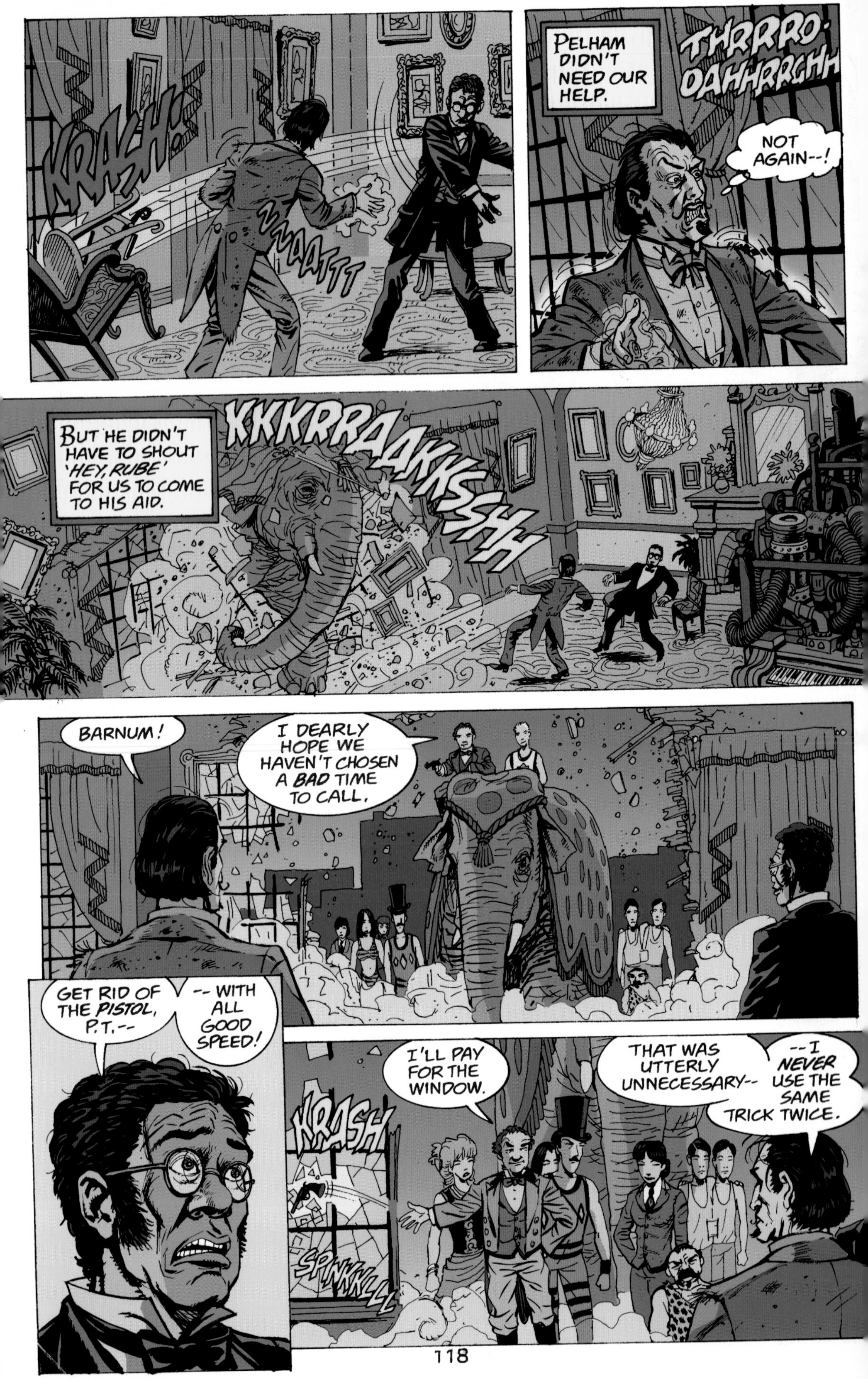

KRASH!
ZZAATTTT
PELHAM DIDN'T NEED OUR HELP.
THRRRO-OAHHRRGHH
NOT AGAIN--!
BUT HE DIDN'T HAVE TO SHOUT 'HEY, RUBE' FOR US TO COME TO HIS AID.
KKKRRAAKKSSHH
BARNUM!
I DEARLY HOPE WE HAVEN'T CHOSEN A BAD TIME TO CALL.
GET RID OF THE PISTOL, P.T.--
-- WITH ALL GOOD SPEED!
KRASH
SPINKKLL
I'LL PAY FOR THE WINDOW.
THAT WAS UTTERLY UNNECESSARY--
--I NEVER USE THE SAME TRICK TWICE.

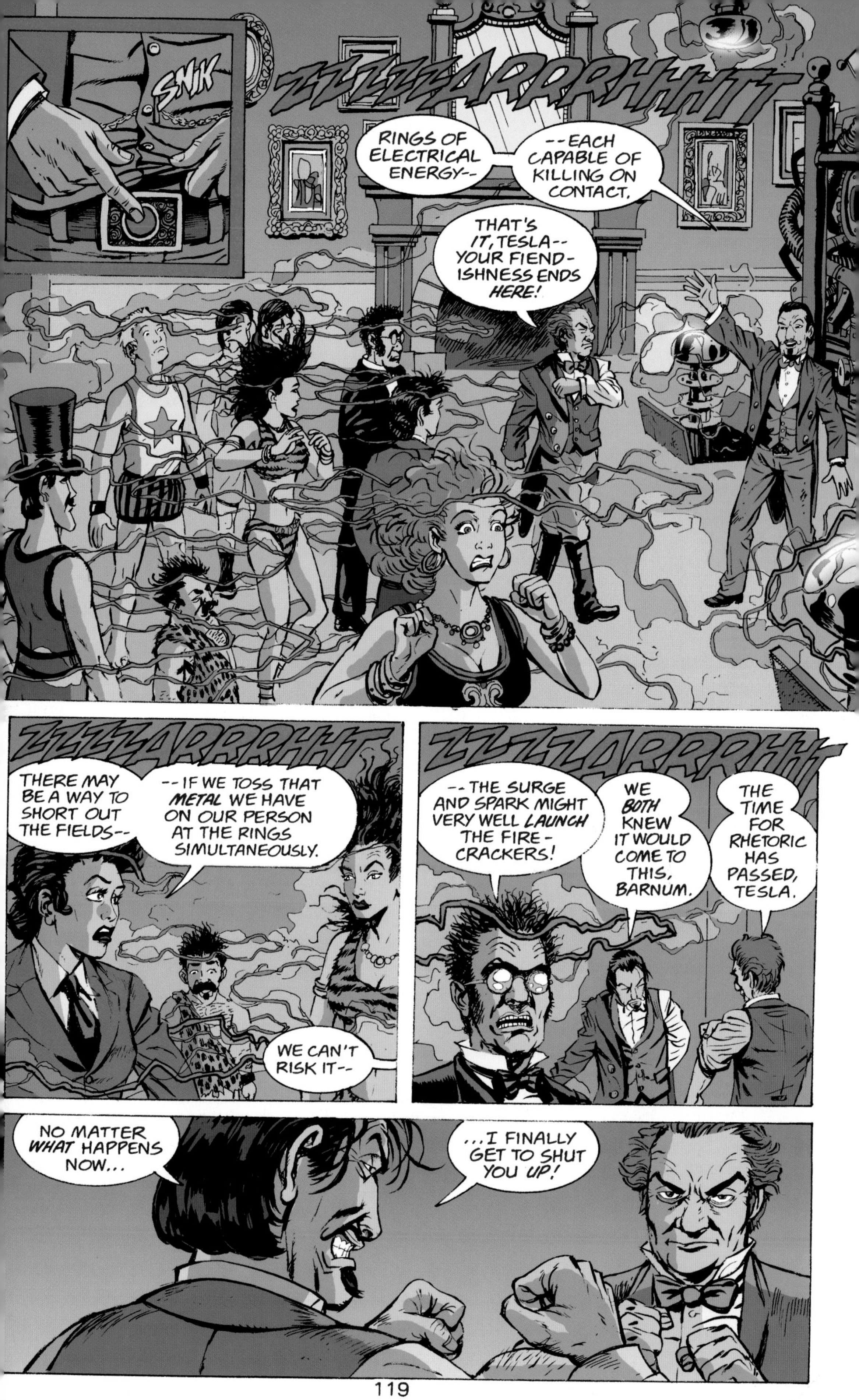
SNIK
ZZZZZZARRRRHHHTT
RINGS OF ELECTRICAL ENERGY--
--EACH CAPABLE OF KILLING ON CONTACT.
THAT'S *IT*, TESLA-- YOUR FIEND-ISHNESS ENDS *HERE!*
ZZZZZARRRRHHT
THERE MAY BE A WAY TO SHORT OUT THE FIELDS--
--IF WE TOSS THAT *METAL* WE HAVE ON OUR PERSON AT THE RINGS SIMULTANEOUSLY.
WE CAN'T RISK IT--
ZZZZZARRRRHHT
--THE SURGE AND SPARK MIGHT VERY WELL *LAUNCH* THE FIRE-CRACKERS!
WE *BOTH* KNEW IT WOULD COME TO THIS, BARNUM.
THE TIME FOR RHETORIC HAS PASSED, TESLA.
NO MATTER *WHAT* HAPPENS NOW...
...I FINALLY GET TO SHUT YOU *UP!*

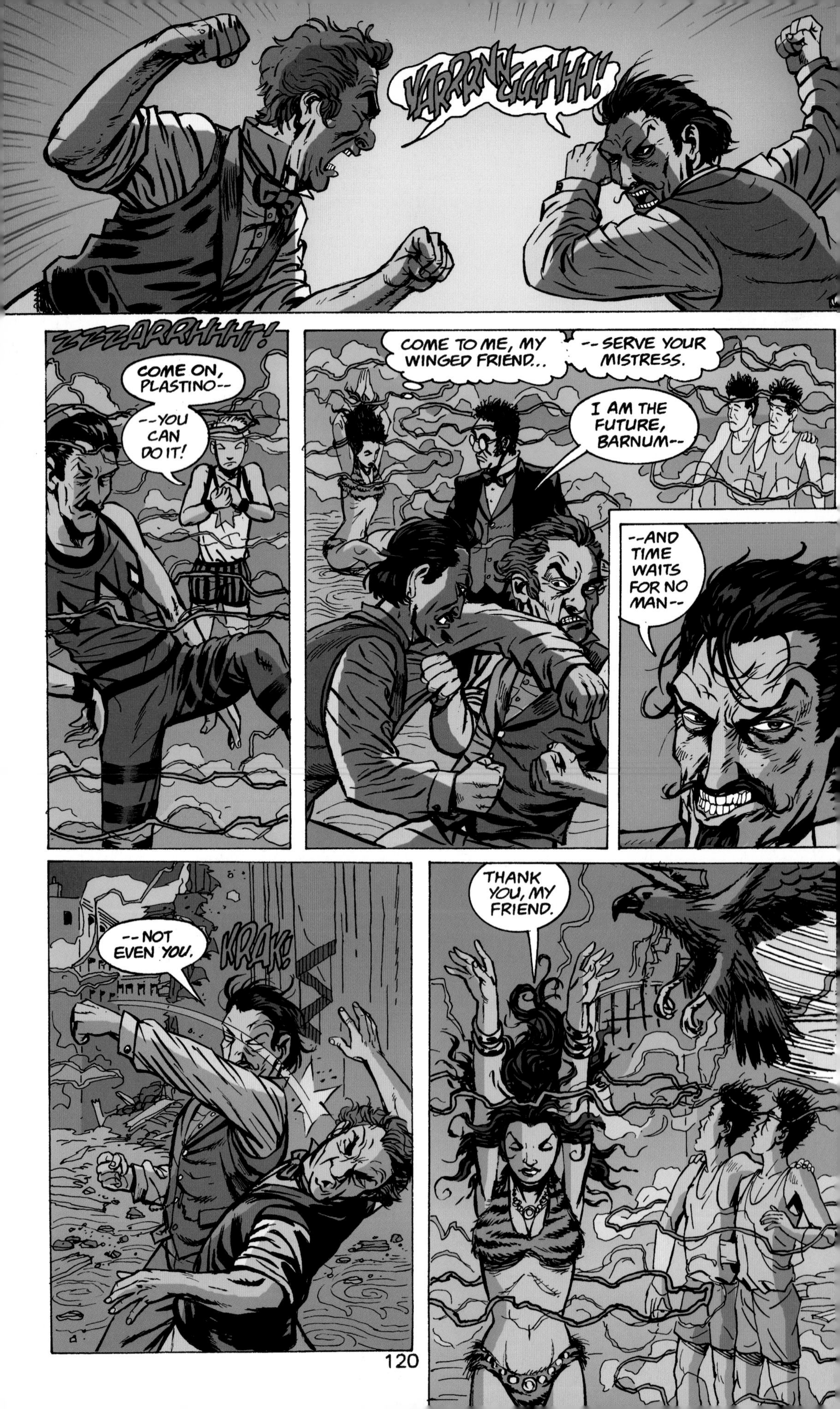
YAAARRNNGGGHHH!
ZZZARRHHHT!
COME ON, PLASTINO--
--YOU CAN DO IT!
COME TO ME, MY WINGED FRIEND...
--SERVE YOUR MISTRESS.
I AM THE FUTURE, BARNUM--
--AND TIME WAITS FOR NO MAN--
--NOT EVEN YOU.
KRAK!
THANK YOU, MY FRIEND.

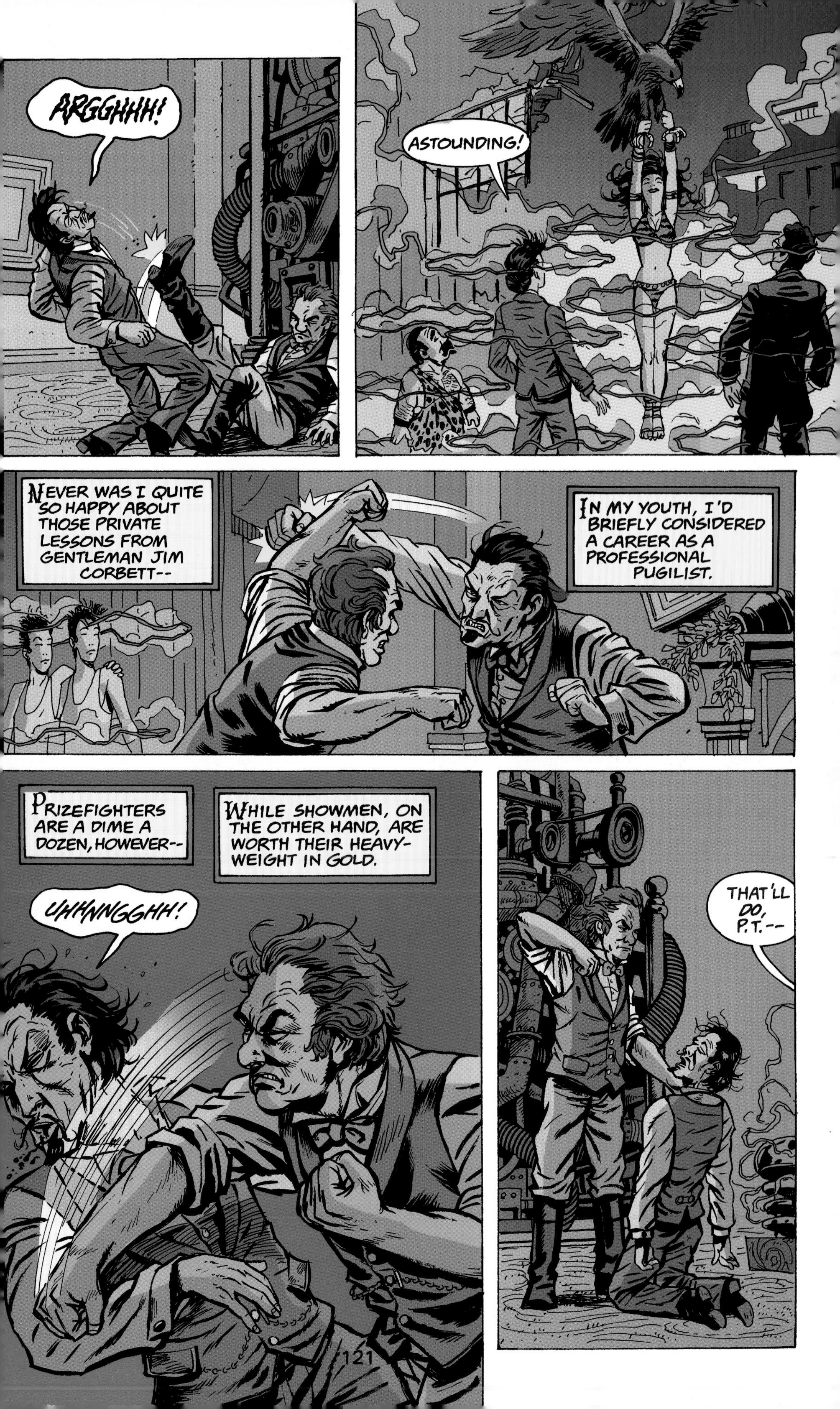

ARGGHHH!
ASTOUNDING!
NEVER WAS I QUITE SO HAPPY ABOUT THOSE PRIVATE LESSONS FROM GENTLEMAN JIM CORBETT--
IN MY YOUTH, I'D BRIEFLY CONSIDERED A CAREER AS A PROFESSIONAL PUGILIST.
PRIZEFIGHTERS ARE A DIME A DOZEN, HOWEVER--
WHILE SHOWMEN, ON THE OTHER HAND, ARE WORTH THEIR HEAVY-WEIGHT IN GOLD.
UHHNNGGHH!
THAT'LL DO, P.T.--

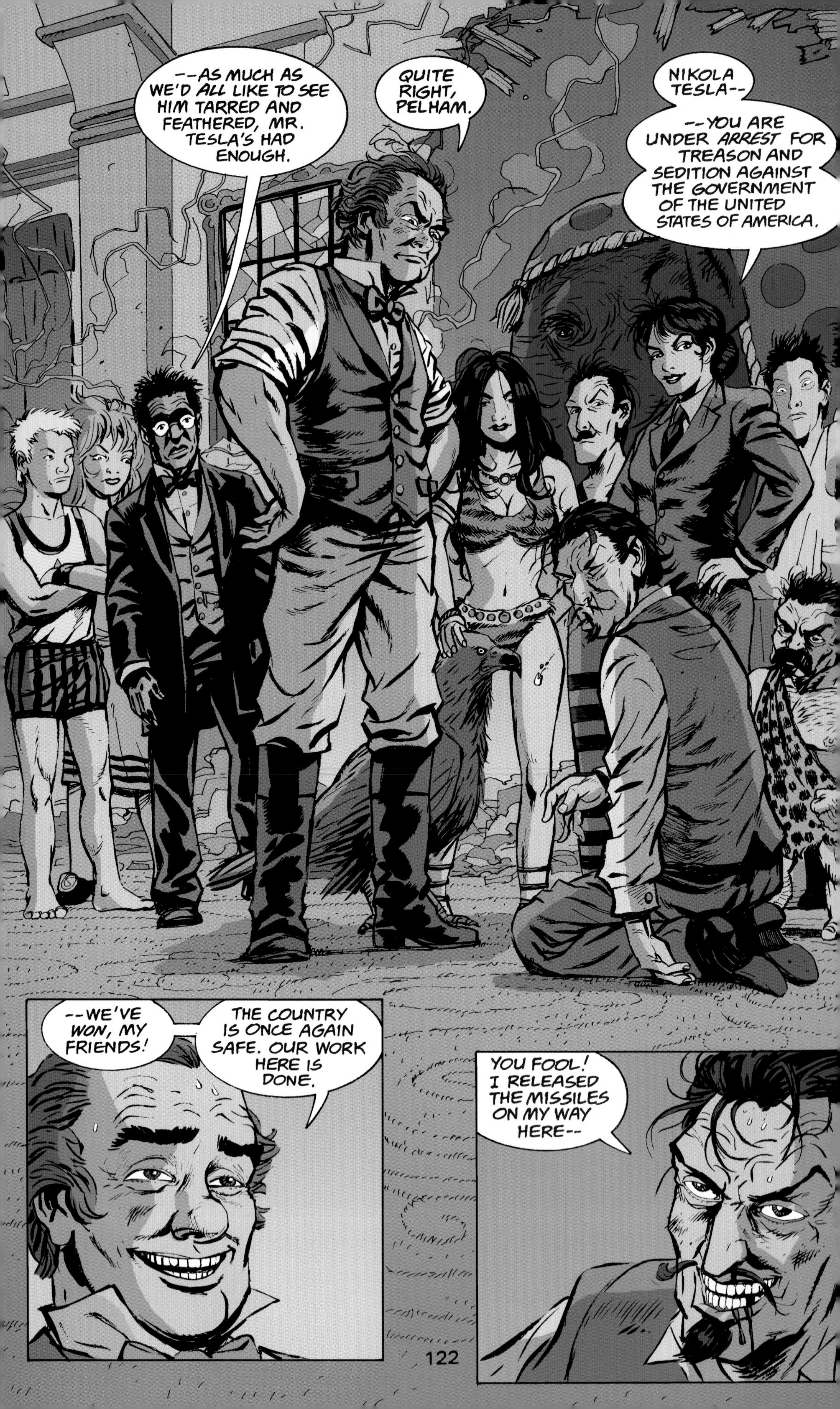
--AS MUCH AS WE'D ALL LIKE TO SEE HIM TARRED AND FEATHERED, MR. TESLA'S HAD ENOUGH.
QUITE RIGHT, PELHAM.
NIKOLA TESLA--
--YOU ARE UNDER ARREST FOR TREASON AND SEDITION AGAINST THE GOVERNMENT OF THE UNITED STATES OF AMERICA.
--WE'VE WON, MY FRIENDS!
THE COUNTRY IS ONCE AGAIN SAFE. OUR WORK HERE IS DONE.
YOU FOOL! I RELEASED THE MISSILES ON MY WAY HERE--

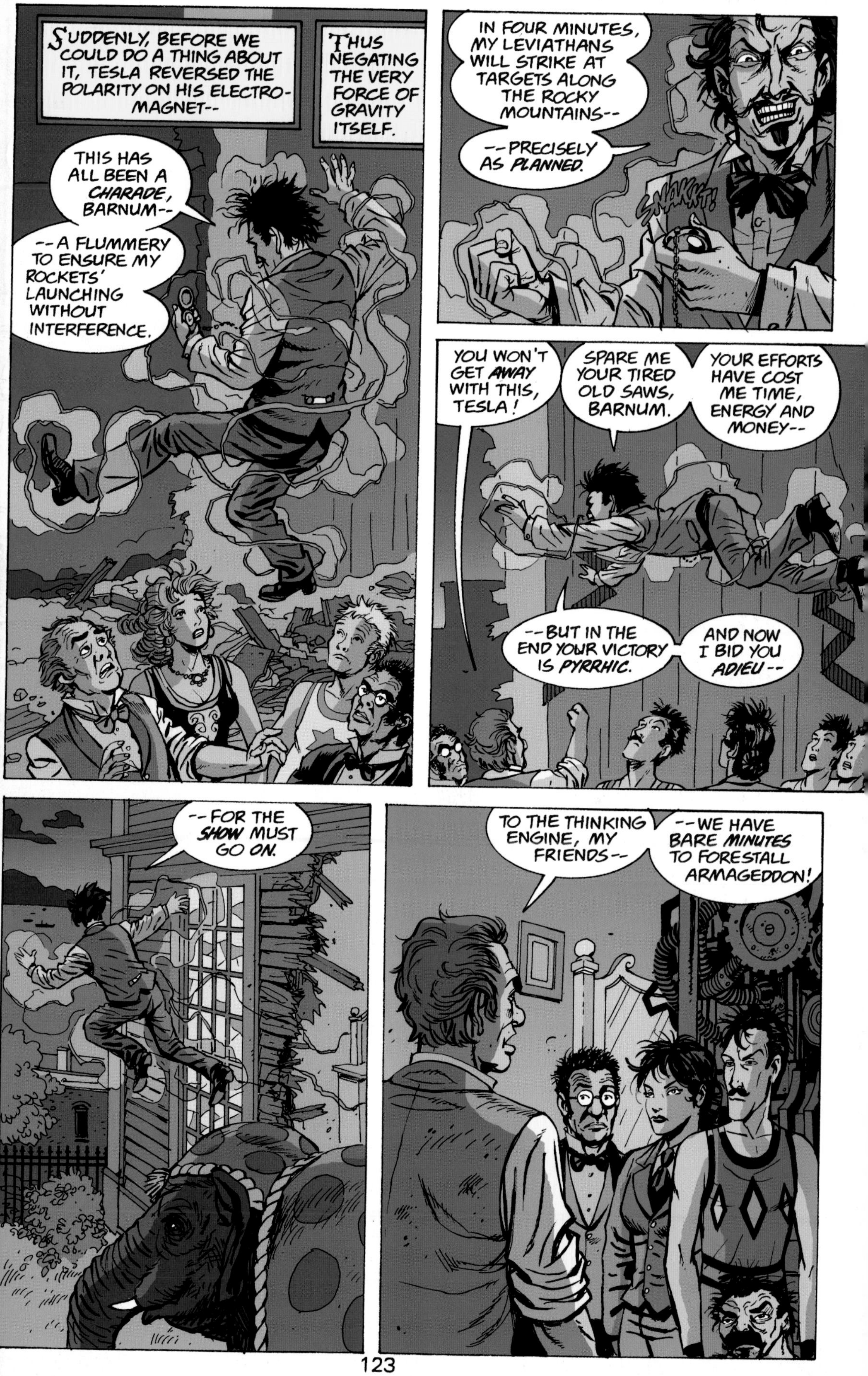
SUDDENLY, BEFORE WE COULD DO A THING ABOUT IT, TESLA REVERSED THE POLARITY ON HIS ELECTRO-MAGNET--
THUS NEGATING THE VERY FORCE OF GRAVITY ITSELF.
THIS HAS ALL BEEN A CHARADE, BARNUM--
--A FLUMMERY TO ENSURE MY ROCKETS' LAUNCHING WITHOUT INTERFERENCE.
IN FOUR MINUTES, MY LEVIATHANS WILL STRIKE AT TARGETS ALONG THE ROCKY MOUNTAINS--
--PRECISELY AS PLANNED.
SNAKKT!
YOU WON'T GET AWAY WITH THIS, TESLA!
SPARE ME YOUR TIRED OLD SAWS, BARNUM.
YOUR EFFORTS HAVE COST ME TIME, ENERGY AND MONEY--
--BUT IN THE END YOUR VICTORY IS PYRRHIC.
AND NOW I BID YOU ADIEU--
--FOR THE SHOW MUST GO ON.
TO THE THINKING ENGINE, MY FRIENDS--
--WE HAVE BARE MINUTES TO FORESTALL ARMAGEDDON!

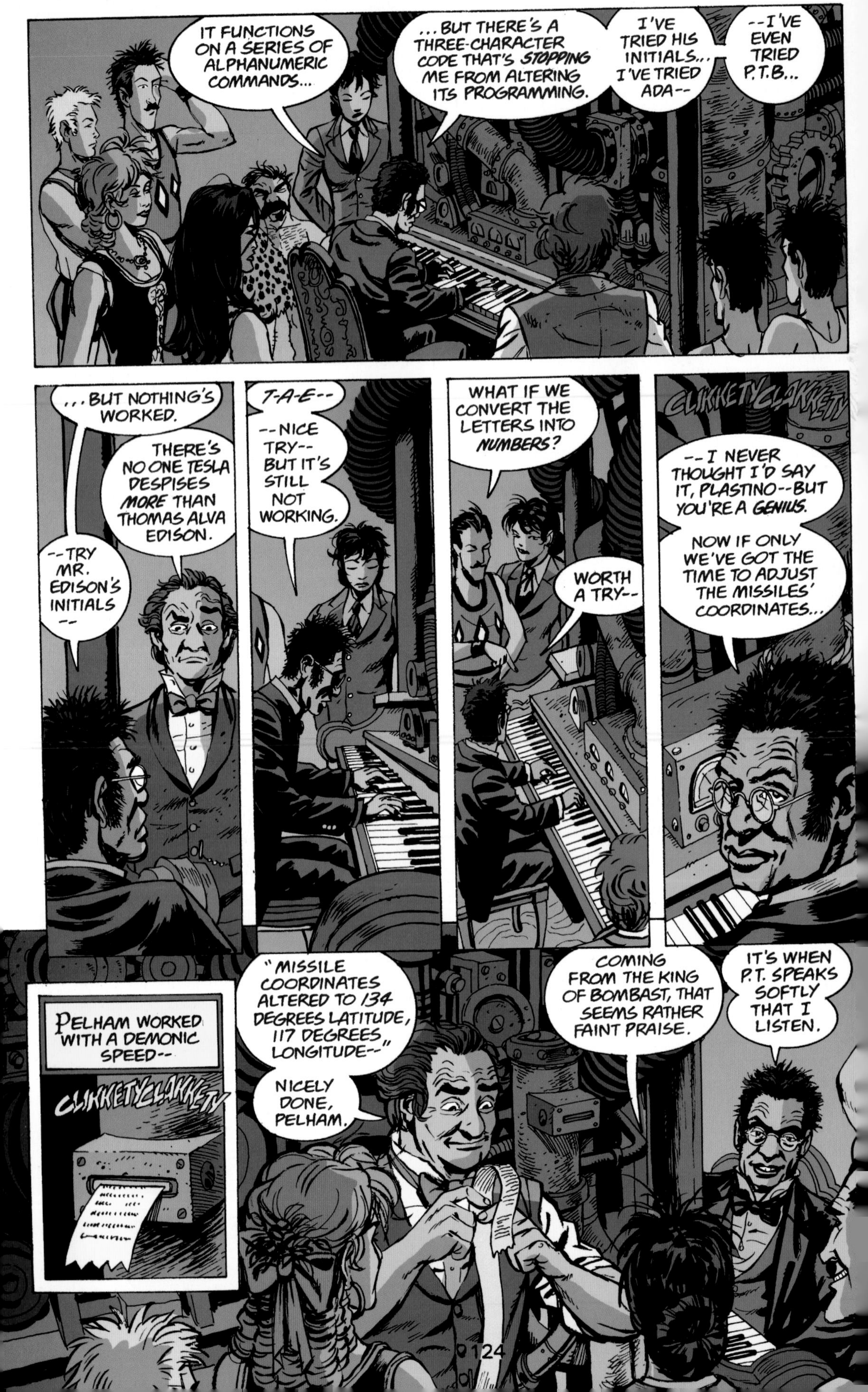
IT FUNCTIONS ON A SERIES OF ALPHANUMERIC COMMANDS...
...BUT THERE'S A THREE-CHARACTER CODE THAT'S STOPPING ME FROM ALTERING ITS PROGRAMMING.
I'VE TRIED HIS INITIALS... I'VE TRIED ADA--
--I'VE EVEN TRIED P.T.B...
...BUT NOTHING'S WORKED.
THERE'S NO ONE TESLA DESPISES MORE THAN THOMAS ALVA EDISON.
--TRY MR. EDISON'S INITIALS --
T-A-E--
--NICE TRY-- BUT IT'S STILL NOT WORKING.
WHAT IF WE CONVERT THE LETTERS INTO NUMBERS?
WORTH A TRY--
CLIKKETYCLAKKETY
--I NEVER THOUGHT I'D SAY IT, PLASTINO--BUT YOU'RE A GENIUS.
NOW IF ONLY WE'VE GOT THE TIME TO ADJUST THE MISSILES' COORDINATES...
PELHAM WORKED WITH A DEMONIC SPEED--
CLIKKETYCLAKKETY
"MISSILE COORDINATES ALTERED TO 134 DEGREES LATITUDE, 117 DEGREES LONGITUDE--"
NICELY DONE, PELHAM.
COMING FROM THE KING OF BOMBAST, THAT SEEMS RATHER FAINT PRAISE.
IT'S WHEN P.T. SPEAKS SOFTLY THAT I LISTEN.

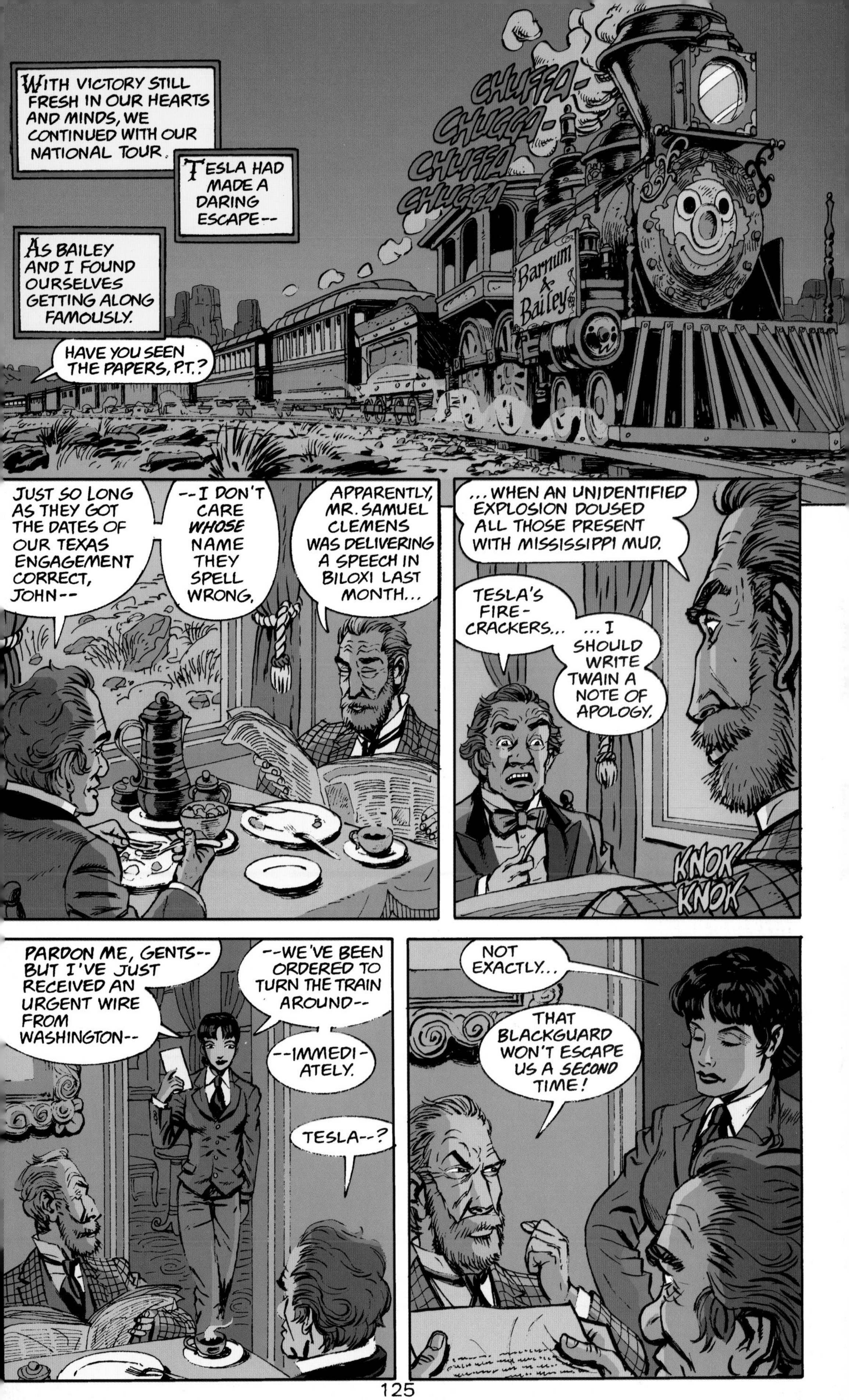
WITH VICTORY STILL FRESH IN OUR HEARTS AND MINDS, WE CONTINUED WITH OUR NATIONAL TOUR.
TESLA HAD MADE A DARING ESCAPE--
AS BAILEY AND I FOUND OURSELVES GETTING ALONG FAMOUSLY.
CHUFFA-CHUGGA-CHUFFA CHUGGA
Barnum & Bailey
HAVE YOU SEEN THE PAPERS, P.T.?
JUST SO LONG AS THEY GOT THE DATES OF OUR TEXAS ENGAGEMENT CORRECT, JOHN--
--I DON'T CARE WHOSE NAME THEY SPELL WRONG.
APPARENTLY, MR. SAMUEL CLEMENS WAS DELIVERING A SPEECH IN BILOXI LAST MONTH...
...WHEN AN UNIDENTIFIED EXPLOSION DOUSED ALL THOSE PRESENT WITH MISSISSIPPI MUD.
TESLA'S FIRE-CRACKERS...
...I SHOULD WRITE TWAIN A NOTE OF APOLOGY.
KNOK KNOK
PARDON ME, GENTS-- BUT I'VE JUST RECEIVED AN URGENT WIRE FROM WASHINGTON--
--WE'VE BEEN ORDERED TO TURN THE TRAIN AROUND--
--IMMEDI-ATELY.
TESLA--?
NOT EXACTLY...
THAT BLACKGUARD WON'T ESCAPE US A SECOND TIME!

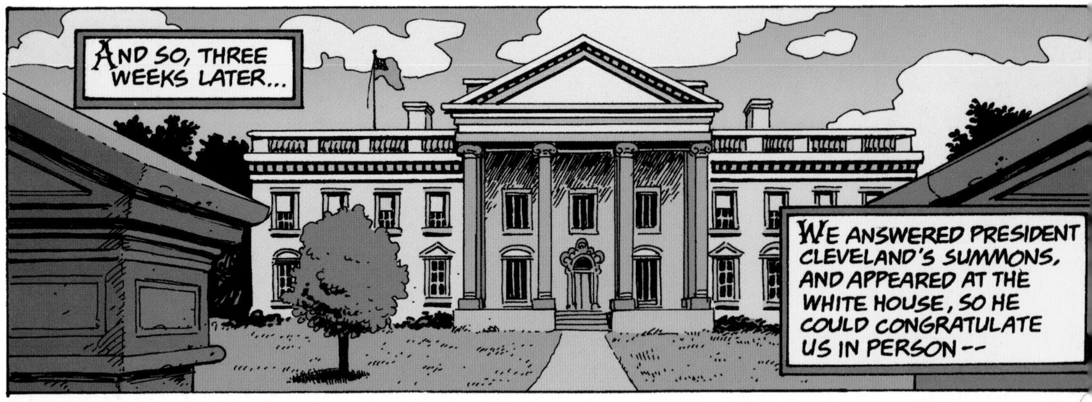
AND SO, THREE WEEKS LATER...
WE ANSWERED PRESIDENT CLEVELAND'S SUMMONS, AND APPEARED AT THE WHITE HOUSE, SO HE COULD CONGRATULATE US IN PERSON --

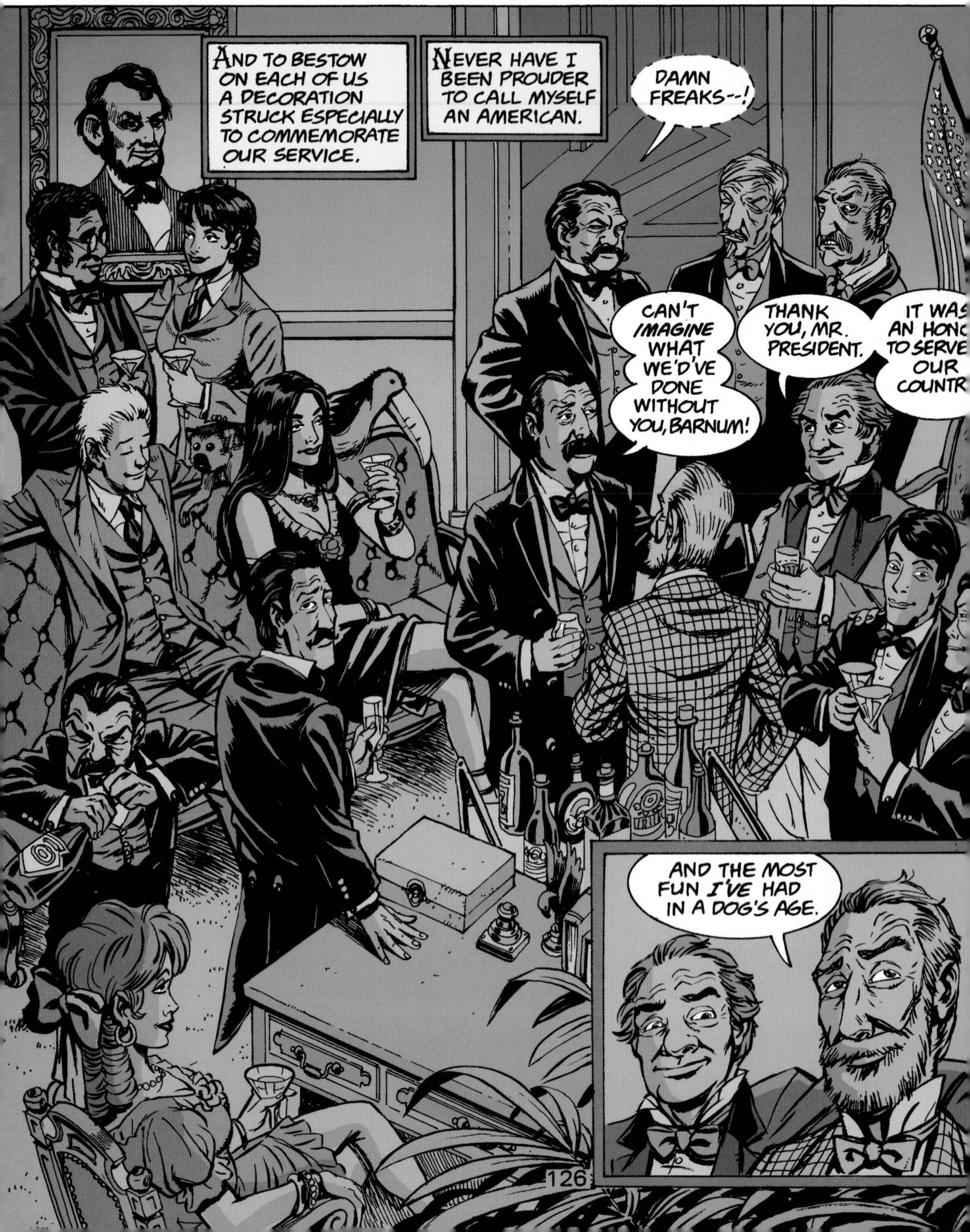
AND TO BESTOW ON EACH OF US A DECORATION STRUCK ESPECIALLY TO COMMEMORATE OUR SERVICE.
NEVER HAVE I BEEN PROUDER TO CALL MYSELF AN AMERICAN.
DAMN FREAKS--!
CAN'T *IMAGINE* WHAT WE'D'VE DONE WITHOUT YOU, BARNUM!
THANK YOU, MR. PRESIDENT.
IT WAS AN HONC TO SERVE OUR COUNTR
AND THE MOST FUN *I'VE* HAD IN A DOG'S AGE.

ANY WORD ON TESLA?

HE POPPED UP IN SARAJEVO LAST WEEK--

--WITH A SWORN AFFIDAVIT FROM THE ARCHDUKE THAT HE'S BEEN WORKING THERE FOR THE PAST SIX MONTHS.

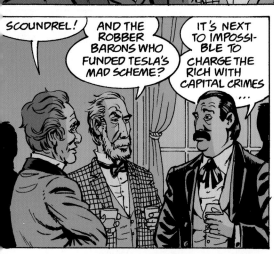

SCOUNDREL!

AND THE ROBBER BARONS WHO FUNDED TESLA'S MAD SCHEME?

IT'S NEXT TO IMPOSSIBLE TO CHARGE THE RICH WITH CAPITAL CRIMES ...

... I AM, HOWEVER, INTRODUCING NEW LEGISLATION TO CONGRESS--

--AIMED AT BREAKING THE TRUSTS.

I'LL DO EVERYTHING IN MY POWER TO SEE WE WON'T BE THREATENED BY THE WEALTH OF THE FEW AGAIN.

POP!

I TOLD YOUR ASSOCIATES HOW YOU SAVED ALL OUR LIVES--

--BUT THEY CONTINUE TO BELIEVE A WOMAN'S PLACE IS IN THE KITCHEN.

SORRY!

IT'S A LONG ROAD TO CHANGE THAT MISCONCEPTION.

THUNGKK

YOU'LL GET THERE--

--CONSIDER WHAT MR. LINCOLN DID FOR ME AND MINE.

THANK YOU, DARLING.

MR. PRESIDENT--

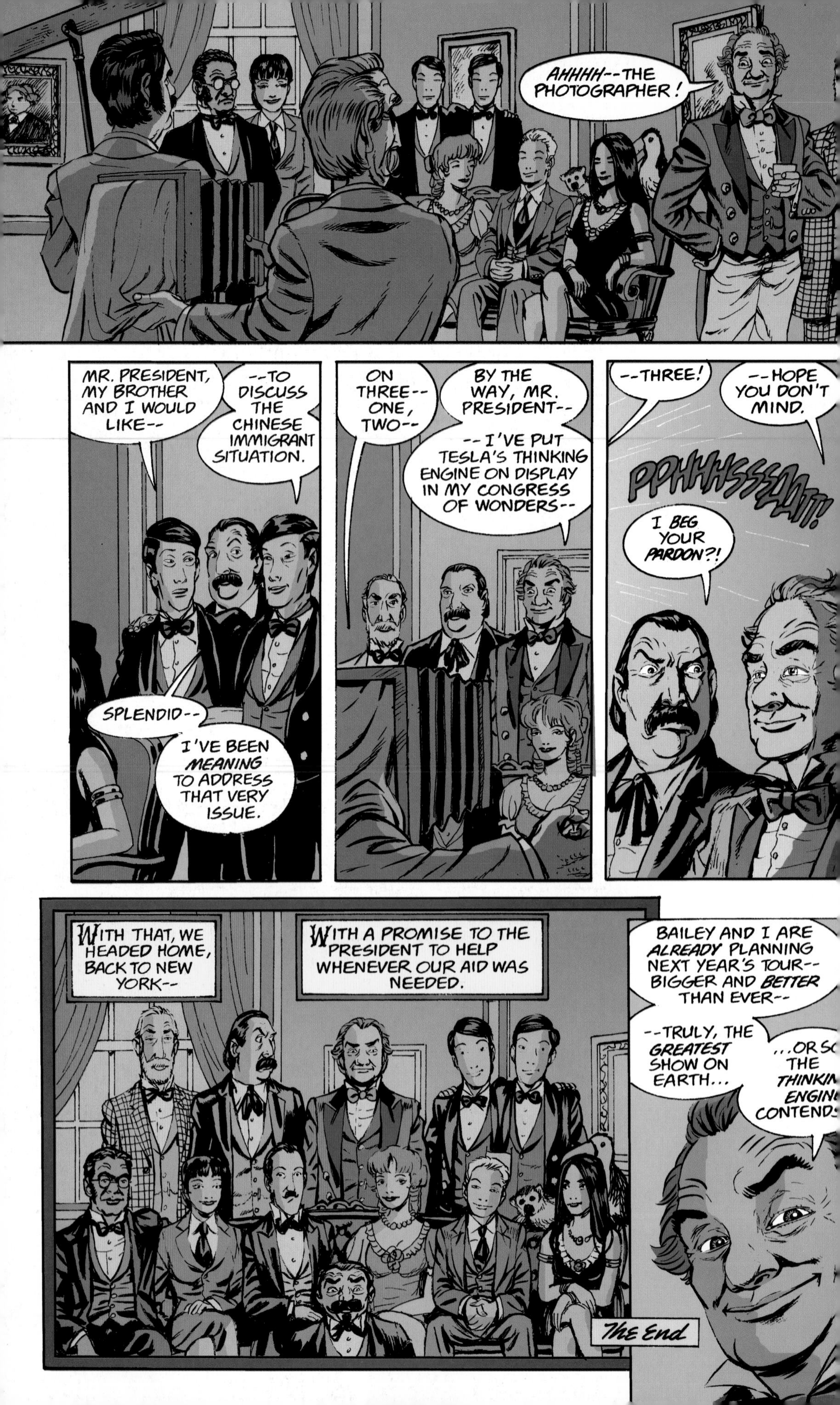
AHHHH--THE PHOTOGRAPHER!
MR. PRESIDENT, MY BROTHER AND I WOULD LIKE--
--TO DISCUSS THE CHINESE IMMIGRANT SITUATION.
SPLENDID--
I'VE BEEN MEANING TO ADDRESS THAT VERY ISSUE.
ON THREE-- ONE, TWO--
BY THE WAY, MR. PRESIDENT--
--I'VE PUT TESLA'S THINKING ENGINE ON DISPLAY IN MY CONGRESS OF WONDERS--
--THREE!
--HOPE YOU DON'T MIND.
PPHHHSSSZAAT!!
I BEG YOUR PARDON?!
WITH THAT, WE HEADED HOME, BACK TO NEW YORK--
WITH A PROMISE TO THE PRESIDENT TO HELP WHENEVER OUR AID WAS NEEDED.
BAILEY AND I ARE ALREADY PLANNING NEXT YEAR'S TOUR-- BIGGER AND BETTER THAN EVER--
--TRULY, THE GREATEST SHOW ON EARTH...
...OR SO THE THINKING ENGINE CONTENDS.
THE END